SHIVER THE WHOLE NIGHT THROUGH

DARRAGH McMANUS

HOT KEY BOOKS

First published in Great Britain in 2014 by Hot Key Books
Northburgh House, 10 Northburgh Street, London EC1V 0AT

A CIP catalogue record for this book is available from the British Library.

ISBN: 978-1-4714-0409-2

1

This book is typeset in 10.5 Berling LT Std using Atomik ePublisher

Printed and bound by Clays Ltd, St Ives Plc

www.hotkeybooks.com

Hot Key Books is part of the Bonnier Publishing Group
www.bonnierpublishing.com

Read the book – and listen to the soundtrack

I've done up a Spotify playlist for *Shiver the Whole Night Through*. It's the music I listened to while writing the book, or that inspired it in some way. Music that I felt chimed well with the tone and mood of *Shiver*; that complemented the story, or expressed something inexpressible about the characters and themes. Music with a chilly, brittle, spooky or melancholy feel. Music that sounded like a strange, eerie nursery rhyme or lullaby. Music that captured the novel's wintry vibe. I guess I see the playlist as a sort of soundtrack to the book, so you can use it as an accompaniment to your reading, making the whole experience more . . . cinematic, for want of a better word.

It's a cool little add-on, an aural embellishment. Listen to it here by typing http://bit.ly/shiverthewholenight into your web browser.

Hope you enjoy both the book and the soundtrack,

Darragh

(P.S. You'll need Spotify for it to work . . .)

For our little buachaillín and cailín beag

My girl, my girl, where will you go?
I'm going where the cold wind blows
In the pines, in the pines
Where the sun don't ever shine
I would shiver the whole night through.

'Where Did You Sleep Last Night?'
Traditional folk song

Contents

Guide to pronunciation of Irish Gaelic words

Sláine – SLAWN-yeh

Siochta – shook-teh

Padraig – PAW-drig

Tús maith, leath na hoibre – TOOSE mah, LAH na HIB-reh

Sliabh – shlee-uv

Cohnda – KUHN-deh

Sioda – SHEE-uh-deh

Amadán – OMMA-dawn

Ráiméis – raw-maysh

Púca – POO-kah

Part I

NEW LIFE

ON THE BRIDGE

I stood on the bridge and tried to get up the courage to jump. I stood there and thought, if it's good enough for Kurt Cobain, it's good enough for me.

I looked down at the freezing, choppy water far below. This Sunday night in November was darker than it should have been with a full moon. But I could see the river, out here on the edge of town, churning like something half-crazy, and knew it'd do for me. I'd die if I leaped in there, and right then, I wanted to die.

I think I did. I think I wanted to die.

I gripped the stone bridge, an ancient thing without a name built long before the town itself. Dated to medieval times, historians said. It was colder than the grave. I kind of smiled at that. The grave. *My* grave. Was I really about to do this?

I got a better grip for leverage and lifted one leg onto the top of the parapet and thought, hell yes I'm going to do it. If it's good enough for that movie director in Los Angeles, it's good enough for me. Even stupid, pathetic, butt-of-every-joke me.

The water really did look freezing, very rough. I imagined myself hitting it at speed, maybe being dragged down by a current, the river sloshing over my head, snaking down my throat. The image made me shiver. I didn't want that, but I didn't want to be here any longer either. I wanted out.

Maybe if I got lucky I'd crack my head off the rocks, lights out, no need to drown, no more coldness and pain. No more memories. No more anything. But I was never very lucky.

I pulled myself fully onto the bridge and stood there, wobbling a bit, caught unawares by a strong wind. Whoa. Wouldn't want to get blown off, I might get hurt, ha ha.

I thought about *her* and what had happened last summer. Thought about the bullying and harassment, the blows and whispers, and steeled myself. Just do it. Do it and be done. If it's good enough for all those celebrities and poets and geniuses and rebels who killed themselves, it's good enough for me.

Me. Loser. Clown. Designated town asshole.

I raised my right leg half an inch and leaned into the wind and closed my eyes and . . . I still don't know if I would have jumped, because then I heard a voice. My movement stalled. I heard it again, definitely, hard to distinguish over the wind and torrents of water but it was real, not my imagination.

'*Hey*. Watch yourself there, boy.'

I opened my eyes and turned around. An oldish man, fifty-five or sixty, stood ten feet away, holding a terrier on a leash. The dog was snuffling around his feet, trying to root something out from under them. I knew this guy. He did work for my parents the odd time, a handyman.

'Mind yourself up there,' he said. 'That wind'd knock a house. Ah, you might come down out of there altogether will you – I'm too old to be lepping into the river to rescue someone.'

3

I nodded dumbly and had jumped back onto the pavement before I realised it. Foiled. I smiled bitterly and thought, not to worry – I have all the time in the world.

I mumbled some vague excuse as to why I was up there in the first place. It was hard to tell if the man believed me. I walked home, not sure whether I felt relieved or disappointed. Thinking, I've got the rest of my life to end my life.

Then I woke the next morning to hear that Sláine McAuley actually had.

My mother gently shook me at eight and said, 'Something awful has happened, Aidan. I'm so sorry, pet.'

I blinked the sleep from my eyes and head, staring at her. What the hell? Was this about me? Had I actually done it? The man with the dog just a dream after all, some part of my brain still working after death? Or maybe that was heaven and he was an angel, my guide. But if I was dead, how could my mother be talking to me?

I tried to focus. You're going crazy, man. You're still half asleep and fully alive. Oh, whoopee.

I smiled at my mother, pretending to be okay. 'Sorry. Say that again.'

She squeezed my hand and blurted out the details. 'That girl from your school, Sláine McAuley. She died last night. Her body was found early this morning. Her family doesn't know what time she left the house, they say she went to bed early and next thing was they heard . . . This must be upsetting for you. Something like that happening your friend.'

Sláine McAuley wasn't my friend, exactly. She wasn't at my

4

school any more, either. I knew her to say hello to – we'd had maybe five conversations and none stretched beyond a brief greeting. She was older than me, eighteen at least, while I'd turned seventeen in July (what happy memories I had of *that* time). She'd also been a year ahead in school. A month ago Sláine had started first year in university; meanwhile I was in my last year at secondary school, without a clue what I wanted to do or where I wanted to go.

Anything or anywhere but here, I suppose. Anything, nothing, who cared?

Now my mother was telling me Sláine was dead. Could that really be true? I put a hand to my face and winced – still tender around my mouth after the punch Rattigan had given me. I couldn't believe it – he'd done that last Friday and it was still sore. At least he hadn't loosened any teeth. I'd told my mother I walked into a road sign when she asked about it. I have some pride. A tiny amount.

Rattigan. The Rat. One of the main reasons I wanted to check out.

I hadn't, not yet. But I was about to discover that Sláine had. 'What happened?' I said.

My mother replied, 'She . . . she killed herself, pet. They found her body in the forest, a good way in. Robert Marsden who works for the forestry was clearing some old growth or something. He found her, lying under a tree. Almost curled around it, the sergeant told your father.'

'How come she was lying under the tree? If . . . Oh right. She didn't hang herself, then.'

'No. They don't know exactly yet. Might have taken poison,

swallowed something. Or pills, something to knock her out. The cold would finish . . . '

My mother broke off; her head wobbled. She looked close to shedding the tears I somehow knew I should have been shedding myself. But I was pretty sure I wouldn't.

Not that I had anything against Sláine. She seemed fine, a nice person despite being by far the best-looking girl in school – wavy brown hair, dark-grey eyes, a classical beauty, like something out of an old painting. She hadn't let that lovely head go to her head, so to speak.

As far as I knew her, which wasn't far, I liked her. She was intelligent and softly spoken. Honours all the way, studying Law in Galway. Popular, well read, played tennis, helped out at a home for mentally handicapped people. That's about all I know of Sláine.

Except, of course, the fact that she had now killed herself and I hadn't.

I felt sorry for her, obviously. You'd feel it for anyone, if you've any bit of heart in you; especially someone so young, who you vaguely knew. But I wasn't going to cry. I was fairly sure there weren't any tears left in me. They'd all been wrung out, and everything else besides. I was empty inside. Hollowed out. Used up.

So me not crying or really *feeling*, even – it had nothing to do with her. Ha. It's not you, Sláine, it's me.

I heard myself mutter 'Jesus' without meaning to. Maybe I was in shock, after all. That'd do things to anyone, wouldn't it, news like that? And the state I was in, close to the edge, all sorts of edges . . . I didn't know what I felt or what was what.

I patted my mother's hand. 'All right, Mam. I'm grand. I'll get up now or I'll be late for school.'

School. I shuddered inside. My mother smiled warmly and left the room. I opened my window and rolled a cigarette, wondering again if I was in shock. Hard to know. I looked out at cold November and thought, for the millionth time, of that day last summer when I really had been in shock. Such an almighty shock I still hadn't recovered from it. I sometimes wondered if I ever would.

Late to school as usual, but for once it didn't matter because everyone else remained gathered around outside. They'd all heard about Sláine McAuley. Ridiculous rumours and wide-eyed speculation running like a virus through the student body. I overheard someone say she'd climbed to the top of the tallest tree in Shook Woods and jumped to her death. Someone else said she ate poisonous toadstools, and they knew this for a fact because Sláine always got A1s in Biology so she'd know what to pick. A third someone reckoned she'd encountered something ungodly, otherworldly – literally scared to death.

None of these kids would have known her well, probably, and they were all talking complete shit.

At the main entrance I met Podsy, my friend – my only friend now, really. He was wiry haired and short-sighted, small, not like me; I was tall and skinny, not bad looking I guess, awfully pale with permanent five o'clock shadow. My father's hairy genes, thanks very much. I had to shave every day if I wanted to look respectable. I'd given up on shaving every day a while ago.

Podsy looked dumbfounded. 'Aidan, did you hear?'

'I heard.'

'Holy crap. Sláine McAuley, I mean of all the people you wouldn't expect to top themselves.'

'Podsy, d'you mind not saying that? "Topped herself." It's a bit . . . I dunno. Don't like the thought of it.'

'Aw yeah, course. Sorry, man.'

Podsy was a sweet-natured kid, he honestly wouldn't hurt a fly if he could help it – he'd even turned vegetarian after seeing a documentary on abattoirs. Maybe that's why he was decent enough to not mind being seen with a dickhead like me.

At ten the principal herded us into the sports hall for what he called 'special assembly'. He stood on the stage and told us he was worried. The principal was decent, he would have been sincere about that.

He cleared his throat and said uncertainly, 'Kids, you've all heard about what happened to poor Sláine in Shook Woods. An awful tragedy, for her family and of course her friends. Many of you knew her last year. Now, I know there's this thing about copycats. I've read about it, and we're concerned about what happens next. Okay? Kids, it'd break my heart if this terrible event was to start some kind of chain reaction, people imitating poor Sláine . . . '

I zoned out and looked around. Girls dabbing tears from their eyes, mascara running although technically students weren't allowed to wear make-up. Some kids sniggering, the callous little gits. A guy called Tommy Fox stared at the floor, ashen-faced, grief-stricken: I wondered if him and Sláine had a thing together. It was clear he was taking it badly.

I looked around, remembering how much I hated this place.

This hall, the school and, except for Podsy, every kid in it. Hated the town, hated the world. Most of all, I hated myself.

Actually no. I probably hated John Rattigan even more, and now I could hear his voice in my ear, that guttural croak, a perfect match for his bulldog face and hulking body.

'I hear there's a carnival coming next weekend. You'll be going along, will you, Flood? You like the carnival, I heard.'

I said, 'Yeah, good one, John. You've used that joke already, but it's still good.'

Rattigan snarled, 'D'you want another thump, do you? Another nice bruise to go with that one.'

I looked down, face reddening, more ashamed than words can say. 'No, John,' I muttered.

'"No, John" is right, and don't forget it.'

Rattigan was standing behind me with his usual gang. His little army of creeps and scobies and borderline psychos. I'd have bet a million that half of them would be locked up, in prison or the mental home, before they reached thirty. Unfortunately, that wasn't much help right now.

Assembly was dismissed and everyone filed outside. Rattigan flicked Podsy on the ear. It looked like it hurt, but fair play to the small fella, he didn't give Rattigan the satisfaction of reacting. I snuck around the side of the school for a smoke – I figured classes wouldn't start for ten or fifteen minutes. Podsy followed, a firm set to his mouth. It had always been slightly wonky – his bite was off or something – and gave his face a comical sort of appearance.

'C'mon, Aidan, come inside. Freezing out here.'

'Leave if you're cold. Nobody's keeping you.'

9

He ignored me. Podsy was good like that, putting up with my crap; he knew it didn't mean anything, I was just taking it out on him because I hadn't the guts to take it out on anyone else.

He stamped his feet to warm them. 'Did you know, there hasn't been a suicide in the town in years? *Years*. Twenty or something. More, even.'

'Yeah? Right.' I wasn't interested in talking but he wouldn't leave me alone.

'Yeah, it's kind of unusual actually,' Podsy said, ''cause generally it's a kid does it, like Sláine? But our last one was that guy, Martin Hassett. The farmer? And he was middle-aged. Up to his eyes in debt, that's why he shot himself.'

He knew all this stuff through his Uncle Tim, the deputy Garda sergeant, who was forever telling Podsy about different cases, things he was working on; probably stuff he shouldn't have shared with a seventeen-year-old chatterbox.

'Your man did it in the nineties – ninety-two or something. We weren't even born. Took out the shotgun and . . . ' Podsy made the sound of a weapon firing.

I grimaced and said, 'Stop it, will you? It's depressing.'

'Sorry, man. Come on to feck, I'm freezing. Finish up that thing.'

I flicked my rollie into a drain and slouched back towards school behind him. On the way we passed Caitlin, standing with a group of girls. I looked away. I didn't want her to see me, but somehow our eyes locked. She blinked and turned her head. She looked embarrassed. I'd like to think she was; maybe she didn't give a damn. You can't know what's inside someone else's head.

One of her friends shrieked and hissed, deliberately loudly so I'd hear: 'Oh my *God*! It's your ex! Oh my God, I mean, is he *stalking* you now?' She laughed and the rest of their group did too and finally Caitlin joined in. I didn't blame her. I blamed her for other things, but not this. This was trivial.

I walked past. Caitlin: she pronounced it 'Kate-lin' in the American style, not 'Cat-leen', which is how the original Irish name sounded. That had always annoyed me about her; it seemed so dumb. A name travels across the Atlantic and gets misheard over there and comes back and we start using the new, wrong version for some reason.

It's stupid, getting worked up over something so small. I couldn't help it. Anyway, it was pretty much the only thing I'd disliked about Caitlin Downes, and you're allowed one thing, right?

Kate-lin, Cat-leen, however you pronounced it: the girl who broke my heart and kind of ruined my life.

WHAT HAPPENED
LAST SUMMER

It had happened earlier that year, on a Sunday in July – the fourteenth, which I remember because, one, that's Bastille Day, and two, it was three days after my seventeenth birthday. It's amazing how your emotions can swing so violently in just seventy-two hours: perfect happiness to the depths of misery.

For once we'd been having a half-decent summer, warm and dry most days. The little rain which fell was light, almost pleasurable on your face. And the day of the carnival incident was a scorcher, as though part of the Mediterranean had relocated to our small town on the Irish west coast.

The carnival. Those two words still have the power to send chills up my spine. No, that's not it: they make me feel sick in my stomach. Make me want to throw up.

They'd arrived in town midweek, a small outfit run by semi-dodgy geezers but they seemed all right. You probably wouldn't trust them with the keys to your house, but the rides were safe and the games weren't rigged too much. They travelled around the country all summer, pitching up for a few days in towns along the way. Dodgems, roulette wheel, ring-tossing, the usual.

Barney McFarney's Big Bumper Funfair: the name I'd remember till the day I died. Which, all going to plan, wouldn't be too long coming.

I don't know if Barney McFarney was his real name or something cutesy they dreamed up to sell the carnival. What I know is that he had a son called Francis: about eighteen, handsome, with shining-brown eyes and dark skin. All the girls thought he was gorgeous. I heard one say he was like how she imagined Heathcliff from *Wuthering Heights*. His personality was that mix of edginess and little-boy-lost sensitivity that drives teenage girls nuts. Looking back, I'm not surprised Caitlin fell for him. If I were her, I probably would've done the same. But that didn't make it hurt any less.

We'd been going together for five months. She first kissed me at the Valentine's disco, out of nowhere; I was so surprised and delighted, I had a big dumb smile on my face for a week. Caitlin Downes actually fancied *me*. I couldn't believe it.

I wasn't the ugliest troll in the world, but I wasn't quite in her league either. I was a nerd, one of those quiet guys you're unaware of until one day you realise they've sat next to you for two years and you barely know their name. I was only noticed when someone noticed they never noticed me. I'd kissed a few people but never had a serious girlfriend.

Caitlin was a babe. Auburn hair, fierce green eyes, ski-slope nose. *Great* legs. So much of a babe, in fact, that other kids couldn't believe she was really going with a geek like me when they heard about it. I fell for her, hard and fast. I thought she

13

felt the same. Turns out I was wrong.

We'd got serious quickly, spending a lot of time together. We talked about all sorts of things – Caitlin opened up to me in a way I imagined she didn't, or couldn't, with her friends. She mostly hung out with a group of catty, nasty assholes. We made plans – not long-term but that summer, or next year. We wondered if we should go to the same city for college, or would a long-distance relationship be doable. We shifted all the time, whenever we could.

We even came close to doing *it*, once or twice. I wanted to, I think she did too, but we were young and immature; whatever else happened, I'm glad we didn't. That would have made what followed even harder to bear: deeper intimacy making for greater betrayal.

That awful day, Black Sunday as I think of it, Caitlin cheated on me with the boy from the carnival. Francis, with his bloody Heathcliff face and wounded rebel image. She shifted him in a meadow outside town, as the afternoon sun beat down mercilessly. Meanwhile stupid, innocent me was at a match with my father.

I hadn't wanted to go but he insisted – he thought we should spend more time together, so fine. We drove to the city and stood on the terrace, getting fried in the heat, crushed by the crowds. Then we returned home and Podsy was waiting for me at the front gate. He looked nervous but willing to say what he had to anyway, which I'll forever be thankful for. Podsy's always been a good friend.

'Aidan,' he said, gulping, waiting until my father passed on inside. 'I heard something about Caitlin.'

'What? Is she all right?'

'Uh . . . *she* is, yeah.'

Meaning, but *you* might not be when you find out what happened.

I still hadn't clicked anything was wrong. I frowned at him. 'Well, come on. Let's hear it.'

'She got off with yer man from the carnival. The son. You know the guy, kinda greasy-looking. Everyone's saying it. I wish I wasn't telling you this, but you've a right to know.'

Straight away, I knew it was true. I didn't bother asking questions or trying to convince myself Podsy was wrong – I *knew*. In my guts, in the very heart of me.

I think I actually went into shock then. The violent shock of it, like a cut that came so fast I almost forgot to bleed. But I felt the cut. Felt the pain. Like someone had driven their hand through my breastplate and torn my insides to shreds.

I fought the urge to vomit as my head started lifting off my body and rising slowly into the air. I was gone, floating away, headed for space. Only me and that cold moon, out there in the darkness.

I think I said thanks to Podsy. Then I stumbled inside, lay on my bed and cried until dawn broke, and for a long time after that.

Incredibly, things got worse from there.

For the first few weeks after Black Sunday, I had to listen to all sorts of sleazy rumours: they'd had sex, she was pregnant with his child, she'd done it with his friends, he'd paid her, he hadn't paid her and she only did it because she'd do it with anyone – anyone except me, clearly.

I put up with veiled jibes and sideways smirks, skin prickling in shame and self-consciousness. I knew everyone was laughing at me, and the fact they were laughing at Caitlin as well didn't console me. I didn't want them laughing at anybody, I wanted things back the way they were.

I'd see that goddamn carnival out the window of my room until they shoved off a few days later. I even had to go there one evening with my kid sister Sheila, because my parents were too busy but she'd been promised. I managed to avoid eye contact with Francis/Heathcliff all night but it was horrendous.

I tried to pretend this wasn't happening as I struggled to make sense of it, to deal with it.

She didn't apologise. That was one of the hardest things to suck up. Caitlin basically ignored me from then on. I'll be kind and assume she was too embarrassed to speak with me, to explain or say sorry (if she felt sorry, I don't know). Certainly, it would have been excruciating for both of us. Whatever the reason, we haven't exchanged one word since.

She refused to take my calls, didn't reply to texts or emails; she'd literally turn and walk in the other direction if she saw me coming. After a while, I stopped trying and gave up on her and me.

But even *that* wasn't the worst part.

For some mysterious reason me, not Caitlin, became the target of mockery. She got a few good-natured slags from her pals, but they *were* good-natured; no intent to hurt. I got the impression one or two were even jealous that she'd bagged Francis.

From early August, though, he was forgotten, by her and

16

everyone else it seemed; unfortunately, *I* wasn't. By the end of that month she was going with someone else – Caitlin moved on while I was trapped in a vicious circle created by someone else's deeds.

A relentless barrage of ridicule and abuse started rolling over me about a fortnight after it happened, and didn't stop. I was openly jeered in the street, the shops, the community centre. Both girls and boys would shout things to me, vulgar jokes, absurd accusations.

I was a faggot, a retard, a wimpy girl in disguise. I'd told Caitlin to shift the guy so I could watch or take photos; I was a perv and voyeur. The fact that she'd cheated with a carnie made it worse, bringing out people's snobbishness as well as their vindictiveness. 'Even a knacker is better than you!' I heard that more than once.

I had notes pushed through the letter box – shit that my mother saw, which really killed me. I got sent hateful emails. A Facebook page was set up called 'Aidan Flood is a dickless loooooser', although it was taken down quickly; someone's parents must have seen and complained. I even had a rock thrown through my bedroom window one night, with a blurry photograph of Caitlin smiling across at Francis wrapped around it.

To this day I don't know how or why it went like this. Why the hell was I getting all the grief? I'd done nothing wrong. Not that I wanted Caitlin derided or scorned either; I hated all that 'she's a slut' junk. I didn't want anything to happen to her, only that she'd get back with me and try to move on from it. At that point, I was still willing to try. To forgive, I think, if she'd given me the chance.

For whatever reason, the hive mind decided to pick on me, and like I say, I can't explain it. Maybe it was collective revenge for my cheek in going with a girl like Caitlin in the first place. Maybe it was the orchestrated masterplan of some unknown weirdo who bore a grudge. Maybe it was conscious, maybe not.

Maybe it was simply my turn. Or blind chance.

The funny thing is, I hadn't been bullied particularly up till then. Yes, I was a nerd, but so were lots of kids. Since childhood I'd been more or less left alone. I got the odd belt on the playground and was slagged from time to time for being poor or skinny or whatever, but nothing serious.

Now, though, it was serious. It was unrelenting, and soon escalated into physical attacks.

John Rattigan was the ringleader, unsurprisingly. He was a violent animal anyway, and probably held no more ill will towards me than any other victim – Rattigan wasn't choosy about who he bullied. But that didn't stop him decking me at least once a week, and others followed.

I had my head scraped along a wall and forced down into a urinal. My schoolbag and books were destroyed several times. I was punched, kicked, had half my hair sheared off. I lost three teeth from three separate blows, one with the top end of a hurley. I couldn't see properly out of my eye for a week after someone threw chemical powder in it, something stolen from the school lab.

On it went. Mostly verbal bullying, sometimes physical. The physical assaults hurt, but the other stuff really tore me apart. I felt so foolish and humiliated all the time, my self-esteem

18

gone through the floor, my existence starting to seem pointless.

I didn't fight back. Even if I was naturally brave, which I wasn't, I wouldn't have retaliated. I couldn't. It was too much, almost overwhelming. Like trying to stop the Atlantic tide.

Not every kid was involved but lots were, if not most. Christ, even the ones who got bullied themselves found a target in me. I really was at the bottom of the food chain. Almost everyone turned on me and rejected me, except Podsy. He proudly, publicly, remained my friend. He got picked on too for that, but Podsy stood tough, he stayed true to himself.

In fairness, Tommy Fox wasn't really a part of it either, nor was Sláine McAuley. She'd left school by then anyway, but even before she always seemed somehow distant from other students in school, more mature; she hadn't much to do with them. Sláine kept to herself.

Caitlin didn't try to stop the bullying, but to her credit, didn't join in either. That was something, a small something. It wasn't her fault really; she'd caused it but she wasn't behind it, as such . . .

Still. It was as if, when she shifted that boy, she suddenly realised just how out of her league I was, and actually, yeah, her friends *had* been right when they asked what the hell she was doing with a yoke like me. She couldn't get shot of me quickly enough.

I didn't bother telling my parents about any of this. I didn't want them to worry. Besides, part of me, a little wormy voice in my inner ear, insisted I was getting what I deserved anyway. Why else would it be happening? Because I was a worthless speck of dirt, and that's what they got: a fist in the mouth or a head full of disdain.

So how's that for a double whammy: I had my heart broken and was turned into the biggest asshole on the planet, all in one wonderful summer. The teen movie from hell, and I was stuck in the starring role.

Finally, by some point in September, I'd had enough – and wanted it all to end.

SHOOK WOODS

School went on as usual that Monday: the day after the bridge, and not jumping, and waking to find out about Sláine lying dead in Shook Woods. The teachers told us that funeral arrangements would be announced as soon as possible – I assumed the Gardaí would want to autopsy her body beforehand. They have to, don't they, when someone is found dead in unexplained circumstances? During afternoon Irish class I stared out the window and tried to guess what Sláine had died from. Hypothermia, maybe, if not something in her system, something she'd swallowed.

It was horrible, whatever happened, too depressing to dwell on. I felt sorry for her and hoped it had been quick. And I wondered why she'd done it. She had everything to live for, as far as surface appearances went. Sláine's life was seemingly going along great. She was beautiful, vivacious, popular, clever . . . happy? Apparently not.

When school ended I retrieved my jacket from the cloakroom – for once, it wasn't ripped or scrawled with swear words in Tipp-Ex; I didn't have to fish dog shit or cigarette butts out of the pocket. In fact, nobody seemed to notice me at all. Small mercies, silver linings, et cetera.

Even Rattigan ignored me as I walked towards the main gates. He was too busy sniggering with his pals, making a foul comment about how he'd still 'give it' to Sláine McAuley even though she was dead. Rattigan said, 'I'd want to get a move on – she'll be getting cold quickly. Getting a bit stiff!'

Disgusting bastard. I never wanted to smash someone in the face so much. Needless to say, I didn't. I kept my head down and thanked God or Sláine or whoever that I wasn't the centre of attention. I let it go.

But Tommy Fox didn't. He stomped over to Rattigan's group, fury on his handsome face, hands trembling as he clenched and unclenched them. I thought, he was in love with her. It was as clear as the dawn, this terrible light all over his face.

He grabbed Rattigan and spun him around, snarling, 'Take that back. Say sorry and take it back or I'll break your ignorant head in.'

Rattigan started in surprise, then regained his composure and pushed Tommy in the chest. 'You'll what now?' He turned to his friends. 'Hear that, lads? Foxy Lady wants a scrap.'

'Take it *back*, you scumbag. *Now.*'

Rattigan smiled viciously and pushed again. Tommy didn't move. Rattigan went to slap him. Tommy caught his hand and bent the fingers back. Rattigan yelped and squeezed Tommy's ear. They both looked in pain but neither was backing down.

I'd never suspected Tommy had this kind of courage. Maybe he didn't, maybe he *couldn't* act differently. Maybe love drove you to recklessness.

One of Rattigan's mob hissed a warning about a teacher

approaching. The two released their grip on each other. Rattigan was flustered and angry, muttering about what he'd do to 'Foxy Lady' the next time they met. Tommy didn't say anything. He looked desolate. If possible, his face was even paler than earlier.

I realised I was staring at them when I heard Rattigan bark, 'What're *you* looking at, you weasel? Want some of that, do you?'

I muttered, 'No,' and scurried off. This time, there was no mocking laughter in my wake. There was only silence as I walked away, not yet knowing where I'd go.

I shivered a little as Shook Woods loomed ahead of me. I'd gone there straight from school; I didn't know why. Something told me, go to the forest. It was as though the wind switched direction and pushed me that way.

Shook Woods. The name came from the Irish word *siochta*, for frozen. I don't know how it got called that. The climate here is mild, like most of western Europe; it doesn't often drop below zero. The Frozen Forest sounds like something out of a German fairy tale, yet it stood a bare mile outside our town. It had previously been known by a different name – Dark Woods or Forest of Dusk or something, I couldn't remember exactly.

You can see it from up the mountains on the far side of town, spreading out over a hundred square miles like a dark blanket. Rising and falling, following the curve of the land over low hills. Small by Canadian or Russian standards, but to us it was massive. It was planted centuries ago by the local lord of the manor; the State took control after Irish independence in the 1920s, but apart from basic maintenance it was pretty much left it to itself, standing there, silent, mysterious. The forest was mainly pine, a few deciduous trees interspersed throughout, like inappropriately cheerful interlopers at a funeral. Those endless rows of tightly packed conifers, reaching to the heavens and blocking out the light down on earth.

There's always been something eerie about Shook Woods. The whole town, actually. As far back as Great Famine times, the English authorities believed it cursed. They called it the Frozen Place, or Death's Shadow. They wouldn't even say its name, and to this day we don't usually use the proper name either; we just say 'the town'. Sometimes the sense that something was *off* about the place could be almost physically felt. (Though other times I assumed this was just how every disaffected, over-imaginative kid feels about their home town. Get me out of this hell, quick.)

But the forest – that was Ground Zero for spookiness; that was the epicentre of our unnameable dread. As kids we were afraid to go there after night fell, or even anywhere nearby: the forest was murky, deep and black. It was scary. You didn't know what went on in there, under the silver moon, and didn't want to know.

One version of the folklore had it that the trees were enchanted, alive. Other versions said monsters lived under the forest bed, in endless networks of caves. Monsters with hideous pits where their eyes should be, four sets of jagged teeth and an unquenchable appetite for human flesh.

Those were just fairy tales and, even for children, not believable. More plausible and unnerving were stories of medieval serial killers and their forest dumping grounds. Stories of witchcraft and devil worship, weird ceremonies in the depths of night. Stories of people turning to cannibalism during the Famine, murdering and eating their own children.

To a kid, *those* were properly scary.

Running through these legends was one theme, a feeling which persisted to this day: there was something not right about that forest. Something cold and strange. Maybe even evil . . .

Right, yeah. 'Evil.' Whatever you say, weirdoes. Shook was spooky but nothing more. There weren't any devils in there, and the only monsters that existed came with human faces and spoke the same language as me.

I reached the mouth of the forest, a road leading in, surfaced with tarmac for the first three hundred yards, a dirt path after that. Just enough of a thoroughfare for forestry workers to gain access if they needed to, not that they did very often.

Two picnic benches stood out front, with an informational sign and rubbish bin – I knew for a fact nobody ever actually picnicked here. The place didn't exactly give off a welcoming vibe. My nose picked up the sweet, sappy smell of the pines. Sharp but not unpleasant: a nice, zingy smell, like the juice of citrus fruits, or the tea tree oil face wash my mother used.

I looked up the path and tried to remember if anyone at school had said where exactly Sláine's body was discovered. Then the wind sort of pushed me again and before I knew it I was walking, right into the black heart of Shook Woods.

It *was* dark in there, though my watch told me it was only four in the afternoon. The trees appeared to lean in and over you, obstructing the weak November light. I knew this was an optical illusion – they were mostly conifers, standing straight

25

as an arrow – but when you looked up, they really did seem to crowd around you, glaring down, shoving each other aside for a better view of the little human below. A cluster of crows rose from the top of the tallest one, fluttering into the air like a splash of ink. Rooks, maybe, or ravens. A murder of crows, wasn't that the proper term . . . ?

I turned back to the main road. It was visible from here. I sighed with relief – that was the real world, out there. I felt still connected to it, physically. The forest couldn't take you while you could still see the road . . .

I laughed and rolled a cigarette. Yo, crazy thoughts, get out of my head. They're just stupid trees. The worst thing that could happen here would be leaving the path and losing your bearings, or staying too late and tripping in the darkness.

The ember of my cigarette flared in the wind and I shivered again.

I walked on, and after a few minutes saw police tape around a tree, marking the area off: Do Not Enter. The tree was a monstrous thing, gnarled, ancient-looking. Unlike most of the plants in Shook, this wasn't evergreen but deciduous, possibly oak – I never could tell the difference.

It stood off the path, ten yards in. I tossed my cigarette, put down my bag and hiked over. There was no indication that something terrible had happened here – except for the tape, you'd never suspect. The body hadn't made a shape in the ground. The leaves and dirt weren't scuffed up.

It was just . . . a tree. A place. A boring spot of ground. Except . . . a place where the worst thing in the world had happened to one girl.

I sent up another prayer for Sláine, then turned around to go home – and my bag was gone. I literally jumped in fright. What . . . ? I glanced around: nobody, nothing to be seen, only those impenetrable rows of trees. But my bag, I'd left it right there, directly opposite, a few steps away. Someone had moved it.

I made to walk back to the dirt path, hesitated, started again. I reached the path and looked left and right and *nothing*. My heart rate clicked up a notch. I gulped and felt something without a name tickle the back of my neck. I looked right once more, towards the main road, and finally spotted it resting against a tree trunk, hard to see in the gathering dusk.

I flung the bag over my shoulder and thought it through. I was sure I'd left it closer to where Sláine was found, but clearly I was mistaken. I'd left it here all along. But man, I was *so sure* of where I'd put that bag . . .

Maybe someone was here. Playing a prank, some idiot, one of Rattigan's gang. No, this wasn't their style. They'd be more likely to bury me under the moss floor of the forest. Someone else, a younger kid . . . ?

I looked around and around, knowing I wouldn't see anyone. There was nowhere for them to hide, and no one else here.

I shrugged it off and hit for home, leaving the forest a little faster than I'd arrived.

The rest of the week passed in a blur. On Wednesday I found out what Sláine had died from. On Thursday she was buried. And by Saturday I was preparing to spend the night alone in dark, eerie Shook Woods.

That first day, passing the funeral home on my way home from school, there was already a long line of mourners assembling, waiting to commiserate with Sláine's family. Even at that early hour, not yet five o'clock. Guess it proves how well liked she was. A guy approached the end of the line and respectfully whispered, 'Who's dead?' I like that, the way we phrase it in Hiberno-English: 'Who *is* dead?' and not 'Who died?' Putting it in the present tense seems to keep the person around in some way, keep some bit of them alive through the mysterious alchemy of words.

My father arrived at the dinner table that evening and pulled off his cap. He worked as a mechanic when there was work to be got, and that black knit cap was part of his tool bag as much as any wrench or oil can. He squeezed it, looked at me, looked away. He said softly, 'They did the autopsy on that poor girl. Your friend.'

I was about to say she wasn't really my friend but didn't bother. Instead I replied, 'Sláine? What happened to her?'

My father had been doing maintenance work on the Garda fleet of vehicles for a few weeks. 'Sergeant was saying it at coffee. Says the coroner found . . . nothing. There was nothing unusual in the girl's system.'

My younger brother Ronan leaped in his seat and hollered, 'Your one, the dead girl? My friend said she was hanging off a tree. Eeugh, *gross*!'

I barked, 'Shut your face, you little troll.'

My mother frowned and said to me, 'Please don't use that language to your brother. Ronan, it's not nice to talk like that. You have to show respect when someone dies. Go on, sweetheart. What did the sergeant say?'

My father shrugged and rubbed his eyes. 'That's all there is. No trace of poison or any other foreign substances. She must have . . . ' He looked at me again. 'She died of the cold. That's the long and short of it, as far as I could gather.'

I nodded, pushed my plate aside and excused myself – I didn't feel like eating. My mother must have understood; she smiled kindly and said not a word.

The next morning Sláine was buried in an old graveyard on the outskirts of town. The council had built a new place a decade ago, which most people now used, but the odd family continued to lay their dead to rest in existing family plots. The McAuleys had a big crypt up there, a statue of an angel standing guard on top. Protecting the souls of the departed, or whatever it was meant to represent. The graveyard was oddly beautiful, something out of a Gothic horror movie: lumps and hillocks, ancient tombstones, grasses run wild, a discordant choir of crows squawking.

Virtually the whole town attended the funeral, including all school students and teachers. Sláine's family were really decent, respected by everyone, which made it tougher to witness their anguish. Her mother and father cried unashamedly, as did four older brothers and most of her friends. There was a good crowd from university, which was nice to see. They carried Sláine's coffin to the family crypt and lowered her into the ground as her music teacher played 'Amazing Grace' on a low whistle: a sad and lovely tune, very moving.

I was with my mam and dad. Podsy was there too, smiling when I caught his eye, out of nerves and upset more than finding anything funny about this. There was nothing funny here.

Tommy Fox stood at the back of the huge gathering, balancing unsteadily on the edge of some long-forgotten person's grave. He swayed and I realised it wasn't just his footing – he'd been drinking. His eyes were red, from crying or alcohol or both. He was taking it very badly. Tommy hadn't been seen in school since Monday. He needed time, I guess.

The priest said the last words of blessing and the crowd started shuffling out. As I passed, Tommy grabbed my arm. I probably just happened to be there exactly when he needed someone. Anyone. I smiled in a way I hoped would seem supportive. He stared into my eyes, his own ablaze like angry suns.

'Why did she do it, man?' he whispered. 'Nobody's telling me anything and I need to bloody *know*. Why?'

'I don't know, Tommy. I'm really sorry for you.'

He gazed into space like a condemned man. Finally he released my arm and patted it, a sort of apology. 'You're okay, Flood. Thanks. I'm sorry too.'

Tommy disappeared into the crowds. I kept walking. After a minute of very slow progress – the crowd was large and the exit small – I found myself abreast of Caitlin. On her own, for once. I stared at the path, weeds poking out of cracks in the stone. Then I heard her speak.

'Did you . . . Sláine McAuley. Did you know her?'

I didn't look up, just shook my head. Caitlin went on, 'I didn't really at all. But I've been crying non-stop for the last three days. Isn't that screwed up? I didn't even know her but I can't believe she's gone.'

This was the most she'd said to me in five months. I was struck dumb. I didn't know how to respond, didn't know if I wanted to.

Caitlin was still speaking, almost babbling now, as though she had so much to get out she was afraid she'd explode. 'Someone our age – dead. Just like that. Gone forever. She's never coming back. And I was thinking, like last night? That could be any one of us. You think it'll never end and then one day . . . ' She choked back a sob. 'I can't stop crying. Have you been crying too? . . . I think I'm going mad, I can't explain it.'

The better side of my nature won out; it told me to ignore my wounded pride, do the decent thing and console this girl in distress. I said quietly, 'No, I haven't cried. I mean I feel sad, though. For her. I wish it hadn't happened.'

We got jostled by the mass of people. We were separated and Caitlin went back to her life without me. I stood motionless for a long moment, staring at those old weeds busting up the pathway. The circle of life, indifferent nature, making a mockery of our grand notions as human beings. It felt an appropriate thought to have on a day like that.

I skipped school for the rest of Thursday – first time I'd ever done that. Even after the thing with Caitlin happened and led to my season in hell, I hadn't mitched. Somehow, I managed to drag my ass to that hated place every day and stay there with those hated people. Today, though, I had somewhere more important to be. As kids and staff went back to class, I hit for Shook Woods once more. Again, I wasn't exactly sure why I was going, or why it felt more important than school.

But this time round I went prepared: food, water, flask of coffee, a pouch of tobacco and rolling papers, an MP3 player should I feel the need for a soundtrack to my visit . . . or for some company if the forest started getting a bit too creepy.

And a notebook and pen to jot down my thoughts, if I had any. What sort of thoughts they might be, I hadn't a clue. The whole thing felt unplanned, even random. I was fine with that.

I got to the tree where Sláine was found by half one in the afternoon. That gave me a few good hours of daylight. To do what? Just be there, maybe. Spend a few hours where she'd spent her final hours. Pay my respects to this girl I didn't really know.

I slipped underneath the police tape and sat against the tree, the moss cold but dry underneath. I rolled a cigarette and let my mind drift.

I pictured Sláine lying here, in the pitch dark of the forest; hard to make out any details. Then I recalled there'd been a full moon that night and adjusted my mental picture accordingly. Now I could see her, softly glowing in that silver-blue light. Placing her hands under her face and closing her eyes. Shivering as the coldness gradually took her.

I imagined her body struggling against its oncoming demise as her mind willed it to come. Did her lips turn blue with the cold? Did she feel tingling pains in her fingers and toes, icy stabs? Did she take her clothes off? We never heard what Sláine had been wearing when she was discovered.

What a way to go: lying down on the pine needles and mulch of Shook Woods, waiting for death to take you away. Why hadn't she swallowed something, made it quicker, made it painless?

32

Then a weird thing happened: my dream kind of took on a life of its own. Because what I'd wanted to imagine was seeing Sláine at peace as she opened her eyes to look at the world one last time. However sad and pointless it might be to kill yourself, I thought, at least it was what she'd desired.

But now I wasn't so sure, because Sláine didn't look peaceful at all: she looked shocked. Afraid. And she was standing, not lying. She was about to run but couldn't. She seemed . . . frozen.

My eyes blinked open. I didn't remember having closed them. The cigarette had quenched. I relit it and took a long drag. Jesus, that was – spooky. I chuckled nervously. It's this place, messing with your head . . . As if to prove my point, a breeze whipped up, making leaves dance and branches flutter, an almost musical sound as it whistled off into the distance: four notes, going up for three, down for one. Obviously it was only random noise, but the tune lodged in my head; I sang it, once, twice, a little cagily in the back of my throat. 'Doo-doo-*doo*-doo . . . doo-doo-*doo*-doo . . . '

I pulled out the notebook and began scribbling down memories of that waking dream, but I couldn't hold on to the details. It dissolved like morning fog. I finished my smoke sitting back against the tree. Thinking about Sláine, not thinking about her; staring into space, listening to the wind through the trees. It sounded like a mother consoling her baby. *Hussshhh* . . .

I stayed like that for a good two hours. At the end of it I rose slowly, stretched my back, had a pee and realised something so profound that it almost felt like a physical blow: I wasn't sure I wanted to kill myself any more.

Maybe it was Sláine, the terrible tragedy of it. Maybe seeing her being buried reminded me how precious life is – even mine, pathetic as it was.

But I had definitely decided, sometime during those two hours, that at the very least I'd wait a while. I had all the time in the world, right? I still hated myself, hated most everything and everyone, but – life *was* precious. Not to be lightly tossed aside. And death, I now understood, was brutal and awful – something that, only days before, I'd been so glib about. I'd toyed with it, flirted with it.

I'd almost embraced it. Maybe I would yet, but not now.

There was another reason for this change of heart: I was intrigued. Curious. I wanted – it felt as if I *needed* – to know what happened to Sláine McAuley, why she died. What drove this seemingly happy girl, her world full of possibilities, to kill herself? I might never find out, but I had to try. If that was the last meaningful thing I did with my life, fine – I was going to do it. If nothing else, it gave me a sense of purpose.

I left Shook Woods as dusk was falling, without the faintest idea how I'd begin to investigate Sláine's last days. I was excited by it, hopeful, but I hadn't a clue where to start.

As it turned out, help in solving the mystery was to come soon, from an unexpected source: Sláine herself.

I DIDN'T KILL MYSELF

By Friday the weather had turned much colder. Frost on the ground, ice on puddles, TV weather warnings of snow to come. Walking to school that day, my head was nearly cut off by a blast of wintery wind. I spent lunchtime with Podsy, eating half a sandwich and smoking too much. He asked if I fancied coming over later to watch a DVD. I told him no, I didn't want company.

That's not exactly true: it felt as if I already had company. For some strange reason that made my skin prickle when I thought about it, I felt Sláine was there, hanging around, somewhere nearby. She wasn't, of course, but it seemed real, or half-real, all the same.

Anyway, I slouched through the rest of the day. No hassle from anyone, not even Rattigan. I wasn't sure if they were preoccupied with this Sláine thing, or had once more forgotten I existed. Whichever, I was happy enough with the situation.

I went home, pushed my dinner around the plate and trudged up to my room. It was tiny, backing on to the rear of our small house. Home was shared with my parents and two siblings, much younger than me: Ronan was twelve, still in primary school, and Sheila only eight. I think I might have felt better about myself, more able to handle the crap in my life, if I'd had a sibling closer to my age. I loved the smallies to bits, but that's exactly what they were: smallies. So there was only Podsy and my folks. But they did their best, I'm sure. I don't blame them for anything.

The view out my window was miserable: our filthy council estate wall, a muddy field beyond that, an old farmer's barn falling apart with neglect. I'd never seen anyone working in there. It was a rusting hulk, left to die.

I put on a CD – Sigur Ros, *Valtari*. Just the job to set my thoughts running free and take my mind off things. I rolled a smoke and cracked open the window. Frost was forming on the glass in intricate patterns. I remembered an old story my mother often told me as a child, about the Snow Queen, how ice crystals were left behind by her touch. That was such a cool story, equal parts frightening and exciting.

I thought about my mother and being a child and how she'd comfort me after a nightmare, wrapping me in a blanket and rubbing my back. I smiled at the memory and slipped into sleep.

When I woke, it was 2 a.m. The house was silent – everyone else long gone to bed. I shivered, noticing that the room was sub-zero; I'd left the window open. I leaned over to push it down, the frame freezing to touch. Then *I* froze, and it had nothing to do with the temperature.

I didn't kill myself.

The words were written on the window. Not written, that's wrong – they had been formed, somehow. They rose off the glass, sixteen letters made of ice, shaped out of frozen water, which struck an icy terror into my heart.

I didn't kill myself.

I slapped my face, pinched my cheek, thinking I was still asleep and this was some unusually vivid dream. Somehow, I knew I wouldn't wake up from it. It was impossible but real.

And more: underneath the words was a symbol, a jewellery design of two hands holding a heart with a crown. I knew it because everyone knew what a Claddagh ring looked like, and more importantly, I'd seen that design just the day before. A photograph in our town's newspaper, under an article paying tribute to 'local girl Sláine McAuley, tragically found dead earlier this week'.

The picture was taken at a hurling-club dance that spring. The ring belonged to Sláine. And this message must have come from her.

I didn't kill myself. Why was she telling me? How could this even be happening? Was I going insane? Was I dead, too? Was I dead and Sláine still alive and this was some bizarre dream someone else was having?

I calmed my mind and *thought*. Okay, you don't know what's going on. You're not sure if you're alive or dead. What *do* you know?

I knew I was here, now, having these thoughts. All right, go with that. Assume this is somehow possible and a dead girl has

37

sent you a message from beyond the grave. Forget the hows and whys, forget about yourself for a second: think about the message. What does it mean?

I didn't kill myself. There was only one logical conclusion – Sláine had been murdered. And just one question can follow that: who did it?

I pulled the duvet around myself and mulled it over. Someone she'd been seeing? The Claddagh ring is a sign that your heart is given to someone. Did Sláine have a boyfriend, and did the love turn sour? Tommy Fox hardly killed her. He was a nice, mild-mannered guy and didn't seem the murdering kind. Besides, he looked in agony at the news of her death.

On the other hand, people always said love and hate are two sides of the same coin. Something I knew only too well.

My mind said, no, not Tommy. Someone else, then. For some reason I imagined this faceless killer to be older. Maybe middle-aged, married – that'd give him a reason, if she was threatening to go public and wreck his marriage. Would Sláine be vindictive like that? But what if it wasn't vindictiveness? What if she genuinely loved the guy and wanted to be with him properly?

What about the man who found the body, the forestry worker? What had my mother said? He'd claimed he was in there clearing vegetation or something? The perfect excuse to 'accidentally discover' a dead girl. Then I remembered him – Robert Marsden. He was pretty old, a bird-like sort of man with a gentle way. If he was a murderer, I was the Pope.

Maybe it was a random killing, some sex beast, a bloodthirsty weirdo. There'd been no mention of sexual assault but that didn't mean anything – they might have kept the information private to protect our feelings, or help the case. But if it was a stranger, how did he lure her out to the woods? Maybe he drugged her. But in that case, it would have shown up in the autopsy. Did I read somewhere about chloroform leaving no chemical trace? Or that other stuff, the date-rape drug . . .

How, though? It all came back to one glaring question: how did this hypothetical man physically kill Sláine? There was no sign of violence. No poisons or drugs in her system. She wasn't hanged or strangled or smothered – even that leaves fibre traces in the lungs, around the mouth. I've watched enough *CSI* to know one thing: it's difficult to kill someone and hide your tracks.

The coroner said it straight: she basically died from the cold. So how does that square with murder?

God, this was exhausting, my brain whizzing around in circles. Ever-decreasing circles, at that. I was getting nowhere. I needed to sleep then come at this from a fresh angle in the morning. I was definitely on to something, but obviously I couldn't tell anyone. They'd think I'd gone bonkers, banging on about magic writing on the . . .

It was gone. Her message, the words and Claddagh symbol, they'd melted from the rising heat in the room. No, no, you stupid *asshole*. I should have taken a picture first. Now there was nothing. I had no proof.

I shut my eyes and thought, to hell with it. *I* know. I saw what I saw. Sláine McAuley didn't take her own life, and I'm going to find out who did. She wants vengeance and justice,

39

and needs me to get it for her.

I slid back into sleep, my body finally yielding to exhaustion, but my mind on fire. It was an electrical storm in there. I smiled as I realised that right then, in a different way, I also felt more energised, more *awake*, than I had for a long time. As if I was about to wake up to something great.

The next morning my family was behaving completely normally at breakfast, which seemed a bit abnormal to me. Then I checked myself: what did you expect, genius? Nobody else saw the ice writing. They don't know anything. Of course they're going to be getting on with business as usual. I guess you always think everyone sees the world from the same perspective as you.

I plonked down next to my father, punched him cheerily on the shoulder, robbed toast from his plate and grinned when he gasped in surprise. He looked warily at me and questioningly at my mother. Clearly this was not *my* normal behaviour. They were used to me moping around, the black cloud of gloominess over my head almost visible.

My parents never asked what was wrong over the last five months, but they surely knew something was. It's hard sometimes for people to have those awkward conversations with their kids, and my dad especially was taciturn at the best of times. As I said, I didn't blame them for anything or hold any resentment.

I poured a cup of tea and checked that the younger kids were in a different room. Then I said, 'Did you hear anything else? About Sláine, you know, from the sergeant or whatever.'

He said, 'No. Just what I told you last night.'

'But they know she wasn't choked or beaten to death or anything. I have that right?'

My mother grimaced and put a hand to her mouth. I said quickly, 'Sorry, that sounded a bit funny. I'm not being smart. I genuinely just want to know how she died.'

My father shrugged. 'You know already. Hypothermia.' He clicked his tongue. 'Awful thing. And her people are the finest you could meet.'

'No, I know that. I just, she definitely wasn't . . . like, they didn't find any wounds or anything, right? Bruises, whatever. Signs of violence.'

'I don't think so.'

'No drugs, poison, nothing like that.'

'No.'

My mother said, 'Aidan, why are you asking all this? You're not . . . ' She couldn't bring herself to complete the sentence.

'Mam, don't worry. I'm not gonna do a copycat or anything.' Not yet, anyway. 'Just – curious. She was my age. I'd like to know what happened.' I paused. 'Suppose . . . just supposing Sláine didn't kill herself.' My mother started to object. I cut across her, saying, 'Let's *say* that's how it happened. For argument's sake. Say someone killed her. How would they have done that? She wasn't stabbed, shot, strangled or poisoned. So how?'

No response from either, although my father seemed to be thinking about it.

I said, 'Would the sergeant know? Could you ask him?'

'No,' he said, very definitively. 'It's not my place. If he wants to tell me things, fine. Wouldn't be right for me to ask.'

41

'Ah yeah, fair enough.'

'Anyway, that job for the Guards is finished. Won't be speaking to the sergeant for a while probably.'

My mother looked at him with worry. These were tough times in our town and my home, tougher than usual. He flapped a hand and said, ''Twill be grand. I have another job lined up, some chap collared me – at the station, in fact. Asked me to fix up some classic cars he has. Vintage.'

'Who is he, love?'

'You don't know him at all – he's new to the town. Only recently moved from . . . blast it, he said but I don't remember. He's bought one of those places on Belladonna Way.'

I whistled. 'Belladona? *Very* swish.'

My mother said, 'He must have money. That's not a cheap part of town.'

'The house is very old, now,' Dad said. 'One of the lads reckons Victorian era. But it's in good nick, doesn't need too much work. The man's own name is Kinvara.'

'Kinvara?' I asked. 'Heh. Like the place in Galway. So he's got some cool cars. Real James Bond stuff, yeah?'

'No, I don't think so. An old Jaguar all right, one of the classic nineteen-sixties' models. James Bond might have driven a car like that, I suppose.'

That was my dad, God love him: full of imagination, cracking sense of humour. I rolled my eyes, finished my tea and stood. 'Gonna head to Podsy's. We haven't hung out much in a while. That okay? I'll study later.'

My father nodded his permission. Mam still looked worried. I caught her look – she didn't even have to say it.

'Mam, I told you. Don't stress it. I don't have some obsession with death or anything. It's just her, Sláine. She's on my mind.'

'You hear these things . . . '

'I know. That's not the case here. Yeah? Stop worrying.'

'All right, pet. Bring a cap, it's freezing out.'

I did as instructed and half walked, half jogged to Podsy's house. He lived in a nice estate on the other side of town, a step up from our cruddy social housing scheme. But he'd never been snobby about it – another reason I was fond of him.

His mother opened the door and let me in, saying only, 'His room. Doing something on the computer.'

I thanked Mrs O'Keeffe and ran up. Podsy was at his desk when I burst in without knocking. He held up a finger and said, 'One second, Aidan. Okay, Hiro? That data's sent to you now. Have a look and see what you think. Sayonara.'

He tapped the keyboard a few times, turned to me and smiled. 'Well. Mister Flood. Anything strange or startling?'

I smiled too, for reasons of my own. Strange or startling, indeed. I said, 'Nah, nothin' much. Who were you Skyping?'

'A pal in Osaka – Hiro. In Japan? He's a great guy. We've been collaborating on a project for SETI. You know, the extraterr—'

'*I* know. Search for little green men.'

Podsy scowled, pretending to be annoyed. 'It's not exactly that, now.'

'So what's the data you're sending?'

'Ah, I've been monitoring activity over the skies in this part of Ireland. Electromagnetic radiation, a few other things. Noticed some weird spikes recently, so I'm sending it to Hiro. He's got better equipment than me for crunching the numbers.'

43

'Hiro's a real hero. Am I allowed to smoke in here?'

'You know you're not, you ape.'

I lit one anyway and Podsy opened his window anyway. It generally goes like this. I said, 'Weird spikes how? Explain that to a bonehead like me.'

Podsy always got enthusiastic when you asked about his science-nerd stuff. 'Basically there were these big pulses of energy. In the flow, you know? Like, the radiation is going like this' – he made a gentle wave motion with his hand – 'and then it went *whoop* like this.' He punched the air a few times. 'A bit unusual, that's all.'

'What's it mean? Are we going to be invaded by giant lizards?'

'Probably nothing. I just record the information and forward it on to someone smarter than me. Actually it was kind of funny cos the first one happened on Sunday night. With the whole Sláine McAuley thing, it was a funny coincidence.'

I felt a tiny shiver. 'When was the next one? The next spike.'

'Last night. Well, this morning. Bit after two?'

The shiver became a tingle. 'Listen, will you let me know if that happens again?'

He said suspiciously, 'Yes. Why?'

'No reason.'

'Is this some stupid practical joke?'

'Podsy boy, do I strike you as the practical joke sort?'

'Nah, suppose not. Yeah, I'll tell you. Be nice to have someone pretend to be interested in it for a change.'

I flicked my cigarette onto his lawn and sat on the bed. 'Can I ask a favour?'

'Sure. What do you need?'

'Can you get on to your uncle and find out all the details about Sláine's autopsy? As in, exact cause of death. What they found on the body, what state she was in, everything.'

He looked at me warily. 'Why do you want to know? I'll ask Uncle Tim, but why?'

I shook my head. 'I don't know. Just . . . call it curiosity.'

'Did something happen? Aidan, what's going on?'

I laughed nervously. '*Nothing*. There isn't anything going on . . . Hey, uh, do you believe in, in . . . like, an afterlife? Life after death?'

'Yes.'

'Well, do you believe that someone can – I don't know. Okay, what do you think happens when we die?'

'We go to heaven, I hope. I mean I believe in God and Jesus, all that. It's probably rubbish, but I still believe. Maybe I'm just too scared not to.' He blew out heavily. 'Gotta be some place better than this, right?'

'I guess so.'

'Why all the questions about life and death?'

'Why all the questions about all the questions?'

'You're a pain.' Podsy turned back to his computer. 'I'll find out what Tim knows and get back to you. Look, I've a stupid essay to do for Monday. Buzz off and I'll let you know, all right?'

I slapped his shoulder. 'Good man.'

At the door I stopped and said, 'Podsy. Thanks.'

He didn't turn around. 'Uncle Tim never stops yakking – it's no big deal.'

'I mean that. Thanks. For everything.'

This time he did turn around. He looked at me, long and

hard. 'I'd assume you were being sarcastic but I can see by your face that you're not.' Podsy shook his head and shrugged. 'You're welcome, you're welcome. Now clear *off*.'

I cleared off.

I spent the rest of Saturday wandering around town feeling like a detective in a movie. Not a very good movie, admittedly, straight-to-DVD at best, but you can't have everything. I was on the lookout for anyone acting suspiciously, who might fit my profile of Sláine's killer. It was unscientific and probably a total waste of time, but I didn't know where else to start.

I saw the usual clowns, morons and ignoramuses I'm forced to share this town with, but none really looked like murderers, much as I might wish it. I passed groups of my peers, kids hanging out, even a few hardy lads from my estate, older lads, drinking in a field near the waterworks. Interestingly, not one made a joke or abused me in any way. The lads drinking even offered me a swig of their cider. I took some, afraid to offend by refusing.

At about four, I spotted a guy leaving a dingy pub in the market area and slipping to his car. He was what we'd call 'shlooky': dodgy, shifty, untrustworthy. The sort of rat-like man who always seems on edge, as if afraid of being arrested by a cop or thumped by someone he's ripped off.

The man pulled a bag from the car and strode off, making for the canal walkway, and I followed. It was an off-white hold all, big enough to hide things in, maybe bloodied clothes, maybe a knife or other weapon. One part of my mind knew none of those things had been used in Sláine's murder but the other part was ignoring that – it was buzzing on the thrill of the chase. The facts didn't add up at all, and that dumb part didn't care.

This could be the guy. Get after him.

I crept along behind him, keeping well enough back that he wouldn't see me and trying to look casual enough that he wouldn't get suspicious if he did see me. We followed the canal, turned onto a side street, crossed a park, skirted a factory that made scaffolding. Finally we reached a run-down housing estate called, ironically, Elegant Towers. Was he going to burn the contents of the bag? Should I accost him, grab the stuff and bring it to the Gardaí? If I was wrong, I'd look like an idiot. Worse, he could probably sue me for slander or something. But if I was right, and let him slide . . .

I made a snap decision and began sprinting towards him as he crossed the green in front of a row of houses. Then a door opened and a little girl burst out, running into his arms, laughing. He whirled her around, returned her to the ground and pulled something from the bag. A stuffed elephant wearing a dicky bow.

I stopped dead. I *was* wrong, and did feel like an idiot. At least nobody else would know.

I walked home, thinking about what to do next. I was passing our nearest corner shop when it struck me: villains often return to the scene of the crime. I'd seen enough cop shows. They get off on it – they're twisted and enjoy revisiting their evil deeds. Maybe I should stake out Shook Woods, in case the murderer showed his face.

It was a long shot, but better than no shot. And better than wasting my time chasing deadbeat dads around town. I'd go back to the forest. I smiled as this new path opened up, then winced as it occurred to me that no killer, no matter how crazy, would return to the dump site during the day. They'd go when darkness would hide them.

I'd have to go to Shook at night. I didn't believe those ghost stories people told about the place, but that was still a scary goddamn thought.

BEHOLD

The forest looked like an old photograph under the moonlight. Everything was bleached of colour – black and white in sharp lines, hardly any shades of grey – except for a subtle blue tint cast by that great rock in the sky. I crouched on my hunkers, trying to ignore the creeping discomfort behind my knees. I waited.

I'd decided at teatime that I might as well go to Shook Woods tonight, Saturday. So I snuck out at eleven, when I reckoned my family were asleep, bag on my back, heart pounding in my chest. I could see no point in waiting, and my nameless killer might return tonight. I didn't want to miss them, although being honest, I didn't want to meet them either.

What was I supposed to do if I saw some lunatic dancing around in the woods, laughing his evil head off? March over there and make a citizen's arrest? I wasn't a fighter – I was a wimp, a coward. I swallowed heavily and let out a tiny wail of anxiety, sounding like a trapped mouse. But I stuck to my position, I didn't run away. For some reason, I couldn't.

I was further in than where they'd found her body. I'd arrived at Shook and gone to where the tape still marked the scene of

49

the crime. Looking at it, that enormous tree, a funny feeling passed over me and I was sure it hadn't happened here. Sláine had been murdered somewhere else, further in, before her corpse was brought to this spot.

Then the wind blew up behind me and almost knocked me off my feet. Not for the first time, it sort of pushed me along.

I'd gathered my courage and kept walking into the woods. My torch wobbled in my hand but showed me the way well enough. I crunched along the inner path, my boots unnaturally loud in the silence. That had struck me as odd: weren't forests meant to have sounds? Owls calling, foxes yelping, animals rustling through the undergrowth. Here the only sound was the wind, rattling those pines.

After a while, and maybe a mile, I stopped in a natural clearing, about a third the size of a football pitch. Not because of some sixth sense or anything like that: it was the wind again. As soon as I entered that space, glowing under the moonlight, a gust blew up around me, swirling like a genie, throwing dust in my eyes. I felt it was telling me, this is the place.

The clearing was oval shaped, covered in long grass and dirt, with trees on three sides and a wall of rock on the other. The rock face was cut sharply at both ends and stepped in shape, making the whole place resemble an ancient amphitheatre that's been let return to nature. Like something they might visit in a TV show about the Greek islands.

I looked around and picked a spot: there, by the far end of the 'wall'. I skipped over and got low, making sure I couldn't be seen by anyone approaching from outside. I killed the light and put it in my bag. I couldn't smoke and couldn't sleep. So I waited, and thought.

What was I doing here? God, if only Rattigan and everyone else saw me now. They really would think I was a complete freak – and maybe they'd be right. Hiding in the dirt of Shook Woods after midnight. For what? Some magical writing I may or may not have seen on my window. Rattigan would almost take pity on me, I looked so pathetic. Yet again, I wondered if I was going crazy.

I didn't kill myself. Had I really read those words? I couldn't have – it was simply impossible. I'd been so sure, though. I'd looked and looked again, running my fingertips over the ice as it rose off the glass. I hadn't just read Sláine's message, I'd *felt* it. It was as real as the hand that touched it.

At least, I think it was.

Okay, I told myself, hang tight here for another while. If he doesn't show by two, go home. What have you got to lose? Apart from your life if you get hypothermia, ha. I was well wrapped up, layered like an onion: thermal vest, long-sleeved tee, rubbed-cotton hoodie, parka with goose-feather lining, wool cap with ear flaps. I was toasty. Everything was set. All I had to do was wait.

Easier said than done, though. This was *tedious*. It was also unsettling and physically uncomfortable. And I was tired. Long day, short night's sleep before it. My eyelids rolled down heavily and I blinked myself into alertness again. I looked around for visual stimulation, anything to keep me awake.

I looked at the moon, half-hidden from this angle. It was spectacularly beautiful. Amazing, really, how a lifeless chunk of stone, hanging up there, can become something heavenly when reflecting light from the sun. The moon didn't create anything – it merely beamed back what hit it. But it was beautiful. A giant silver coin suspended in space and time.

I wondered if Sláine noticed the full moon on her last night. We'd both have been looking at the same satellite: me being distracted from my wish to die, her dying whether she wanted it or not. Creepy thought.

A raven landed across the clearing and gave me the dread eye. That didn't help. I barked, as loudly as I dared, 'The hell're you looking at? Get lost.' The bird waddled a few steps in my direction – heart rate *spiking* – then changed its mind and flew off. Heart rate slowly coming back to earth.

But this was good, I was doing all right. Holding my nerve. Now all I had to do was stay awake for another few –

I woke with a violent jerk – I think I yelled out. I put a hand to my mouth. Christ. Did anyone hear that? No sound, no sign of any movement. The place was as lifeless as a grave.

And as cold. My body realised the temperature had plunged and began violently shivering. It was *freezing* now. The clearing was like a huge icebox. But how could I be this cold, with my layers and thermals and goose-feather parka . . . ?

What time was it? Ten to two. I'd been asleep for over an hour. How could I have been so stupid? Anything could have gone on in that time. My faceless killer could have returned, seen me, cut my throat and smeared the blood all over his bare backside, and I wouldn't have noticed. Out for the count, lost in the sleep of the dead.

I patted my body, up and down – nothing unusual, no tears

or cuts. No wounds, no blood. I stopped myself: what are you doing? Nobody had been here. This place was as bare as that bloody moon, and I was an idiot with an overactive imagination.

I clambered up the rock wall and sat there, rolling a cigarette. I'd imagined the writing on the window. There hadn't been any murder. Poor Sláine had simply lain down to die, and I'd never understand why.

Being here in the middle of the night, on my hare-brained stake-out: that was ridiculous. *I* was ridiculous.

I lay on the rock, eyes closed, feeling more foolish than I'd ever felt. I blew out a long plume of smoke and felt tears beginning to well up. I thought about the bridge. Suddenly, it seemed inviting once more.

Then I heard a voice and my heart just about stopped beating in my chest.

'Behold, I will bring a flood of waters upon the earth to destroy all flesh in which is the breath of life under heaven. Everything that is on the earth shall die.'

Who *said that*? I feared I was going to wet myself. The voice was strange, kind of a whisper but at the same time louder than that. It seemed to fade in and out, as though someone was fiddling with the volume on a stereo. And it sounded like a human being but somehow not; warm but icy; like a girl but old, even timeless. A noise coming from a throat and the rush of wind through tree branches.

That voice was as much a feeling as a sound.

I was still too afraid to sit up and look in that direction. I didn't want to know who or what was talking. I wanted to wake from this terrifying dream.

The voice spoke again and I bit my tongue to stop myself crying out. 'Flood. That's your surname, isn't it? Aidan Flood.'

Oh God. It knew my name. Forget the bridge, I was already doomed, I was dead meat.

The voice said, 'You sweep them away as with a flood; they are like a dream.' A gentle laugh, the sound of dried-out autumn leaves. 'I didn't know those lines when I was alive. Isn't that funny? I know them now. I seem to know lots of things now. Sit up, Aidan. Look at me. I won't hurt you.'

After a million years I forced myself to obey. I pulled myself into a sitting position and slowly, *slooooowly*, opened my eyes. There, in the clearing, stood Sláine McAuley, looking more beautiful and brilliant than the moon ever could.

She was glowing. I mean literally. Not like a neon sign, something gaudy: this was softer, a diffuse glow surrounding her whole being, as if she were shrouded in mist. Oddly, she was dressed all in black but it *felt* as if she was in white, if that makes sense. Her clothes were dark but this light seemed to be emanating from deep inside, from the core of Sláine. Or this presence in front of me that looked just like her.

'You dropped your cigarette.' She pointed to a spot next to me. I went to pick it up and hesitated.

She said, 'Go on, it's all right. I'm pretty sure second-hand smoke can't harm me now.' That uncanny, lovely laugh again.

I relit the cigarette and looked at her. Sláine was wearing what she'd been buried in. Full-length coat, high collar, intricate patterning, closed from neck to thigh with antique-style buttons. Trousers and long pointed boots, also adorned with old-style buttons. Her hair held in an elaborate bun by various pins and grips; one lock curling past each ear, brushing her cheeks.

She looked as young as me but simultaneously older. Her skin was extremely pale. Her lips were bruised red. Her eyes were dark and shining. She was breathtaking.

'Are you going to say anything? Or just stare at me.'

I blinked. Tried to think of something, make my mouth form the correct shapes and my lungs breathe the words out of me. Then I said the first dumb thing that popped into my head: 'Your clothes. Not the usual things people get . . . um –'

'Buried in?'

I paused before nodding.

'My cousin Carmel dressed me for the funeral,' Sláine said. 'She knew what I'd have wanted to wear. We used to talk about it a bit, you know – how would you like to be buried, if you *had* to choose . . . People have a fascination with all that stuff when they're young, don't they? I suppose because you never actually believe that one day it'll happen to you for real.'

She gave me a steady, piercing look, her head slightly tilted. I wondered if she somehow knew I'd considered that very thing myself, a week before. How could she know, or get inside my mind? Then again, how was this possible anyway? How could she stand here before me as – what?

I said uncertainly, 'Are . . . are you a . . . a ghost?'

She smiled softly. 'I'm not sure what I am. All I know is that I died a week ago. Now I'm . . . here.' She spread her arms wide and gestured around her.

'In the forest?'

'Yes. Mostly.'

55

'You – live here now? Sorry, that sounded so stupid.'

Sláine laughed. I went on, 'You're here, though? This is where you . . . stay now?'

She nodded and thought for a moment. 'It's hard to explain. I don't . . . Time doesn't seem the same as it used to be. It's not as if I spend all day and night walking around Shook Woods. I don't get bored the way I might have . . . before. I sort of just *exist* now. I'm aware of my own existence and in control of it, but it's not how it was when I was alive. It's a strange feeling. Almost more a state of mind than an actual thing. Can you understand any of that?'

'I don't think so. I'm sorry, I wish I could.'

'It's all right. Are you still afraid of me?'

I realised that I wasn't. I said, 'No. I feel . . . comfortable talking to you, I think. Does that make sense?'

'It does.'

'So the forest, is *this* a state of mind to you? Is that what you meant?'

'You know how I'd describe my existence now? Like a waking dream. I don't sleep any more but all the hours feel like I'm walking through a never-ending dream. Except the dream, as you see, is very real.'

She gave a little ironic bow. I rolled another cigarette and said, 'It is, isn't it? It's really real. Christ. Weird and all as this is, I'm glad you're real. I thought I was going mad. With the sign on my window, what you wrote on the glass, the message . . . That *was* you, wasn't it?'

'Yes.'

'So you can leave here?'

'Yes.'

'Whenever you like?'

She thought about this. 'Mm . . . sort of. Yes. I'll say yes, to all intents and purposes.'

'And go where you want?'

'No. I can't – something seems to be stopping me from actually entering places. Buildings, or even an enclosed space, like a yard or someone's garden? I can come right up to them, and no further. Don't know why.'

'But you can touch them. I mean you must have touched my window, the outside. Made the ice do something on the inside. I don't know. Caused some parts of the glass to get very cold or whatever. Made the words form like that, turning condensation into little streaks of ice?'

Sláine nodded and smiled. She seemed pleased I'd worked out the mechanics of it. So was I: surprised and pleased.

A crucial question marched to the front of my brain, begging to be asked. 'Why me? Why did you contact me? We hardly knew each other.'

'I saw you here, that day. You came to the tree where they found me. You seemed . . . lost. Alone. And I was alone, so . . . ' She shrugged. 'I reached out to you. Do you wish I hadn't?'

'No. Definitely not.' A thought struck me. 'My bag. You moved it.'

Sláine giggled playfully. 'My little practical joke. I didn't lose my sense of humour when I lost my life.'

I wanted to ask her about that but I couldn't, it felt too early, as if I'd be intruding somewhere I didn't yet have the right to go. Instead I said, 'Your voice – it's amazing. Sounds like nothing I've ever heard. Hard to describe.'

She looked proud, and happy, that I'd said this. 'Yes. I like it. It reminds me of wind chimes. But wood. Not the metal ones.'

'Yeah, I can see that. Can I ask you something else?'

'Anything you like.'

'Are you physical? Do you have, like, a physical body any more?'

'In a way. Watch.'

All of a sudden I was hurled backwards by a strong force, *whoomp*, landing me flat on my back. It hadn't hurt, though, that was the thing. It was the closest I'd ever come to an out-of-body experience. Sláine had shoved me but hadn't seemed to move herself. And I'd felt the shove but didn't feel it. It was as if she'd acted incredibly quickly, pushing me, then rushing around behind and catching my fall, before tearing back to her starting point.

A line from some book came to me: 'The dead travel fast.' Unexpectedly, I found myself laughing. I sat up and said, 'That was, uh . . . interesting. How did you do that?'

'I'm not sure. Yet.'

'Was it speed? You went so fast I didn't see it?'

'No. That's the funny part. I didn't really move at all.'

'Ha. Well, it was impressive. So is that your only party trick, then?'

She smiled like a poker player who's full sure she's got an unbeatable hand. 'I think I have a few more up my sleeve.'

I hopped off the rock and brushed dust from my coat. She moved away from me in a weird sort of gliding motion. I couldn't really say that I saw her doing it – one moment she was here, the next over there – but I saw her do it.

I think I did. This was all a lot to take in. I shivered inside as a shadowy premonition of something great and dreadful ran through me. I felt a little afraid, but not of Sláine.

I asked, to get this feeling out of my mind, 'What was that you said earlier? Something about a flood.'

'It's from the Bible. Noah and the Ark, all that. I thought it might be a good way to . . . introduce myself. Doesn't mean anything – just some lines I liked the sound of. It didn't scare you, did it? Maybe I should have picked something less ominous.'

'No, it was . . . To be honest, you could have been reciting *The Three Little Pigs* and I would have nearly peed in my pants. You gave me some shock.'

'Your name *is* Flood, right? I'm sorry, I only knew you to see you around town, really. I wasn't sure which one you were.'

I said bitterly, 'What, you don't know Aidan Flood the dickless loser? I'm a celebrity – how could you not know all about me? Shit, they put up a Facebook page in my honour.'

'I'd heard some vague stories. I didn't pay any attention. They seemed pretty mean-spirited.'

'They were.'

'Your girlfriend went off with someone else, I think?'

I sighed heavily. Raking over the ashes of my Caitlin disaster wasn't pleasant, even under such unusual conditions. 'Yeh. She shifted this guy behind my back. Guy from the carnival. We were supposed to be a couple. *Supposed* to.'

'I remember him. I went there one evening with my niece. He was very good-looking.'

She was smiling mischievously. I smiled back, in spite of myself.

'He was. Ah, you know what? I think it was the best thing for us anyway. Looking back now. I'm not just, I don't know, making excuses for her or whatever? I mean I hated her for what she did, and what it brought on me. Maybe a bit of me still does. But if Caitlin cared that little for me to make an asshole out of me like that, then . . . Pff. Feck it. No loss.'

'Caitlin. Is that how she pronounced her name, that American way? It's all wrong.'

'Yep.'

'You should have told her it's "Cat-leen".'

'I couldn't. I was in love.'

Sláine regarded me with a cool eye. 'Were you, though?'

'Wha—? God, I *think* so. I mean I thought I was. I don't know . . . maybe not? I don't know much of anything. Sorry, that's not a very good answer. I wish I wasn't so dumb.'

'You're not dumb,' Sláine said. 'You're unsure, and a little timid, and you don't like yourself – in fact you partly hate yourself. But you're not dumb, Aidan. You're just normal. Like the rest of us, ha.'

I laughed too, both at her joke and the craziness of where I found myself. How typical, I thought: I finally meet a confidante and she's a dead girl who spends her days and nights haunting a creepy old forest. But I was going with the flow, not fighting it, not worrying or overthinking. My brain told me this was fantastical and absurd, but my guts told me it felt natural. It felt right.

'What about you?' I said.

'What about me?'

'I mean your . . . this. Your situation, what happened to you. What did happen?'

'Leave that for a minute. Tell me about the bullying.'

'Oh, so you *have* heard about the famous dickless loser.'

'Tell me.'

I sighed again. 'What's there to tell? I used to be a geek that everyone ignored. Then the thing with Caitlin happened and I became a geek everyone picked on. That's it, full stop, nothing more to say.'

'I think there's a lot more to say.'

I snapped, 'Yeah, well I don't really feel like talking about it.' I looked at her nervously. 'Sorry. You're not going to wallop me again, are you?'

Sláine said, laughing, 'Not unless you ask me to. It's okay if you don't want to talk about it. Raking over old coals – there's no point, I can see that. No point dwelling in the past. Life has to go on, right?'

'Yeah,' I drawled. 'So, uh . . . You. What's the story? You said you didn't kill yourself. Then who did?'

'I can't tell you that.'

'Was it someone I know? I mean, should we be alerting the cops that there's a killer on the loose?'

Sláine smiled. 'I can't tell you because I don't know. I have some of the how, but not the who – or the why.' She frowned. 'And to be honest? I don't think there's much the Guards can do about it.'

She must have seen some empathy or pity on my face, because Sláine reached out and put a hand to it – her touch

61

felt like snow, very cold but not unpleasant. She said, 'Don't be upset, Aidan. It's all right. There's nothing you can do. Things will work out, don't worry.'

'I feel bad for you, though. I don't even know you but I feel bad.'

'I understand that. And appreciate it. Look, there are things you can't know yet. I don't think you're ready. That's not being patronising – this is heavy stuff. But when the time is right . . . Now go home.'

'Will we talk again? Can we meet?'

'Of course. I'll contact you. You'll know the sign when you see it.'

'Okay. But soon, please. I'd like it to be soon. If that's cool with you.'

She said wryly, '*Everything* is cool in my world. Soon, yes. Now go to sleep.'

Sláine reached out again and her index finger touched my forehead and then I –

SHOCK AND BLOOD LOSS

I woke at home, feeling more rested than I had for ages. Feeling energised, electrified, on fire. *Alive.*

I guess that's what spending a few hours with the dead will do for you.

I stretched and it felt great. I hopped out of bed, went to the bathroom and looked at my reflection: I was smiling broadly. I couldn't remember the last time I'd seen that. And another thing – a mark on my forehead, barely visible but definitely there. A little pink ellipse. The shape of a fingertip.

So it wasn't a dream. I'd worried that the whole thing had been invented by my mind. How pathetic would that have been? To not only retreat from the disappointments of life into a fantasy, but for that dream to be about a dead girl you didn't even know? It wasn't fantasy, though. It was real. *She* was real, and I bore the physical proof like a tattoo.

I brushed my teeth distractedly and thought back to the night before. The last thing I recalled was Sláine touching my forehead, then *pow*, lights out. She must have brought me home. Hadn't she said she couldn't enter buildings? But clearly she did, because I looked down and saw I was wearing pyjama trousers and a T-shirt – what, she'd even got me dressed for bed? And undressed.

I smiled again. Oh, this was too weird. Weird but very cool.

I skipped down to breakfast but the kitchen was empty – and it was one in the afternoon. My mother had left a note for me:

Aidan we are gone to visit Granny didn't want to wake you you looked bushed make yourself a sandwich see you later.

I made it and ate it and basked in quietness and good thoughts. No, not good, that wasn't right: Sláine was dead, it was horrible what had happened to her. It *couldn't* be good. Yet she hadn't seemed terribly unhappy, or traumatised. She'd seemed – at peace? Maybe. *I* certainly felt more peaceful, more content, my heart beating slow and steady, my guts not burning and twisting as they often did. I didn't understand it at all but I liked it.

I took a walk around town, seeing it through new eyes: it looked different. I suppose it *was* different now, because I was different. Something had changed in me. I couldn't have said what that was, but I felt it: change for the better.

I noticed things that had escaped my attention before, or perhaps remembered them afresh. How small the town was, how cramped its streets, though in a charming kind of way. A quaint little place that tourists would appreciate, if we ever got any. I noticed a lot of cracks in the pavement and dog shit on the ground, but surprisingly little rubbish. How the town was built in a bowl, the centre streets running flat and the outlying streets leaning in, flowing to its heart like mercury in a dish.

I also noticed the ruined bell tower of the church, bricks

falling away to reveal the split, rusted bell inside. It was never used any more, and that spot was surely unsafe – loose bricks could crash to the ground at any time. For some reason, I wasn't bothered by it. Nor, apparently, were the bats swooping in and out of the bell tower. Honest-to-God actual bats, looking weirdly large from this angle, like cartoonish angels of death amassing on an abandoned holy site. Guess they can fly off if it all falls down, I thought.

A car was parked out front of the church, engine idling, a man inside checking a map. Beautiful machine, dark-green, sleek and muscular, exactly like a big cat. It might have been a Jag but I'm hopeless with car marques – can never tell them apart. I wondered if the Jag my father would be working on looked like this. The man raised a finger in salute as I passed, without looking up.

I debated whether to tell him to move his car in case the bell tower came down on it like the plunge of a giant hypodermic needle. Nah, he'd be all right.

Town was quiet, this being Sunday. On the main street, however, a Garda squad car zoomed past, blowing a tiny hurricane around my head, siren squealing, heading out of town. I figured it was a traffic accident and blessed myself, more from habit than anything else. I didn't have religious belief but old superstitions die hard; it feels nice to make a blessing for someone in trouble. I hoped nobody was seriously hurt and walked on.

I thought about that – belief. If someone had told me last week that another world existed beyond this one, I'd have told them to see a psychiatrist or get off whatever drugs they were taking. (Or give some to me, ha ha.) But it did – I'd seen it. A world where the dead aren't gone, where they can talk and laugh and touch. A world where ghostly girls move through the shadows of the dark woods, glowing like stars fallen to earth.

I passed an old gent I vaguely knew and he gave a big cheery wave. I waved back, just as cheerily. I heard the sirens again, whooping through the air, over in the distance. I guessed they were skirting the town, coming around by that estate near the golf course. It was hard to tell for sure.

After a while I went home and chilled out in front of the TV, doing the bare minimum of homework. Study could wait. Revision for my Leaving Cert could wait. The whole bloody thing could wait, while I waited for another message from Sláine.

At around six I put on the TV news and the second story, most unusually, was from my town. A grave-faced reporter in an ill-fitting suit was standing across the road from the golf club, a line of trees running behind him. I knew the spot. The river's course partly took it along there, and the whole area was a sort of nature reserve, marshy and overgrown, with walking paths and a car park. Families went there for picnics.

Also, assholes went there to shoot ducks, looking ridiculous in their army fatigues and those stupid caps they wear. I smiled vindictively and wondered if one had shot his friend in the backside. Hope springs eternal . . .

I turned up the volume and the reporter said, 'Full details haven't been released yet, but investigating Gardaí are not looking for anyone in connection with this incident. The victim,

Chris Harrington, was found by a jogger this morning, lying unconscious in this stretch of marsh behind me. It is believed he was mauled by one or more large animals, probably dogs. Sources are telling us that, due to the severity of injuries received to his face, the teenager was unrecognisable. He was identified by an eagle tattoo on his right arm. Mr Harrington was rushed to hospital, where his condition is described as "critical but stable". His family was being consoled by local priest Father –'

I killed the sound. What the hell? Chris Harrington. A good-looking sleazeball, the year ahead of me at school. Unlike Sláine, Harrington hadn't gone on to college; he hadn't gone on to anything but hanging around town, collecting his dole and keeping a string of casual girlfriends on the go. Some people said he did some small-time hash dealing, but I only smoked the legal stuff so I wouldn't know.

I rang Podsy's mobile but it went to answerphone. I opened my laptop and went online. If anyone would know the details of what had happened, social media would.

After half an hour of searching and reading, I'd pieced together the basic facts, allowing for the usual distortion and Chinese whispers of the internet. Harrington went out last night at around half ten. He was drinking in a scuzzy pub that serves scuzzy people until they all got kicked out sometime north of one. Harrington headed home alone. After that, a gap in the narrative.

Fast-forward to this morning. He hadn't come home. Then this guy, the runner, stumbles across Harrington's body around nine: mangled, unconscious but still alive, just about. According to the online rumour mill – everyone *swore* their information was good – he'd been attacked by something, a pack of dogs maybe. Torn apart. His handsome face shredded, innards half-spilled from his body. Harrington had since gone into a coma, caused by shock and blood loss. Doctors doing all they could, et cetera.

I tried Podsy again and this time he answered: 'Aidan. You heard about Harrington, obviously?'

'Yeah. Man, this is nuts. What did it? I know you asked your uncle.'

'I did. He says they *think* it was wild dogs. They're not sure. Uncle Tim says it's hard to tell because the wounds are so bad. The feckin' guy was ripped to bits. Like, I don't think there's a lot of him left to examine, know what I mean?'

'God. I don't even want to think about it.'

Instead I thought about something else, as Podsy rambled on: Chris Harrington, and what an absolute prick he was to me. He'd been one of the prime movers in my four months of harassment. A smart mouth, always looking to make himself feel good at the expense of someone else, and for a while, I was that someone. Harrington was relentless and merciless. It was never physical with him, but any chance for a jibe or sneer, he took it.

Harrington was a bully and a jerk. I hated him as much as any of the others. And the world would probably be a better place without him in it. But was I happy that he'd been seriously injured? I didn't honestly know.

Podsy's voice shocked me back to reality, my ear honing in on one word: 'Sláine.'

My blood chilled. Did he know something? He couldn't, but he'd said her name. I tried to play it cool, replying, 'Sorry, what? Other phone went off there – I didn't hear you properly.'

'I was saying first Sláine, now this. It's shocking, really. Not a good time to be a kid in this town, Aidan! You better watch out, you might be next!'

I knew he was fooling around to break the tension. I was about to say my goodbyes when Podsy spoke again, quieter: 'I didn't like what he did to you. Harrington – that wasn't right, the way he treated you.' Silence hung between us, thick and heavy. 'I'm not saying he deserved it, but . . . ' His voice trailed off.

I said, 'Yeah. I know what you mean.'

'Listen, I've to go. Mum's calling me. I didn't get the full story on Sláine from Tim yet, I'll do it soon as I can.'

'All right. Talk to you at school, yeah?'

'Take it easy, man.'

We hung up. I closed my laptop and then my eyes. One of my tormentors, a guy I'd wanted to batter with a hammer every time I saw his face, was now clinging on to life in the emergency ward. It didn't really make me feel better, knowing that. But being brutally frank, it didn't make me feel any worse either.

School was ablaze again the next morning. Another weekend, another young person struck by disaster, this time in radically different circumstances. And this time, of course, not dead – yet. Harrington wasn't our schoolmate any more, but everyone seemed pretty shook up. What had Podsy said: this was a bad time to be a kid and we should all watch our backs? I laughed uneasily to myself and tried to concentrate on what my teacher was saying.

We were in History, studying the Great Famine with Mr Lee. Everyone knew the basics of the story: between about 1845 and 1852, a potato blight caused mass starvation and social breakdown throughout impoverished Ireland. An estimated million people died, another million emigrated. It was a catastrophe, a huge scar on the Irish psyche which remained to this day. The Famine was still remembered, commemorated, lamented.

What I hadn't known, until this morning, was that our town suffered worse than most during those terrible times. We're cut off by the sea on one side, the forest on another and mountains on a third and most of a fourth. Back then there was really only one route in or out – through and over those mountains – and hardly anybody was taking it.

When the English authorities finally got their act together and came to help in the bleak midwinter of 1851, they arrived in a ghost town. As Mr Lee explained, virtually every last person was dead by the end: of hunger, disease, exhaustion, cold. The few who survived made for safety across the mountains, a perilous journey with low chances of success.

The company of Crown soldiers found a group of mangy dogs picking at the few corpses that weren't already eaten by wild animals. Clusters of bones, scraps of clothing; a piece of cheap jewellery here, leather boot there. Makeshift headstones dotted the edge of town, a pathetic attempt to mark the passing of parents, children, friends. But only a handful; probably by the end people hadn't the energy to do anything but wait there for death.

Just like Sláine. What a strange thought. I shivered, as though a thousand frozen hands were reaching out to me across the centuries.

Mr Lee also mentioned how the English thought our town was cursed, calling it Death's Shadow. I already knew that, we all did; not the sort of nickname you shrug off too easily. Even worse, I thought sarcastically, than 'dickless loooooser'.

Anyway, the man in charge decided to start afresh – to slay whatever demons might be present, genuine or imagined. The whole place was razed to the ground, burned into obliteration, and completely rebuilt. Rebuilt for whom? Those few dozen who'd escaped over the mountains – and somehow survived. They returned, in dribs and drabs, bringing others with them, and people passing by decided to stay . . . and over the years, the town was repopulated and reborn.

But it never forgot: the cold, the hunger, the ever-present unstoppable death.

Mr Lee finished his talk and called for questions. A girl called Yvonne raised her hand and said, 'Is anything left of the old town, then, sir?'

'Well, we have the bridge on the coast road,' he said, 'though that's a little outside town, of course. Built sometime in the fifteenth century. Apart from that, no. Not one thing was left standing.' He began gathering his things, a sign the class was drawing to a close. 'I mean, there's underground. There're all sorts of stories about tunnels and passages and catacombs, deep underneath the town. Dating from long before Famine times, possibly as far back as the Dark Ages. They wouldn't have been destroyed in the fire –'

I was listening intently when something odd happened: Mr Lee's voice sort of stretched out into a low droning noise, like an Aboriginal didgeridoo. My vision went black at the edges, reforming into a tunnel of light on the teacher's face. He turned to me, looked me right in the eye, and said, 'Tonight. Midnight. You know the place.'

Only it wasn't *him* – Mr Lee – saying it, it was Sláine. I'd know it anywhere, I'd never forget it. That voice which sounded like the tinkle of ice, which you felt more than heard.

I thought I heard her whisper something else; it could have been 'heart'. Then she laughed and there was silence. I snapped back to reality. Mr Lee was still talking: 'But nobody has any *proof* that they exist. Probably just legends, you know. A bit of local colour. All right, is that it, so? Okay, off you go.'

I looked around. No one else appeared to have noticed anything strange. What was that, a hallucination? Is that what those feel like? I remembered reading that epileptic fits and brain seizures are often preceded by some bizarro out-of-body type feeling. Aw God, I wasn't going to be struck down by one of those, was I? As if I didn't have enough crap to be dealing with.

I met Podsy after school and we walked part of the way home together. He'd talked to his uncle late last night. God bless you, Uncle Tim, and your free-and-easy way with confidential information.

According to Podsy, Sláine had been fully dressed when they found her, although not wearing a coat. Her parents said they didn't think one was missing from her room, so I assumed she'd gone there without. That'd back up the suicide theory, but of course I knew by now this wasn't the case.

Her feet were bare – they'd turned blue from the cold, become swollen. Other than that, the medical examiner found no marks on Sláine's corpse, no signs of violence, self-inflicted or not. The one thing of note they couldn't explain yet was the state of her skin and eyes. Sláine's skin was marked by tiny light-blue lines all over her body, as if the blood vessels underneath had somehow petrified. Tim said the girl looked like she'd been tattooed.

And her irises had changed colour: from her natural dark-grey to the same icy-blue as the lines on her skin. The coroner was baffled, hypothesising that the freezing temperatures had had some radical, mystifying effect.

I didn't recall noticing marks on her skin when we met on Saturday night. Having said that, I wasn't exactly in the right frame of mind to notice much of anything, beyond the fact I was having a conversation with a girl who was dead and now appeared to be alive once more. Also, her eyes had seemed dark to me, not blue. I'd have to examine her more closely tonight.

I thanked Podsy for the information and turned to go. He stopped me by the arm, saying, 'What's all this about? All this wanting to know about Sláine McAuley. Did you fancy her or something before?'

I laughed unconvincingly. 'What? No way. I didn't even know the girl.'

He eyeballed me, clearly suspicious.

I said, 'I'm just curious, I told you. Like, it's weird, the way she was found and all. How they don't know what happened to her.'

'They *do* know, though. She died of the cold. Anyone would, out in Shook Woods in winter, middle of the night. Your body temperature drops below a certain point, you can't metabolise nutrients and your organs start to fail. Eventually you'll slip into a coma. Then you die.'

'Did Uncle Tim tell you that?'

'Nah, just know it myself. From Biology, you know.'

'Right.' I paused, not sure if I wanted to express the thought that had just popped into my head. 'I, uh . . . this's going to sound awful, but you want to know something?'

'Uh-huh.'

'I kind of don't give a shit that Chris Harrington got his ass torn up like that.' I looked at Podsy, feeling ashamed but not ashamed. 'Does that make me an evil person?'

He smiled wryly. 'Yeah, I noticed you weren't too concerned about him, all right. No, I don't think so. I mean I'm not happy the guy got attacked. But he was an asshole. Is, sorry. Still is an asshole. Not dead yet.'

I smiled at Podsy and punched him lightly on the arm. 'I mean I guess I want him to pull through.'

'Sure, yeah. Me too.'

'So what did happen, anyway? Harrington. What was it, a pack of wild dogs or something?'

Podsy said indifferently, 'Mm, think so. Don't know where they came from, though. Do we have wild dogs around here?'

'Maybe from the forest.'

'Yeah. You wouldn't know *what's* hiding out in that bloody place.' He gave an exaggerated shudder. 'Man. Shook Woods. Wouldn't catch me going there for love nor money.'

'No? You believe all that stuff, then? Legends about the forest?'

Podsy glared at me as if I'd just said the dumbest thing ever. 'Eh, *no*. Of course not. I'm not a child. But there's something really creepy about the woods all the same. Don't you think so? You never got that little shiver up your spine out there?'

I smiled inside. 'I suppose so, yeah. The odd time.'

Podsy muttered, 'Whole *town* gives me a weird feeling sometimes.' Then he smiled. 'But it's home, right? For good or bad.'

He waved goodbye and headed off towards his own house: Hiro the Hero was Skyping from Japan again this evening, so he had to prepare. I walked in the direction of my home – I had things to prepare for too.

COLDER, WARMER

This cold snap wasn't going away. We were in the last week of November now, not normally a freezing time of year on the west coast of Ireland. Chilly, yes, usually windy, and rainy of course. It's almost always rainy in this country. But never so cold in November, temperatures hovering close to zero.

If anything, it was getting colder. Those days were sunny, motionless and perishingly cold. There hadn't been any rain in weeks; even the wind had eased down. Still no snow, but we had crystals on windows, frost on the grass, spiders' webs glistening icily. Everything felt *caught* in a sort of stasis of coldness: the molecules which form matter slowing down and slowing more and then stopping, *kaput*. It was all quite beautiful.

I was doubly wrapped up when I hit for Shook Woods at ten past eleven that night. My mother heard me leaving; she was up, smoking a cigarette and doing the crossword. I told her I was feeling insomniac too and going for a walk to bring on sleep hopefully. She may or may not have believed me; all she said was, 'Mind yourself, love. It's treacherous out there.'

I didn't know if she meant the weather conditions or the world in general.

Sláine was waiting when I reached our place. *Our place.* Wow. Did we have a 'place' now? And what did I mean by 'we' anyway? What exactly was going on here? A mystery, an intrigue, a freaky experience that I still wasn't one hundred per cent sure was actually taking place.

The most exciting thing that had happened to me in a long time.

Whatever it all meant, there I went and there she stood, exactly in the centre, as beautiful as before. Her clothes seemed a slightly lighter colour, probably a trick of the moonlight. Her eyes, I quickly confirmed, were dark-grey, and her skin was flawless. It glowed like white alabaster, cool, exquisite. I don't know what that coroner was talking about.

A little smile played on Sláine's lips as she beckoned me towards her. The air was thin in our Ancient Greek amphitheatre in the forest; I had to labour that bit harder to draw enough oxygen from it. I shuffled over.

Sláine said, 'Hmm. You look like you've got something to say.'

I started rolling a cigarette. 'That was a cool trick you pulled in History class. Getting your voice inside my head like that.'

She mock-curtsied, then said, 'No. Something else.'

'Heh. I've got so much to say, I don't know where to start.'

'No, this is something in particular. There's a question on your mind that you want to ask but you're afraid to. You think it might upset me.'

Was there? I realised that actually, yes, there was. How odd. 'How'd you know what was in my head before I knew it myself?'

'I'm not sure. Maybe I'm telepathic, ha! . . . That was a joke,

77

Aidan. I can't literally read your thoughts. I'm not Edward Cullen.'

'So how then?'

She shrugged. 'I think I can read you pretty well. You're easy to read anyway, and that's a compliment. You're an open, genuine guy. You don't dissemble all the time, like a lot of people. Am I right in saying this?'

I gave a shrug of my own, signifying, 'Sure, I suppose so.'

She went on, 'I read your body language, maybe? Or something in your eyes, the way you looked at me a bit warily . . . I don't know how I knew. I just did.'

I smiled. 'Maybe I'm wary because of . . . Well.' I threw my hand around the open space. 'This. You. Me and you. It's a pretty goddamn weird situation, don't you think?'

Sláine smiled back – it made her look younger. She said, 'Maybe. You're probably right to be wary. But you still haven't asked that question you're afraid of.'

I changed tack. 'How did you get me home the other night? Into my room. Thought you couldn't go into, like, people's houses or whatever.'

'Yeah, like Dracula. Not until I'm invited . . . ' She looked off into the darkness. 'I don't know. I *couldn't* before, now I can. Your house, at least. I'm not sure about other places – except for one . . . Maybe it's because I met you? Met you, touched you – made some kind of connection, right? Like that enabled me to some extent, gave me power? But I don't really know. "Ours is not to question why, ours is but to do or . . . "'

She left the last word out – the Tennyson quotation was seared into my brain from English class, rote learning, and I unthinkingly finished it. '"Die." Shit. Sorry, that was . . . '

'Don't worry about it. Now come on, you're stalling for time. You realise that, don't you? Ask me the question you *really* want to ask.'

I said it out straight, finally: 'Your body. Is it still in the graveyard? I mean, I'm . . . I presume that this' – I gestured towards her – 'isn't you. As in, the old you. Do you know what I mean?'

'I do.' She thought about it. 'I think . . . I think it's still there. *I'm* still there. But that's not me any more, like you said. It's just decaying flesh. *This* is me. And I'm free now.'

'Is that how you feel? Free?'

'In some ways. Not entirely.'

'Someone told me that your skin was all blue when you were found. Little blue lines all over. They said it looked like a tattoo. What was all that about?'

'I don't know. I don't remember that.'

'What *do* you remember? About – you know. Dying. God, it sounds so messed up when I say it out loud. Kind of absurd.'

Sláine threw her head back and laughed, gorgeously. My heart quickened half a beat. She said, 'Some of it. But I'm not going to tell you about that yet. Like I said, not until the time is right . . . Don't get that disappointed look, Aidan. You trust me?'

'I guess.'

'Then trust me on this.'

'Sure. All right . . . Hey, I also heard that your eyes had changed colour. They were blue too, like the lines on your skin. But that couldn't have been correct. I mean I can see them right now. They're dark.'

'Same as the day I was born. Again, I can't explain what they saw. I mean, I wasn't there when they did that – that examination, whatever you call it. Elvis had left the building, as they say. I was long gone, my spirit . . . How do you know all this?'

I answered, 'My friend Podsy told me. His uncle's a Guard, blabs all the time.'

'Do I know him? What's his name again?'

'Podsy O'Keeffe. It's a pet name for Padraig. I don't know if you do. Probably not – he'd be younger than you. Bit younger than me. Small fella, kinda nerdy? He's a good guy. Podsy's a good friend – he's been really decent to me.'

The clearing shimmered from the moonlight, but the forest surrounding us was totally black, as though dipped in ink and left to dry. The trees were massive and unmoving. I had an unnerving feeling that they were listening to us, conscious in some way. A creature flapped into the air, beyond my vision; something told me it was a bat, not a bird.

I hopped onto the wall of rock and began pacing it to distract my thoughts. Shook Woods *was* creepy, no doubt about it. And moonlight made everything kind of strange and spectral; I read it described once as not so much a light, more 'a state of things'. Still, while I continued to find the forest unsettling, I was beginning to feel comfortable there. It might have been the fact that Sláine was with me, and for whatever reason I was coming to see her as a protector of some sort. My gut instinct told me, she'll look after you, whatever happens. At any rate, I was positive she wouldn't do me any harm herself.

Standing in our space, the shining moon above us like a celestial spotlight, I felt secure. The trees were outside this blessed circle, they couldn't get in to us; we were safe here. I was even a tiny bit happy in this place. It almost felt like home.

'Okay, my turn for a few questions,' she said.

I nodded and muttered, 'All right. Yeah, fine.'

'First off: are you happy?'

'Right now, or life in general?'

'Either. Both.'

'Right now, yes. I think I'm happy, being here, talking to you. Which is a sad reflection on where my life's at, I have to tell you.'

We both laughed. She said, 'So in general . . . not so happy?'

'You could say that.' I finished my smoke and flicked it into the shadows. For an instant I had a ludicrous fear that one of the pines would lurch forward and clobber me for littering. I went on. 'I don't know. I mean things aren't as awful as they were, so that's progress, right? I used to be *unbelievably* . . . Like, I'd just feel so bad all the time. Angry and upset and lonely. Basically like the world's biggest asshole. As if I was cursed or something. Probably was clinically depressed. I don't know why I'm telling you this. Laying all this doom and gloom on you.'

'Because I asked you to. Go on.'

'Well I haven't really been hassled much since . . . uh, for the last while. Don't know why but I'm being left alone for the time being. So I guess I'm happier now? Or less *unhappy*, anyway. I don't feel . . . '

I left that unexpressed. Sláine must have read my mind again, metaphorically at least, because she completed the

81

sentence: 'Like killing yourself any more.'

A long silence stretched out in the still cold darkness. Finally I said quietly, 'Yeah. Like . . . doing that, yeah.'

She spoke so softly it was barely a sound. 'You were going to do it on Sunday week, weren't you? Jump off the bridge. End it all.'

I didn't reply.

'That would have been a stupid thing to do. I'm glad you changed your mind.'

I snapped at her, 'What do you mean, stupid? What the hell d'you know about my life anyway?'

'I know it's worth more than to throw it away because a group of malicious little babies decided they didn't like you.' She sighed. 'You're right, I don't know everything about you. But I know enough, Aidan. I know you're a good person and they're not. You're more precious than they'll ever be.'

I sighed too. 'I suppose you're right.'

'There's no suppose. I *am* right.'

I smiled up to meet Sláine's own smile, and jokily bowed before her great wisdom. I thought to myself, man oh man, you're parleying wits with a dead girl at midnight. And you like it. How did *that* happen?

She hovered closer to me, that funny moving-that-wasn't-moving. 'Tell me about it now. The bullying.'

'Do I have to? To be honest I'd sooner talk about you. You and this and how is it even possible.'

'That can wait. I'm not going to suddenly be alive again, don't worry. There's plenty time.'

'I didn't mean anything by that.'

'I know. Now tell me.'

So I did. The whole sorry story, beginning to end. Caitlin, the carnival guy, the sneering, the punches, the shame, the isolation. The stupid Facebook page, the brick through my window. That night at the bridge. The way I wanted a massive hole to open up and the earth to swallow me completely. The way it made me hate them all, like an unquenchable fire in my belly, and hate myself for hating them.

The way it made me hate myself, full stop.

Sláine let me talk myself out. It could have lasted ten minutes, it could have been an hour. All I know are two things. I was freezing by the time I'd finished, because I hadn't moved throughout the telling. And I didn't cry, which surprised me a little. Maybe the tears inside had chilled to ice too, along with everything else in this frozen midwinter.

'Actually,' I finished, 'one of them got attacked yesterday. One of the bullies. This complete and utter knob called Chris Harrington. Sorry, that's not a nice way to talk about someone in hospital.'

'Hospital? That's serious. What happened?'

'He got . . . they think an animal or something. Or a pack of them, wild dogs maybe. They tore him up pretty viciously. He's in ICU, hooked up to who knows what. I think he's gonna pull through, but still. Harrington got messed *up*, you know? Really badly.'

'Did he deserve it?'

'What? To get himself attacked?'

'Mm-hm.'

I considered Sláine's question, and the answer came slamming into my head with the weight and violence of that brick hurled through my window. I looked at her and said evenly, 'Yes. Yes, he did. Harrington was a horrible bastard to me. Just, a really nasty piece of work, you know?'

'I do.'

I said warily, 'And, like, if he *hadn't* survived last night? He did, but just say he hadn't . . . ' I gulped heavily. Did I believe what I was about to say? 'People often go, "Oh the world's a better place without such-and-such." I don't know if that's the case here. I mean Chris Harrington isn't a serial killer or Hitler or anything. He's just an asshole. But . . . *my* world might be better without him. I know that sounds awful. It makes me sound like a vindictive psycho. I can't help it. I hate him. Probably a part of me *wanted* something bad to happen to him – and now it has. Maybe I should be careful what I wish for . . . But feck it, that's how a bit of me thinks. And Harrington's not the only one.'

'I think I know how you feel.'

'Why, were you bullied too? I gotta tell you, that'd shock me. You always seemed so – popular. Confident.'

'No, I was never bullied. But I have a heart and eyes, which means I can empathise with people and can see things happen. I saw a lot of that stuff going on, and I felt sorry for those on the receiving end.' She clicked her tongue and added regretfully, 'Never did anything to stop it, though.'

I waved a hand, dismissing her self-criticism. 'Forget it. Nobody ever steps in, really. I wouldn't feel bad about it, Sláine.'

'But I do.'

'Well, don't. People keep their head down and mind their

own business. All of us do it. I'm no better than anyone else. It's only in the movies, in a book or whatever, that some hero stands up for the little guy. Doesn't work like that in real life.'

'Maybe it should.'

I shrugged again, this time in agreement and resignation. It should, Sláine, but it never will. An owl hooted in the distance, sending its soft, eerie call into the darkness. Another call, a third. What cool music those birds made. It sounded almost human. No, not human exactly – more like a peculiar version of a person. I pictured a man with huge owl eyes, like pools of oil, staring at me through the trees.

Sláine said, 'Barn owl. Male, eight-and-a-half years old. Nest about a mile from here. Bright-white face, but with an unusual dark line running diagonally between its eyes.'

'Wha—? How do you know that?'

She smiled, playfully triumphant. 'I know lots of things, Aidan Flood. My gaze penetrates deeply into the black heart of Shook Woods. *And* further.'

I looked into those shining dark eyes. 'You know, I don't doubt that.'

The owl hooted once more and Sláine said, 'There goes the whistle. End of our working day.'

'Oh yeah – like a factory whistle. That's pretty clever.'

She said drolly, 'Yep. The deader I get, the more clever I am.'

I laughed because it was expected of me, but I wished she hadn't said that. I didn't care to be reminded of the one undeniable, unalterable fact here: this girl *was* dead. And I didn't want her to be. Because if she was dead, then we . . .

'Come here. I want to show you something before you leave.'

I snapped out of my thoughts and forced myself to joke, 'Oh, I'm leaving now, am I? That's it. "Aidan, you're dismissed."'

'Aidan, you're dismissed. But I want you to see something first.'

The next thing I knew I was standing in a different part of the forest, much further in. Blacker in here, the trees closer together, but still moonlight to see by. No paths, though there were some gaps between the trees, wide enough to walk through.

Sláine had somehow brought me here in a split second – whisked me up and whooshed me through the woods. I had a vague memory of an even vaguer sensation of high speed, the way your stomach lurches, but at the same time no conscious recollection of actually travelling over the ground or through the air. Had she used some sort of teleportation, or was that a fantastical notion from science fiction?

I said, 'Did you . . . ? You did something.'

'I did.'

'What was it? How did you get us here so fast?'

'I clicked my magic heels and said, "Home, James, and don't spare the horses." Come on, it's over here.'

Sláine walked in front of me, towards where she was pointing. I noticed a ring on her index finger. Blackish in colour, maybe tarnished silver; a long oval shape like a tribal shield; and a raised design, what looked like a molecule of some sort, or a crystal, perfectly symmetrical and encased in a circle.

We pushed through the undergrowth and brambles – I say pushed, it felt more like the plants themselves parted to clear a path for her – and as we made our way I said, 'What's the design on your ring? Does it mean something special to you?'

'This old thing? Mm . . . means more to someone else than me, maybe. I'll tell you about it another time.'

'You've a lot of things to tell me about.'

'I've a lot of time to tell them.' She stopped. 'And here we are.'

A small square building – a shack, really – made of cut stone with a flat timber roof, small door, teensy window. It looked very old but very solid. Ivy curled all over it like falling hair, moss crept up along it like a second skin. The place was part fairy-tale cottage, part redneck's hideaway in a horror movie. *Hansel and Gretel* meets *Texas Chainsaw Massacre*, maybe.

There was an inscription over the door: 'It does not trouble the wolf how many the sheep may be.' Wolves? So, more of a fairy tale, then.

I pointed to the writing: 'What's that mean? What is this place?'

'An old hunting lodge. Built by the lord of the manor back in whenever. Years ago. They used to sleep here overnight if it was a really big hunt, like a few days of it. The lord and his pals, they hunted wolves. Can you believe that? They were so ignorant back then. Those beautiful animals. Ireland used to have lots of wolves until we killed them all.'

'Okay. And how did you find this? You "just knew"?'

'I stumbled across it. It's been abandoned for years – over a century probably – but still habitable enough inside. It's dry at least. Have a look.'

She pushed the wooden door and it swung open with a creak, echoing louder in the night air than it would during the daytime. Everything sounds louder at night, doesn't it?

Inside, the place was lit by two antique oil lamps which gave off a welcoming orange glow. It was about the size of a decent sitting room. Stone walls, small fireplace, table and two stools, various old tools and things hanging by nails on the wall. There was also a wreck of an armchair, which looked like it'd catch fire just by someone *thinking* about a naked flame, and an ancient iron bed with what seemed to be a new mattress and blankets on top. Hardly any rubbish or leaves or dirt, which surprised me for some reason. And the plants which caressed the outside of the building hadn't managed to break through the stone and set up residence indoors.

It was rough and ramshackle, not to mention bitterly cold, but Sláine was correct: the hunting lodge was liveable enough. It had been *made* liveable – which meant she'd been inside.

I said, 'How did you . . . I mean you went in there, right? You crossed the threshold.'

She nodded. 'This's the one other place. Don't know how I was able to pass inside. It's very odd. I got kind of drawn to it and then I pretty much just walked on in.'

'Curiouser and curiouser. Anyway, I'm glad you did.'

We went in, Sláine first. I said, 'That mattress and stuff's not centuries old. Where'd that come from?'

'You'd be amazed at the gifts this forest provides. Once it knows you're a friend, of course.'

'Uh . . . okay. I'm going to assume that you're joking. Cos if I don't do that, I'm in danger of pooping my pants and having a nervous breakdown. Hopefully not in that order.'

She laughed. 'I've been busy. Redecorating. Giving this old place a woman's touch. You approve?'

'I do. Seriously, though: how'd you get all this gear?'

'Persuasion and female ingenuity. It's surprising, how easily manipulated some people are. A man working at a furniture warehouse, for example. Gets a whisper in his ear to drop off a mattress at the entrance to Shook Woods, only he doesn't *hear* it as a whisper in his ear. He doesn't hear it at all. Doesn't even know he's doing it, and doesn't remember it afterwards. Or a different man, who owns an antique shop that sells battered armchairs and old lamps. He won't even miss them the next time he does the inventory.'

I whistled, impressed. 'Wow. So you can do that? Like, control people's minds. Their actions.'

'Eh . . . kind of. For a very limited time. But long enough for my purposes, I guess. I'm better at sort of *reaching* into other people's consciousness and "talking" to them. Inducing hallucinations. Visions, if you like. But you already know that.'

'Shit, that's impressive. I mean I thought it was pretty clever speaking to me inside my head! But to actually persuade someone to do what you want them to . . . Can you do it to me? *Would* you do it to me!?'

'No. Never. Anyway, I thought we could come here the next time.'

Next time. I liked the sound of that.

'We can set the fire and you'll be warmer here,' she said. 'Won't have to go lugging that big old duvet around.'

I tugged at my parka. 'What, this? This's a class coat. Real goose feathers.' I grinned smugly. 'Warm as toast. Actually do you . . . ? Do you feel the cold?'

Sláine gave a wistful smile. 'All the time. Sometimes I feel that I'm nothing *but* cold. No physical body any more, just a mind or a soul living inside this great mass of coldness. A voice on the north wind.' She paused. 'You know the funny thing, though? I don't mind. I don't *feel* things the way I used to. The way you do still. I'm cold right through, unbelievably cold, but it's not unpleasant. It's just how things are now. And it's as easy to accept as my eye colour or the shape of my hands.'

A piece of poetry bubbled up in my head and I muttered, half-consciously, 'There's a line like that somewhere in a Paul Éluard poem. About his girl having the colour of his eyes, the shape of his hands . . . ' I looked at Sláine. 'Do you know it? French surrealism. Really nice. It's . . . it's, you know, a love poem.'

I coughed uncomfortably and began rolling a cigarette. Sláine smiled and said, 'He'd have to be French. Something romantic and melodramatic like that. No, it sounds lovely. Oh, I almost forgot.'

She reached behind the bed and pulled out a bottle: frosted, dull-grey glass, holding a dark-coloured liquid. 'This is wine. Incredibly old and valuable wine, at that. This bottle alone is worth . . . what? Three thousand, maybe?'

'Three thousand what, *euro*? You're kidding.'

She shook her head. I said, 'Huh? You're *kidding*.'

Sláine said, 'I thought we could wait before opening it. Wait for a really special occasion, you know? We'll drink this wine to celebrate something wonderful.'

'All right. Yeah, that sounds coola-boola. Celebrate what, though?'

'I'm not sure yet. We'll know when it happens.'

'Can you . . . ? I mean are you able to, uh . . . drink?'

'Not sure of that either. But you can have a glass for me anyway, can't you? Actually, bring two glasses the next time you're coming.'

'Hey, I thought you were the girl that could get her hands on anything.'

'I am. But it'd be nice for you to bring something. This is going to be *our* place, not just mine. You get to decorate it too.'

I nodded. 'Okay by me. So when's next time? And when are you going to – to . . . '

'Hush. All will be revealed in due course, don't worry. As much as I know, anyway. I promise. Now go home. You look tired.'

I expected her to do that magic trick from before, to touch my forehead and spirit me away by some unknowable, supernatural force. But she didn't. Instead, Sláine leaned in and I realised that she was nearly the same height as me and I was wondering how much shorter she'd be without those boots on, and then I forgot absolutely what I was thinking because she was kissing me on the mouth.

Her lips like soft snow. An icy tingle on my lips. My heart a jackhammer thumping in my throat. I opened my eyes wide in shock and then I –

HISTORY LESSONS

The week passed quickly. Before I knew what was what, it was Saturday morning and I was sitting in the town library, poring over old newspaper reports and other documents. Reading up on the Famine for an essay. Interesting stuff of itself, and more importantly, it took my mind off everything that had happened in the last while. I needed a breather.

Chris Harrington, I'd heard during the week, was out of the coma, still in intensive care but slowly recovering. He'd live, and more or less return to full health – but he'd never be pretty again. The scarring was awful, by all accounts. I didn't visit him in hospital. I couldn't stand the guy anyway and felt no obligation to sympathise or empathise with his misfortune.

Also, a trip to hospital would have probably meant blowing off school, and amazingly, I looked forward to going these days. The atmosphere had changed for me, subtly and without fanfare but it was definitely different.

The bullying seemed to have faded away to a large extent. Nobody spoke to me much at all, admittedly, but nobody did anything mean either. I even got a smile or nod of the head from time to time. In any case I didn't care. To hell with them:

if anyone did want to make up now, they could stick it where the sun don't shine. Podsy was enough friends for me. Podsy and, of course, Sláine.

My marble-white friend with lips of ice and fire. Friend? Or something else . . . ?

The Guards couldn't say for sure what attacked Harrington. Their best guess was a pack of feral dogs, hiding out in Shook Woods or some other uninhabited place. Why they would have gone for him like that, nobody could say; wild animals are usually more afraid of us than the other way around. Maybe they didn't like the smell of him. Maybe Harrington gave off a sour, bad odour, because he was sour and bad inside.

I didn't want to think shitty things like that. I couldn't help thinking them.

Meanwhile, my investigation into Sláine's death seemed to be on hold. That hadn't been a conscious decision; it's just that with everything going on, this whirlwind of events lifting me up and spinning me round like the girl in *The Wizard of Oz*, enquiries had been pushed to the background. Not forgotten about, exactly, but the pause button was definitely pressed. I'd wait, I figured, until she told me what she knew. We could then work out together where to take it from there.

Now, on Saturday, I sat in the library – a disappointingly modern building, but filled with the wisdom of ages – and reminisced about that kiss. What a shock it had been. Not an unpleasant one. Not exactly enjoyable, but not unpleasant. In fact, it was hard to describe at all. When Sláine pressed her lips to mine, I'd had the strangest sensation that part of me was leaving my body, being transferred to her, as if she was squeezing it out of me, inhaling something of my essence into herself.

Which is weird enough. Even weirder is the fact that I hadn't minded.

That kiss . . . It was just a friendly peck, right? A mark of affection between two people. Friends kiss each other, don't they? Didn't necessarily mean anything . . . Although, you know, if it *did* mean something, that might not be . . .

I shook my head, banished Sláine from my thoughts and got back to business. It was the weekend – I didn't want to spend all day on homework. I'd already taken notes from a bunch of history books: national and local, academic and popular, professional and amateur. All were about the Famine, most telling me things I hadn't already known. Now I clicked to the next page on the library's microfiche. Old newspapers, scanned and stored on computer. The past brought bang up to date with the present. History coming back to haunt us.

It really was haunting. The Famine was a horrible time in this country, especially our part of it. Death stalked the land for years. People must have known it was on the way, it was coming for them. They must have looked at their own gaunt faces, their children's hunger-swollen bellies, and *known*. They must have shivered like newborns as the cold filled their bones and drained their lives away, and been certain the end was near.

What an awful way to go, I thought, and how lucky we are to live nowadays. Even someone like me, struggling with personal problems or whatever. At least I wouldn't be frozen or starved. I wasn't going to wake up dead.

Mr Lee had asked us to present a personal history of someone's experiences during the Famine. Not just regurgitate what we read, but imagine ourselves as that person. We could use a composite of different stories, reports or recollections. That's what I was doing, collecting those stories. The assignment wasn't due until sometime in January, but I wanted to get going on it – 'tús maith, leath na hoibre', and all that.

After a while I'd shifted my focus to records specifically dealing with our town and surroundings. I'd come across a few notable, even downright peculiar, tales.

First, the sea froze over at one point. This was during the winter of 1851, around the time that company of English soldiers arrived. Some remaining straggler found the strength to record what happened, probably because it was so unusual. Ireland is in a temperate climate. The Atlantic can get cold enough to kill you but this isn't Norway or the Antarctic – we don't have ice-entombed seas. Yet that's what took place: the ocean froze solid, further than the eye could see, for several days, possibly weeks.

Secondly, all the crows died. Every single one, of every type: raven, rook, hooded crow, jackdaw, jay, magpie. As far as I could gather, piecing different bits of information together, this was about a month before the sea seized up. All of them, thousands, found dead within a few days of each other. In fields, streets, yards, farms, everywhere – as though they'd more or less simultaneously keeled over and fallen to the ground. There was no explanation for it. No other bird or animal had perished in such huge numbers.

Thirdly, and here's where my interest was really tickled, one of Sláine's ancestors had refused the chance to leave town with that brave group who made it over the mountains – who made it out alive. The McAuleys were pretty well off, by the standards of the time, and her great-great-great-great – I think – grandfather contributed money and whatever provisions he could spare to the expedition.

So, naturally he was invited to join them. When he declined, he was begged to join. Still he said no. William John McAuley instead put his wife Eleanor and three children into a cart, waved goodbye and settled down to welcome death, which surely wouldn't be long. He was never seen again and they never found a body – I guess the dogs had him for a finish.

I wondered why he stayed. Like virtually everyone else, he must have known he couldn't survive. There was no food left, disease was rampant, the town was in the grip of the worst cold spell in half a century. He was a dead man already, waiting for his body to catch up with reality.

Maybe he wanted to die where he'd lived, or under circumstances of his choosing, instead of halfway up a mountain while on a hare-brained flight to freedom that might never succeed. Some people are stubborn like that. Maybe he didn't want to witness his wife and children dying, although if that was true, he still should have manned up and gone with them: they needed him more than he needed himself.

Whatever the cause, William John stayed behind to die; some of Sláine's forebears lived and later returned to their home town. On down through history the line of family went, ending with Sláine and her siblings. Now she had joined the old man in death.

What would she say to him, I mused, if she were to meet him in the afterlife? 'Should've got on the cart, dummy,' probably ...

I jumped as someone tapped my shoulder, whirling around on the swivel chair. A handsome middle-aged man in a smart suit was standing behind me. He raised his hands in apology and whispered, 'Sorry. Didn't mean to give you a fright.'

'No,' I whispered back, 'you're okay. I just didn't hear you for some reason.'

He gave an easy smile and said, 'I should have coughed. Tapped my feet. I was wondering if you'd be long more on the microfiche?'

'Huh?' I checked the clock on the wall: I'd been sitting here for over an hour, hogging the machine. I said in embarrassment, 'Aw, *feck* it. My apologies. I didn't notice the time going.'

'That's all right. Time has a funny way of getting away from us, doesn't it? "*Tempus fugit.*"'

I clicked off the page I was reading, muttering absentmindedly, '"Time flies." Sure does.'

The man said, not hiding his surprise, 'You speak Latin?'

I laughed and gathered my things. 'Nah. Learned that from an old *Batman* cartoon.'

He laughed too. 'Latin is . . . useful sometimes. In helping to understand very old texts, that sort of thing.'

'Right. Are you an academic or something?'

'Of sorts.' He added, self-effacingly, 'More of a dabbler, really.'

He left it at that so I left him to it and found a desk nearby to jot down a few more notes while they were fresh in my head. I reckoned I had enough now for a really good piece. I'd bring in the flight over the mountains, freezing sea and crow wipeout, and mix them with general facts about the Famine. I'd imagine myself as a boy of seventeen, same as my own age, desperately trying to survive in 1851.

Perhaps one of the last people left alive, but sadly, no room for me on the convoy heading out of town. Or perhaps I'd chosen to stay, one last act of defiance against my own mortality. Bite me, Death. Come and have a go if you think you're hard enough.

The hunger, fear, misery, cold . . . it shouldn't be too hard to conjure up those feelings. Especially not if this bloody weather got any worse.

I continued working for another twenty minutes, then had enough and decided to blow the gaff. En route to the exit I checked out a few books, an obese lady with a sweet smile doing the needful, bipping them through the security-tag scanner, stamping the date in royal-blue ink. I gazed around lazily, waiting for her to finish, and noticed the handsome man who dabbled at being an academic riffling through a stand of ancient yellowing newspapers fixed to a steel pole.

I said, really thinking out loud, 'Wonder who he is . . . ?'

The librarian looked up. 'Pardon me?'

'Uh, the man over there. Going through the old papers. Sorry, I just haven't seen him before.'

She took a good look then went back to her work. 'Mr Kinvara? He's often in here. A real scholar, that one.' She smiled, handing over my books. 'Some of the books he takes out, I'd say he's the first person to read them since they were published. *Ancient* old manuscripts, they're practically falling apart. Good job we kept them, all the same. Maybe all these old things are coming back into fashion. Now, that's you done.'

I thanked her and strolled off, glancing over at the man, now reading one of the pages intently. The famous Mr Kinvara – our resident James Bond, with his presumed wealth and old Victorian pile and taste for classic cars. I wondered how my dad had got on working for him; he didn't say, I didn't ask. 'Twas always thus between fathers and sons, and always thus would be.

I trotted down the steps outside, thinking, should have told Kinvara who I was. Carefully, carefully: it was hazardous outside, a film of ice making every surface slippery. I couldn't get over how cold it was. Temperatures now remained below zero all the time, around minus two during the day and down to minus ten at night. This, in Ireland. Heavy snowfall every day for several days. It was unprecedented, according to TV climatologists.

The worst Big Chill since, it so happened, the winter of 1851. How's that for coincidence?

Even stranger, they reported, was that the cold snap was unusually localised: basically, our town and its hinterland. We were situated in a funny spot anyway – as I said, hemmed in by the sea, forest and mountains – which I presumed had created some kind of microclimate or whatever they call it. I didn't know the causes – I didn't care. I just wanted it to warm the hell up. My fingers were turning an angry blue already, starting to hurt, and I'd only just left the building.

Turning towards home, I saw one of my former tormentors, a fat girl called Clara, staring into space outside a closed-up record store called Music Sounds Better With You, after that song. She looked a bit freaked over something, muttering and pressing one hand to her head. A cigarette was perilously close to her hair, and with all that peroxide it'd go up like a fireworks display, but I wasn't feeling very charitable towards her. At first I thought she was speaking into a phone but as I got nearer I saw there was no phone and Clara was talking to herself: 'Who – who are you? What do you want? Get . . . how are you doing this? This isn't . . . it's not *funny*. Go away. Go away go away go awaaaaay.'

Whatever. I didn't stop to ask what was wrong – screw her. I continued on, past a little park, bag swinging on my shoulder, thinking about Sláine. I hadn't heard from her since the start of the week, that Monday night. I'd woken up in bed the next morning and checked my lips in the mirror to see if her kiss had left any mark. Maybe something, there on the bottom lip – was that a slight bruise . . . ?

Since then, not a word. I wasn't massively offended by this – I figured she'd contact me when she was ready – but it annoyed me. I was impatient. I wanted to see her again. And a whisper in my mind made me the tiniest bit afraid: what if I didn't? What if something had happened to her?

Ha. Something *happened* to her? What exactly, genius, do you think might have happened to a girl who was already dead? Sláine was going to get *more* dead, and this would stop her being able to talk to you?

I shook my head, laughing at myself. Then I turned a corner and bumped into John Rattigan. Oh no.

A can of beer jumped in his hand, splashed his coat and fell to the ground. Rattigan followed its flight with a look of shock and dismay that would have been endearing in anyone else. He muttered, 'Huh?' and glared up at me, the old anger and aggression abruptly back in place, his eyes bloodshot from cans already drunk.

When he clocked who it was, the look of shock returned for a moment, as if he couldn't believe a maggot like me had dared to knock his drink away. If I'd done it on purpose, I wouldn't have believed it either. As it was, it had been a total accident, no fault on my part. And though I knew concepts like logic and fairness didn't hold much sway with Rattigan, I felt obliged to point this out anyway.

'Sorry about your beer. It was an accident.'

I held my palms up in a show of peace. That only stoked the rage inside him further. Shock got pushed off his face for the second time, aggression returning again. That bastard's ugly mug was having a real emotional tug-of-war today.

Rattigan spluttered, 'You – you – clumsy *asshole*. Look what you did.'

'I said it was an accident, all right?'

I made to move past. His arm shot out and stopped me.

'Why am I not surprised?' he said. 'The dipshit you are, can't even watch where you're going. Who else would it be but the Carnival Boy?'

I didn't reply. A small crowd had stopped to watch, shoppers and construction workers, kids with their mothers; even a hunched old crow, wings tucked back, leaning forward as though listening in. Everyone was keeping their distance: they all knew Rattigan's reputation as a thug – nobody wanted to get involved.

He went on, 'Moping around like a little faggot. What's this?' He grabbed my bag with his other hand, keeping the first one on my chest. 'In the library, were you? The faggot spending his Saturday reading. Jesus Christ. No wonder your girl left you for that knacker of a carnie. The only thing I don't get is why a fine bird like that was going with a mopey little puke like you in the first place.'

He flung my bag to the ground. Stupid Aidan, you left the top untied – books and sheaves of loose paper spilled onto the ice in almost geometric patterns.

Rattigan stepped back and smiled, as if to say, 'Well, what do you think of that?'

I thought of a few weeks ago, when he'd punched me in the face just because he was an ignorant Neanderthal and got the notion to do it and I was too weak to stop him. I thought of all the times he'd made me feel pathetic and afraid. I thought of Sláine, what she'd said about my life being worth more than any of those 'vindictive babies'.

And I had a realisation, it washed over me like a blast of fresh air: in most cases, other people only have power over you if you let them. They can strike or tease or ignore you, yes. But their *power* over you is dependent on your acceptance of it. Once you stop giving a shit, they've got nothing.

I realised that I'd stopped giving a shit about John Rattigan. He had nothing. And he *was* nothing.

So I said it to him: 'You're nothing, Rattigan.'

He stared at me, boggly eyed, incredulous. Before he could speak I continued, 'You're *nothing*. You're a bully and a cretin. You're scum. You are nothing, and you offer nothing. You're a waste of oxygen and a drain on society. If you were to drop dead right now, you know what everyone in this town would do? They'd celebrate. They'd throw a big party and celebrate. Then they'd forget you ever existed, because you're nothing, and who remembers nothing? Now take your filthy hands off me.'

To my amazement, he complied. Probably to his own amazement too, if he gave it any thought, and the amazement of everyone watching – they stood open-mouthed, motionless. I couldn't believe that I was saying all this stuff either, but there it was, pouring out of me. It was almost like someone else had taken control of my mind and was using my tongue. But no, it was me, the real me. Some newfound courage was making me face up to him. Making me honest and unafraid.

'Yeah, I was in the library,' I went on. 'Know why? Because I'm a human being with a brain that I like to use from time to time. I'm not an animal, Rattigan, like you. In ten years I'll be doing some job that you won't even understand what it is, living far away from this kip. But you'll still be here, still stupid, still acting like an animal. Drinking cans in the park and trying to prove how tough you are. What a great future you have to look forward to.'

I heard one of the workmen chuckling, probably happy to see Rattigan get what was coming to him, finally. For the first time, I looked him right in the eyes; and for the first time, Rattigan looked away. He couldn't hold the stare.

I said, 'All you have is brute strength and the willingness to use it. That's *all* you have, and all you are. I know you can beat me up, you're stronger than me. That doesn't change the fact that you're a shitty person, nobody likes you, and hopefully you'll be dead soon so we can have that party I was talking about. Okay? So I'm going now. Take it easy, jerk-off.'

I turned to leave. He looked in shock again. I was pretty sure that was going to win the tug-of-war; aggression had slinked away for good. Rattigan muttered, 'I should . . . should bust your bloody teeth out for . . . talking to me like that . . . '

'If that's what you need to do, Johnny boy, knock yourself out. Knock *me* out, I can't stop you. Won't change a goddamn thing. You'll still be a supreme asshole. Still be nothing. You'll always be nothing.'

I left him, hunched, staring at the ground, his lips moving as he tried to process what had just happened. I wasn't fully sure myself. I crouched and picked up the books and things that fell from my bag; a little old lady hobbled over and helped, smiling kindly. I smiled back and said, 'Thanks.'

And I nodded and smiled to the crowd around us as I stood, now separating and returning to their lives – it was all smiles today. Including the man from the library, Kinvara. He must have left soon after me. He grinned mischievously, tipped his finger off his forehead in salute and said, 'Bravo.' I gave a little bow.

Kinvara added, 'From the Latin. Look it up.'

I said back, 'I will.'

One of the children smiled at me too, as if I was his big hero, and I wondered if he was a victim of bullying. So many poor kids getting hassled; it was always the way. But for once, I wasn't one of them. For once I had the power.

I walked off with a light step, heart pumping, head buzzing, a surge of energy through my whole body. It felt like I was being lit up from inside with a thousand electric lights.

Then I burst out laughing. Holy crap. You just *owned* John Rattigan. What the hell's going on with you, man?

I felt pure happiness, an adrenaline shot, *boom*, straight to the heart. I only wished I'd done it months ago. Although maybe I couldn't have. Maybe I was only now rediscovering the strength inside me. Becoming a different person.

I heard a voice behind me, aged but not weak, medium-pitch. It was the old dear who'd helped me gather my things off the snow. Once more she hobbled towards me – it sounds like the start of a literally lame joke – held out her hands and gestured for me to give her mine. She took my fingers and looked deep into my eyes. Her own seemed a bit funny, gone blooey, very distant, as if she were high on something. I smiled self-consciously, wondering what this was all about. But I kind of already knew.

The old lady said, 'Now look at your hand.'

She left and I looked down. There was writing on it. Tiny veins under my skin had redirected the blood, filled themselves with it, which made them rise up and form words.

Sláine was doing this. It wasn't really happening, I was hallucinating, yet it was as real as anything I'd ever experienced.

'I think you're ready to know what happened,' the words read. 'How I died.'

HOW I DIED

'Another cool trick this afternoon, by the way. You're building up a real repertoire, Sláine. You could go on stage, put on a magic show.'

'Oh?' she said vaguely, pretending not to know what I meant.

'With that old lady. Hypnotising her or whatever you did. It was good, I was impressed.'

She smiled. 'I aim to please.'

'Were you nearby?'

'Mmm . . . sort of. In spirit, let's say.'

Two wine glasses clinked as I placed them on the table in the hunting lodge. I'd pinched them from home. I was sure my mother wouldn't mind – they were cheap old things, though free of cracks. It was past midnight on Saturday, Shook Woods was frozen and motionless, Sláine was sitting on the bed and me on a stool, and we were talking. Or rather, not yet talking about the big issue. Her death. I didn't want to force it so decided to go along with the flow of conversation, wherever she wished it to travel.

She had prettied up the place further: a large colourful rug covering half the floor, a Picasso print in a frame on the wall, even some sprigs of holly in a vase on the table. An ashtray for me, some toilet roll if I felt the call of nature. There was also a gas heater, giving off a lovely warming glow. I couldn't begin to guess where she'd got this stuff; it didn't matter. The whole world had been reduced to this stone-and-wood shack, the two of us in one moment, and that was all that counted.

Sláine somehow knew about my researches into the Famine, although not exactly what I had found out. How? I don't know. By this stage, nothing about that girl came as a surprise. I just accepted it as the way things were, the way she was.

She leaned against the wall, getting comfortable on the bed. Interestingly, she had a physical presence, in that she didn't fall through the wall – she wasn't a ghost in the traditional sense. Yet at the same time, the mattress didn't depress under her, the blankets weren't shifted or scrunched; Sláine had no weight, as such. She kind of floated on that bed, as light as a pillow feather.

I gave her a quick precis of my discoveries that afternoon and she said, 'Actually I knew that already. About my family fleeing for survival, and William John staying behind. But it's an odd coincidence – I didn't know until recently. I started researching the family history during the summer. For no reason. It was just something I felt . . . compelled to do. You know what I mean? Nothing to do with college or anything. I just had an urge to know.'

'Sure. I mean I don't really know – I have exactly zero interest in tracing my family tree. Couldn't give a rat's ass if they were all a pack of murderers and rum smugglers.'

'I used to feel like that. Didn't interest me at all. But last summer, yeah . . . Soon after the Leaving. I was at a bit of a loose end anyway, no summer job lined up – that's probably why.'

'Well, at least it was pretty cool material,' I said. 'The Famine, like it's awful but fascinating too. And your guy, the ancestor? He was an interesting character.'

Sláine looked at the low ceiling, cobwebs stretching across corners like supports in a tiny suspension bridge.

'He was . . . It must have been unusual, their relationship. Eleanor – my great-great-whatever grandmother – she was poor, relative to William John McAuley. He owned a shop and land, which I suppose made you rich for those times. She wasn't from absolute poverty, but they would have been small farmers, like tenants of someone else. I think it was a step down in social class.'

'So McAuley, he sounds fairly forward-thinking for that time?'

'Yep. And he was very well educated, apparently. Had a room full of books in his house, a whole library really. He read all the time, everything and anything. He was famous for it. Probably *infamous*, ha! "That weirdo McAuley, what's he wasting his time with all those books for?"'

'Ugh. People were so dumb back in those days.'

'He was into all sorts of stuff. This's according to family lore, you know. History, philosophy, eastern religions, astrology, Classical civilisation, Celtic civ . . . Even things like witchcraft, seances, mediums, all this far-out stuff. Different cults, old gods, like the old Irish gods? The river gods or whatever. That's what people used to say.'

'Ouija boards are such horseshit, aren't they? They never

work. Sorry, that's a totally irrelevant statement. I'm sorry, carry on.'

Sláine smiled. 'Anyway, his wife and kids survived the Famine and eventually returned to town and found him . . . dead, missing, who knows. Dead, I suppose. They inherited his property, his land, the business . . . And here we remain.'

We were still dancing around it, the reason she'd summoned me. Sláine had said she'd tell me how she died, as much as she understood it. But she hadn't broached the subject yet. She didn't even explain why there'd been no contact for several days. All she said was, 'I needed to rest . . . I was very tired. I needed time to rest.'

What was that supposed to mean? Did dead people really 'need to rest'? Sláine admitted that she didn't sleep any more, so what did she mean by 'rest'? Chillax in front of the telly with the feet up, a cup of tea and a few fags? Somehow I couldn't picture that cosy little scene taking place here in gloomy Shook Woods.

Of course Sláine didn't stay in the forest, though, did she? This was her home but she could travel other places as well. And she'd 'brought' me home, somehow, twice. I wondered where else she'd been since becoming what she was now. Could she enter properties besides my house, or was this – our friendship, relationship, whatever – making it possible? I debated whether to ask, then decided to switch gears by telling her about the Rattigan incident instead.

She listened to my story, then said, 'How did it make you feel? To do that.'

I laughed. 'Gee, I'm not sure I'm comfortable going there

just yet, Doctor Freud. Maybe another few sessions on the couch first. Maybe you could *get* a couch first.'

Sláine frowned at me, almost maternal, and I remembered again how much older than me she often seemed. She said, 'Don't hide behind sarcasm. I'm not a psychiatrist and you know that. I'm just – interested in you.'

That was a nice thing to hear. One of many. I said, 'Okay, sorry. I'm a moron, I admit it. How did it, uh . . . You know what? It felt feckin' *great*. Every bit as good as I'd imagined. I didn't even mind that I haven't the balls to, you know,' – I chuckled – 'smash his face in too. I have to admit, that little fantasy has kept me warm on many a night. John Rattigan's face at the business end of a lead pipe. And me standing over him, screaming – no, not screaming. Saying it really quietly, you know – it's more menacing that way. "How's it feel, asshole? How's that taste of your own medicine going down?"' I laughed louder, partly embarrassed but happy too, almost giddy. 'That would've *ruled*. But hey, what happened today wasn't bad either.'

'Do you still want to punish him? Do you want revenge, I mean?'

'On Rattigan?'

'On all of them.'

'Uh . . . I dunno. Like, walking away today, having just *destroyed* him, basically, with nothing but the power of my intellect . . . That felt good. And it proves I'm the bigger man, right? I'm better than him, I don't need revenge.'

'You still haven't answered my question.'

'Yeah, I know, I know . . . This is called stalling, Sláine.

Playing for time.'

'That's fine. I can wait.'

I sighed and pulled out my tobacco. 'Then you might be waiting a long time. Because I'm not sure I know the answer to that myself.'

Sláine looked at me for a good while, then nodded to herself as if something had been settled in her mind. She stood up and crossed the room, turning the oil lamps down. The room dimmed to a twilight blur. I liked it better this way. Now it felt even more like a place of seclusion, a womb, somewhere warm and safe, to hide away from the rest of the world.

She floated to the wall opposite me, brought her hands together and pursed her lips. In this darker atmosphere, weirdly, she seemed to be glowing more than before. Her skin, impossibly pale. Her clothes becoming whiter every time I saw her. I squeezed my eyes shut and told myself it was the light playing tricks again. I opened them.

Finally Sláine spoke the words I'd been waiting for all evening, for days past: 'I said you were ready to know how I died. So here it is.'

'I can't explain everything because I don't understand it all myself,' she said. 'Not yet. Hopefully I will, eventually. For now, I'll tell you what I know.'

'All right. That's fair enough.'

'And I'm sorry, again, that you're only hearing this now. I was . . . worried. For you. How you'd react. I wanted to build up to it, gradually. It's . . . this is outside everything you've ever known. There might be some – what can I call it? "Psychic disorientation." So, you know. Brace yourself.'

'All right. Braced.'

'That night . . . the night I died,' Sláine began. 'It didn't feel special in any way. The whole day, the weeks leading up to it – my life was carrying on as normal. College was good, I was enjoying the course, staying with a nice group of girls in Galway. Heading out, having fun. No romance going on. I'd had this thing earlier in the year, it got a bit serious on his side and I didn't feel the same. I knew I never would, so I'd called it off about two months before.'

I felt a prickle of jealousy. Was she talking about Tommy Fox? Was that why he was so cut up? Some sense of unfinished business, maybe . . . *She'd* ended the relationship – that was a good sign, right? But hang on, Aidan, why do you care anyway? You and Sláine are just friends, no . . . ?

She was still talking; I ordered my inner voice to quit yapping and listened.

'Things were good. Life was good. Ha. *Life*. Remember that, Sláine? Another life, another Sláine . . . I remember it clearly, that Sunday. Visiting an old friend in the afternoon. Coffee in that place on Main Street, you know it, with the old black-and-white movie posters. Home, did a bit of reading. Funny, I don't remember what book it was. Something by Borges, I think . . . Anyway, I felt pretty tired by about nine, so I went to bed early. Said goodnight to my parents, brushed my teeth and lay down to sleep. That was the last thing, really, I ever did. As the old me.'

I held my breath.

Sláine went on. 'I'm not sure I actually *did* anything more after that. Of my own free will, you know? I was sort of aware that things were happening around me, but I didn't have any power myself. To move, to react in any way. I was just *there*.'

A pause. I said quietly, '"There" meaning Shook Woods.'

She nodded. 'I woke up in the forest, deep in the heart of it. I say woke, but it didn't feel like that, the way you sort of surface slowly out of sleep. This was more like – like being shocked into consciousness by a great cold. As if my body took a huge, sudden breath . . . ' She opened her eyes wide and gasped violently to demonstrate what she meant. ' . . . And my eyes were open and I was standing in the middle of the forest. Much further in than they found my body – it must have been moved. It's hard to describe how it felt. I suppose – try to imagine you're asleep, and someone throws you into a freezing pool: the way you'd just *leap* back into wakefulness, your entire body screaming. Except there was no water, and no screaming. I couldn't speak, couldn't do anything. I just stood there, under the moonlight.'

Sláine paused again. Jesus, the tension was becoming unbearable.

'I was fully dressed. Had I gone to bed in my clothes? No. So either I'd dressed myself or someone else had done it for me. How had I got to Shook Woods? Walked there, I guess. My feet were bare, blue with the cold, but I didn't seem to mind. Maybe because the rest of me was so cold too. More than cold, that seems such a puny little word, those four letters . . . I was beyond cold. I felt literally *frozen* inside. All the blood frozen in my veins. My heart frozen, not beating. My eyes frozen, I wasn't blinking. My whole body frozen, I mean I wasn't even

113

shivering in response to it. I was a statue. No, an ice sculpture. The only thing not frozen, it seemed, was my mind – and that wasn't working the way it usually did, either. Everything felt weird and kind of dreamlike. I was present but detached from it too, the way you feel in a dream. How you're part of it but at the same time watching yourself from a distance. The creator and the audience, all at once.'

She looked at me, brows raised in a question. I nodded that I knew what she meant.

'I don't even know if I was still alive or had already died by this stage. That's how strange it was. I stood there for what might have been an hour, might have been thirty seconds . . . no movement around me, the whole forest frozen like I was, although I thought I heard birds crying in the distance, like a raven's cry, but probably just imagined that. And then . . . '

Her eyes misted over as she was transported back in time to that fateful moment: 'I felt a . . . presence. Nearby. Hard to describe, again. Not a *being* as such, like a person or some other living thing. But not something inorganic either, you know. This wasn't just the wind blowing . . . A *presence*. I don't know how to . . . Maybe if the wind could have a personality, or the sun or moon, that might describe it. If some element of the weather had a mind or soul . . . The cold. It felt as if the physical state of coldness had come alive. And I realised that the same coldness I felt inside, it was outside me now as well, pushing against me. Pushing to get in. The coldness inside pushing to get out. The two of them moving towards each other, pushing me, pushing *through* me . . . And then I *was* the coldness – it was me, we were one and the same. It settled in me and I was part of it. And I knew for sure that I was dead.'

I gulped painfully and supressed a squeak. Oh man, this was heavy. I was out of my depth. I wanted to run, I wanted to stay. I wanted to hear the rest of the story. I told myself to grow a pair and managed to hold my position without running off, wailing like a baby.

'I don't remember anything else for a while after that. I must have blacked out or something. Don't even remember falling to the ground, which I must have. When you die, you fall down, isn't that how it goes? No memory of my body being brought to that tree, near the entrance. No memory of being buried or rising from the dead. No Jesus-style resurrection stories to tell, I'm afraid. I was dead, I knew I was . . . and then I was still dead but also awake, lying on that wall where we first met. It was night. I felt as cold as before, but like I said, I didn't mind now. I didn't seem to feel things in the old way. That was all gone. *I* was gone, and yet I was right there. Looking like this.'

She gestured down her body, pointed to her face, tilted her head and smiled distantly. I chanced a joke, to lighten the mood for me if not her: 'Well, you look pretty good for it, I must say. For a dead girl, you look grand.'

'Thanks. And that's it. You wanted to know; now you know. Bet you're glad you asked, huh?'

'I *am* glad.'

'Thanks again. Sorry, though: it doesn't really answer your questions, does it? I mean I still don't fully know what happened. Or why.' Sláine shrugged. 'But at least you know as much as I do.'

'So basically – you *did* die of hypothermia? Like the autopsy said.'

'No. That would suggest a natural physical reaction to extreme conditions. This wasn't just low temperatures, Aidan. This cold, it – it almost had a mind. It *wanted* me. And I think it came for me.'

'Why?'

'I don't know that either. But I'm convinced of it. Something, someone, I don't know – it drew me here that night, from my home. It *lured* me.'

I had something then, an idea, a theory: 'Maybe . . . hypnotised you? Persuaded you to come out here. Like how you can sort of do it to others.'

'Maybe. Yeah, that's possible. Anyway, it got me here, then it took me. Took my life and changed me into this. Tch. Whatever this is.'

She looked a bit disgusted saying that. I retorted, 'Hey, *this* is you. You're not some monster or ghoul. You're just a girl. And a pretty cool one at that.'

'Really?' she drawled, totally sceptical.

'Yes. You're still Sláine. Just . . . I don't know, in a different package. Same you. I *know* it. I didn't know you before – this is all gut instinct but shit, gut instincts are usually right. You're a good person with a big heart. Even if you've got trouble believing it yourself. *I* believe it.' I muttered to myself, 'You *couldn't* be a monster, cos if you were a monster . . . '

I stopped myself. She smiled and diplomatically changed tack, saying, 'Why did *you* come here? We can come back to my story, but just answer this for me. You were here a few times after I died. Why? That night we met, you looked like you were on stakeout.'

'I sort of was . . . I'm not sure. Something drew me here. Not like with you, I don't mean some presence. I just wanted to see where you'd been found, that was the start. I was curious. Also I felt shitty for what'd happened to you. You always came across as all right – it didn't seem fair. I came back, decided to try and find out exactly what had happened. Facts didn't seem to stack up, you know? And then . . . you left me the message and I thought, oh she was murdered, and basically at that point I was trying to catch the killer. That's why I was here the night we met. I'd read that killers often return to the scene of their crimes, so . . . ' I chuckled. 'Christ. As if I'd've been any good anyway! Like, me? Bringing down a murderer one-handed? Anyway, that's it. End of report.' I looked at Sláine. 'So was it . . . *were* you murdered, then? Sorry, that's – I'm sorry, can't think of a better way to put that.'

'It's all right. The answer is, I don't know. Something made this happen to me. But was it a some*one*? There, my lad, lies the question.'

I grimaced and swallowed hard again. This was getting crazier by the minute. I felt ever more out of my depth.

She said, putting some cheerfulness into it, 'Ah, it's not *that* bad. Being dead. Hey, I probably would have never met you if I was still alive.'

We smiled at each other, bittersweet. Sláine added, 'I didn't choose it and I'd prefer if it hadn't happened. But it's not so bad. Honestly.'

'Do you feel – sad? About it all.'

'I don't think so. Not happy, but . . . no. Not sad. Although it kind of feels as if I've gone past all that altogether. Those simple emotions. Happy, sad. They don't seem to apply to me any more.'

'Okay. I won't pretend to understand that, but I can accept it.'

'Actually,' she said, 'it's funny. After the first day or so, once the mental shock of it wore off and I'd adjusted to my new . . . life, whatever this is. Once I accepted that this was how it was now, there was nothing I could do about it. A change came over me. I realised that I felt different. It wasn't scary or depressing so much. It started to feel . . . as if I was *returning* in some way. Coming back to something, some previous state of being. It almost felt like going home.'

I looked around the old hunting lodge and smiled. I kind of knew what she meant by that.

Then I turned back to Sláine and was shocked – not the usual 'how can this be happening?' stuff I'd got accustomed to, but in a far more normal, *human* way. For the first time since I'd met her, she looked tired, despondent, even a little afraid. Her shoulders were slumped, her gaze landing at a spot on the wall or some distant point in the uncertain future. If I hadn't assumed it to be impossible, I would have sworn she was about to start crying.

I said, concern making my voice shake, 'Sláine. What is it?'

She didn't reply for what seemed an age. Finally she said, barely above a whisper, 'I need your help, Aidan. You have to help me.'

***

118

She needed *my* help? This was unexpected. If I'd been asked to summarise the Sláine I'd come to know, it'd probably be along the lines of 'capable, unflappable, self-reliant, self-contained'. It hadn't occurred to me that she could need anything. She liked me, I knew that, and appreciated whatever our friendship gave her; but actually *needed* me? I was dumbfounded.

There it was, though. Sláine had asked for my help, and I guessed it hadn't come easy to her, either: some kick of simple pride making the words stumble in her mouth; some trace of the mortal ego she once possessed lingering on in this new incarnation. She'd asked for help, and I'd give it, no hesitations.

'Of course,' I said. 'Anything I can do – what, tell me what.'

'I'd hoped to work it out for myself: who killed me, why they did it. What this all means. It must mean something. And I want to know, I *need* to. But I . . . I can't do it by myself, I'm not able, I need you to help.'

I moved closer to her, sitting on the bed but leaving her some personal space. 'Sure. I told you, whatever I can do, I will.'

'I can't enter buildings, right? Properties. Except your house, for whatever reason, and here. And I can't be everywhere at once. I can't go into town during the day, in case someone sees me – I don't think they would, but the risk isn't worth taking. I can't be away from the forest for too long. Not really sure why, it just . . . draws me back. Like a magnet, I'm not able to stay away for long. So, you have to do some of that for me. Going into specific places. Being my eyes and ears out there.'

'Cool. What are you thinking exactly?'

'Research. Investigation.'

Sláine sort of shook herself down then, stood and began

pacing around the room as she mentally worked it through. 'As far as I can see, there are only two possible explanations for what's going on, essentially. One, this thing, this presence I felt: it's some weird force of nature, beyond human control. Or two, it's being manipulated by someone. A person.'

'Who lives in our town.'

'Almost certainly. There isn't another for miles in all directions.'

'And it'd make sense, wouldn't it? If you were up to some black magic bullshit, then you'd want to be right there, where the action is.'

She nodded. 'So those're our two options. There may be more, but we have to be practical. We have to assume all this is down to one or other. Otherwise it's needle-in-a-haystack stuff.'

I nodded too. 'Okay. Makes sense. It's a start, anyway.'

'Right. We have to start somewhere.'

'So, what? You want me to check stuff out in the library? Bookshops? Maybe second-hand shops. Like, research into local folklore, legends of supernatural events, stories, rumours.' I clicked my fingers. '*Specifically*, any mentions of people dying from the cold, under mysterious circumstances. I could look at microfiche of old newspapers, that sorta thing.'

'Yes. But not just local. Anything along those lines, anywhere in the world.'

'Like Bella in *Twilight*. Yeah? That scene where she's reading about vampire mythologies across the planet cos she suspected yer man of being one, the guy with the hair.'

Sláine smiled for the first time in ages. 'Big *Twilight* fan, are you?'

I scowled. '*No*. It was, uh . . . one of the girls in school was on about it. Go on, what's next?'

'What's next is the possibility that someone is behind it. Controlling this force of . . . coldness, whatever it might be. But the person we could be looking for, we've got to narrow it down. Can't just interrogate everyone in the town and ask them, "Are you a murderer?"'

'Agreed.'

'The way I see it, our hypothetical killer fits the following criteria.' She ticked off the list on outstretched fingers. 'One, a man, almost certainly. Because most killers are men – that's a statistical fact. But more than this, I felt something . . . *masculine*. That night, when I died. When he – he, it – lured me out here. There was something male in the air. Something sour and cold and male.'

I chanced a joke: 'Could describe virtually every asshole I go to school with, to be honest.'

Sláine smiled again, thank God. She went on. 'Two: living locally. Three: with an interest in the occult. Paranormal, supernatural, stuff like that. Sorry, I can't be any more specific – my mind feels like it's on go-slow or something. You know what I mean anyway.'

'I do.'

'And four . . . Screw it. I don't really have a four.'

She looked tired once more, plonking back onto the bed beside me.

I felt this mad urge to raise her spirits again, cheer her up, say *something*. 'Well, well, four could be, like . . . anyone acting suspiciously. I'll keep my eyes and ears open for anything dodgy.

Get on to Podsy again too, see if the Guards heard something.'

'He can't know about this. About me, I mean.'

'I'll be discreet, don't worry . . . Sláine, did you *really* feel this? That there was someone out here that night, a man, a human being. Or is it some kind of retrospective thing?'

She shrugged. 'I'm not sure. You might be right. Look, let's assume there was. Again, we need to fix on a start point. Let's make it that.'

'Good enough.' I asked, nearly as an afterthought, 'You reckon it's anything to do with this weird weather we've been having?'

Sláine raised her eyebrows, as if the thought hadn't struck her, which surprised me. '*Yeah*,' she said. 'Good spot.'

'Well it's so feckin' *freezing*, you know? It's not normal for Ireland to be this Baltic. And then what happened to you, the cold . . . *Ergo ipso facto*: possible connection.'

'Definitely. Good spot, Aidan. Bad Latin, but good spot.'

'Yep. It ain't easy being this brilliant.' I stretched my back out. 'Should I go now? You want me to go?'

'No, just . . . stay here. For a while longer, stay with me. I don't . . . ' She sighed deeply, a sorrowful sound that set my nerves on edge. 'It's not just the logistics of it. Asking you to help me: that wasn't the only reason. I do need your help, the practical stuff I mean. But I also need *you*. Someone to share all this with, another . . . Heh. Another *person*, if that's even what I am any more. I don't want to feel I'm in this thing by myself, you know? That I'm all alone.'

'Whoa. You are *not* alone. I'm here for you, Sláine. Always.'

She smiled at me and it was even sadder than that sigh.

I thought my heart was going to crack. My mind scrambled around for some words of comfort, anything to salve her spirit. Providence or blind chance landed on these: 'On that third day, you said you were lonely; you knew I was lonely, like that purple star glowing on the rail track. Could we rupture the fabric of space and time again? We are hearts talking across continents.'

My voice trailed off. I felt embarrassed, and knowing that I'd no reason for it didn't make me feel it any less. Sláine caught my hand; hers was freezing but I left mine there.

She said, 'That was beautiful. I don't know it. Where's it from?'

'You don't know it cos I wrote it. Unpublished poet, thus far anyway.' I grinned crookedly and looked away.

'You wrote that for someone else, I presume?'

'Yeeeeah,' I drawled, reluctantly 'fessing up. 'But she doesn't deserve it, you do. So I'm offering it to you now. No obligation to accept.'

'No, I accept. Gratefully. Thanks, Aidan. For everything.'

I accepted her acceptance in silence. We stayed sitting there, silent, easy together in the silence, silently struggling towards some imperfect form of peace or contentment. Her silent touch burning my hand like core ice, exhilarating and elemental, as if I'd plunged it into the centre of the frozen silent earth.

CHANGING

Time passed then. Days, weeks, and I hardly noticed them. I was wrapped up in this other world, wrapped up in her. Sláine. I was lost in dreams and magic and intrigue, as the earth got ever colder and the woods froze over.

We met several times a week, sometimes during the day but mostly at night. Outside of those hours – and school and time with my family and snatched morsels of sleep – I was also burrowing into our investigation, trying to get some handle on what the Jesus happened in the forest that fatal night. By the end of December the sleep deprivation was starting to affect me, all this added work and sneaking out in the witching hours. But I didn't care, and got the energy to keep going from somewhere. From her, maybe.

Not that I actually *got* that far, to be honest. I found a few things of potential interest, but by the end of the year we hadn't come any closer to solving the riddle of Sláine's death. The library was a dead end: no reports of anything hinky in our area, as far back as newspaper records went. Microfiche, local history books, old journals so fragile and desiccated from age that they were crisp to the touch: I read as much as I could

124

and found zip, except for those strange incidents around 1851 when the sea froze over and all the crows died.

I waded through an ocean of information, misinformation, conjecture and pure horseshit on the internet, and came across a few references to unexplained deaths, at least superficially similar to Sláine's. An Inuit settlement in Canada told legends of people being 'taken' by the cold, their bodies turned to ice and dust. An eighteenth-century French traveller to the Baltic Sea claimed to have seen a corpse with 'lines of blue about the skin, not to be found on any natural human form; and eyes turned grey or white, shining in death more than ever this or any man's did shine in life'. One inmate of a New England mental institution, in the 1890s, apparently said he had worked out a way to cheat death and live forever, 'if only these ignorant bastards will allow me and my acolyte the freedom to conclude our experiments in commanding the cold'.

All very vague, and probably as deranged as the New England guy's cellmates. Most likely fiction, although my experiences of recent months had taught me to keep an open mind. I continued the search. Found a list of various cold snaps in Ireland down the years on some amateur-meteorologist discussion board – nothing to make your hair stand on edge. Whatever else was going on in Shook Woods, this glacial weather seemed little more than a naturally occurring anomaly.

I hunted down books, online and in the physical world, on the paranormal, the occult, demonology, necromancy, telekinesis, ESP, divination, the Tarot: all those freaky-deaky areas of human enquiry that made me uneasy just reading about them. Reports of spirits moving objects during a seance, voodoo raising bodies from the grave, cults and sacrifices, Satanic rituals, naked men and women smeared in goat's blood and howling at the moon. *The Magus*, the *Corpus Hermiticum*, transcripts of Mesopotamian cuneiform tablets, Osthanes, Zoroaster, the *Grand Grimoire*, the *Eighth Book of Moses* . . . Semi-interesting to me, in an abstract way, but seemingly irrelevant to my search.

I talked to the ancient geezer who ran a New Age-type store on one of the town's main streets. He seemed offended that I'd imply he had any knowledge of a dark side to the supernatural world, then gave me the address of an even more ancient lady to visit. He said she was his sister, she said they were cousins. Whatever – she was as much use as the proverbial ashtray on a motorbike, even having the cheek to finish by offering a palm reading for the 'bargain price' of ten euro. I mentally showed her the facing side of my hand, middle finger raised, and skedaddled.

(I also, in the midst of this, followed Mr Kinvara's suggestion and looked up the meaning of 'bravo'. The online dictionary told me it was originally an Italian word, itself derived from the Latin, as he'd said: a combination of *pravus* and *barberas*. Funny, actually, where this term of hearty congratulations or praise had come from: the first part meant 'wicked or corrupt', the second 'savage or outsider'. Well done, you wicked outsider. What the hell, I'd take it as a compliment anyway.)

I tapped Podsy on a regular basis for skinny from Uncle Tim and the Gardaí. No reports of anything that seemed germane to Sláine's case. Nobody else found frozen to death. Certainly nobody with ice-blue markings on their skin, irises changed in colour. Sláine, so far, was the only victim of this . . . thing, whatever it was. That made me feel better, and kind of worse, all at once.

However, the Guards *were* keeping an eye on a few unusual incidents, Podsy told me one evening after school. A smattering of other attacks, presumably animals; a bizarre situation going on with some hallucinating girl. Another idiot found with his ass hanging out of a big oak tree – I didn't even want to *know* what that was about. Strange days, I guess, but I wasn't really paying attention: none of it had anything to do with me and Sláine – it didn't help us.

Neither did my beady-eyed impersonation of Sam Spade, keeping a close watch on the streets. Aidan Flood's on the case, dirtbags, tremble in fear. If there was a dirtbag behind Sláine's killing, I didn't see him. No cabal of weirdoes summoning Beelzebub from the pit on a moonlit night. Nobody dressed like Merlin the Magician on Rattle Street, having sex with a chicken and then cutting its throat, or maybe the other way round. No black magic that I could see. Nobody in control of this cold spell that just refused to end.

Playing the private detective made me feel pretty sharp, like I was some cool son of a bitch in a film. I even trailed a few blokes around, to their homes, their offices, lonely old factories on the outskirts of town – but it came to nothing. The worst I saw was a married father of four nipping behind one of the storage sheds in his lumberyard to do the wild thing with his twenty-year-old secretary. Were they not *freezing*?

I stored this information away, mentally and in Word files on my laptop, assuming I'd never use it. And I discussed it with Sláine, regularly. At first she'd be annoyed with our lack of progress, even angry or bitter, which wasn't like her – but trying to hide it from me, which was. After a while, that passion cooled to disappointment, then resignation. Our investigation had more-or-less ground to a halt by Christmas; both of us seemed to tacitly accept it.

In the meantime, me and her talked and talked, about everything and nothing. Sometimes deep conversations, sometimes the usual trivial rubbish any young couple come out with. Sometimes we didn't talk at all, just sat quietly in each other's company, listening for an owl call or the sound of snow falling off a pine tree's branch. Those times, the silent times, were almost as pleasurable as when we spoke. But we did speak, a lot, growing closer as each week went by.

Sláine would tell me about what it was like to be dead. She described the early days of her new life, before and after she met me. It was weird at first for her; she felt isolated and exhausted, at a loss as to what she should do now. How exactly do you fill your days when time has ceased to have any consequence? Do you plan ahead, when the future no longer means anything?

Worst of all, she said, was how she missed her family. Sláine didn't cry any more – she didn't think she could, the tears feeling frozen in her. Something else we had in common, though in my case that was more metaphorical. But she certainly felt that pain of separation, of knowing she'd never speak to her folks again.

She'd been tempted to make contact, but dismissed it out of hand, almost immediately. It wouldn't have been fair. How could you do something like that, to your parents or brothers? The shock of it, she said with a smile, might have killed her mother. So she left them be, in their grief and mourning. And dealt with her grief and mourning all on her lonesome.

I think this was one of the reasons Sláine reached out to me in the first place. We didn't know each other particularly well when she was alive, so there was no baggage from the past. No memories of what she'd once had, mercilessly pointing out that this, now, here, was inferior. You can't bear your existence at all, dead or alive, if you're constantly being reminded that the past was better than the present. I was someone new, a fresh start. I was more than happy with that.

So, Sláine was dead, alone. But there were some advantages to it. She told me how she started noticing things she'd never have done when alive. Her senses seemed amplified to an extent – hearing, sight, smell. (Not touch, obviously.) She felt stronger, faster, more powerful. And, Sláine said, she could kind of 'move' through space in giant leaps – as though she was bypassing large chunks of it, skipping from A to Z without using the rest of the alphabet. That's how she had transported me home those two times, I assumed, although she didn't confirm that. She didn't understand *how* she could do any of this – she just did it.

Sláine also felt a change inside, mentally or spiritually or something – she was vague about it, didn't quite understand it herself. The best way she could describe it was 'As though I'm opening up to the universe, and it's opening up to me. But slowly, very slowly. We've only just started our little dance.' Whatever that meant.

Sláine spent most of her time in Shook Woods. At first she'd been bound within the confines of the forest by some invisible barrier, but very quickly – within a few days – could travel beyond, able to leave whenever she wanted, though as she'd said before, not for long. Some compulsion dragged her back, and she wasn't unhappy about that. This was where she felt most at ease, most herself. The forest never got boring, she said, or bleak. It was silent and unchanging, and that's how she liked it. She spent long days and nights wandering around, not for the sake of exploring but simply to *be*. At times, Sláine admitted, she was even unsure where exactly she ended and Shook Woods began.

She showed me different parts of it, guided me along invisible trails, pointed out its camouflaged beauty. I was never that much into nature and stuff, but with Sláine as my guide, I came to properly see and appreciate the forest's wonders. The pines, of course, were its star attraction, shooting into the sky like the pointed contrails of a rocket. But there were other trees, stripped now of their leaves and all the more enchanting for it. And down on the ground, richer than rich, moss and humus, funguses, fragments of branches and leaves, stones and gravel, uncountable quantities of microorganisms. A whole world lived there. Sláine revealed it to me as she told me her story.

And I told her mine in reply. About my relatively contented early years, which sound like something from a novel: we were poor, but there was a lot of love in that house. How I grew out of childhood, and grew and grew, so I ended up too tall, too skinny, and *way* too shy and insecure for the battlefield of adolescence. How I limped along through secondary school, not deliriously happy, not miserable either. Your typical, mildly disaffected kid.

I expanded on the bullying, the break-up with Caitlin, our relationship such as it was. It wasn't embarrassing, at all, from the beginning, to lay myself bare like that. From the moment we met, I'd been completely comfortable in Sláine's company – I felt I could tell her anything and she wouldn't judge, mock, make me feel stupid. She listened and, if I asked, gave an opinion on what I'd said.

As I talked about it, over those weeks, I realised some deep truths – about myself and other people. First: the worst thing about youth, and how we interact with one another, is that it's all conspiracies and shifting allegiances. Whispered conversations, designed to exclude. Muted giggles, but just audible enough, aimed in your direction. Friends becoming enemies and you never know the reason why – possibly there is no reason. The strong eating the weak. There's something brutal and Darwinian about adolescence.

And we're dishonest, at this age. Books and films are fond of scenes where the sincere, straightforward teen is shocked on discovering the hypocrisy of adulthood. But in reality, as far as I could see, youth is just as deceitful. You're putting up a front from an early age – eight or nine years old and there you are, bullshitting your friends about your score in a video game or how much money your aunt gave you for Confirmation. Then you get older and your interests change slightly, but the bullshitting remains. You lie to your friends, or at least exaggerate, about shifting some girl, how much you drank last night, how unlucky you were not to make the football team. It's all bluster and untruths.

I always hated that, the fact that you couldn't be yourself

as a kid. You had to play a role, and worse, not even a role you'd chosen. You had to go along with the collective script and make sure to bloody well *fit in*. Most teenagers who are properly authentic and present a true self to their peers, are derided as anti-social weirdoes. What an irony: for all our declarations about 'keeping it real', kids can't handle sincerity. We don't want real.

Secondly, I realised something about myself that left me slightly embittered, but at the same time filled with a delirious sense of freedom. There was nothing wrong with me, and there never was. It was others who had the problem. I was fine, I was normal and decent and well-adjusted. Mostly good qualities and a few annoying habits, same as anyone else. I wasn't even as much of a dweeb or an oddball as I always assumed. I was just a regular guy. *They* were the ones with social or personality disorders.

It's the kind of thing parents would say to console a bullied child, and you appreciate the sentiment, maybe even agree on an intellectual level – but you don't really believe it in your gut. Now, though, I didn't only believe, I *knew*. The bullies were the screw-ups, not me. Now I actually liked myself again.

Oddly, everyone else seemed to have come to the same conclusion, because the bullying had ended completely. Not only that, I was being treated 'normally', the way I was before; which is to say, generally being ignored, with some friendly words.

Tommy Fox did more than that, and I didn't quite know why. He began spending some time with me, initiating conversation. Not that I minded – he'd always been all right to me. I was curious, though. I wondered if he had an inkling, on some mysterious level, that I was in contact with Sláine. But he couldn't know that, could he?

Whenever he spoke, Tommy would steer the conversation around to *her*. Again, I didn't mind, although it was sad, almost depressing, to see that look in his eyes: the pitch-black of heartbroken desperation, illuminated only by a flickering hope that he must have known could never come through for him. I remember thinking one day, this is what it means to lose someone you loved, lose them to death. I thanked my lucky stars it hadn't happened to me.

One evening in the forest I asked Sláine about Tommy, after a particularly emotional tête-à-tête which had him in tears. She brushed it off, saying they used to hang out but it was nothing really. At first I was annoyed; it felt so callous, her obvious disinterest. She seemed almost bored by another person's pain. But then it occurred to me that Sláine meant nothing by it – she didn't feel much for Tommy now because she didn't feel much for anyone . . . except maybe me. She wasn't herself any more. As she'd explained, regular human emotions didn't really apply to her.

Anyway, it appeared all the other kids had forgotten I was the designated town asshole. I wondered vaguely if some other poor fecker had been chosen to fill the slot. I hoped not, though it didn't occupy too many of my thoughts. In fact, life in general, interacting with my schoolmates and neighbours, had come to seem less and less important, less real. The woods and Sláine were more solid in my mind. I made an effort to stay connected to my family, Podsy, a few other people. I kept in touch with the world through school, my research, trips to the library, chats with demented old palm readers. Other than that, I let it kind of drift away.

I was happier, more confident in myself. I looked better too, healthier, although I felt tired because of lost sleep. I even put on some weight for the first time since infancy. I wasn't eating any more than usual – indeed sometimes I'd go all day without food, my tummy tingling with such anticipation about the night's meeting that I couldn't stomach a thing. But I got a bit heavier anyway. Maybe it was the absence of stress: all that anxious energy which used to burn up the calories, gone from my life.

As was any love I may have once felt for Caitlin. I stress 'may'. I was starting to suspect that I'd never truly loved her at all, that it had only been a youthful folly. She must have noticed these changes in me too, because the day before Christmas she approached me outside the chipper, a funny expression on her face, as if she was very nervous but trying desperately to seem cool. For once, Caitlin was on her own, not with the gang, which made me feel more certain of myself. It didn't even bother me that I'd stuffed my face with garlic chips, which I'd have to wolf down if I didn't want to speak with my mouth full. I couldn't remember the last time we'd talked. Sláine's funeral?

Caitlin made chit-chat, asked me how I was doing, referenced how she hadn't seen me around much, stuff like that. She even asked after my parents. I let her ramble on for a bit. Somehow, I knew what was coming, and it amused me to see her struggle for the words and the courage to say them. This time, I thought,

I'm the one with the power. And it feels goddamn good. I'm not proud of this – it was petty, I know. I couldn't help it.

Finally Caitlin asked if I was seeing anyone. When I gave a deliberately ambiguous answer, she mentioned, faux-casual, that there was a Christmas dance that night and maybe, you know, if I didn't have anything else on, like if I *wanted* to, maybe she and me could go together, or meet up there, whatever, it didn't matter, she'd be going anyway so might see me there.

I smiled and told her sorry, I did have plans for the night, but I'd maybe see her around sometime. Or, hey, maybe not. Then I sauntered off, munching my chips in the freezing air, leaving her behind, as cold and still as a glacier. And yes, this felt pretty good too. I'm not proud of that either, but I'm not going to lie.

All the while, the weather kept getting colder, and colder, and much, much colder. The meteorological people were increasingly perplexed. Our town, and its hinterland, was in the grip of virtually Arctic conditions. By Christmas we'd had snow every day for weeks. Huge drifts piled up outside houses, smothering streets and cars, making everything look like candy figurines on top of a cake that was covered in white icing. Water pipes seized up or burst constantly, the power cut out periodically. Irish towns weren't built to deal with Scandinavian temperatures.

Grown-ups moaned about it all the time, bitching that the government wasn't doing enough to help. Children revelled in it, having countless snowball fights and building snowmen, now that schools were often closed. Experts pondered it, media commentators debated it, farmers worried about it, shopkeepers cursed it, council workers battled against it, religious people saw it as a sign or prayed for it to end.

I loved it. This winter wonderland. Time felt frozen, along with the physical world; the two were in perfect harmony. And more: as the world turned whiter, so too did Sláine. Her clothes, once black, had by now shifted to a sort of pearl-white, with a trace of ice-blue. She glowed more than ever, everything about her. The clothes, her skin, the brilliance of her smile. She was like a photograph that somehow contained both the image and the flash.

We walked the length and breadth of Shook Woods, as well as spending time inside the lodge and a second favourite clearing we'd discovered – smaller than the Greek amphitheatre, more cloistered, a little sitting room set aside by nature in the many rooms of this forested home. I'd crunch noisily over the fresh snowfall, Sláine would float like a spectre. Usually there was nobody around; nobody came to the forest, certainly not in this weather, and never so far in. I did see Robert Marsden once or twice, the guy who found Sláine's body – in the distance, towards the exit, barely spotted through the massed trees. Doing whatever it is he does for the forestry service. I'm sure he didn't see us.

The second time this happened I asked Sláine if anyone *could* see her, besides me. She said it depended on her wanting to be seen. For some reason, I wasn't sure I believed her. But I had no reason not to – and there hadn't been any reported sightings of ghosts, no horror stories of girls rising from the dead.

We walked the forest, over days that blurred one into another. Shook Woods, its name now completely appropriate: the frozen forest. The place was even creepier with all this snow and frost; daytime felt as enchanted and perilous as the small hours. It reminded me of a scene out of some eerie old fairy tale, as though Jack Frost or the Snow Queen had become real. But I wasn't scared; I could never be scared once Sláine was with me. She was my guardian angel, my protector, my comfort and best friend.

We walked and talked and *were*. Just us two, the snow falling softly like confetti being thrown from heaven, pines closing in around us. The difference between these times in the woods and my increasingly brief visits to 'real life' was stark and mesmerising. It honestly did feel like I was stepping between two separate worlds. Back there was mundane waking life; here was an intoxicating dream.

On Christmas Eve, exactly at midnight, we opened that bottle of wine, the expensive one that she'd got God knows where. I hadn't lied to Caitlin about having other plans. This was where I had to be, the only place I wanted to be.

I poured out two glasses even though only one of us would be drinking, then took a long sip. It tasted delicious. Sláine smiled and raised her untouched glass.

'Happy Christmas to you, Aidan.'

'And to you, Sláine.'

We smiled at each other. A fraction of a second passed and suddenly our glasses were back on the table and she was holding me six inches above the ground, her mouth close to mine, her freezing hands at my face, a wash of coldness coming off her like a slowly rolling mist. It made me shiver from head to toe. It was wonderful. I was almost delirious.

I caught my breath. I wished I knew what to say, and realised that nothing needed to be said. We stayed like this for ages, the moment teased out, petrified in space-time.

Finally I whispered, 'Sometimes I wonder if you're a dream, a ghost . . . or a demon.'

Sláine said, 'Sometimes I wonder that myself,' and didn't let go.

I also wondered, from time to time, if I'd fallen in love with her. Funnily enough, it didn't seem to matter that I couldn't really answer the question. Whether I was in love with Sláine was outside of all this. By the same token, I didn't know or care whether she was in love with me.

And I wasn't sure if I felt sexual attraction for her. She was beautiful, no doubt; her smile made my heart leap in my chest. (There was an irony to it – no way would I have got with a girl that good-looking under normal circumstances.) But did I *want* her, in the sexual sense? I don't know. Maybe. Maybe the fact that I assumed it was impossible sort of killed those passions before they had a chance to take root.

I didn't really think about it. Such terms and concepts had no meaning in our world. There was just us, safe inside our frozen little universe, and that's all we needed.

I did think about the future, though. Not our future, whether there was one or not; that, too, seemed hazy and meaningless. I told myself I'd be all right with whatever happened. I'd accept it, like Sláine had accepted her death and new existence.

But I was beginning to think about my life, where I wanted it to go, what I wanted to do. Not exactly making concrete plans, but I was definitely more positive and enthusiastic about it. For the first time since before the bullying – perhaps the first time ever – I had ambitions for myself. I wanted to do things, not waste my life. I'd already decided to chat to Podsy in January and get some advice on college courses, what he felt I should apply for.

As December 31st came and went, and time rolled forward into the next twelve months, I took stock of where I was. I felt . . . happy. I had plans. I had a future. *We* had a future. I think.

That night, on the cusp of a new year, Sláine took my hands and said, 'Hey, about all that. Trying to work out who killed me, or what happened. Forget about it.'

I was surprised. 'Huh? You serious?'

'I am. I think I've come to terms with it. We should move on now.'

'I thought you really needed to know.'

'I thought I did too. Guess I didn't. Or don't any more. Seriously, it's fine. Nobody else has died, I don't think? I was wrong about it meaning anything – it was just some freak accident. Like this weather we've been having, it's meaningless, there's no big story behind it. It is the way it is. I died and somehow came back to life. There's nothing more to it.'

'Yeah.' I chewed this over. 'Yeah, I think you might be on to something there. I mean I didn't find shit, really, in all this time. No clues, nothing. Maybe it *was* just a freak.'

'Are you okay with that, so? Forget and move on?'

'Whatever my lady desires.'

So that was that. Everything was really great. It was peachy. It was close to perfect. Except for one thing, one little stone in my shoe. Life, as it so often does, got in the way.

Plans are fine. Plans are great. But the gods, as they say, laugh when men make plans. And my best-laid plans went out the goddamn window when, early in January, three things happened. Big things. Things that changed everything.

People started dying of the cold, the same as Sláine had. The Guards accused me of running a violent hate campaign against several local kids. And on the upside, I think I got a break in solving the mystery of Sláine's murder. That's life, I guess: always giving with one hand, taking with the other.

PART II

ANCIENT DEATH

MY STRANGE CONNECTION

The cold had begun killing again, but I didn't know this just yet. I had a more immediate problem. And Podsy was telling me exactly what that was, in detail.

I hadn't thought much of it to start with. Over a month and more, a bunch of kids from the town had been attacked: brutally, swiftly, inexplicably. Nobody was dead, but most were very badly hurt. Now a few people, for some crazy reason, thought I was behind it.

I'd heard about these assaults, of course. Podsy had mentioned them on occasion, although I wasn't really listening half the time. Besides, you couldn't avoid getting the news in a small place, something as dramatic as this. But for whatever reason, I hadn't given any of it much attention. It sounds callous, but I basically pushed it out of my mind. I was so engrossed in everything going on with Sláine that I was ignoring all else. I knew about it, but it didn't impinge on my life to a great extent. I felt bad for the victims, probably, in some vague way, then forgot about it. I definitely didn't grasp the full extent of what was happening.

But when Podsy called to my house one Sunday morning,

second week of January, and said people were beginning to suspect me, I *had* to give it some attention. All my attention, my keenest attention. The sort of attention that makes your head spin and your stomach lurch.

It started, he explained in my room, with Chris Harrington, the guy who got shredded opposite the golf course, thought to have been savaged by feral dogs. A few weeks later, towards the end of November, more of these incidents started to follow, drip-drip at first, then quickly escalating into a torrent.

Several other youngsters had been found mauled by, presumably, the same wild animals that did Chris Harrington. Podsy reckoned there were more than a dozen attacks by now. No one was killed, but all were seriously injured. Lacerations, broken bones, cranial trauma, blood loss. At least three of the victims needed transfusions, one had a leg amputated because of infection, another was rumoured to have suffered brain injury with long-term consequences. One guy went blind in his right eye. One girl had her left ear torn off. The victims were discovered, dumped and mostly unconscious, in different places: the sand dunes, the edge of Shook Woods, the long grass that runs by the river, abandoned yards. Messed up, violently shivering from the cold.

So how did this connect to me? It didn't, I would have said, until that morning when Podsy arrived at my door and said urgently, 'I *absolutely* need to talk to you. Right now. This is serious.'

I raised my eyebrows in surprise and gestured him inside. 'Well, good, cos I need to talk to you too. About college stuff. I want some advice from the biggest nerd I know.'

143

He frowned and said darkly, 'Man, if this doesn't get sorted out you can forget college. You can forget *everything*.' He grabbed my arm: 'Aidan, I think you're in trouble.'

That got my interest all right. We went up to my bedroom where Podsy sat his smallish body on the study chair, I lounged on the bed and he laid it out for me.

'Okay, you know how there's been a pile of kids attacked,' he said.

'Ummm . . . yes? Sort of? I guess.'

'This is *super*-serious stuff. Those kids were found all torn up. "Ravaged" was the word Uncle Tim used. One of 'em had her ear ripped off, you heard that? Another one got sliced right down the cheek, I mean eyeball to jawline.'

I didn't really want to hear the disgusting details, but Podsy insisted. For such a gentle, easy-going guy, he had an iron stomach and insatiable appetite for gory stories.

So, these fourteen or fifteen young people had fallen victim to . . . well, there was the thing. None of them could accurately describe their assailant. All they remembered was being somewhere, wherever, walking along in the dark – it always happened at night-time – and then *something* assaulting them, pouncing from the blackness behind them, crashing, slashing, beating, tearing, at massive speed. Each attack happened so fast, the victims had barely time to register it was happening before they passed out or were knocked out.

The Guards didn't know the cause. Their list of suspects was long. Wild dogs were the most obvious, but not the only one. Some people said they'd heard about a leopard escaping from a city zoo. Others reckoned it was a madman with a big collection of bigger knives. Someone else claimed there were still wolves in isolated parts of Ireland. The Guards were said to be investigating a rumoured trafficking ring of exotic pets: large cats, alligators, Komodo dragons. Somehow they'd escaped and gone on the rampage. There was talk of a clandestine dog-fighting circuit – a bloodthirsty pit bull or Doberman let loose.

Most people didn't know who to believe or what to think, including me. I couldn't see what Podsy was driving at here either, and I hadn't the mental space to figure it out anyway because something else was gnawing away in there, some unsettling thought or half-thought.

I said, 'What's all this got to do with me?'

Podsy laughed curtly. He looked bemused and nervous. 'Aidan, man . . . Some people are saying it's *you* who's doing it.'

I laughed too but there was no mirth in it, because that unsettling thought had firmed itself up in my head and now I could sort of see their point as Podsy added, 'All of the victims, of all these attacks, are people who bullied you. Every single one.'

He then recited their names – he had them listed on what looked like official Garda headed paper. And I instantly recognised each one. You don't forget the names of those who've tortured you, who made your life a daily hell. You don't forget the people you wanted so badly to hurt so badly. And maybe even wished were dead.

After six or seven, I was involuntarily flinching at Podsy's litany of names. *Them*. The monsters of my personal anguish. The ones who singled me out and made me pay for nothing at all. I remembered my history with each one, vividly – too much so. I wanted to forget all that, it was in the past now, but I guess your memory doesn't necessarily go along with your wishes. I remembered all their crimes, such as they were, against me. I even remembered specific incidents, and couldn't help automatically tying each victim's name to their history with me.

Sally Cribbin. Three broken ribs, broken femur. She wrote a poem about what a pathetic shithead I was – her words – and recorded it for YouTube. Then she arranged for the video to be played in front of our class while the teacher was out of the room.

Daniel Moynihan. Lost an eye. He put cat vomit (God knows where he got it) in my shoes while I was in gym class and tossed my trainers down a rubbish chute. I had to walk around in my socks for the rest of the day. Needless to say, each one had a hole.

Aileen Aacheson. Serious lacerations across her face and torso, punctured lung. Aileen and her stupid alliterative Irish-German name. She made a move on me outside the chipper one night, shoving her tongue down my throat, only it wasn't a move because she laughed like a hyena in my face and told the watching audience she was going to be sick.

More, there were more, Podsy droned on and on. All bullies. All remembered. Now all given a taste of what it feels like to be on the receiving end. A serious goddamn taste.

Podsy went on, 'Someone obviously figured out there's a connection. These kids, they're all around the same age. And by all accounts they'd each picked on someone who maybe has a good reason to hurt them now. Or feels he does, anyway.'

'What?'

'They think you're getting revenge on the bullies. You went crazy from it, lost your mind and now you're getting your own back.'

'*What*? I'm actually committing all these – these major *crimes*, because a few assholes picked on me?'

Podsy shrugged. 'That's what they're saying.'

'But how would . . . How do they know that I'm some way linked to those kids?'

He winced in discomfort. 'Uh . . . I think everyone kinda knew, Aidan. About the bullying? It was sort of well known. You know, around the town. Pretty much everyone knew who you were and what was going on.'

God, I felt mortified all over again. What a colossal joke I'd become. Not only my peer group but the entire town. I muttered, 'Yeah. Everyone knew and nobody did squat.'

'Hey, I didn't like that either.'

'Ah, I know. I'm not having a go at you.'

I didn't quite know how to feel about this. Was I in some way responsible? I *couldn't* be, I wasn't doing anything . . . I was certainly dumbfounded by it, creeped out, and to be honest, a little nervous with what Podsy was telling me. They each had an undeniable connection to me. I was the common link and I couldn't for the life of me work out why this was. But some others, apparently, thought they could.

Podsy said, 'There're rumours. Whispers. Around town, like. This's only a few people shite-talking, but you know how it goes with rumours. Something gets said enough times and all of a sudden people treat it as gospel truth.'

'Who's spreading these rumours? Do I even want to hear any more of this?'

'Different people. A couple of kids at school – though who cares what they say. But grown-ups as well. Aileen Aacheson's father, he's one. He's a tool bag, all mouth. But Jonas Woodlock – I know he wasn't very nice to you but his folks are fine and they've said it too. I heard them going on to my mum and dad the other night. They thought I was out.'

'What happened to him again?'

'Got cut to bits out the old mountain road. Barely alive when they found him.'

'Jesus. What did his parents say?'

'That someone had to be doing these things, like a person – they didn't believe it was any animal because wouldn't a dog or whatever have been caught by now. And what about that young lad of the Floods, which means you . . . '

'I figured that.'

' . . . He got an awful doing at school last year and they knew Jonas was involved. "Oh don't worry," they said, "we made sure to take him to task for it." Anyway they said it was possible you were doing it all out of revenge, you were sick in the head and maybe it was hard to fully blame you but you couldn't be doing that in a civilised society and they were thinking of going to the Guards about it. My dad talked them out of it, told 'em they can't go making wild allegations without evidence, that it was slander if they can't prove it and they'd end up in court themselves. Said he'd pass it on to Uncle Tim though, keep an eye on you.'

148

I said, 'They didn't tell you not to come here, then? Your mam and dad.'

'No. Why would they do that?'

'So they don't believe this theory?'

'Not for a second. But some do. And if I know the people of this town, that's a number that is going to *increase*, not go in the other direction.'

This was so absurd, it was laughable. Obviously those kids had been mauled by an animal, or several. The wounds, the bloodletting, the mindless savagery of these attacks, it was totally clear. The way their attacker seemingly stalked them from the darkness before springing out – that's how animals do it, isn't it? Lions, wolves, large beasts, wild things.

Not *me*, for God's sake. But if it was all so bloody laughable, why wasn't I laughing? I felt a noose of panic being fitted around my thin neck, and needed to shake the thought before it started to tighten.

Rolling a smoke I said to Podsy, 'It's *ridiculous*. I'm amazed anyone is giving this a second thought. The whole notion of it, me as some kind of psycho terrorist, it's so daft I won't . . . Besides, I couldn't even do that stuff. I mean literally, I wouldn't have the strength to – didn't you say people were basically torn to ribbons? Sure, how would I be able to do that?'

Podsy said, 'The sergeant reckons it might have been "the strength of the insane". That's a direct quote. He says, "You'd be amazed what people are capable of when they're not in their right minds". Also a quote.'

'The sergeant . . . He doesn't believe this too, does he?'

'Uncle Tim says he's "keeping an open mind", again a quote.

149

Tim doesn't think there's anything in it himself, he knows you, but he can't give an opinion officially. But, Aidan, listen, I have to tell you: I'm getting the impression that more and more people are starting to feel there's something to this.'

It was crazy. The whole world had turned upside down and everyone's marbles had fallen out and rolled away on them. A thought struck me. '*You* don't believe it, surely to God?'

He glowered as if I was the biggest dumb-ass on the planet. 'Would I be here if I thought you were some axe-wielding maniac? Telling you all this?'

I smiled at him. Good old Podsy. 'No, s'pose not.'

'I dunno, it's just . . . strange, you know?' he said. 'Some wild animal on the loose – it's like something out of a horror movie.'

You have *no* idea, Podsy.

He stood and absently ran his fingers along the bookshelf. 'Then all that other weird shit that's been going down . . . God. Crazy days in our sleepy little town, huh?'

'What do you mean, "weird shit"?'

'Just all the bizarre things that've happened. Like those three meatheads each getting a fake text from the other – you know what happened there. Or Clara Kinnane going bananas, hearing voices. 'S just weird, is all.'

I cast my mind back over the last several weeks, piecing together memories and parts of memories, things I'd overheard but disregarded, bits and pieces of knowledge I'd accrued and obviously filed away without knowing I was doing it. Things Podsy had told me. Different incidents which I now recalled with an increasingly sickening feeling.

At the end of November three lads had become embroiled

in quite a serious scrap outside a pub – the same shithole Harrington had his last pint in, though that was probably coincidence. All of them claimed that one of the others had sent malicious text messages, insulting their girlfriends (or sisters, mothers, goldfish, whatever); all denied ever sending such texts. They each took an equally bad beating, in some weird form of karmic balance, street-fighting style.

A week later, a teenage girl was institutionalised by her parents and doctor, after suffering a psychotic break: she'd imagined she saw someone hovering outside her window over several nights, which wasn't possible because they lived in a fourth-storey apartment overlooking the river. The figure, she babbled, was 'beautiful and terrifying like the face of death, the face of hell'. It called to her, telling her the river was waiting.

Then a guy who lived near enough to me had his car set on fire and, beside it, a message was scorched into the ground in burning petrol: NEXT TIME YOU MIGHT BE SITTING IN IT, SWEETHEART. There was something blackly comic about another incident: a young lad was found, coming on for midnight, doped up to the eyeballs and stripped to his underwear, his *head* rammed inside a hole in this giant tree that stands across the road from the town's 'Welcome to . . . ' sign. He was hospitalised for hypothermia, drug intoxication and mental trauma. He's lucky he didn't die of the first, and was still suffering from the last.

Even my old pal Clara, that fat fucker, had gone a bit doolally, as Podsy said – she kept hearing voices in her head, so she thought, tormenting her, trying to drive her maaaaaad. She got bundled off to the same 'rest home for the terminally bewildered' as the other girl.

At first I didn't see a link between any of this: stolen phones, prank texts, religious hallucinations, drugs and abduction, burned-out cars, ghostly voices, whatever. Or between those events and the animal attacks. I resisted this dawning awareness, but it slowly rose within me like creeping damp.

I actually started to shake a little as I realised: Jesus Christ, *I'm* the connection. Again.

'They were bullies too.'

I'd whispered that, my words barely rising above silence, so Podsy asked me to repeat it. Something stopped me. Some instinct of caution or self-preservation made me mumble instead, 'Nothing. Sorry, just talking to myself, it's nothing.'

Meanwhile the thought was getting louder and *louder*: all those kids had also bullied me. The fake texts guys, Clara, that dipshit McGuinness getting his crappy car burned up, the girl who thought she saw the devil, Marina Callaghan, that was her name . . . She was one as well. God help me, they *all* were.

What was I saying here? I didn't know. But something *very* strange was going on. Just as with the animal attacks, these other victims had picked on me. Which meant, of course, that I'd hypothetically want revenge on them too.

I raised my eyebrows, blew out carefully, interlaced my fingers, cracking them loudly.

Podsy said, 'You all right, man?'

Careful, Aidan. *Careful.*

'Yeah. Uh, everything's fine. Just, you know, pissed off at this. These allegations, me attacking people.'

'Don't worry. I know you couldn't pull some crap like this.

You're too much of a wimp for starters, ha ha. Daniel Moynihan would probably beat you and me *together* in a fight. But . . . clearly something is off here.'

Podsy thought about it for half a minute while I held my breath and tried to calm my hands long enough to roll another smoke. I told myself, don't mention the other stuff, whatever you do: texts, arson, Clara, that moron inside a tree, the rest of it. Nobody else seemed to have made the link to me, not the Guards nor concerned parents, not even Podsy. I assumed it was because those incidents were so dissimilar. There was no obvious pattern to them . . . except my strange connection.

Finally he said, 'Occam's razor.'

'Whose what?'

'Occam's razor. A philosophical principle. Basically it can be reduced to, "The simplest explanation is usually the correct one."'

'Uh . . . right,' I said. 'So according to your buddy Occan –'

'Occ*am*.'

'What*ever*, the explanation here is . . . ?'

'You didn't attack those kids – but someone did. It's too much of a coincidence otherwise. Yes, a wild animal could do that, but to only choose people who'd bullied you? Statistically, it's impossible.'

'Go on. I know you have a theory, you always have a theory.'

Podsy said, 'They all picked on you – now someone's getting them back on your behalf. Either with their own two hands or using, like, trained animals or something. That's the less likely scenario, in my opinion.'

'Someone? Who?'

153

'Beats me.'

'It's not you, is it?'

He didn't even laugh, that's how ridiculous the idea was. I said, 'Sorry, that's stupid. Who, then?'

'I haven't a clue. Have your mum and dad seemed a bit on edge lately?'

'Very funny, Podsy.'

'Hey, maybe it's you. Some split-personality thing, like in *Fight Club*. Maybe Evil Aidan's getting revenge on behalf of Wimpy Aidan, who doesn't know the other one exists.'

'And that's even funnier.'

'Joking, obviously. Although you have been acting a bit weird lately,' Podsy added. 'I haven't seen much of you for a good while. You look like you haven't slept in a month. And, and, *aaaand* . . . your kid brother told me he sometimes sees you creeping out of home at night.'

'The bloody little sneak.'

'Don't be too hard on him. I got it out of him through low cunning and bribery. He thinks you're some sort of vigilante, by the way, like Batman. Which obviously isn't the case, cos Bruce Wayne is Batman.'

I looked Podsy right in the eye. 'No. So what do you think's going on if I'm not Batman?'

He looked right back. 'I don't know, Aidan. I'm not sure I even want to know. All I know is you're my best friend . . . my only friend, prob'ly. And you're not capable of hurting anyone. *Really* hurting, like. They're a shower of pricks but even bullies don't deserve to get assaulted that badly. And I know you think that too.'

'I do.'

'Look.' Podsy sighed. 'Something is happening with you, something else, besides this . . . whatever. Vigilante-slash-revenge thing. What that something is, I haven't a clue. Like I said, maybe I don't want to. Don't even know if it's good or bad – I'm thinking a bit of both . . . I assume you're not going to tell me?'

'Eh . . . no. Sorry, I can't.'

'What I figured. That's okay. But it's definitely *something*. You seem . . . different. These last few months, you've kind of changed. I mean in a good way – you're more . . . grown-up. More sure of yourself. And that's cool, I'm happy for you. Just . . . you know. Watch yourself, man.'

'Thanks. I mean I will.'

'If you need my help – and it's help I can give – you know where I am.'

'Thanks,' I said. 'Again. I know that, thanks. Third time.'

'And don't worry, nobody else knows. Sneaking out at night or whatever, it's just me and the kid. Maybe make up some story for him, swear him to secrecy.'

'All right, I'll do that. Listen, Podsy, I'm gonna have to bail on you. D'you mind? Got loads of things to do. But thanks for giving me the heads-up on what people are saying.'

'It's only *some*, now, in fairness. Most people I'm sure know the whole thing is rubbish.'

'Yeah, hopefully. Talk to you at school, all right?'

'Cool, yeah. I'll let myself out.'

He did, while I finally lit that smoke and inhaled and exhaled a dozen times, hardly aware of either. This was *mental*, it was crazy. Not just the bizarre revelation that people thought I was capable of mutilating other kids or beating them into comas (capable in either sense: morally or physically). Even weirder, I thought now, was the second tranche of victims, the other connection to me that I'd kept from Podsy.

Apart from my link with it – and the queasy suspicion that some demented stalker was out there, wreaking havoc on my behalf – parts of it simply didn't make sense. They didn't seem possible. The arson on McGuinness's car, yes, that was doable. It was also possible, albeit difficult, to steal or hack someone's mobile and fire off incendiary messages about their mate's girlfriend. Even abducting someone, drugging them to the gills, ramming them into an oak tree: that could conceivably be carried out by someone. Not me, but someone strong and daring and ruthless.

But the thing with whatsherface, Marina Callaghan: how could anyone have done that? Her family lived four storeys up, for God's sake. Floating outside her window, it was inconceivable. Unless, unless . . .

My mind casted around for plausible explanations, and amazingly, suggested one: you could slip a psychoactive substance into her food, after laying down subtle prompts about what you want her to think she's seeing. Plant the seed of an image over a few weeks, then water that seed with a hit of acid or what have you. So she *thinks* she's seeing the scary-beautiful face of death, when there's nothing outside her window.

A long shot, but possible. Was it? Just about, *maybe*. And it still didn't explain how poor old Clara heard voices in her head. How'd my avenging angel get those in there?

Oh, this was pointless. I knew I wouldn't be able to untangle the mystery on my own, and I couldn't hammer it out with Podsy, my parents or anyone else . . . Sláine might be able to help. We'd arranged to meet that night, in our hunting lodge, right at the stroke of midnight. Two days since we'd spoken, and I'd been counting down the hours with the impatience of a kid on Christmas Eve. But now I was buzzing on an even sharper sense of anticipation. I wanted to know what was going on. Maybe Sláine could help with that.

In the meantime, I decided on the spur of the moment, I'd do a bit of schoolwork. It would take my mind off things, these unsettling developments. Might even knock some insights into place – lateral thinking, or whatever they call it.

My decision sharpened to a narrower focus: I'd work on that History essay for Mr Lee, the one where we imagined ourselves as a Famine survivor. The due date was within a fortnight, and I hadn't written so much as a word. I hadn't even opened the folder filled with notes since I scribbled them in the library that day. I smiled tenderly and thought: Sláine, you're interfering with my education now. How long ago was that? The day I'd softened Rattigan's cough, by the park. It seemed a long while past. Anyway, today was as good as any to get back into it.

I scrabbled around under my bed for where the folder lay – for some reason, I remembered sliding it in there on my return from the library, to keep that stuff separate from other school notebooks and things. My fingers felt it, sharp-edged cardboard. I pulled it out, sliding 'ssshhh' along the carpet.

Pale grey, two punched holes, secured at the top by an elastic band. I popped the elastic and opened the folder.

And nearly dropped it again when I saw, sitting on top, sheets of paper that were not in my handwriting, not of my doing, and by the looks of them, not even from this century.

OLDER DIVINITIES

to be something of an amateur historian. I stress 'used to', because I shall shortly be dead; or at least, no longer in the form I now possess. I am unsure of what precisely will result from this thing I now attempt. I hope for success, of course. I would pray for it, if prayer remained open to me. It may kill me. Or it may refashion me, making me into something new. One way or the other, the man who currently exists, the one whose hand shapes these words . . . soon, he will be no more.

The handwriting was elegant, ornate, done with, I'd guess, an old-fashioned fountain pen. Dark-blue ink, flamboyant loops on the letters f and s, the words slanted quite a bit to the left. The paper looked ancient, though I guessed it had been of high quality when first bought. It was stiff and frayed at the edges, turning a sort of burned-brown colour from age. I handled it gingerly as I read, fingers holding the small pages gently but firmly, like those robotic hands they use for delicate, precise surgery. I reckoned some of the document must have been missing, because the text began on that lower-case word 'to', and apparently in the middle of a sentence. So I didn't have the beginning, which was annoying; I didn't even know how much was missing. Still I read.

An amateur historian, I call myself. But I was more than that, much more. I read widely and voraciously, my life entire. The ignorant peasantry mistrusted me to some extent because they didn't understand why I sought knowledge and wisdom. The priests mistrusted me precisely because they did understand. I had no grand intentions or designs in the beginning, by the by. I was just a man, intelligent, curious, with an open heart and open mind. But knowledge is power, and reading makes us greater beings.

It even – you may find this hard to believe, considering what you read in these pages – it even brings us closer to God. And I wanted that. I wanted to be as close to God as was imaginable, and be the most fully realised man I could be. Noble ideals, I'm sure anyone would agree.

How did I come to have these pages in that folder? I tried to remember back to the day at the library, how glacial the weather was outside, all the fascinating stuff I came across about the Famine and Sláine's ancestors, the freaky cold spell that had encased the area like a snow globe. Had someone put this document into my bag when I went for a smoke break or nipped to the toilet? No, wait . . .

The old lady. The one who carried Sláine's message, but prior to that had helped me pick my stuff off the ground after Rattigan slapped the bag from my shoulder. She could have slipped these small pages into the folder, on top of my foolscap-sized notes. I read on.

Then the Great Hunger came and destroyed all that, for me and everyone else. Lives, dreams . . . yes, those noble ideals. We were reduced to savagery, to the level of beasts. When you are starving, nothing matters – nothing – but getting food. Love, decency, family, God himself . . . all of that pales to insignificance beside the primordial biological imperative: to feed.

I have watched almost everybody I know die slowly, in agony. Agony. Death by hunger is as bad a death as there is. And if starvation didn't get them, disease or exhaustion or this infernal cold did. My friends, my workers, business associates, people I loved, people I hated . . . they were all fellow human beings, and they all died. I cried out to God for help – but God wasn't listening. Or if he was, he never replied to me.

The Great Hunger. Another name for the Famine. Something was telling me that this had meaning, it was a message, it was trying to make me *see* . . . See what? I didn't know. Keep reading, damn it. The Famine, the cold, all that death, loitering everywhere with the baddest of bad intent. This man calling out to God. His desperation, his rage . . . His. Who wrote these lines? Who are you? I kept reading.

161

He never helped us! We, his children, dying in our thousands . . . and he let it happen. Thus my heart turned against him. My wife, my beautiful Eleanor, often asked if I still believed in God, the Christian one of her devotion. She is nervous-tempered and worries too easily. Her question surprised me. Certainly I do; I will always believe. But once, I also loved God. Then love turned to hate – and anger.

And I went in search of aid elsewhere. I returned to our own gods – the older divinities – the ones who'd ruled this land for thousands of years before that Middle Eastern usurper banished them all. In desperation, I have appealed to these older forces. I had heretofore studied necromancy, demonology, all manner of arcana. I was, you might say, already prepared. Strange – it is as though I knew this crisis would one day come. Now it has, and I alone was ready.

I stopped, paused, some fraction of a thought echoing from the deepest recesses of my mind. Demonology, necromancy, the study of obscure disciplines and dark, dangerous arts: why was that familiar to me? I read back to the top, and there it was, black on white or blue on yellow, the starkest confirmation. *My beautiful Eleanor.*

William John McAuley wrote this. Sláine's great-great-something grandfather, I remembered now: his wife's name, the breadth of his reading, his interest in what were considered, back then anyway, 'questionable' subjects. He filled these pages and must have left them somewhere, in the hope that another might read them after his ... death, whatever. He'd seemed to think he could somehow circumvent death, hadn't he, there at the start? What had he written ...? I scrolled back the pages, quickly. *This thing I now attempt ... It may kill me. Or it may refashion me, making me into something new.*

Jesus. I shuddered, an involuntary reaction. What the hell did *that* mean? And why, again, did I now have McAuley's last testament in my hands? I hadn't a clue of either answer, but that nagging sense remained in my nervous system and heart, getting stronger all the time, insisting this was connected, in some as-yet-unexplained way, to what happened to Sláine ...

I raced to the end, my eyes flicking over the words like a careering skater on thin ice.

I have let my wife leave with our children. She would never have appreciated what I was doing, or agreed to it. I love that woman like I have never loved another, but she is too pious in her devotion to the God who has failed us. She wouldn't even blame him for the hell we were living in! Too pious, too timid. She would have tried to stop me in this; I think she might even have killed me, had she known. She loves her husband, but she loves that capricious God more. So I let her go.

Shortly after Eleanor left, the English soldiers came – help finally from the Crown. Too late for her aid, and too late for me: I have also left. I am gone to Shook Woods these past seven nights, far beyond the reach of any mortal authority. And there in the forest, I summoned something more ancient than the Christians' deity.

Something of the land, that dwelled in the very rocks themselves, in the elements: wind, snow, ice. The weather has been cold enough, these long months; I took it as a sign that I was justified. I summoned this presence and told it what I needed and heard what it desired. Now I wait for

There it came to an abrupt halt. The back end of this letter or diary must have been missing too. I dropped to my knees and searched around the floor, thinking loose pages might have fallen under the bed, unseen and unread. Knowing they hadn't. Perhaps this was all that survived of McAuley's epistle. Perhaps this was all they wanted me to know.

They. He, she, them, whoever. I now knew, at least, who wrote this stuff, but still wasn't sure who'd given it to me. Or what it meant. All I knew was that it meant *something.* I felt, as certainly as I've ever felt anything, that part of the solution to our riddle lay in these words. At least a clue to guide us towards that solution. The cold, he mentioned it more than once – that was crucial, I was sure. McAuley summoned something, or tried to, or thought he did; and he needed freezing weather to do it.

I couldn't wait to talk to Sláine about all this; how excited she'd be, fired-up like me. I knew she'd said at Christmas that she was cool with not knowing exactly what happened to her, that we should move on from the past, but I didn't truly believe that. Anyone would want to know, wouldn't they? It's beyond a choice, it's down in the guts, it's in your blood as much as white cells or platelets. You *need* answers. We all do.

Midnight seemed an eternity away. I grabbed my coat and hit

for the door. A walk, while there was still daylight. A blast of fresh air to clear my mind, blow the cobwebs out, get a better handle on this, freshen me up in readiness for a big discussion with Sláine about what I'd found.

Two words popped into my head, McAuley's words, unbidden and very unwelcome: 'refashion me'. That shudder again, juddering through my body like a convulsion. I told myself to ignore it and left.

I ambled through town, aimless and directionless, just walking to be out walking, listening to music on my headphones, deliberately not mulling over what I'd read. I could discuss it with Sláine all in good time, see if she had ideas. Two heads are better than one, and so on. Besides, she was a clever girl in life, far more than me, and her mental powers seemed to have grown since her new life began . . .

'New life.' Hadn't McAuley mentioned that, too? My pulse rate ticked up a notch and I thought, we're close, sweetheart. We're *close*, I'm certain of it.

Passed the local industrial park – tiny, depressing, with its peeling paint and vacant units – then two housing estates, a very plain and modest Protestant church, something else, an empty patch of real estate overgrown with weeds and discarded bottles, something else again, I forget what. After another few minutes I came to Belladonna Way, the poshest street in town. Belladonna, aka deadly nightshade – only in this kip would the fanciest area be named after a poison.

Gorgeous houses, though. Lots of money went into restoring these beauties, renovating them, building them in the first place.

Some of the properties on Belladonna were ancient, dating back to the nineteenth century. A range of architectural designs, though all scrupulously tasteful and, especially, 'traditional': Gothic and Neoclassical here, Georgian and mock Tudor there, and none of your ugly Modernist rubbish, thank you very much. A few crows, brooding in the shadows, motionless and black, completed the mood of time-worn, spooky elegance.

An upstairs light went on in one of the houses exactly as I passed. I stopped, and it went out again. That *might* have been the home of Mr Kinvara, I wasn't sure. There was a spacious garage to the rear anyway, and no car out front, which would suggest a man with a collection of vintage motors that he didn't want getting keyed by some boozed-up knacker staggering home from drinking jungle juice in a ditch. A faint sound of music drifted from somewhere deep within the house – the rear, presumably – a four-note piano motif, vaguely familiar to me. Rising steadily from a mid-tone for the first three, then crashing down, hard and very low, for the fourth. Dum-dum-dum-DUMMM . . .

My father had mentioned Kinvara in passing a few days before; maybe that's why he was in my head. He'd asked Dad to drop over and collect some extra money for that job he did on the cars. My father was a proud man but not too proud to refuse hard cash in straitened times. Kinvara tactfully called it a 'delayed Christmas bonus'. Dad described the house as 'smashing', inside and out; that's literally the best he could come up with. Said it reminded him of the library of a gentleman's club in London where he once did maintenance work, decades ago, when he lived in the UK. I guess this meant a lot of plush leather, hardwood bookcases and expensive brandy running hot and cold. The building was, according to my father, a 'converted something-or-other'.

Flash bastard, and his own piano too – Kinvara really *was* like James Bond.

Dad also said Kinvara was 'very charming' and 'a real gentleman'. And the guy's first name, it turned out, was Sioda, which sounds like it should be a girl's name, but apparently isn't. I'd never come across it before. Means silk, or fairy folk, or something. I'm a dumb-ass when it comes to languages.

Sioda Kinvara, super-spy! Women swoon for his dapper good looks, men for his sexy cars and a house that looks like Bill Gates' boardroom. The international man of mystery, hiding out in a sleepy Irish town . . . Actually, what *did* he do for a living? My father hadn't said. I kind of got the impression that Agent Kinvara was a man of independent means and didn't need a job, so didn't have one. A perfectly sensible approach to life, really.

I quit my mental rambling and shuffled on further up Belladonna Way. I thought I heard a car pull out behind me, but it didn't sound like the souped-up growl of a Jag. As far as I knew. I was as *au fait* with cars as I was with languages. I kept walking.

This being dead midwinter, dusk was already beginning to crawl across the sky as I travelled out of town and continued along Distillery Road. So-called because it once was home to a whisky manufacturing business, long defunct, this led in a straight line along one edge of Shook Woods – the far side to its main entrance.

The album on my MP3 player had ended, I belatedly noticed. Silence in my earphones; I decided on a whim to take them out. I stopped walking and did that and found my tobacco and rolled a smoke. And I heard a clicking noise.

Faint, distant . . . but definitely there. I finished assembling the cigarette and listened, and it continued to sound. Maybe a little nearer? A regular click, a tap almost, probably louder in this still, chilled air, minus five degrees and dropping. I lit the smoke and looked up. A man was walking in my direction, same side of the road – cheap-looking overcoat, and no hat despite it being as cold as the proverbial witch's tender parts.

Almost dark, I realised. And nobody around, on foot or in a car. This road was hardly used by anyone, since they shut the distillery down. It didn't really go anywhere, just out to the surrounding countryside, with a number of winding boreens branching off to farms and houses. Nobody in sight, just me and this guy coming towards me. Not in a rush, a steady pace, brisk but casual. His feet hitting the asphalt, that clicking sound now changed into a slap that almost twanged through the air, as if made by someone keeping rhythm on the body of a guitar. Cold air makes acoustics go all screwy.

I drew on my cigarette and realised I had tensed up slightly. At some point in the preceding two minutes, my nerves had got on edge, just a bit. My heart rate was a little faster. And was that sweat I could feel, surfacing through the skin of my back? I resumed walking, out of embarrassment more than anything else. Can't stand here indefinitely, it looks suspicious and makes you come across as a hysterical idiot.

The man's whole face was in shadow. Why can't I see your

face? I thought. His head wasn't angled away from me, he didn't wear a broad-brimmed hat, yet I couldn't see him properly. It was as though he carried a shadow with him, a personal cloaking device. Something shifted across his face, a wisp of light, and I thought I saw his eyes twinkle, maybe the flash of a smile.

We continued to approach one another. A creepy feeling of dread, not quite panic but with panic definitely in its future plans, washed down through me. Who was this man? Why was he here? What business did anyone have on this lonely, disused road, in the freezing cold, as night fell?

We came closer.

My feet crunched on slush and snow and I wished they'd shut the hell up, stop being so *loud*, and the man was within twenty yards and I still couldn't make out his face. I flicked my fag onto the road and found that I'd bunched my hands into fists and was as tense as bejeesus, my heart kicking like a mule and sweat steaming inside my coat and vest and this goddamn guy was almost on top of me.

Then we met and he stopped and drew in a few paces so I could pass, and I felt like the biggest baby in the world. He smiled and said, 'Nice evening for a walk,' his voice faintly familiar or maybe that was my heightened imagination, and I almost laughed with mortification. My face was red, I'm sure, as I recognised how ridiculous I'd been. I mumbled some semi-civilised response and went to go by. He took a step too and stumbled on a tree root, falling against me, lightly touching really, and muttered something, maybe an apology. We carried on our separate ways and I heard his footsteps receding into the distance – the sound of relief.

This whole mystery thing is getting to you, man. Now you're

imagining things. Guy was out for a walk, dumbo, like you are.

Half a minute up the road I stopped with a jolt as I realised I still hadn't seen his face. Weird. We'd passed within two feet of each other, we'd actually touched, and there was still a watery trace of light in the sky, but I couldn't for the life of me give any part of any description of what that man looked like.

Was that weird? Probably not. I was on edge, and twilight's a funny time anyway. People think they see all sorts of crazy shit at twilight.

I'd talk to Sláine tonight, hopefully put some shape on all this. That'd help, that'd plane some of those edges down. Even if we didn't come to any conclusion, just talking to my girl would relax me, ground me on this solid earth once more.

And that was worst-case scenario. Best-case was that together we might be able to work it all out, solve the big mystery. Another case closed by Aidan & Sláine Investigations! Book 'em, boys, and throw away the key.

I dashed home with dreams of heroes in my head, lay that same head down for a nap so brief it barely warranted the name, showered, ate, drank a gallon of coffee, retired to my room and pretended to be asleep. When I was sure everyone else really *was* asleep, I made a calm, smooth getaway – I was getting to be a real pro at this.

I reached our place in the forest by about half-past twelve, hollering a greeting to Sláine as I approached. I noticed with a subconscious tickle of anxiety that the light wasn't showing. I went in and lit the lamp and looked around. And then realised, through the evidence of my eyes but especially through the sickly quiver I felt vibrating deep, deep in the marrow of my bones . . .

Sláine had disappeared. And I was alone.

UNDER ARREST

'Am I under arrest?'

'No.'

'Do I need to call a solicitor or someone?'

'No. We're just talking, Aidan. There isn't any need to bring in the heavy guns. This is nothing official. Like I say, we're just . . . having a little chat.'

A little chat, my ass. The sergeant, named Parkinson, and Uncle Tim sat opposite me behind a desk in the former's surprisingly small office in the town Garda station. Uncle Tim had the look of a man who personally regretted the circumstances but was determined to meet his professional obligations, whatever discomfort this may cause him. Of course I wasn't calling him Uncle Tim – he wasn't my uncle anyway, and down here, wearing that uniform, he was Deputy Sergeant McGlynn. Tim McGlynn, it almost rhymes. Silly-sounding sort of name. I suppressed a smile. This wasn't the place for levity, and besides I didn't feel too light-hearted myself.

Despite the sergeant's rehearsed reassurances, I was potentially in big trouble and I knew it. John Rattigan had been found, torn up like the other animal attacks. He was currently on life support in hospital; the scuttlebutt said it was fifty-fifty whether he lived or died. And someone had told the Guards I wanted him dead.

The sergeant said in his broad Kerry accent, 'No school today?'

I mumbled some excuse about the building being closed due to snow. I could tell by his expression that Parkinson didn't believe me but he let it slide, saying, 'Okay, let's go through this one more time. Clear it all up. You said to Mr Rattigan, "You're a dead man," or "You'll soon be a dead man," – words to that effect. Is our information correct?'

'No, it's not bloody correct. I didn't say that at all. Who told you that?'

Uncle Tim said, 'Aidan, never mind who said it. Trust us, we have reputable witnesses to this. More than one. So will you answer the question please.'

'Unc— I mean, Deputy Sergeant McGlynn. I never said anything like that. Not to Rattigan, not anyone.'

'You call him by his surname,' the sergeant said. 'Not "John", but "Rattigan". You sort of spat it out there. I take it that means you don't like the lad?'

'That doesn't mean anything. It's just a name . . . All right, I admit it. I *don't* like him. He's an asshole, he was really crappy to me. Me and loads of other people. I mean the list of suspects, if you're including everyone who had a reason to get John Rattigan? That's a pretty long list.'

A young guard opened the door and blurted out, 'Sergeant, the coroner's here about Mr Blue Skin . . . '

Parkinson glared at him and shot his eyes in my direction.

172

The officer blushed and muttered, 'S-sorry, sir. Uh, whenever you're ready, sir, sorry.'

He reversed out. I leaned back and looked out the door as it was shutting, trying to see what was happening, my interest pricked by his flippant comment. The coroner, blue skin . . . it made me think of Sláine.

But the door closed, the sergeant calling through it, '*Knock* the next time, you *amadán*.'

Uncle Tim added in a quiet voice, 'And show some bloody respect for the dead.'

I turned back to them as Parkinson glared at Tim too, before brusquely saying to me, 'Now, let's return to this matter before us. The two of ye had a row outside the public library and you threatened to end Mr Rattigan's life. Yes or no?'

I said forcefully, 'What? *No*. One hundred per cent no way. What I might have said, I think I told him, "I hope you'll be dead soon and we can all have a party." It's a figure of speech. I was just ragging on him.'

The sergeant said, '"I hope you're dead soon," "You'll be a dead man soon," . . . to be honest, son, I don't see a big difference there.'

'Well, that's too bad because there *is* a big difference. There's a world of difference. Anyway, he's not dead, is he? So why are you quoting, no *misquoting*, something I supposedly said about wanting to kill him? He's still alive.'

'You sound disappointed.'

I smiled grimly and didn't respond to that, only saying, 'Do I need a solicitor?'

'We already told you, no. This is a voluntary interview

process. You came here of your own free will. You're not under arrest or anything like that. You can call your parents, by all means, but you've no need to.'

It *was* voluntary, Parkinson had that much right. They'd collared me outside the station as I was walking by, eyes scanning the scene around me but head in the clouds, in bloody outer space. I don't know if Parkinson and Uncle Tim had been waiting for me – it looked as if they were, but perhaps it was simple happenstance. There I was, so they asked me to come in for a few questions. If I hadn't gone past at that moment, they'd have called to my home. Whichever: they asked, I went in. Now here we were, going around in circles.

I said, 'Look, he was hassling me that day and I snapped. He'd been at me for months. That's all there was to it. Rattigan, I let him have it. Told him he was a worthless piece of . . . uh, you know, like he was nothing and if he was to die – *if* he was, not when – the whole town would celebrate because everyone hated him.'

'So you admit you hate him?'

'No!' I rubbed my eyes. This was becoming exhausting. 'I told you: I don't hate him. I don't hate anyone. I don't like him either. Nobody does, his own parents probably can't stand him. But for the last time, I did *not* attack John Rattigan.'

I stared at the cigarette-scarred desktop. This must be an old piece of furniture; smoking had been banned in Garda stations for donkey's years. Pity – I could really have done with a fag. I thought of Rattigan: his unconscious body had been discovered by a geology student two days before, semi-buried in ice-encrusted dirt halfway up Sliabh Cohnda, the tallest mountain of ten or so which bordered our town on its north side. And the Guards, evidently, had decided to act on those rumours about me.

Rattigan came from what's known as 'a bad family'. His parents didn't give a rat's ass about him – I'd had that right. They hadn't even reported him missing. But of course they were all, right now, in the station lobby, loudly and aggressively bellowing at the desk sergeant, demanding 'justice for poor Johnny' and threatening reprisals on 'the bad bastard who done this on our boy'. Uncle Tim had whisked me in the side entrance; was he worried one of them would make a go for me? Jesus, that was all I needed: a horde of lunatic Rattigans out for my blood.

By all accounts 'poor Johnny' had been really messed up, even worse than the previous victims. His face, someone said, was unrecognisable – because it was missing several parts. I didn't know how much of this was true.

Parkinson was still worrying away at me like a dog at a bone. 'What about the others?'

I knew what he was referring to but some inner stubbornness made me play dumb. 'Huh? What about what others?'

Uncle Tim said gently, 'Aidan, you know what others. Several people have been assaulted in a violent manner over the course of the last two months.'

'Yeah. By wild animals.'

'Probably wild animals. We don't know for sure yet.'

Parkinson corrected him: '*Possibly* wild animals. And possibly not.'

He raised his eyebrows at me. I smiled, looked away, trying

175

to appear cool and reasonable, not shifty or nervous. I hadn't done anything wrong but that meant sweet FA in a police station. The atmosphere itself, the awareness of where you were, made you feel you had.

I forced myself to speak. 'What about it? What's it got to do with me?'

Parkinson said, 'What it's got to do with you is that many of them had bullied you, if not all of them. We know this. There's no shame in it. You were the victim, we understand that. It happens to a lot of very fine people, more's the pity. You're not the first and won't be the last. Bullying is an awful scourge in our society.'

Embarrassment coloured my cheeks a lurid crimson. I said quietly, 'So . . . ?'

'So, my boy, that gives you reason to want to hurt them. Revenge is a powerful motive in many crimes. And do you know, it's an understandable one, too. We can't condone it – indeed we must come down hard on it – but our common humanity allows us to empathise at the same time. The desire for revenge: it's a strong one, Aidan. And it makes seemingly normal people do extraordinary things.'

I looked at him. 'Do you really believe that?'

'I don't have to believe it – sure, I've seen it with my own two eyes.'

'No, I mean about me.'

'I'm not sure, to be honest. You might say I'm keeping . . . '

' . . . An open mind. Yeah, I get it.'

Parkinson and Uncle Tim looked at each other, a little bemused. Tim's phone vibrated; the sergeant gave him the evil eye yet again. He flipped it open and listened, then turned away and whispered, '*Another* one? Good Christ. Yeah, hold on there. We'll send out a CS unit – be with you in an hour.' He added to Parkinson, 'I'll tell you about it after.'

I cut in, saying, 'I actually *do* feel like calling my parents and getting them to bring in the solicitor. But if I do that, I'm thinking it makes me look guilty. So . . . it's a bit of a catch-22 for me, isn't it?'

The sergeant leaned in. 'And do you feel guilty about something, Aidan?'

I puffed out my cheeks in exasperation and for a moment forgot how worried I was. 'Oh *come* on. That's the best you've got? That's your big psychological play, to try and trick me into confessing to something?'

Parkinson actually looked embarrassed. I could have sworn Uncle Tim was biting back a giggle. I went on, 'Man, you *know* I didn't do any of this. Didn't, wouldn't, and damn sure couldn't. Look at me, for Christ's sake. I weigh about ten stone. You think I've got the upper-body strength to beat someone into a coma? To get the better of John Rattigan in a scrap? God Almighty.'

Parkinson raised his hands. He said, 'Well, who knows what anyone could do, if pushed to it? If the inner motivation is strong enough. People lift cars off trapped children, they rush into burning buildings to save Granny, not caring a fig about the flames. Not feeling them, even. We just don't know, Aidan. What we're really capable of.'

'May I go, please? I don't think I want to stay here any more.'

'You may. But don't get any ideas about skipping town or heading to England or anything like that. We might want to speak with you again.'

'So I'm officially a suspect, then?'

'Not officially. Yet.'

I shook my head in disgust. 'This is ridiculous. I'm going.' I stomped to the door and turned back. 'Could you . . . Listen, please don't say anything to my parents. I don't want them worried over nothing. And it *is* nothing, I'm telling you.'

The sergeant shrugged again. 'We'll see. But don't fret, your mam and dad won't hear anything from us. For the time being.'

Uncle Tim gave me an encouraging smile and said, 'D'you need a lift home, Aidan?' Parkinson scowled at him. I got Tim out of this self-dug hole by saying no thanks, and left quickly. He called after me, 'Go out the back way, there might be some of those bloody eejit Rattigans still hanging around the desk.' I did.

'For the time being.' Such menace in those four simple words. And such weight, the deadweight of potential disaster, so heavy I could almost physically feel it dragging me down.

I went outside and the sun was blinding. I started walking some random route; air and exercise to clear my head, a cigarette to steady my nerves. This situation was getting serious, but the funny thing was, I had a more immediate problem: Sláine.

More specifically, where the hell she'd got to. I knew in my heart on Sunday night, when I found the lodge empty, that she was properly gone – not detained, or on her way, but *gone*. Where, for how long, I couldn't say. I couldn't fathom what was going on. Now it was Tuesday, past half-three in the afternoon, and there'd been absolutely no contact. She was off the grid lost on the wind. She was, to use a word so appropriate it made me feel uneasy, a ghost.

That night, I'd taken a moment to accept she was gone, then mentally shrugged and trudged back home. I didn't know what else to do. On Monday I woke at dawn, before dawn, and waited in the fading dark. For want of a better plan, I skipped school and stayed in my room, staying out of sight, thinking, not thinking. Thinking when I didn't want to think, and vice-versa. Not for the first time, I felt in over my head. As if I were drowning in a sea of confusion and mystery. It was too large, too powerful. This whole thing was coming at me again and again, giant waves of it, and I was powerless to resist. It was surely only a matter of time before I slipped under.

Lunchtime rolled around and I was still waiting. There'd been no sign of her, no ice writing on the wall or voices in my head, nothing. So I headed out, striking into the heart of Shook Woods, in search of her. Every place we visited, every path walked, every tree passed or rock sat on. She wasn't there. I walked the roads around the forest, then every other road in the area that I could. I hiked up the mountains as high as I was able. I crossed beaches and sand dunes. She was nowhere to be seen.

Later I'd slept in the hunting lodge, exhausted, all night through, in the forlorn hope she'd return and explain that, oh my God, it was all a terrible mix-up and everything was fine! I fell asleep on the old bed dreaming that Sláine would stride in the door and tell me the whole story, and how silly I'd feel for worrying, but so deliriously happy that the silliness not only stopped being an embarrassment, but added to my happiness, perfected it, like a spot of cream on an ice-cream sundae.

That didn't happen. She remained gone, gone, far gone.

By Tuesday morning I was walking the streets, cutting school again, during the daytime, which was ridiculous because Sláine was hardly going to materialise in broad daylight outside the shopping centre or Supermac's. I did it anyway. It hadn't worked, except to draw me into the clutches of Parkinson and Uncle Tim.

All along I continued to wait because what else was I supposed to do? I didn't have a choice. I felt paralysed and useless and waited some more.

Now I sat on a park bench and whispered, 'Where *are* you, Sláine?' A squad car rushed past across the street – one driver in uniform and two forensics types in those padded white onesies they wear – as I considered the question.

Was she dead? As in, properly dead, no more afterlife, no more strange existence as a shadowy entity, haunting the forest and my dreams? Maybe she had an allotted time after her mortal death and then, *click*, it truly was all over. Maybe Sláine hadn't foreseen this happening, it came too fast and she was gone before she knew it so there was no way to warn me.

Or *maybe*, genius, she sodded off and left you without bothering to say goodbye. I didn't believe that. I think I didn't. Even if I had, I wouldn't have admitted it to myself.

I felt lost without her, I realised. She'd only been missing a day and a half, and already my life didn't seem to have the same purpose. It was on pause while I awaited her return, a state of limbo made worse by anxious uncertainty. And . . . and . . . I think I knew then that I was in love with her.

The park was practically frozen solid, as was everywhere else. The temperatures, incredibly, had continued to fall: now the daytime average was around minus five, nights dipping as low as minus twenty. For Ireland, this was unparalleled. My mother had fallen on the treacherous ground the day before and sprained her wrist. I thought I'd get her something, a gift to cheer her up and a little mission to distract me.

So I wobbled across town, cautious on that slippery surface, to an old antiques shop in an alleyway. I'd never been inside before. I'd never even seen the owner, but had passed more times than I could count. They always had a collection of interesting-looking things in the window: all sort of gewgaws and trinkets and dideys, a piled-up mass of bric-a-brac collapsing on itself, the relics of hundreds of forgotten lives.

I went in, a bell tinkling to announce my entry, and had a look around. There was as much dust as objects for sale in here, but I didn't mind. It kind of gave the place a romantic atmosphere, like something out of an old movie about Victorian times. Jack the Ripper might dash in here, fleeing from the bobbies. Pity the street outside had no cobblestones, just boring concrete slabs.

A voice spoke, small and quavering but quite strong. I almost yelped in shock. 'Flood. Isn't that it?'

I whirled around. A tiny woman had come through an alcove and stood behind the counter. It reached her chest, so high that she looked slightly out of scale with the rest of the shop. I squinted through the gloom and thought I'd seen her before, but not in here. Where . . . ? She sort of resembled the woman Sláine had 'hypnotised' into coming over to me, outside the

181

park, after I'd given both barrels to Rattigan; the same one who might have slipped William McAuley's letter into my bag.

Then again, maybe it wasn't her. All old people look alike, don't they? Babies and old folks – we look the same as everyone else at the start and end of life.

She gave a small smile and said, 'I know who you are. Our two families go a long way back in this town.'

'Um . . . thanks. I mean, okay.'

'I'm Meredith. Your parents will know me if you want to give them my regards.' She waved a hand around the shop. 'Have a good look. Take your time and decide what you want.'

I did as she suggested. There were some pretty things on those shelves, the sort of stuff my mam would definitely like. After a few minutes of browsing I narrowed it down to an old brass bell shaped like a woman in a ballgown, and a piece of coral embedded in a half-sphere of glass. I held each in my hand, getting a feel for them, their weight and balance, how they reflected the light.

The old lady spoke again, almost to herself, her voice drifting across to my ears like dust motes in the still air: 'I will bring a flood of waters to destroy all flesh in which is the breath of life. Everything on the earth shall die.'

My skin crawled. Those words . . . where had I heard them before?

Sláine. The first night we met.

I spun around again. 'How do you know those lines?'

Meredith said, 'The Bible. I'm sure I have them a bit mixed up, but that's more-or-less the way it goes.'

'But –' I stopped myself from asking, 'How did you know

that Sláine had spoken them too?' Because of course she didn't know – it was a coincidence. Lots of people read the Bible, and she knew my name was Flood, and that was a quote about *the* Flood, the Noah's Ark one. You'd have looked a right eejit, I told myself, making some wild hypothesis out of this lady reciting part of a book.

As if supporting the argument, she said, 'I just remembered that because of your name. Flood, it's a lovely name. Not common in Ireland, I don't think?'

My mouth recited some vague reply while my mind asked itself, but *is* there such thing as a coincidence? All the extraordinary events I'd experienced over the last few months proved that this was a far more weird and fantastic world than we imagine. There were unexplained connections between things, which may not be recognised but are very real . . .

'Anyway don't mind me babbling like this,' she said, 'I'm just filling the silence with speech. Have you chosen what you want to do?'

'Wha—?'

'Those two. Have you picked one to buy? You needn't make any purchase by the way. At this stage of my life I'm as happy to have some company in the shop as to make a sale.' Again she gave that small, enigmatic smile. 'That's probably why I keep it open at all. There's no money in it any more really. I do a bit of cleaning work to make ends meet, casual, you know. Big houses around the town. Knockmore Road, Belladonna, DeLacey Heights . . . Those people are too busy to clean, I suppose. They just give me the house keys and let me work away.'

I nodded sympathetically and made a snap decision: the bell. I handed it over and Meredith wrapped it nicely in a box and coloured paper.

'Thanks,' I said. 'How much?'

'Ah sure, we'll say . . . five. Have you that?'

'Yeah, no worries.' I paid her and was about to go when the old lady frowned and tapped her forehead.

'Oh. Do you know, I might have something here for you. Free of charge. Hold on one moment, like a good lad.'

'For me?'

Meredith reached under the counter and, without looking, pulled out a small disc made of brass or copper. She flicked a clasp and it sprung open: a locket, used for holding photographs. Two oval spaces to place pictures. It was old and, although plain, quite beautiful.

'It mightn't be the kind of thing young men like, I suppose – I wouldn't be well up on the fashions nowadays,' she said. 'But I saw you and thought you might be interested. It's a pretty little thing, isn't it?'

I nodded.

'Dates from Victorian times . . . around the Famine, as far as I know. I couldn't *tell* you where it came from or how long we've had it. My father ran the shop before me, and his before him . . . We're around a long time.' She smiled ruefully. 'Anyway. You might find some use for it. Maybe put in a nice picture of your sweetheart. Go on, take it. Think of it as a gift for a valued customer. A *rare* customer, ha ha.'

I mumbled thanks and shoved it into my inside jacket pocket. I'd put in photos later, maybe a passport shot of me and that one of Sláine from the newspaper report on her death.

Meredith smiled. 'That's it. Keep it close to your heart.'

I left the old lady and her dusty, romantic shop, a bit discommoded by the experience but not sure why. Anyway the feeling soon faded because, two steps past the entrance door, I bumped into international super-spy Sioda Kinvara.

Literally: we collided and he almost fell on the ice. I grabbed his arm. The soft sleeve of his plush cashmere overcoat was chilly to the touch.

Kinvara regained his balance and smiled, saying, 'Thank you.' Then he did a double take and the smile changed to bemused recognition. 'The lad from the library. The park there, you gave that other boy some dressing-down.'

I said, 'The –? Oh yeah. That was me.' I smiled awkwardly. 'Ah, he deserved it.'

'I have no doubt . . . Enjoyable to watch someone beat a bully with the power of words, I must say. It pleases a mild-mannered bibliophile like me.'

I shrugged and harrumphed, the usual Irish way of accepting a compliment. 'John Rattigan's brain, now . . . it wouldn't take much to outsmart him.'

'Perhaps . . . Still. The pen really is mightier than the sword. Sometimes.'

'Yeah, sometimes. Sorry, am I blocking your way?'

I moved from the door. Kinvara said, 'Not at all, I'm just browsing. Killing time. Yourself?'

'Uh . . . pretty much the same. Got something for my mother, you know. Little present.'

I held up the gift box Meredith had given me. Kinvara said

appreciatively, 'Good man yourself. It's lovely to see a boy looking after his mother. Family is . . . ' He frowned and sort of stumbled on his words. After a pause he went on, 'Family is important. We . . . we do have to take care of family, don't we?'

I shrugged again. Guess so, man.

'You can't . . . you have to stay loyal to your own, don't you?' he said. 'Yes. That's right, I think.'

'Sure.'

I stared at the ground, a bit perplexed and a bit uncomfortable. Then Kinvara's face brightened, as though whatever clouds were darkening the sky inside his head had blown away, and it was all shiny blue in there now.

'Speaking of family,' he said. 'I think I know your father. It's Aidan, isn't it?'

'That's me. Dad did the job on your cars, right? You're Mr Kinvara.'

'Live and in person.' He stuck out his hand – I shook it. The hand was even colder than his overcoat. 'Sioda, please.'

'Nice to meet you, Sioda.'

'Likewise.' His phone sounded, the tone for a message, a familiar tune. Did I know that from somewhere . . . ? Four notes, three up before the last one comes back down as far as notes can go . . .

Kinvara must have read my thoughts or noticed my expression of curious concentration. His eyes twinkled as he said, 'The ringtone? I love that tune. From a film I really like. I downloaded it off the internet.' He hummed the melody, 'Dum-dum-dum-DUMMM,' and I remembered, of course, hearing it play inside the house on Belladonna Way. So that was Kinvara's home after all – I'd got that right.

Now he was off on a different tack, saying, 'He did a grand job for me. Your dad. That man knows cars, *whoo*.' He whistled, a low and somehow mournful sound. 'Are you into all that yourself?'

'Cars? Not in the slightest,' I said proudly, chuckling. 'Music and books'd be more my thing.'

'Well, I'm the same as you. Which of course is why I needed your father in the first place. I mean I *love* to drive them. Those vintage machines – beautiful. It's an almost narcotic experience, you know? Actually, I hope you *don't* know.' He smirked. 'But as to how or why or what they do . . . pff. Might as well be Coptic Greek. No, I'm a man of letters, like yourself.'

I rolled a smoke, saying, 'Yeah, I love to read. Like, I get real pleasure from it, as well as . . . broadening the mind, whatever.'

'Absolutely. That is *absolutely* it. There's an unbelievable power in books. Literal power. Books can change the world. Marx, Darwin, the Bible, Shakespeare, sure where do you stop . . . ? Such possibilities. Language and words, I mean they actually create consciousness. They're what make us human, not just dumb apes that can stand upright . . . Do you know, I thank God, or whatever's out there, on a daily basis for books and reading. Don't think I could exist without them.'

'Um . . . yeah. Me too, like I say. Love reading.'

I pulled on my fag and sort of half-moved onto the road. Kinvara ducked in the opposite direction, towards the old curiosity shop. He stopped with his hand on the door, saying over his shoulder, 'Come around to my house, any time you like, and pick something from my library. I have thousands of books, all sorts, you can borrow some. If you want to – no obligation. But there might be something to pique your interest, maybe a book that's hard to find elsewhere, you know.' He raised a finger. '*Only* if your parents say it's all right. If you want to drop by, have your dad ring me beforehand to verify. The door won't be opened unless I get that call.' He turned to me and flashed a smile. 'Wouldn't want people getting the wrong impression. Don't worry, I'm not some sort of weirdo. It's just books. But you seem like the kind of lad who'd be interested in alternative stuff, so . . . ' Kinvara shrugged. 'The offer's there, whatever you decide is fine by me.'

I shrugged too, the best non-response I could think of in a situation where a response was required. Something felt slightly hinky about it: his offer, this whole conversation. Not in the predictable sense – I didn't get any dangerous pederast vibes off Kinvara. Quite the opposite. If anything, he seemed strangely asexual, a bit of a cold fish. It was just . . . something.

I sighed. Probably your imagination, Aidan. Again. The man knows your dad, knows you like reading, he's offering to loan some books. He's even said he won't let you into the house until your parents phone to verify it's all kosher. Stop looking for shit when there's none there. You've got enough shit to deal with as it is, ha.

'Sure,' I said. 'We'll see. I mean I'm pretty busy right now.'

'Of course you are. As I say, whatever you want. Good luck to you, Aidan.' Kinvara depressed the door handle and stepped into the shop, his final words trailing out behind him like a lace veil: 'We might even let you behind the wheel of that old Jag for a test drive. I know your dad enjoyed it when he took her out . . . ' He laughed roguishly and was gone.

This guy really was too smooth . . . If Bond ever gets tired of the 007 gig, M, we've got a ready-made replacement over here. He's even got the debonair hairstyle and everything.

Walking home with my little surprise for Mam, a thought came to me, totally unrelated, out of nowhere. One of those tiny bursts of electrical energy in the brain which seem to spontaneously create themselves from nothing.

I recalled Sláine saying she'd contacted me because I appeared lost to her, the first day she saw me in Shook Woods. It occurred to me that, while this was true, it was only part of the truth. Sláine took pity on the lonely boy poking around the forest by himself, yes – but she was also lonely. Despite what she said about a new life, and old emotions not applying to her any more, I think she was lonely. She wanted company. A friend, a human being to touch, literally and figuratively.

And there was something else – this unsolicited thought wasn't finished with me yet. I knew now – not suspected or wished, but *knew* – that Sláine had fallen in love with me too.

The revelation should have filled me with joy. Instead, I was sort of numb inside. Where was she where was she where was she. The words repeated in my head like some hellish mantra. No message, no sign, no contact, no *her*. That wasn't like Sláine at all. Yes, I was worried.

I told myself it was unwarranted, I was overreacting, things would be fine, it'd only been two short days, she'd come back soon . . . I half-believed it. I made myself believe it, enough at least to squash that worry down to the bottom of my stomach and pretend it didn't exist, for a little while anyway. I sighed heavily, my breath blowing out in front like a cartoon speech bubble, and trudged home.

KILLED BY THE COLD

Wednesday arrived: Day Three of a World Without Sláine. Still no sign. I lay in bed as the clock moved past half-eight in the morning, staring at the ceiling, where a spider remorselessly crawled towards a fly trapped in its web. Good for you, spider. At least one of us is going to feel happy today.

Her timing, I reflected bitterly, could hardly have been worse. Not only did I miss Sláine for her own sake, but I also had this apparent breakthrough, the McAuley letter, and she wasn't around to help figure out what it might mean.

Aaargh, this was excruciating. I didn't feel depressed, but I was tense, and concerned for her whereabouts. I lurched out of bed, sleepwalked to school – gotta keep up appearances, and I'd missed two days – and sleepwalked through those seven hours. Teachers taught, my classmates chattered, the bell sounded several times, a car engine noisily died in the school car park, and I hardly noticed any of it.

Funnily enough, I did notice one thing that day. It came to me with a clarity that was almost shining – it sort of knocked me off my feet when I realised it. The bullying had definitively ended for me, and didn't look like resuming even though the new, confident Aidan had been partly subsumed into old, nervous Aidan once more. I'd become 'normal', it seemed, somewhere along the way, and normal I had stayed in the eyes of my peers. No more hate mail, no dog shit through the letter box, no antagonism at all. I was becoming a bit of a wreck with anxiety over Sláine, and it must have shown on my face, in the dark bags under my eyes. But my peers continued to treat me exactly as they had for the last two months, i.e. with a basic level of courtesy and common decency. It didn't exactly help with any of this crap, but it didn't hurt either.

I walked home from school, chewing this over, and *whammo*, a second moment of insight, even more energising than the first: the idea of killing myself never entered my mind now. It hadn't for several weeks, and even then had been instantly rejected. Literally, in the same moment as the notion drifted across my thoughts, I'd shot it down mercilessly. I chided myself for even considering it before. How stupid you were! How stupid and selfish – and self-defeating in all kinds of ways.

That would have just proven their argument, Aidan, that you're weak and spineless and pathetic. If you had killed yourself, they would have won. Do you want that, you idiot? No you bloody well *don't*. So you stay around and stay the course, you little maggot. No matter how hard it gets, or how bad you might think you're feeling, you *will* endure it. You'll stick it out and survive. Got me?

Yes, *sir*, I got you.

No, I wouldn't be checking out by my own hand, soon or at any stage in the future. I knew this as definitively as I knew my name. Maybe Sláine going AWOL had fortified me yet further, somewhere in the heart of my heart – it had stiffened me, put a certain steel in me . . .

'Aidan.'

I almost bumped into her, lost inside my head. Caitlin. She was standing in front of me on the path; it looked as though she'd been waiting here. She smiled nervously, twisted her hands into one another. She was wearing a woollen beret, red hair spilling over her shoulders, and looked very pretty.

I said nothing. I didn't want to talk to her right now, or talk to anyone; I was preoccupied with Sláine.

Caitlin shuffled some more and finally said, 'Um, are you, like . . . ? Is everything all right? You weren't in school yesterday.'

'Yeah?' I said absently. 'You noticed.'

She laughed nervously. 'Yes, I . . . I noticed. Aidan, what's wrong?'

I looked at her, properly. A welter of conflicting feelings suddenly bubbled up inside me, like a pot of stew boiling over: irritation, tiredness, apprehension, boredom, awkwardness, physical desire, maybe some residual anger or loathing for this girl and what she'd done to me. A sprinkle of pity, wherever that came from.

I said, in a soft and weary voice, 'You know what's wrong, Caitlin-with-your-stupid-incorrect-pronunciation-of-your-own-name? Nothing, that's what. Or nothing I'd want to discuss with you anyway, no offence.' I moved past her and walked away. 'Thanks for asking, though. I'm going home now. See you around, maybe.'

That evening I sleepwalked – yes, again – through dinner and

192

conversation with my parents, and possibly even sleepwalked through an hour of homework, which is a pretty impressive achievement in its own right. Around eleven I schlepped downstairs for a bedside glass of water and my mother was sitting at the kitchen table, wrist thickly bandaged, plonked heavily on the wood. Dammit, the gift. The bell figurine, I'd forgotten to give it to her. I said, 'Hang on a second,' then briskly tiptoed upstairs and retrieved it. Mam took the package with an expression of happy surprise. I flopped onto the chair opposite and said, ''S nothing. Just a little pressie – cheer you up after your fall. How is it anyway?'

I pointed at her wrist. She said, 'Ah, not too bad. Still sore but they say it should be fine in a few weeks. This looks very nice.'

She wrestled with the wrapping but it was awkward, her movements clumsy on that side, so I opened it for her. I held up the bell and said drolly, 'Ting-a-ling.'

My mother gasped and gave a lovely smile – it took twenty years off her. That made me happy.

'Aw,' she said. 'Aidan, it's perfect. Aw, you shouldn't have.'

'Nah, seriously, it's nothing. I got it in that place, you know the little curiosity shop there off the square? Actually the lady, Meredith, the owner? She said say hello to you and Dad. So, uh, hello from Meredith.'

'Oh, yes. A real lady, she is.'

Mam began hauling herself off her seat. 'Would you like some tea, pet? I find it's good for sleep. You look tired, you need to sleep.'

'Sit down, I'll get it.'

I filled the kettle, water drumming against metal like an

193

equatorial monsoon, and set it to boil. My mother fired up a smoke and held the packet back to me.

'Go on, sure. You might as well do it in front of me.'

I took a Silk Cut – a change being as good as a rest, and all that – and lit it. Silence for a few minutes, oddly calming, just the loudening hiss of the kettle and our soft smoky inhalations. I made her tea, none for myself, and sat. More silence. More calm. This was nice.

Then Mam broke the surface of that calm, shark's-fin-style, by saying, 'Is everything all right, Aidan?'

I replied, guarded, 'Uh . . . yeah?'

'Are you sure?'

'I think so, yeah. Sorry, what . . . ? Yes, Mam, everything's fine.'

'Because you know you can tell me if it's not. Don't you?'

Like hell I can. 'Sure.'

'Anything at all that's bothering you, you can say it.'

Yeah, I can see that working out well. 'Uh-huh.'

My mother sipped her tea for a long moment, watching me. I pretended to be fascinated by a comical postcard on the fridge.

'It's funny,' she said. 'When you're in the middle of something, especially if it's bad, it feels like the biggest thing that could ever possibly happen. Then a while later, when you get some perspective on the whole thing, you realise, oh it wasn't such a big deal after all.'

Right. Where was this leading . . . ?

'And when you're a teenager, I mean, *everything* feels like the biggest thing that could ever happen. It's all very dramatic and exciting at that age.'

Okaaay . . . I muttered, 'Uh . . . I guess so.'

194

'You know, Aidan, people come and go. Into our lives, I mean. And you're very young. There'll be a lot of people in your life. You're so young, you're only a child still.'

I saw her smiling at me, kind and melancholy, out the corner of my eye. My discomfort was sliding towards embarrassment as Mam went on. 'All I'm saying is that nothing is ever as bad as it seems. A broken heart, say. We're never really broken. We're just . . . waiting for someone to make us whole again.'

Ugh. That humorous postcard was getting ever-more interesting. I kept my eyes fixed on it.

'I'd my heart broken once,' she said. 'This was long before your father, now. A boy called Tiernan. Beautiful, he was. Dark hair, dark eyes, just *gorgeous* . . . like someone you'd see in an old picture. I thought I loved him. Heh. I thought he loved me too.'

Life lessons and personal revelations, a mother–son heart-to-heart. Save me, Jesus, *pleeeeease* . . . I don't do emotional honesty with my family. I'm Irish, not a Hollywood TV character.

My mother said, 'And it hurt. I thought I'd die when he broke it off. Went to bed for a solid week! My parents were afraid I was having a nervous breakdown.'

I was actually squirming by now, physically. I stared at the postcard and wished to hell Mam would stop talking, even though I appreciated why she was doing it.

She paused, then said, 'That girl Caitlin. You know I never put the two of ye together anyway. I don't think she was meant for you – ye didn't fit right together.'

Finally I looked at her. 'Wha—? Caitlin, what are you on about?'

My mother seemed perplexed. 'Aren't you . . . ?'

'What? No. Caitlin?'

'Yes, isn't that . . . ?'

Ah. Got it. Right situation – sort of – wrong girl. I smiled. 'No, it's not her. I mean it's not anyone. Everything is cool, swear to God.'

'Is it?'

'Yes. The Caitlin thing, it's all over and done with.' I tweaked the truth a little by adding, 'Sure, I only met her today, chatting after school. It's all fine. *I'm* fine.'

'All right, well . . . I worry, you know? About all of you.'

'I know. Thanks. It's grand, honestly.' I stood and kissed the top of her head. 'Finish your tea, I'm off to bed. And quit worrying.'

She seemed half-reassured when I left. My own anxiety continued running at full steam. I slept badly. The next day I went back to sleepwalking. Same thing Friday. By 8 p.m. I was sitting at my desk again, gazing dully at some textbook, not reading it, only scanning my eyes across the pages, back and forth, like an empty swing in a breeze.

I abruptly shut the book, moved to the window and opened it. A shot of chilly air, like a drug being injected to the heart. It woke me up somewhat. I rolled a cigarette and thought, I need to get some purpose back in my life. For sanity's sake, if nothing else.

Sláine's gone, all right. But it's only been five days. She might come back – she will, goddamn it, *will*, not might – and when she does, you should be ready. There's no point putting everything on pause while you wait. Keep moving forward, it's the only way to exist. So: continue with the investigation. Follow up this McAuley thing. The letter. The cold. Something strange and malevolent which took place in the woods . . .

Gah. I didn't even know where to *begin*. I had nothing, pretty much. Just a handful of whispers and suggestions and possibilities. My head was spinning, a vortex of confusion, and it spun worse when a second stream of thought joined in – those bloody animal attacks or psycho-revenge attacks on my behalf – and then a third stream, the freaky connection between me and the text messages and Clara's mental voices and the girl who dreamed of the devil on her acid trip from hell . . .

Coffee. I'd read in one of the Sunday newspaper supplements that coffee was a good aid to thinking. My parents only had crappy-quality instant that looked and tasted like dust swept off the floor, so I texted Podsy and asked if he'd meet in a cafe in town. Might as well have someone to drink with. Fair play to him, he agreed on the spot. He must have known I needed some company.

As it happened, my nerdy little friend gave me a whole lot more than that.

'What'd you tell the young fella?'

'What the what now?'

'Your little brother,' Podsy said. 'What'd you say about those night-time excursions? You know, you being Batman and all.'

We sat across from each other in a booth, in a place called Fiver and Dimes, a confused mixture of Irish food and small-town American decor. Podsy had arrived first and ordered coffee. Double-shot Americano for me – he knew what I liked. We let the drinks cool and I tried to remember what excuse I'd given Ronan about sneaking out of the house at all hours.

Then it hit me. 'Ah. Right. Told him I was birdwatching. Owls and things that only came out at night.'

'He bought it?'

'He bought it. God bless the gullibility of youth.'

I smiled, Podsy didn't. Instead he said, 'And are you going to give me the real reason?'

I winced. 'Eh . . . no. I can't, Podsy. Sorry, boy, I just . . . '

'Can't, won't, whatever. Look, 'tis grand – your own private business. But I am curious. And nosy.'

He shrugged, making an end to it there, and blew across the top of his coffee, his wonky little mouth in the shape of a wonky little O, giving him a comical appearance. 'Hey, did I tell you about what's happening with Hiro?'

I said, 'Hiro the Hero. With the cool name.'

'Cool guy too. I told you we've been tracking electromagnetic radiation for SETI, this project I'm involved with.'

I nodded. He went on. 'You asked me a while ago to let you know if there were any more unusual patterns in the flow. You know, spikes of energy?'

I *had* asked him, I remembered that. And good on him, Podsy remembered too. I felt like a heel for keeping him out of the loop so much about everything. Then again, what exactly was I to say? 'Okay, *don't* jump to any snap conclusions about this? But I've been in a relationship with a dead girl for a few months. Seems to be going all right so far.' There was nothing I could do; he had to be kept in the dark. Everyone did.

Now I said, 'Uh-huh. Patterns in the flow. Sounds like a lame-ass prog-rock band. So did you get any?'

He replied, enthused, 'Yeah, actually. What we're dealing with here are irregularly occurring phenomena in the electro—' He stopped, seeing the genuine look of bafflement on my face. 'Okay, look at it like this: you have the normal flow, quote–unquote, of energy out there in space. Over us, here, in Ireland. But what we've been seeing –' He smiled proudly. 'What *I've* been seeing, and Hiro has been processing, is these unusual spikes. Weirdest thing is, they're coming at quite regular intervals? Which really is weird.'

'What's weird about it? I'm still a bonehead, Podsy, just like the last time you told me about this stuff.' I gave a small smile. I think it was the first time I'd smiled – properly, happily – since Sunday afternoon. Whether through the coffee, the conversation or the distraction, I felt a bit better, the mental load slightly lifted.

He said, 'It's weird cos . . . *usually*, with something like this, it's gonna happen randomly. The usual thing with unusual events, ha. But here we have what kind of looks like a pattern. Two or three of these spikes, every week, for about two months now. And that, as it happens, coincides with the cold weather. Which I have to say I'm ticked off that it doesn't look like going away any time soon.'

'What does Hiro the Hero make of all this?'

'He's still sifting through the data. But it's picking up – that's the other weird aspect. The rate of these spikes, their frequency, it's accelerating. Last week we had four, this week so far six and it's only Friday yet. So . . . that's it, that's where we stand.' He added as an afterthought, 'There was one night actually, *man*, the bloody thing nearly went off the scale. Just this huge, I mean a *massive* surge of energy. Few nights ago. Haven't seen anything like it since.'

My curiosity was piqued now. I said casually, 'Oh, yeah? D'you remember what night?'

'Yeh, it was Sunday. Which I know cos I was Skyping – yes, you guessed it – Hiro at the time. We chat online most Sunday nights. Our time, obviously, they're already into Monday by that stage.'

Sunday? That could have been Sláine. Whatever happened to her, whatever she did, maybe it had been recorded in electromagnetic radiation, as her mortal death appeared to have been. Written in some invisible ink across our outer atmosphere. For an instant, my heart was kindled with some vague, unsettled feeling that I couldn't put my finger on.

Then I thought, what difference did it make anyway? So her disappearance was recorded on a graph somewhere in SETI headquarters. Big deal. That didn't change the fact that she was gone – and I was miserable without her.

I went for a pee and ordered two more coffees on my way back to our booth. Podsy picked up a sugar sachet and twirled it in his fingers. He said, 'Any follow-up from the Guards?'

I chuckled. Of course he'd know about my little chinwag with Parkinson; no secret was safe from Uncle Tim and his enormous, uncontrollable gob. I didn't mind. In fact it was quite amusing.

'Nah,' I said. 'I think they were fishing.'

'Me too. I wouldn't worry about it.'

'Easy for you to say, pally.'

'No, but seriously. Anyway there hasn't been another incident since Rattigan. Maybe the wild animal or whatever was behind it has died of the cold. Maybe it *was* just coincidence all along.'

'How's he doing anyway?'

Podsy pouted. 'Rattigan? Tch. He'll pull through. Cockroaches are virtually impossible to kill off, didn't you know that?'

'Yeah, well . . . I'm not unhappy about that, I have to say. Wouldn't want the guy *dead*. Despite what the sergeant might think.'

'Mm, I suppose so . . . Anyway. You're off the hook, I'd say. The Guards have bigger fish to be frying now.'

'Oh, right? Like what? Banditos riding into town to rob El Banco. Shoot-Out at the Fairly Shitty Corral.'

'Nah, man. The hypothermia deaths.'

Something gave me the chills as though my mind had seen an awful future looming on the horizon. The worst thing of all was that this something was telling me I'd have a part to play in it.

I said slowly, 'Podsy. What deaths?'

He looked at me in surprise. 'The bunch of people killed by the cold? You know about this, right? Wakey-wakey, Aidan. Everyone's talking about it.'

'Talking – what?'

'All right, not everyone. Some people. In fairness the cops're trying to keep a lid on it. They're bullshitting people a little, so's not to emphasise too many similarities between the different cases. They're afraid it might start, you know, a panic or whatever.'

'Killed when?'

'Last week or so. More, maybe. Ten days?'

How had I not heard about this? Maybe I had, but dumped the information without paying it any attention, like deleting spam email. Christ, I really *had* been sleepwalking through the last few days. And now it appeared I'd woken up into some real-world nightmare.

Podsy went on, warming to his theme. 'They didn't think anything of it at first, Tim and them. Okay, someone's found frozen to death out by Shook Woods. Whenever, say ten days ago. Which, I mean, isn't crazily surprising of itself, with the big freeze we've had for the last eight weeks. People die from hypothermia in winter, that's a fact of life. So a one-time happening, in this weather? Not a bad percentage. An isolated tragedy, as they say.'

I said, a sinking feeling in my tummy, 'Go on.'

'This's where things get weird. That was the first one. Then another body was found within twenty-four hours. *Then* . . . another. Okay, you're still talking isolated tragedies. A bit of a trickle to start with. But at the beginning of this week it just, *whoa*, suddenly there's a *flood* of these things. Bodies, bodies, everywhere. More being found each day.'

'How many?'

'I think about two dozen so far, but they're not sure. Hang on, though, I haven't got to the really weird bit yet.'

He gave me the full story, and my heart grew colder with each new revelation. This wave of deaths didn't involve either elderly or homeless folks, as would generally be the case with hypothermia. Most of those who'd perished, literally, were young enough – all under fifty, the majority from about twenty to early thirties (none younger than that, nobody from school). Besides, as Podsy pointed out, our town didn't really have homeless people – it wasn't big enough. The odd chronic drunk might spend the odd night sleeping outside in the rough, kicked from the house by an angry wife, but none of those had passed away anyway; somehow they'd survived a night in the cold. Maybe the old gag about a 'drink overcoat' had some truth to it after all.

Some of the victims were people I knew. Some were strangers to me, their names unfamiliar. Some men, some women. Students, workers, parents, on the dole, about to emigrate. As far as I could tell they were decent people, cool people, stupid people, annoying people, creeps and sweethearts, assholes and angels. All in all, it was about as random a selection of townsfolk as you could get. As though some giant computer was arbitrarily selecting names off a list and designating them for death.

They had each been found in the morning, frozen, by loved ones or passers-by. None of them were in their homes – all outside, whether that was their front doorstep or on some road far outside town or anywhere in between. (That must have been what Uncle Tim was whispering about on his phone the other day, organising to send out a crime scene unit to where another corpse had been discovered.) The bodies had all turned partly blue with the cold. Some had their eyes closed, and looked almost peaceful; others were staring into the infinite emptiness of death, a horrible grimace on their faces.

Podsy continued to run through the details. I zoned out his voice and thought, not for the first time, he's right – it *is* strange. Done in by the cold: not disease or a car crash or some tragic accident. Not a 'normal' death, for want of a better word. Of course, on a very simple level it wasn't strange at all: that's what happens if you lie down, outside, with the temperature ten below and dropping. But on a broader level it was so peculiar as to put a shiver – appropriately enough – up my spine. All these youngish people freezing to death, within less than a fortnight, some inexplicable compulsion making them leave their house and lie down to wait for the cruellest of deaths.

And that shiver turned to an eerie prickle in the back of my mind with what Podsy said next – more confidential information from ever-reliable Uncle Tim – all the victims looked the same post-mortem. What he didn't add, but I obviously thought, was: yes, Podsy, the same as Sláine. Their eyes and skin bore the identical marks of each one's demise: those thin light-blue lines covering their bodies, as though death had used them as canvases for a sinister tattoo, their irises changing colour to the same icy-blue as *her*.

Now he said, 'There has to be something to this. It can't be a coincidence. That sort of biological reaction simply does not take place under regular circumstances.'

I fobbed him off with a non-committal reply. I was running this through my head, this Sláine thing, hoping to find some structure to it.

Podsy continued, 'Parkinson's really losing his shit over this. Trying to work out why it's happening, and more importantly I guess, to stop it happening again. This – I don't know – phenomenon. Is that the right word?'

I shrugged, another non-committal response. I wasn't sure I trusted myself to say the right thing here, or rather, not say the *wrong* thing.

'Those animal attacks, that's one thing,' Podsy said. 'As my dear Uncle Tim declared the other day, "Regrettable, of course, but comprehensible at least." I love when he tries to use big words like that, he's a gas man . . . But this thing with the cold is just bananas. Like, think about it, Aidan. Why are all these people coming out at night-time in the middle of the worst big freeze for a hundred and sixty years? Some sort of communal madness? Are they sleepwalking? Pff.' He threw his hands in the air. 'Nobody can say for sure. And the other thing, I mean, none of the victims were suicidal, right? Or at least none had shown suicidal tendencies. As far as the Guards know, nobody had a reason to kill themselves.'

Police and civilians both, he said, had been trying to make sense of these 'cold' deaths through speculation, deduction, wild guesswork. Such-and-such, it was insisted, must have tripped while walking on the ice and hit his head. Someone else, they reckoned, had been mugged and left unconscious with tragic consequences. A third fatality fell asleep on the road with a feed of drink in his belly. Then the ice and frost got them all.

One guy – this clown called Delaney – had died on the beach, on a wind-blasted, Arctic night the previous weekend. He'd gone there to shift his girlfriend, sheltering behind an upturned rowing boat, and they were in the middle of it when he pulled away. She laughed at first, she later reported, thinking he was playing the fool. Then he gasped and stiffened and finally keeled over onto the sand, unmoving. Still she thought he was joking, until she noticed that no condensation was coming from his mouth. He wasn't breathing any more.

205

She was totally hysterical talking about it afterwards, Podsy said, babbling about a 'white spirit' swishing past extremely quickly and what she described as 'a lightning bolt of fog' shooting out of nowhere and going right down her boyfriend's throat. It was unintelligible gobbledegook – she wasn't making any sense. Nobody took her story seriously. They assumed she was drunk or high, and besides, had suffered a great trauma, so it was to be expected she'd be mentally unhinged for a while.

The authorities were apparently about to make a public announcement, suggesting that everyone lock all doors at night and keep an eye on each other. According to Uncle Tim, they were even considering a legal curfew on anyone being in a public place after eight in the evening.

I wondered to myself, what would be the point of that? There didn't seem to be any rhyme or reason to this phenomenon anyway, so why would some dictate of the law make a difference? If locked doors and watchful eyes, even their own sense of self-preservation, weren't enough to keep people safe . . .

I laughed cynically and said to Podsy, 'Ha. Well at least they can't blame *me* for it, right? I mean, I can't manipulate the weather, can –?'

Hold on. Can *I*? No. But then I remembered Sláine's theory that someone was controlling 'the cold', as she called it: that element-with-a-mind which had killed her in Shook Woods. Controlling the cold . . .

Sláine. Whose body bore the same eerie marks as these other dead.

Sláine. Who'd spoken about some unseen force drawing her out of her home that last night.

Sláine. Who felt a presence, neither living nor dead, in the forest when she died. A presence that pushed into her and pulled out of her and turned her into something new.

I muttered to Podsy that I needed a smoke and stumbled outside, into the cold, the *other* cold, the workaday, sane, climatological one. I rolled a fag blindly as fresh elements popped into my head, banging around in there like silver balls in a flashing pinball machine.

McAuley's letter. The cold. Death all around. Blue tattooed skin. Arcane lore. The Famine. Inuit legends. Sláine ancestor's flight. The seas frozen over. Older gods. The New England lunatic. Command the cold and cheat death forever.

McAuley. God. Hatred. Desperation. Ice-blue irises. Demonology. The cold, the cold, the cold. A Frenchman in the Baltic. 1851. Crows falling from the sky. Sláine's murder. That killing presence.

People dying from hypothermia. Someone to blame. Someone in control.

Command the cold.

Cheat death.

McAuley.

Demonology.

Part of his letter flowed into my mind – I swear I recalled it verbatim. How this was even possible I do not know but it was *there*, screaming inside my head:

There in the forest, I summoned something more ancient than the Christians' deity. Something of the land, that dwelled in the very rocks themselves, in the elements:

wind, snow, ice . . . I summoned this presence and told it what I needed and heard what it desired. Now I wait for . . .

A tap on my elbow. I literally leaped in fright, shrieking, 'Jesus!'

Podsy laughed and took a step back. 'Whoa, horsey. What's got you so jumpy, jeez. It's only me.'

I giggled out of embarrassment – and an escalating sense of horror. I managed to whisper, 'Sorry. Hate being surprised.'

'Well, here's a surprise you might welcome: I got those coffees.'

'You shouldn't . . . '

'Nah, I owe you, I'm pretty sure. Borrowed a tenner a while back. Anyway I gotta head. Catch you at school, yeah?'

I nodded yes, almost struck dumb. Podsy shook his shoulders and rammed his hands deep into his pockets, saying, '*Sheeee-it*. Bloody freezing. This weather is killing me.'

He loped off into the night. I stood there on that bland modern street outside that cafe with its absurd decor and tried to gulp, but my throat was as dry as sand and it hurt to do that and I had no saliva in my mouth and I think I knew real, elemental terror for the first time in my life. If this was true. If what I thought. If this could be real.

Jesus. Anything can be real, everything is real. Everything in the heavens is everywhere, anything is all things, the sun is all stars and every star is all stars and the sun . . .

'This weather is killing me,' my friend had said. Podsy, you might be more right than you think.

If this is true we're all fucked.

IT'S REALLY YOU

I staggered home, grunted at my parents, fell onto my bed. The room spun around me. The whole universe had come off its axis and was hurtling into space at a frightening, unstoppable velocity.

The truth. Oh God, the truth was horrifying, it was unbearable.

I forced myself to say the words aloud, to make them real and face my darkest nightmare: 'McAuley raised a demon. I don't know how or what exactly, but it was something very bad. He did this, back in 1851, and now he's returned to haunt us all.' I swallowed heavily. 'William John McAuley is killing those people. He's come back from the grave, and he's brought coldness and death with him.'

Okay. Okay, keep cool. Tell yourself to keep cool, Aidan.

I muttered weakly, 'Keep cool, Aidan.'

It was all much too much to handle, especially without Sláine. Exhaustion, both physical and nervous, overcame me, and I swooned into a sleep blacker than death itself.

Soon I was in the REM state and dreaming furiously. I saw myself wandering through Shook Woods and Sláine appeared before me, her back turned. I called to her and she ignored me so I ran towards her, but no matter how quickly I moved my legs, I couldn't seem to get any closer, even though she wasn't moving at all.

Then she turned and began to shamble in my direction and I was happy at first, only I realised that it wasn't her, this wasn't my Sláine: it was a hideous creature, an undead monster, and it wanted *me* . . .

I must have willed myself to wake up. Some primitive fear – a deep-seated memory of reading somewhere that death in a dream can kill you in real life – must have forced me to snap out of sleep. Was that true? I don't know. It felt like it could be, though. I felt as if I might have died in that dream if I hadn't woken.

I sat upright, my heart banging like a hammer on a sheet of steel. God, what was that all about? Something to do with Sláine, I was positive – I needed to talk to her about . . .

And then, of course, I realised – with a familiar feeling of nausea in my stomach – that she wasn't there. I wanted to tell her about this dream but couldn't. I wanted to ask her those questions which were now queuing up in my mind, like impatient customers in line at the bank, pushing their way to the front of the queue, waving their arms, demanding to be heard.

Were there others like *her*? Had some of these victims of the cold risen from the dead, as Sláine did? Had she met them? Were they the same as her, beautiful spectres floating through the forest?

And most fundamentally, was she with them?

It was all too much, again. My head was spinning, again. I

needed to get it clear. I needed, again and again, some fresh air. So I threw on a coat and went out to get it.

The town was as silent and empty as an abandoned planet. Absolutely nobody about. This weather, presumably, was keeping people indoors at night, unless they had a damn good reason to come out.

The temperature stubbornly stayed below freezing. We were locked in this never-ending deep winter, although the town had by this stage come to terms with the situation. It was coping, sort of. Snow fell periodically, most days in fact, but a gentle snow. It floated softly to earth, renewing the piles of snow already there, like a regular reminder of the state we were in. We hadn't, thankfully, suffered any major storms. I don't know what people would have done if that happened. By now the town had got used to the big freeze: pipes were properly insulated to prevent them from cracking all the time, lanes were regularly cleared to allow vehicles and pedestrians to move about.

There was no longer that childlike delight at living inside a winter wonderland – it was just the way things were now – but neither was there the same trepidation and worry. People didn't worry about how they would deal with the weather because, well, they *had* dealt with it. Life went on, different to before but with the same pressures and enjoyments, the same obligations and reliefs. It was just much, much colder.

Still, a vague anxiety persisted, regarding the medium-term future. Even though everyone knew it was impossible, that this freakish cold snap would have to end at some point, a gnawing whisper remained at the back of the collective mind: 'What if it doesn't? What if we get stuck like this – forever?'

I smiled grimly. Bad weather? That's the *least* of our troubles, folks.

My mobile phone told me it was coming on for eleven. The streets were piled with snow, up to two feet in places, but the council had done a decent job of keeping them clear for traffic, foot or wheeled. It wasn't snowing right at that moment, although you got the sense that this was just a reprieve. The sky was blacker than black, a host of stars twinkling up there like lights on a theatre backdrop. I half-heartedly tried to make out different constellations – the Plough, the Hunter, those geometric outlines we're taught in primary school. I failed – didn't recognise a thing. It was just a shapeless collection of distant lights, albeit a beautiful one.

Where was I going? I asked myself. No reply came, so I continued to put one foot in front of the other, shuffling through the whiteness, my breath frosting in front of me as if it were the reins of some invisible horse that was carrying me through the streets.

I scurried past the scuzzy council estate on the far side of town – that was where the Rattigan clan held court, so it probably wasn't a good idea for me to hang around. After a while I reached the ancient graveyard where Sláine had been buried and realised I had travelled outside the town. I didn't remember leaving it, but ... appropriate enough. I was still half-dazed and half-dozed. I guess my legs chose a direction because my brain wasn't giving them any instructions. I went through the open wrought-iron gates and walked up the long driveway.

The place was even quieter and more lifeless than cemeteries usually are, but it looked incredible, under weeks and months of accumulated snow and ice and frost. The elements gave it a ghostly pallor, accentuating every crypt's curved edge, every grave-top statue, every listing tombstone. It came across more than ever like the deserted set of a Gothic horror movie: angels and shadows and cold and ruination all mixed together, the moon up above like a spotlight on an open-air shoot, bats and ravens flying here and there like CGI spirits.

I took a step forward to better appreciate the scene, and something moved behind a towering headstone in the shape of a cross, on top of a hillock at the far end of the cemetery. What was –?

There. It moved again. A chill rippled up and down me as though icy fingers were using my spine to play the piano. That wasn't a bird, or a bat, some small animal. It was much too big. It was moving on two legs. And it was as white as snow.

And oh Christ, it was looking at me.

For an instant my eyes locked with those eyes, two hideous pits simultaneously glowing white and dark as pitch, and then there was another flash and the thing, the person, whatever it was, had gone. I stepped back, two steps, three, four. I wanted to run but I couldn't, my brain was giving the instructions now all right, urgent goddamn commands to *go go go*, but my stupid legs wouldn't or couldn't obey.

Silence. Stillness. No movement, over there or down here.

Then a wave of terror crashed through me, so violently that I was sure I'd faint clean away, as I realised the thing was almost on me. Charging at me from the side, emerging out of the shadows like one of the four horsemen of the apocalypse, and holy *shit* it was the monster, the one from my dream. Its skin was frozen stiff in some places and had turned black from frostbite in others, and was covered in tiny blue lines. Ice encrusted its eyebrows and hairline. Its eyes were a terrifying Arctic blue-white, its mouth open to reveal teeth shaped like jagged icicles. The thing was skinny, hunched over, moving with the jerkiness of a clockwork toy, but rapidly. I couldn't tell if it was male or female. Its clothes were slightly torn and very dirty but more or less all there: a smart jacket and trousers, shirt, no shoes.

It resembled a corpse that had been stuffed in a freezer for years but now, somehow, had escaped and was coming for me.

I screamed. No sound came out. I was *paralysed*, frozen in terror, and the ice-thing was coming closer and closer . . . It reached out for me, a horrific leer creasing its face, this creature from the depths of the worst nightmare. Still I couldn't move. And then the monster's fingers were on me, digging into my shoulders. I could feel the absolute freeze of it through my clothes and jacket. Such power in those skeletal fingers, drilling down through flesh and fabric, right into the heart of me.

Oh no. *Oh no* . . .

The thing leaned over, its mouth almost on mine, and breathed in deeply and I could feel the air being sucked from my lungs but not just that. This was worse than suffocating. The oxygen was being replaced – as the creature drew each breath out, it pushed something else in.

Cold.

Perfect, implacable, deadly cold.

Hair follicles electrified, skin tightening against the freezing burn of it, blood vessels petrifying, blood-flow decelerating, lungs hardening, crystallising, organs going into shock, folding in on themselves, slowing, *slooooowing* . . . And then my heart – the cold gone right to my heart, and that great muscle seizing up, the engine of the body breaking down, the thing that drives us, that warms the blood and stirs our passions and makes us what we are, makes us *live* . . .

My whole system freezing. Shutting down. Dying.

Is this what happened to you, Sláine? Is this . . . this . . . what . . . you . . .

Terror-stricken panic had left me on the brink of madness, but my brain and ears still functioned enough for me to make out that the thing seemed to be talking to me. A voice, not a voice, a rasp that somehow conveyed words, came at me, horribly intimate. It said just four, excruciatingly slowly.

'No more. Aidan. Flood.'

So this was it – no more of poor old me. I was a goner. I'd like to think I possessed enough self-composure, even under such duress, to wryly reflect on the irony of my situation. A few months before I had stood on a bridge and considered throwing my life away by one cataclysmic action, one simple jump. The lure of killing myself had lingered for quite a while afterwards, a seductive perfume hanging in the air. And before that I'd spent months moping because my heart was broken and my ego was battered; moping, hibernating, withdrawing, but not *living* in any meaningful sense of the word. Now here I was, really on the edge of my mortal coil, about to breathe my last . . . and I had never desired life so much. I would have given anything, done anything, to earn more time. But I couldn't. My time was up. After all those wasted hours, countless hours, I had mere seconds left. There's irony for you.

I'd like to think that's how I reacted, with calmness and a touch of gallows humour. It wouldn't be the truth, though. I was babbling like a lunatic and screaming like a baby.

So much so that I barely registered when those icy fingers were pulled off my shoulder. When the creature, the thing, was violently wrenched from the ground where it stood and hurled into the shadows. My legs started to wobble as I saw a bright blur move across my eyeline at barely conceivable speed and heard an ungodly screech from those shadows, and the monster emerged from them, leaping towards the blur which I could sort of see now was a person. The creature bared its teeth and charged, claws out, at the person in white, and there was another crazy-fast blur of movement and my head was spinning and then the thing's head was spinning too but literally, torn clear off its shoulders and flung into the air. The rest of its body, the corpse or whatever the hell it was, slumped to the ground.

Long pointed boots, decorated with antique-style buttons, came down hard on the body and pounded it into dust in seconds. Then they strode across to where the head lay – sickeningly, it seemed to still be alive, staring at me – and slim hands reached down and lifted it, and with one swift, brutal movement crushed it to powder. They smacked off each other, up and down, knocking off the residue of that thing. That's the correct word, I think – residue. There had been no blood, no wet organic matter of any kind. The creature seemed to be

216

made out of ice and rubble.

The person turned to me and my eyes trailed up along the familiar boots, the overcoat with the high collar, the set of her body, the way she held herself even in repose, and finally the face I knew from my tortured dreams.

Sláine.

I whispered, 'What – the – *fuuuuck*? Sláine, what was . . . ' I collapsed to the ground on all fours and gulped for air. 'Sláine? *Sláine*, Jesus. You're here. What are you doing here?'

'Hello, Aidan.'

'What was that thing?'

'You mean who.'

'Wha—? That's a *person*?'

'Was. Not any more. Now they're . . . changed.'

'Oh God. I don't even . . . Oh God, I think I'm gonna be sick.' My stomach heaved but nothing came up except a thin line of drool, slowly dropping from my lip to the ground.

I looked up at her. 'Is that you? It is. It's really you.' Tears filled my eyes for the first time since Caitlin broke my heart last summer. Only half a year previous, but that time now felt like a lifetime ago. I suppose in one sense it *was* a lifetime ago.

Sláine gave a small smile. 'It's really me.'

'I'm so happy. You're here. Back.'

'I am. It's me.'

'You came back to me.'

'I came back to you.'

My system was going into meltdown, adrenaline coursing through me, limbs shaking, head whirling like water sluicing down the sinkhole. I retched again and croaked, 'Jesus Christ.

This is . . . I feel like I'm stuck in some deranged nightmare.'

'It's no dream, Aidan. It's all very real.'

'Have I gone mad, then? Am I bloody crazy?'

'No. You're not crazy. My poor Aidan. You look so pale.' She smiled sadly. 'As if you've seen a ghost.'

I stared at her. I couldn't even manage a smile back. Sláine had returned, like I knew she would. She'd returned and saved my life from that . . . that . . . I didn't finish the thought – my mind wasn't able to process it any further. I tried to stand, and failed. She looked different somehow, but I couldn't put my finger on exactly how, because I couldn't see straight. My vision was blurring and doubling, swimming in front of me.

'I think I'm in shock. Holy shit.'

'It's the adrenaline. You'll be okay in a few minutes. You're not hurt.'

'No, I mean – you're *back*.'

'I am. I'm right here.'

'You're not . . . dead,' I said faintly. 'You know what I mean . . . '

I thought I was going to pass out. And then, at last, I did.

'Aidan, we have to go.'

She was cradling my head. I came around gradually, woozily, and saw I was lying on the ground in that old graveyard and Sláine was sitting beneath me, nursing my head on her lap. Oddly, her body felt *almost* warm to me, as though it retained, or maybe remembered, a trace of the lifeblood that once gave her force. But that was probably just my mind playing tricks, because the ground itself was so perishing – an iceberg would have felt warm by comparison.

She said again, 'We have to go. It's not safe here.'

I smiled up at her, remembering her superwoman rescue act . . . when was that? How long had I been out? I said, 'What do you mean it's not safe? I saw what you can do.'

'I meant for you. We have to go. Now. I didn't want to . . . *move* you while you were out. Didn't know what effect it might have.'

'How long was I unconscious?'

'You weren't unconscious, you just fainted. I don't know, a minute or two.'

My smile grew broader, expanding from a small grin to a face-covering beam. 'You saved me.'

Sláine didn't reply. She looked around, not anxiously but with a very serious expression. A real taking-care-of-business kind of look.

I said it again: 'Sláine. You saved my life.'

Finally she graced me with a tiny smile in return. I went on, 'Not for the first time. You've saved me before. You're my guardian angel, you know that?'

She frowned. 'I am *far* from being anyone's guardian angel, believe me. I'm more like . . . like the bringer of bad luck.'

'I don't believe you. You're my guardian angel and that's that, whether you like it or not.'

I wanted to stay there forever, resting in her arms, but Sláine had said we needed to move ass, so I moved mine off the ground and shook myself down. I took a few deep breaths and searched my pockets for the makings of a cigarette. I pulled out the tobacco and said, 'I got time for a smoke? Sort of think

I need one, you know?'

Sláine waved her hand yes and looked away. I studied her surreptitiously while assembling the fag. Her hair wasn't pinned up high any more; it hung loose around her face, onto the shoulders, curled and shining, a thin braid at either temple; I wondered if she had done those herself. Her eyes were decorated with dark smudgy kohl, or at least the impression of it. And under the surface, she also seemed changed, indisputably. I still couldn't quite put my finger on it. Something intangible – hard to say exactly but it was definitely *there* . . .

'So what the hell was that?' I said around the column of smoke billowing from my mouth. 'The thing that attacked me. You said it was a person, right?'

She stood and nodded. 'That used to be a woman called Rita O'Leary. She was thirty-nine when she died last Monday night. Her body was discovered the next morning by her husband on one of those laneways that run from the road down to the beach. She'd frozen to death.'

I said hesitantly, 'And this . . . it has something to do with you.'

'In a sense, yes.'

'No, it does. Sláine, I know what's going on,' I blurted out. 'I've worked it out, this whole thing. I even know what . . . what killed you.'

She stared at me, her expression unreadable. I ploughed on, 'It's, aah . . . Okay, this is going to sound a bit crazy, but bear with me. It's your ancestor. William John McAuley. I *think* – I'm pretty sure. I mean I don't have any proof? But you know, when your gut instinct says something, it's usually, like, bang on, isn't it?'

Another smile. Sláine made that 'hurry up' gesture with her hand.

'Sorry,' I said. 'Just feels a bit weird to me, you know, *me* being the one telling *you* something, and not the other way around.'

She tilted her head. I could see her patience was running out.

I took one big breath and launched into it. 'Okay, here it is: McAuley conjured some kind of demon or some shit. Like, one of the old Celtic gods, or demons, some supernatural force. Some awful creature or presence, a thing made of the cold itself. He wrote about it in this letter that I found, that someone gave me. He was dying, it was the middle of the Famine and he knew he'd die, and he'd turned to hate God cos God didn't help them when everyone was starving, and McAuley basically said, "Screw you, God, I'm getting help somewhere else." So he went into Shook Woods one night and conjured up this *thing*, this demon, and basically cheated death that way. I don't know where he's been hiding out ever since, like that was a long time ago and he's only resurfaced in the last few months. But he has, William McAuley's definitely back, and he's the one who killed *you* that night. Why, I don't know – maybe because you're related to him? Or he was lonely – the demon and him weren't getting on so well, there were definite cracks in their relationship and McAuley was wondering if this really was the right person for him to spend immortality with.'

I laughed nervously. Sláine didn't. Okay. I hammered on. 'He knew about this black magic voodoo from his reading – you said yourself he was into all that malarkey. He knew what to do and how to do it. So, that's what happened. Like I said I don't have cast-iron proof for this, but it's a good theory. It's more than a theory – it all stacks up, everything. There are some gaps, I accept that, but you might be able to fill those in. I've read a pile of stuff over the last few months and then tonight Podsy told me there'd been a rash of other deaths from the cold in the last week and a bit, and their bodies were similar to yours and the Guards couldn't explain it and, you know, it just all came together in my head. Fell into place. This stacks up. He's the one.'

Still no response. I took a pull on my cigarette and said evenly, 'Soooo . . . what do you think?'

Sláine looked around, continuing to scope the place out for danger. Finally she turned back and said, 'I think you're actually right. Good work.'

I smiled proudly, dumbly. Sláine was impressed and I felt happy. Even now, at the end of the world, her opinion counted for everything.

She raised a finger to indicate 'but' and added, 'Except for one important point: it's not William John McAuley. He lies dead in the ground, where he's lain for the last century and a half. Not even that much: McAuley's body was found and eaten by animals. There's nothing left of my ancestor.'

'But the rest of it, I got that right? Aw, shit. I was kind of hoping you'd tell me I was full of crap, I was insane and there was some banal explanation.'

''Fraid not.'

'Pity. I would have preferred the other explanation. You know, the one that *didn't* involve demons.'

I could hardly believe I was making jokes about all this,

but there you go: the human heart is strange, and mine had evidently been filled with courage and bravado at Sláine's return. Speaking of which . . .

'Where were you since Sunday?' I hadn't meant to ask it yet, but it was out now, I couldn't rewind time or suck the words back into my lungs.

Sláine said, 'I'll tell you, but not here. We need to go somewhere else. You were obviously followed to the graveyard, tracked. We can assume they've been watching out for you.'

'They?'

'There may be others, we don't know.'

I gulped heavily. 'Others . . . ? Right. Of those things. And actually, it knew my name. That monster, it said my name, Aidan Flood. Uuuugh. So it was sent here. After me.'

'After you. I think so, yes.'

I forced myself to make another joke, anything to quell this rising swell of panic and fear in my chest. 'Gee, wasn't I born under a lucky star? Life just keeps getting better and better. What next? I'm gonna get Satan for a roommate? "Bunch up, Aidan, there's plenty room in that bed for two."'

I was babbling a little. Sláine frowned at me. 'You'll be fine. I won't let anything happen to you.'

I sucked hard on the cigarette and tossed it aside. 'All right. I believe you. So where to? Shook Woods? The lodge, yeah?'

'No. Further than that.' Sláine scooted over and wrapped her arms tightly around me. That shivery embrace, as comforting as a mother's hug and as thrilling as a first kiss.

'I'm going to bring you somewhere quite far away, very quickly,' she said. 'All right? So close your eyes and brace

223

yourself. This might feel a little . . . weird.'

We'd already done this, when she'd whooshed me through the forest that time; it felt a bit disorientating but not too bad. I expected it to be like that again, only magnified. I could cope with that. I held my breath and readied myself.

''Kay. Ready as I'll ever be.'

And as my eyes closed on Sláine, it struck me, what was fundamentally different about her, how she'd changed.

Her shift from dark to light had been completed. Only her eyes, lips and hair retained colour and shade. Now she was fully white, a brilliant white, like the inside of a supernova.

BLACK SKIES AND
REVELATIONS

When I was a boy, eight or nine, my father brought me climbing on Sliabh Cohnda. I say climbing, but it wasn't quite that – there were no crampons or ropes, and we didn't climb so much as half-crawl, half-stagger up the mountain's gentlest slope, which faced the town. But we made it to somewhere near the top and rested there, gazing on the panorama unfolding below: roiling green-blue sea, other mountains curving around at either side of us, streets and houses we knew from daily life as intimately as our own faces, and of course Shook Woods, on the far side of town. A balmy summer day, pleasant wind, the sun gently toasting our faces. He had brought snacks, coffee in a flask, Coke for me; he'd even rolled up a towel to use as a picnic spread. We laid our food out and smiled at each other and enjoyed the view. Then he lit a cigarette, and I still recall the aroma of the smoke as it wafted across on the breeze. The smell of warmth and affection.

That day forms one of the absolute best memories from my entire life. My father was – is – a very decent man and was perfectly nice to me growing up, but we never *did* a whole lot together. I don't have any lingering resentment over this. I'm not some petulant kid in a movie whining about how 'Daddy missed my big softball game'; there simply aren't that many memories of him in there. The day on the mountain, though: I'll never forget that. It was just lovely, a few hours of pleasurable exertion followed by well-earned rest. The two of us together, a simple day, a happy day.

A blast of wind came careening down out of the north, almost knocking me off my feet, and I put away that treasured memory and returned to the present. I was back on Sliabh Cohnda again, near the top of this highest peak in the range, but the similarities ended there. This time I was with Sláine, the sky was black and the weather was pitilessly cold – up here the wind never stilled, like it had done below at sea level for months. The view, which I couldn't see anyway, had been changed utterly because everything I remembered from that childhood climb was covered in snow. And unlike then, I wasn't happy and relaxed in the cocoon of childhood; now I was afraid for my life, and everyone else's too. I was no longer a child. Now I was on the cusp of adulthood, with all the heavy responsibilities and frightening possibilities that promised.

'Are we safe?' I asked, not for the first time since Sláine had whisked us here from the graveyard.

'I think so. For the time being.'

We'd sheltered on the far side of the mountain, away from sea and town and forest, facing the yawning valley that headed north. The same stretch of land crossed by Sláine's ancestors when they made their famous flight to freedom during the

Famine. Sliabh Cohnda roughly translated as Brutal or Savage Mountain, which gives some idea of the conditions to be found there. Endured, rather. The entire top half of the mountain was bare rock, scrubbed clean of vegetation by millennia of relentless winds.

Now it was snow-covered, sealed in frost, encased within a glacial cocoon. Sláine had landed us, or whatever the term was, in a kind of cave at its rear side, just in from a cliff edge, close to the peak.

A 'cave' – that doesn't do it justice at all, that flat, one-syllable word. The place was magical, accentuated by shimmering moonlight, literally taking my breath away in a delighted gasp when we arrived. It made me forget everything, for a moment. The full space inside was covered in ice: ceiling, walls and floor. The sides of the cave were thick with long, fat tubes and globs of ice that resembled melted candlewax. Spiky white stalactites hung from above, looking like some modern art installation, or the decor of a painfully hip club in Tokyo or Osaka, somewhere you might see on a Channel 4 travel show. The floor was glassy, clear and smooth, though for some reason, I didn't seem to be having trouble keeping my balance. Underneath, I could see large shards of crystals, pointing upwards. And oddly, they appeared to be glowing faintly, as if lit from within.

I wondered if Sláine was responsible for it, creating this masterpiece by rearranging the molecules of frozen water. I'd half-asked her when we got here; she'd ignored the question so I let it lie.

'There was no blood,' I said, out of nowhere. Sláine raised an

227

enquiring eyebrow. I went on, 'The thing you destroyed. You said it – she, sorry – a woman called . . . O'Leary? There was no blood, or guts or anything. Like she was made out of stone.'

'She was, in a way.' Sláine leaned against the side of the cave and wrapped her arms around herself. If I didn't know better, I'd have sworn she was both tired and colder than usual. Maybe stepping away from the wall of this ice installation would help.

She said, 'That's what happens when they – die. When they're taken by the cold. They turn, more or less, to ice. Their flesh is petrified, it becomes breakable. Not soft and flexible like yours. They're turned almost to stone. Frozen stone.'

'But that didn't happen to you.'

She shook her head. The obvious question was why? What makes *you* so special? That could wait, though. I had more urgent matters on my mind.

I said, 'They can't come after us here, right? These others.'

'I don't think so.'

'So we have time,' I said. 'To talk.'

'Some.'

Sláine seemed out of sorts, almost regretful in some obscure way, and I couldn't tell why. I could always ask straight out, of course – she never refused to answer a question or took offence at any of them, even my dumbest ones – but something was stopping me. I had the strongest feeling she was reading my mind, even though she swore she was unable – that she'd guessed my intentions, what I wanted to know.

Suddenly a giant raven landed a few metres away, coming in on down drafts like a helicopter. It skittered along the icy floor and turned its baleful eye on the two of us. Sinister and black in ancient grace; inscrutable, an ancient face.

'Look at this guy,' she said airily. 'Size of him.'

Okay, so she was trying to change the subject, apparently? The bird shrieked, a surprisingly low tone to it. I shuddered and rolled a cigarette with cold-bitten hands.

'Ravens,' I said, indulging Sláine's reticence. 'Don't know what to make of 'em. Sometimes think they're kind of cool, you know? Like, they're very intelligent. Only animals besides us to use tools.' I lit my fag. 'Then other times, *ech* . . . Other times I imagine someone like that fella eating the eyeballs out of my head.'

Sláine laughed softly. 'Ah, he's all right. He won't harm us. Will you, little man?' She held out a hand and the raven flew across to land on it.

I gasped in shock. 'Wha—? Are you able to control animals now?'

'I don't think so. I didn't make this raven fly to me. He just wanted to, didn't you? My handsome little man.'

'Not going to start tickling that thing under the neck and saying "coochie-coochie-coo", are you?'

Sláine flung the crow out the cave's mouth, sighing heavily. I muttered, 'Guess not.'

'Go on,' she said quietly, looking at the ground. 'Say what you have to. I know you're biting back on it. You needn't do that.'

'Okay, then tell me where you were. I know everyone's in danger and all that, but sorry, I'm a typical self-centred adolescent and I'm putting myself first. Everyone else can wait. I need to know: where the hell did you go? And why?'

Sláine didn't reply. I wondered why she was hesitating. Vague feelings of impending rejection squirmed in my tummy like insects. *Please* don't say it's over, I silently implored her. Don't return to me only to leave again. Don't don't just don't . . .

Something clicked in my head. Aidan, dude, you're asking the wrong question. Find out what you really want to know. Hear her say the only words that count – or not say them.

'No, forget that,' I said. 'I've a better question: do you love me?'

Sláine looked at me, her head going back on that elegant neck like a wary swan. She seemed surprised.

'Do you love me, Sláine? Yes or no, straight answer.'

'Why are you asking me that?'

'Because *I* love *you*,' I said urgently, words spilling out of my mouth as though I'd drunk too much water and there wasn't enough room in there for all of it. Or maybe it wasn't water but wine, wine that had made me loose-tongued and reckless. 'I don't know if I've ever said it to you – you know anyway I'm sure, you must, but I mightn't have said it out loud. Sláine McAuley, I love you. I'm in love with you. You're the most fantastic person I've ever met. I can't imagine life without you – it'd feel so empty. It *did*, these last few days.' I took a step closer, gliding along the ice. 'I love you. Do you love me back?'

She held my gaze, held it, held it, a wistful look in her eyes. *Finally*, after about a thousand years of nervous agony, she broke the stare and answered quietly: 'Yes. Happy now?'

Relief flooded my system like a wash of chemicals, precise, targeted. I was giddy, almost euphoric. I think I knew then what heroin must feel like. 'You mean that? Truly and honestly?'

'Yes.'

I smiled widely. 'Well, *shit*, yeah. Then I'm happy. Course I am.'

She smiled wryly. 'Me too.'

'Really?'

'*Yes*. Jesus, Aidan, yes.'

She laughed heartily. There was my old Sláine, returned to me. I gulped and glanced away to hide the strength of my emotions.

I said, 'Uh, okay. So back to the "where you went" bit. Where, why, the whole deal. I thought you were dead. Like, *dead* dead.'

Sláine stepped in the cone of moonlight shining into the cave. '"Why" is easy: I had to. So you can put those fears to rest, Aidan.' She smiled warmly. 'I didn't abandon you, or reject you. I wouldn't do that. I couldn't. You're . . . ' She paused, then gently thumped her chest. 'You're in here now. For good.'

That wash of placid euphoria again. Sláine was still mine. And she'd said she always would be.

'Cool,' I said dumbly. 'I mean great. I feel like that too.'

'I left . . . because something happened, and it made me afraid. Not for me – afraid *of* me.'

'What do you mean?'

'I did something and . . . I was frightened where it might lead. What I might do next.' Sláine broke off, stared hard at the ground. I was itching to know what that was but didn't want to force it.

'I had to leave you,' she said. 'Go away for a while. Be on my own. I'm sorry. This is hard.'

I shushed her, saying gently, 'It's all right. When you're ready.

231

Do you want to tell me at least where you got to?'

'Somewhere around,' she answered vaguely. 'I basically hid out. Walked into the desert like some wild-eyed mystic, looking for the face of God . . . I found an isolated space not far from here and sat on the ground, arms around my knees, eyes closed, breathing as slowly as I could. Trying to calm myself. To get *beyond* myself, like the Buddhist thing? Subdue the ego, destroy all desire . . . I hunkered down into myself and – waited. For the feeling to pass. The desire. The *danger*.'

'So,' I said cagily, 'you *don't* think you're . . . dangerous now?'

She shook her head. 'No. But he is. Aidan, listen. It's not just you – everyone is in danger now. A great menace is coming. That's the second part of where I was. After four days of isolation, regaining control of myself, I came back. I returned to the forest last night, our lodge. I thought maybe you'd be there.' She smiled. 'Silly, I know. To expect you'd wait for my return.'

'I did wait.'

'I know.'

We smiled at each other. She said, 'Someone had been in the lodge. I recognised it, that presence again. But different to before. More . . . concrete now. It had shape and personality. I could feel it reverberating off the walls. I said to myself, this is *it*. This is what killed you, Sláine. I knew it in the deepest part of me.'

'"It" being a demon.' I winced, it sounded so absurd. 'God, I can't believe I'm saying this. Devil, demigod, whatever. I'm right, aren't I?'

Sláine nodded. 'The demon – and man. Both had been in

232

our lodge.'

I went on, 'And you say it's not William John McAuley who's behind it. The one who's raised this thing.'

'No. You're not totally off the mark, though. My ancestor has a part to play.'

'How do you know who it really is?'

'He wanted me to know. He gave me this.' Sláine lifted her hand and showed me her ring, the one with the strange design. She pulled it off. 'That man placed this on my finger after I died. I never took it off until last night. I knew it wasn't mine – someone had put it there. I *wanted* to remove it, examine it – I simply couldn't. It wouldn't budge.'

'Why didn't you say something before?'

'What would've been the point? If I couldn't get it off, no disrespect but you wouldn't have been able, either.'

'Eh . . . yeah. Fair enough.'

'And I didn't want to worry you,' Sláine said. 'I guess I assumed it'd be explained eventually. You know, take the philosophical view, accept the way things were. And it was explained: last night I looked down and for some reason knew it would move now. It came off my finger smoothly. Want to know what the inscription inside the band reads?'

I groaned. 'Not . . . really?'

'"To my beloved Eleanor. Bound forever, beyond the cold shores of death. From your devoted husband, William John. Winter 1851." I think he inscribed this ring *after* she left him, and kept it somewhere. As a sort of pledge to her, that they'd be together again.'

'Why didn't he just go with her? Instead of all this eejiting around with rings and pledges, crappy poetry.'

'Maybe he thought the trek over the mountains was doomed, so it was better at least one of them survived, stayed behind to . . .'

'To do what he did. Conjure up a demon.'

'No. That's the part you got wrong. William John *tried* to do that – but failed. Too weak, probably. Starvation, exhaustion, the man would've been half-dead by the time he went to Shook Woods. He left it too late. Should have done it weeks before – probably wanted Eleanor out of the way first.' She smiled wanly. 'Trying to protect her, I suppose. That's something.'

'Yeah,' I rasped. 'A pretty small goddamn something. Go on. McAuley failed. Whereas . . .'

'Whereas this guy – our villain, let's call him – did a little better. For him, the ceremony worked.'

It was all becoming too real. Mad imaginings and theories were one thing. Even though I knew deep in my gut that they were essentially true, I didn't *know*. I had no hard evidence. Now, though, Sláine was handing me that evidence on a platter. I felt dizzy. I was afraid I'd fall off that bloody cliff edge.

Block out reality. You're still a kid. None of this is happening.

'He wanted me to know all this,' Sláine said. 'Not at the beginning, not until now. That's why the ring wouldn't shift before. He's happy for me to know now, which suggests one thing: whatever his plan is, we're coming near to the end.'

A hellish blast of wind whipped up around us. I separated from her and stepped further back into the cave, as far as I could go, which wasn't far. I could still see the cliff, and imagined the terrifying drop off that edge. Definitely not a jump you want to make, Aidan. They'd be scraping you off the rocks with a trowel. I sat, my bum bumping hard on the glassy floor with the groovy subterranean crystal lights.

I said quietly, 'But how d'you know this stuff? That McAuley messed up, and now someone else is driving the bus.'

'He came to me.'

I snapped to attention.

'Last night, after I left the lodge. I went to our other place – the Greek amphitheatre, as you call it. Waiting, not waiting, I don't know. I might have had a sixth sense he would show up . . .'

'So who is he?'

'That's the problem,' Sláine said regretfully. 'I don't know. I'm certain it wasn't William John, but who this guy is . . . ? He didn't tell me. I mean, he didn't exactly walk in there either. More . . . drifted over to me. His spirit, his thoughts, something.'

'You felt a presence.'

'Yes, but different to when I died. I told you I felt this great wash of coldness that night, joining me to it. But something organic, as if it possessed a mind. That time, the *thing* – the demon – was more to the forefront, if you know what I mean? It accosted me, with someone, a living man, directing it from the distance. Whereas last night . . .'

'Our boy was riding the horse.'

She nodded. 'Pretty much. The demon's spirit was there too, somewhere. Hanging in the air like a bad smell. But the man felt much more *obvious* to me. As though he was out front, and the demon tailing behind him.'

I tutted in fear and disgust. 'Like a goddamn dog on a lead.

Lovely image. So what'd this asshole say? Say, communicate, beam out brainwaves, whatever.'

'He told me everything except who he was. He's using this supernatural being to kill people, you got that right.'

Realising my ass was in danger of sticking to the ground, I stood. 'I knew it. Didn't I say I knew it?'

'Our villain came across William John's writings,' Sláine said. 'I'm not sure where – it doesn't really matter. My ancestor had kept extensive diaries all his life, written hundreds of letters, even several books although they were never published. Wrote them for himself, I'd imagine. A lot is harmless nonsense, the ravings of a borderline lunatic really. But in the midst of all this *ráiméis* . . . '

'Granddad left instructions.'

'He did. Precise directions on how to conjure up demonic forces. This other man found McAuley's work, studied him . . . followed the path until it led to Shook Woods. The forest is the key. It's beautiful – but there's something menacing about it at the same time. Something truly dangerous. Its heart is dark in more ways than one.'

I didn't want to believe that; I'd got quite used to hanging out in Shook, my eerie home from home. I said, 'So now this creep controls the demon's power.'

'Or maybe it controls him to some extent. Or they're in some symbiotic relationship, where each needs the other equally. I'm not clear on the specifics.' Sláine frowned. 'I guess, in a way, he has *become* this devil. It's become him. They're bound together in cold and death. Whichever – that's what he's done.'

Something clicked on in my mind, some dread I didn't

want to recognise. 'Oh my God. Uh . . . Are you . . . one too? Now. Are you . . . ?' My voice had receded to a hoarse croak: 'A demon.'

'No.'

'You're not . . . *involved* in any way? With all this death.' I laughed nervously. The timeline of these cold killings, it struck me, dovetailed to some degree with Sláine's disappearance.

'Of course not. None of those attacks had anything to do with me.'

I didn't think much of this at that moment, the words just flowing in my ear and out again. In hindsight, though, I should have clocked it, the significance of that word . . .

Anyway, the thought didn't have time to lodge itself in my mind because Sláine was still speaking: she said dryly, 'You know, most people would have asked *that* question first. About me being a demon?'

'Yeah, well . . . ' I shrugged. 'I'm not most people.'

'No. You're one of a kind, Aidan Flood.'

I bowed. 'I thank you. So are there others? People who've risen from the dead.'

'You met one tonight.'

'Nah, you know what I mean. People who're – the way you are. Thinking, feeling. Powerful. *Improved*.'

'Like me? I don't think so.'

'You haven't met any, then? Weren't tearing around with a big gang of beautiful angels all week?'

This time Sláine bowed. 'No. I told you – I was alone.'

'Until last night. When our mystery man shows up, still wearing his mask though cos that makes it more exciting I guess, and gives you the full skinny on his evil doings.'

'Essentially.'

'Go on, then. Might as well have the whole of it. Before I run shrieking from this mountain top.'

'He told me what he does, and why he does it.'

'Do I want to know why?'

'Why else? Immortality.'

Sláine ghosted over and placed her arm around me. I fixed my vision on that ring on her finger, its long oval shape, the raised image suggesting some type of crystal.

She said, 'He extends his life by consuming the lives of others. It's as simple and horrible as that. This man is deranged, driven crazy by lust for power and an absolute refusal to admit that death is . . . Natural. Necessary. Life has no meaning without death at the end. Everything must end, that's how it has to be. But he can't see that, or won't. He wants to live forever, and he's prepared to kill for that.'

'So he drew people out of their homes and took their lives. Like he did with you.'

'Yes. Some form of telepathy. Thought transference. He kind of . . . squirms in there, you know? Into people's minds. Hypnotises them to leave the sanctuary of their homes. I don't think he has the power to enter buildings any more than me.'

'What happens to them? Afterwards.'

'Most of the victims perish,' Sláine said. 'Just gone forever. Whatever was in them, their soul or spirit, it's devoured by him. The body is left behind, a husk.'

'What about that yoke who attacked me tonight? She looked pretty full of bloody spirit.'

'I'm not sure. He seems to be keeping a few . . . animated. But only partly. They're like zombies, unthinking, half-dead. His slaves. I guess everyone in power needs someone to hold it over.'

I nodded slowly. 'Okay, so again: where do you fit in? You're still here, your soul I mean. And you're definitely nobody's slave.'

'He obviously has other plans for me. Don't know exactly what yet. Although I'm thinking, why *me*? Why did I turn out like this, but not the others?'

'That's what I was gonna say . . . ask. What makes you different?'

'I don't know. All we can be sure of is that this man, and his demonic ally, will keep killing unless they're stopped.'

'Yeah,' I drawled. 'Stopping them. That's the part I don't like the sound of.'

She stepped to the edge of the cliff. For an instant I feared she was about to leap off it, swan-dive to some romantic and absurd doom. Then I realised that wouldn't kill her, not in a million years. And Sláine wasn't the romantic-doom type anyway.

I called over, 'How'd this conversation end? Your little chat with Demon Boy.' I checked myself: 'little chat'? What was that supposed to mean? I was acting like a jealous idiot boyfriend, and I wasn't even sure if I *was* her boyfriend. I moaned softly. Oh, Aidan Flood, what a life this is you've got.

Sláine grimaced, her teeth bared a fraction, and I could have sworn the 'lights' inside those crystals underneath my feet pulsed to a brighter shine. She said with a tight voice, 'He told me to be ready – he'd be coming back for me soon.'

I squeezed my eyes shut, the old child's trick: if you can't see it, it's not really happening. I squeaked, 'Great,' my words the echo of an echo from some distant part of my heart, unknown, it seemed, even to myself.

DEEPEST DESIRE

I thought the worst of it might be over, for now at least. The howling winds tore strips off my skin and the sky seemed to slide into ever-deeper shades of black and I was tired and shivering and, I belatedly realised, very hungry – when had I last eaten? But still, I can handle it, I told myself. We'll talk it through and get some rest and Sláine will work out a brilliant plan to defeat the bastard and we'll be okay. If that's as bad as this night is going to get, I can deal with it. *We will be okay*.

Unfortunately, that wasn't as bad as it was going to get.

I rolled another smoke and said, to occupy my mind and blot out the horror of all I'd learned, 'Man. This is . . . just *beyond* the beyond, you know? I wish it wasn't true. I *really* wish you'd've told me I was dreaming. But I'm not, am I? It's all real.'

'It's all real.'

'Don't know why I'm surprised. I mean it's inexplicable, people dying of the cold. Nobody could understand it, the Guards, no one. But I knew it had to be connected to you, what happened to you.' I laughed wryly. 'If only we could figure out those other attacks we'd be on the pig's back. Solve

241

two mysteries at once, then off for a celebratory garlic chips. Bing-bang, job done, thank you and good*night*.'

'Yeah,' Sláine said hazily. 'That . . . '

'Me and Podsy reckoned most of 'em were just some wild animal. It was awful, but I guess things like that are sort of *normal*, you know?' I laughed again. 'At least it wasn't anything to do with you. God, that'd be too much to take in! What a head-wreck!'

I chuckled some more, then stopped because I noticed that Sláine wasn't laughing along. Something made my throat tighten and my stomach start to wobble. I told them, stop doing that, there's no reason to do that because I'm only talking about wild animals and attacks and Sláine and . . .

And the fact that they all came back to you, Aidan, remember? There was a link that you couldn't make sense of, and other incidents too – freaky ones which couldn't be explained by science or logic – that Podsy didn't know also connected to me but *I* knew. A beautiful angel hovering four flights up. A girl driven mad by whispers inside her head.

And then my world sort of crashed in on itself as Sláine gave a lopsided smile and said, '*Actually* . . . it kind of is.'

Time slowed, not quite to a stop but near enough and time didn't matter anyway because I was dissolving into molecules. I was drifting apart into long strings of nothingness under the gargantuan, unpreventable force of this *thing* I was about to find out but deep down knew that I already knew.

Chills along my spine, dryness in my mouth, pressure mounting behind my eyeballs like a tsunami rushing in to break on land. I knew what was coming but didn't want to

hear the words. I didn't want to admit it to myself. I *couldn't*.
Still the dreaded moment hurtled towards us, it didn't care
how I felt. This was almost worse than discovering the truth
about that bloody demon and the lunatic who'd raised it. This
was like watching a lorry spin out of control, you knew what
was about to happen, you'd already *seen* it, and you wanted
to stop it but the sick feeling in the depths of your stomach
told you there was zero chance of that.

Too late. No escape.

I forced myself to say it: 'What exactly do you mean by
that, Sláine?'

'I think you know what I mean.'

'You . . . you did it,' I whispered. 'You attacked all those kids.'

She nodded. Her expression was impossible to read.

'The ones who'd bullied me. It wasn't animals at all.'

She shook her head.

'It was you.'

Sláine nodded again.

'None of *those* attacks . . . That's what you said, about folks
being taken by the cold. None of *those* were down to you,
meaning maybe others . . . *were*.'

Another nod.

'For Christ's sake can't you speak to me?' I spat. 'Stop nodding
like a bloody toy dog. Use words, like a normal goddamn . . . '

I stopped talking. She placed her hand over mine. It was
freezing, like an ice pack placed against my skin, yet the touch
was oddly comforting. So, I realised, this may not have changed
anything. This terrible revelation, and yet it appeared I still
loved Sláine. I wondered what that said about me. I wondered

if I believed in the soul – and whether or not mine was damned.

I pulled my hand away and fell to the ground, quivering like a newborn calf. I thought I'd throw up if this tension wasn't released soon. Better to know it all now, I thought. Better to know the worst than imagine it.

I said, 'Tell me.'

Sláine said flatly, 'I assaulted those boys and girls who'd bullied you. One at a time, quickly, violently, without remorse then or since. And I did it for you.'

For *me*. Oh Jesus, don't say that. Don't tell me this at all. Say I'm imagining it, I'm hallucinating, we're stuck in a nightmare together but don't worry, we'll wake soon and this will have never happened.

Except it did. And you know it, Aidan. No more squeezing your eyes shut. No more kids' tricks. It's time, as they say, to put away childish things.

I mumbled, 'Go on.'

This time, I swear, the lights at the heart of those underfoot crystals really did flare up, glowing like the three mouths of Cerberus the devil-dog, as Sláine said vehemently, 'Revenge. Pure and simple. Mankind's basest instinct in some ways, yet one of our most sublime pleasures too . . . I did it so you could have revenge.'

'Pleasure?' I said weakly.

'All right, pleasure is too strong. I won't deny it gave me some satisfaction, though, getting payback. But please believe me, I did it with the best intentions.'

'The road to hell,' I recited in a monotone, 'is paved with good intentions.'

Sláine ignored this. Instead she said, 'I knew how far to go. I didn't cross that final line.'

'Tch. *How* did you know?'

'I just did. Nobody died, did they? And nobody will.' She added playfully, 'Al*though* . . . ' and clicked her tongue in a way that annoyed me intensely. How could she be so flippant about this?

I growled, 'Although what?'

'I'd gone through them all, one by one, until there was just one more on my list. Your old sweetheart Caitlin. With her silly name and pretty green eyes. I was leaving her until last. She hurt you the worst, so it was appropriate to finish with her. And I think – yes, I'm almost sure – I intended to kill her. Her death would make the perfect ending. Of course, I didn't. I left before that could happen, and Caitlin escaped.'

I glared at her. 'Man, the way you said that. Just recited it off, like you were reading the ingredients on a soup carton.'

'I nearly *did* kill John Rattigan. I tore him asunder and at that moment, honestly? I didn't care whether he survived or not. I didn't care.'

A warm look came to Sláine's eyes, and I remembered again who she was. I remembered that girl I'd fallen in love with.

'Aidan, don't you get it? That's why I left. I was afraid I couldn't control it any more. Especially with Rattigan, it was almost a taste in my mouth, but the attacks were all getting increasingly violent, I felt more rage, it was becoming uncontrollable . . . I needed to be on my own, because being around *you* made this fury rise in me, again and again.'

'Don't blame me for this.'

'I'm not. I'm trying to explain. You're the source of my power, but I guess everything has a flip side. So you're the source of my rage too. I was afraid to make contact for the last week. I wanted to, so *badly*. It physically hurt me to be away from you. But . . . it was necessary.'

'Yet here you stand.'

'I *had* to come back – to you.'

I shook my head, rose and started stomping about the cave. I'm sure I looked like a Neanderthal but didn't care. Just as, it appeared, Sláine didn't care about these awful things she'd done.

'Don't you feel bad about it at all?' I muttered over my shoulder.

'Of *course* I feel bad,' she said. 'I'm not a monster. But I don't regret doing it, my love. I won't ever regret it. They deserved what happened. They did you a terrible wrong. Don't worry, I made it quick. Nothing sadistic about it. I just – hurt them. Like they hurt you. I mean it might have *been* a wild animal, for all they knew. And if an escaped lion attacked those kids, would you be making moral judgments? You'd say it was awful but there you go, these things happen. Well, this happened. Look, I didn't get a big kick out of doing it – but I'm glad I did. It was *right*, Aidan. Natural justice demanded it, every bit as much as nature demands the lion kills its prey.'

'It wasn't a lion, though. That's the whole point. It was you. The girl who . . . the one I love.'

'Love? Not past tense, then?'

I lied: 'I don't know.'

'Can you accept this? You had the right to know. Can you accept it? And me?'

246

'I said I don't *know*.' Another lie.

Oh, Sláine, oh, sweetheart. My dream, my ghost, my guardian angel and personal demon. What have you done?

What have *we* done?

'How did you know who the bullies were?' I said. 'I don't think I mentioned any names besides Caitlin and Rattigan.'

She shrugged. 'Just did. I'm not sure how, exactly. Maybe I read your mind. And saw your deepest desire. Something you wanted so badly but couldn't admit to yourself.'

I flapped my hands wildly, like that stupid raven waving its wings. 'Whoa, whoa. I didn't want anyone badly *hurt*, Sláine. I might have hated them, but holy shit. Not hospitalised, for God's sake.'

'Didn't you? All right, then. I'll take you at your word. And I'll stop.'

'Yes. Stop, please.'

'You want Caitlin to go unharmed? Definitely, no doubt in your mind.'

'Yes. *Yes*.'

She laughed, as sparkling and beautiful as the first time I heard it. 'To sail on through life, and enjoy the happiness she stole from you? The *life* she almost stole. Do you remember the bridge, how you felt standing there?'

I recalled the few conversations I'd had with Caitlin in recent months, when she'd tried to reach me and I'd blown her off. I suppose she was attempting to make amends. But goddamn it, I thought now, she didn't need to. None of them did. That was all in the past, there was nothing to atone for any more, no revenge had to be taken. I just wanted the whole sorry saga to . . . die.

I said, 'I don't think she is that happy. Caitlin, I think she's wracked with guilt about what she . . . what happened between us. But I don't feel good about that. I don't *want* her unhappy. It doesn't matter to me now. And I don't want her hurt. She can carry on with life, let her off. That's what we should have done with all of them. Just let them off to Jaysus.'

'You're saying "we" now.'

I snapped, 'Just a figure of speech.'

Was I as much to blame as Sláine? I didn't think so. But that didn't stop me feeling awful about what had gone down – and the fact that hearing all this hadn't changed my love for her. I don't think anything could have by this stage. I hated what she'd done, I feared what she was capable of . . . and I loved her just as much and would go on loving her. I guess the heart doesn't get to choose these things.

I laughed bitterly. 'Had you any plans to tell me about this? Like, drop it into conversation at some stage: "By the way, I've been on a rampage of vengeance against a bunch of kids, so, uh, just thought you'd like to know."'

'I'm telling you now.'

'What about the Guards? What might happen to me? They had me down for it, you know. Brought me in the other day and fired a pile of questions at me. I could have been flung in jail.'

'You weren't.'

'I *could* have. I was a good suspect. All these kids turn up cut to bits, kids I'd a reason to hold a grudge against . . . Hell, *I* would have suspected me.'

'No,' Sláine said firmly. 'What evidence did they have linking

248

you to any of it? None, because you hadn't done anything. But you're right, I should have thought of that. It caused a problem for you, and I'm sorry about that.'

'But not about actually doing the deed, right?'

'Afraid not.'

I sighed loudly, feeling beaten and beat. Maybe what she'd said held a splinter of truth. Maybe an evil part of me wanted something awful to befall them.

'Probably some bit of me was glad when those bastards got what was coming,' I confessed. 'I don't know any more. But . . . I do want you to stop. Please.'

I looked at her, imploring. Sláine said gently, 'You don't have to plead. You've said it, so that's how it'll be. I'll do whatever makes you happy.'

'Yeah. Okay. Can we go now? I mean . . . Ugh. I don't even know where we're gonna go. Or what we're supposed to do. But I don't want to stay here any longer, if that's all right.'

'In one minute. Listen, I have to say this: I still have a sense of right and wrong. I need you to know that. But it's . . . changed now. I'm more harsh, I suppose, in my feelings towards others. Less forgiving. I used to be a real softie, always quick to forgive. Now I see things in black and white. Literally, but in the emotional sense too.' She thought for a moment. 'When you die as a person, I guess a lot of that hesitation and ambiguity dies with you. Heh. You might say I take a *colder* view now. But absolutely, I still have a – moral code. I'm not evil, Aidan. I wouldn't hurt just anyone; I *didn't*. Only those who deserved it . . . Well. Got what they deserved.'

'Deserved. And this decided by you.'

Sláine folded her arms in a defensive posture, the crystals glowing brighter, matching the rising passion in her voice. 'Do you disagree with my choices? Is there someone on that list who didn't make your life a misery? Have I made a mistake?'

I didn't answer. She went on, 'I wouldn't harm someone innocent, or decent or kind. Someone who'd never done anything really bad to a person I cared about. I'd never hurt your family, or mine. Anyone, really, your friend Padraig, anyone . . . I'm like Michael Corleone: I only kill my enemies. "Kill" used figuratively, don't worry.'

'Who's Michael Corleone?'

'Never seen *The Godfather*?'

'What's that, some Mafia thing?'

'Doesn't matter. Look, it was just those few. The names on my list.' She smiled. '*Our* list. Be honest.'

I winced. 'Please don't say that. Even jokingly . . . What was with all that other stuff, anyhow? The way you hit some kids in a different way. Clara Kinnane, the Callaghan girl . . . that numpty McGuinness – it was you who torched his car, correct?'

Sláine nodded and shrugged, saying lazily, 'A bit of variety, nothing more than that. To be honest, I'd have been happy just beating them all up. But . . . life after death gets boring sometimes. I wanted to spice it up. And it amused me, I must confess. Driving that girl Clara half-insane, little by little – I'm sorry, that *was* funny.'

'Fully insane, by all accounts.'

'Fully, then. Even funnier.'

Was she pulling my leg? I couldn't tell any more.

'Those kids were the lucky ones,' Sláine added. 'They got

away lightly.'

I thought of gouged-out eyes and amputated limbs, deep wounds to faces and abdomens, brain injury, drooling vegetables being fed by tubes, and felt queasy. I wanted this sickening montage of images to get the hell out of my brain but it wouldn't.

Sláine looked towards the horizon – blue-black in the moonlight, no sign of dawn inching its way towards us. She said bitterly, 'That idiot whose car I burned out . . . tch. He should count his blessings he wasn't tied to the bonnet.'

There went the crystal lights again, pulsing in tune with her anger. I yelped, 'Jesus Christ, are you *serious*? Will you stop saying things like that, *please*.'

'Those bullies didn't suffer,' she said quietly. 'Not like they caused *you* to suffer. It was right they be made to pay. I know it was – so do you. Like I said: it was your deepest desire. You just didn't want to admit that.'

I put my head in my hands, pulled at my hair – I could feel it lifting at the roots but kept pulling. 'Was it? God help me if that's the case.'

Sláine whipped her arms around me and guided us to the cliff edge. I braced myself for transit. She smiled and touched her cold lips to my forehead. Then she mumbled into my hair, my hands, 'God can't help you now, sweetheart. But I can. I'll take care of everything, don't worry.'

It was impossible not to worry. She must have known that. By this stage, I was nothing *but* worry. Then Sláine did something I couldn't even begin to imagine, and the universe shifted and we –

My home, my bedroom. I was lying on the bed, coat zipped up fully, hood over my head, a blanket covering my legs. The room was very cold although I could hear the clicking of a storage heater somewhere. I looked around in surprise.

'How . . . ? This is my house. Is it safe for you to be here?'

'Yes. We're safe for now. Close your eyes. You need to rest.'

'No, I mean what if my parents come in? Or someone hears us.' I automatically lowered my voice.

'Nobody will hear us.'

I whispered, 'What if you're wrong?'

'I'm not. Rest.'

'I need a smoke.'

I fumbled for my tobacco but it wasn't where I usually kept it. It was in Sláine's hands and she was rolling a cigarette at bewildering speed, white fingers a blur of movement. She passed it to me and placed an ashtray on the floor nearby.

I rolled onto my side, lit the fag and spoke at a normal volume – guess I'd have to trust that her voodoo was working and we couldn't be heard by anyone else. 'Since when have you been able to roll cigarettes?'

'You'd be amazed what I'm capable of, pumpkin.'

I shuddered and didn't try to hide it. 'I don't think I would.'

I took a long drag – it hit like a punch of pure relaxation, if that makes sense, to my throat. 'Man. That's good.'

Sláine tutted. 'You shouldn't smoke. Those things will kill you.'

I smiled wryly. 'You're never more alive than when you're

on the edge of death, that's my motto.' It was a joke but, I was realising, that line sounded a note of truth too.

Silence hung between us. I broke it by saying, 'Hey. This is the first time you've been in my room.'

'First time *you* were aware of.'

'God, what a joke. Something like that is supposed to be romantic . . . '

'It *is* romantic. Come on. We're together, aren't we? Sláine and Aidan, the two of us together. We can take on the world, can't we?'

She didn't sound that sure of it herself and I didn't respond. Further silence, as heavy and impenetrable as a shroud. Sláine wanted to say more, I could tell – I could always tell. In some ways she was a deeper mystery now than during those insane, is-this-really-happening early days. But I still knew when she had something on her mind and was steeling herself to voice it.

Finally she said, 'Snap decision.'

Nothing more was added. I said, 'Are you going to explain what that means, or will I guess?'

'That's why I attacked the first one. A snap decision.'

'Chris Harrington.'

'Yes. Him. I went for a wander that night and passed Mr Harrington, stumbling along the river walk. Some gut instinct told me he was one of them, that he'd hurt you . . . His handsome face. I think that's what pushed me over the edge. He had this arrogant sneer. The kind of self-regarding asshole who treats girls badly because he knows he can. And I thought, fuck you, Chris Harrington. This is where all that ends.'

I shuddered again. 'So you'd torn Harrington to bits. But

there was a gap then, a few weeks.'

'After that first attack,' Sláine said, 'I got tired, if you can believe it. Not immediately, but when you left on the Monday, I suddenly felt exhausted. I needed to rest. Not sleep – I never sleep – but lie down, rest.'

'I remember that. I didn't believe you. Thought you were blowing me off or something, ha.'

'It was true. I was *wrecked*. Sort of zonked out for a few days. Absolutely drained of energy.' She thought. 'I guess it takes it out of you. Tearing another body apart. There's actually a lot of resistance to flesh and bone, you know. It's not like in movies where everything happens easily. You really have to *work* at—'

'Sláine, stop! For God's sake will you stop right there. I don't want to know the details. Bad enough what I *do* know.'

She smiled, embarrassed. 'Sorry. Anyway, next time I recovered much more quickly. Now I'm fairly confident I could do it whenever I wanted and it wouldn't take anything out of me.'

I laughed, a faintly hysterical edge to it. 'Well, feck it. That's good to know, isn't it?'

'Not really.'

I stubbed out my smoke, got up and walked to the shelf by the window. I couldn't look at Sláine right then. Instead I gazed over the trinkets arrayed there: bits and pieces I'd accumulated over the years. Junk mostly, but each held some enduring attraction for me, spoke to my sentimental side. A lighter shaped like a Chinese warrior. An ashtray with the London Underground logo. Two metallic stones my sister brought me as a gift from somewhere. A resin gargoyle sitting cross-legged, tongue out, a malevolent raspberry at the world.

Was this a life, I wondered? A collection of knick-knacks, their provenance long-forgotten and their meaning non-existent, and little more than that. But were they meaningless? They had some meaning to me. And I guess I had meaning to others, if not always to myself. Didn't I?

Finally I said, 'So the Harrington thing was spur of the moment. Why the others?'

Sláine said, 'I started thinking about everyone else who'd wronged you and it hit me: why should they get away with it, when Harrington didn't?'

I rubbed my eyes, tiredness making them scratchy, uncomfortable in their sockets. I thought I heard someone approaching and stiffened, then remembered it was the middle of the night and it was only the house shifting. Forty years old, and this piece of crap was still settling into its foundations.

'The supernatural vigilante,' I said. 'Justice from beyond the grave. I should sell this stuff to Hollywood . . . You did all this just with your hands, or your mind? What I mean is, you don't do this bloody – *freezing* thing? Like . . . like he does.'

'No. A normal attack, for a want of a better word. I don't even know if I *can* freeze someone. I don't want to. That's a terrible death. It kills the soul as well as the body. I don't go that far. Didn't. Past tense. Won't be going anywhere from now on, scout's honour.'

'But you didn't lose your soul? When you froze to death.'

'I don't think so. Still *feels* like I've got a soul.'

I turned to Sláine, reached for her hands and stared deep into her eyes. 'You *really* don't feel guilty about it? Be honest.

255

I need to know the truth, for good and all.'

She shook her head.

'Okay,' I said. 'Oh, shit. Sláine, I think I'm going to hell.'

She smiled.

'Because I think I can forgive you. I think I *have*.'

She smiled more broadly.

'I think I've already put this nightmare behind me. In my head, and my heart. I think . . . '

Her by-now enormous smile told me she knew what I was trying to say, but I said it anyway.

'I think I still love you and am willing to overlook basically anything you might have done. I know you're a good person, and why you did it. It was wrong, I'll never stop thinking that, but . . . it's done now. We can't undo the past. All we can do is move on. But *no* more attacks, no more revenge. Okay? No more.'

She kissed me. Frozen delight sending messages of thrill and desire from my lips to my heart to every tip of every limb.

We broke the kiss. I smiled back and continued to hold Sláine's hands. Man, I *was* going to hell. And I didn't really care.

SNOWBLIND

Dawn was creeping over the horizon, which told me it was coming on for half-eight and we'd talked through the night. I must have dozed off once or twice, though I didn't specifically recall doing it. I was crashed out in my lumpy old armchair by the door, surfacing groggily into wakefulness. Fragments of dreams lingered in my mind like the crumbling ruins of an ancient civilisation. I must have fallen asleep, at least for a short while. And Sláine, well . . . as I knew, she never slept. She had watched over me instead, steadfast and immovable, my eternal guardian of the night.

Now I did hear people shuffling around outside. My parents, getting up and making brekkie for the smallies. A step, right outside my door. I tensed and sat bolt upright in the chair. I glanced at Sláine, then back at the door. The handle turned and it opened and my mother stepped in before I could stop her.

I spluttered, 'Mam. Uh, listen. Uh, this is . . . this is . . . Okay, let's start again. D'you remember that girl . . . ?'

She regarded me with a cool look you might expect to see on a psychiatrist as they debated whether or not to have you committed for tragic and irreversible softening of the brain.

257

'Are you all right, love?'

I looked behind me. Sláine was gone. Of course she was, *dumbkopf*. As if this powerful, immortal being was going to get caught unawares by your mam stumbling in to offer you a cup of tea. I laughed, letting the tension out. 'Sorry. Just woke up, I'm still a bit . . . you know.' I twirled my finger around my temple. 'What's happening?'

Mam took in my location, the deep bags under my eyes, the fact that I was still wearing an outdoor coat and my boots were fully laced up.

She said wearily, 'Sleeping, right. I can see that . . . Aidan, do you want to –?'

She stopped herself. I knew what she was going to ask: did I need to talk about anything? Probably, yeah, I did – but I wasn't going to. Instead I said cheerily, 'Do I want a cup of tea? *Love* one. I'll see you downstairs in five minutes, all right?'

My mother nodded slowly and backed out the door. I sighed and turned to my chest of drawers. I didn't know when I'd last changed these clothes – they were practically standing up by themselves at this stage. I jumped in surprise at Sláine standing there, leaning against the furniture, a sardonic smile on her beautiful face.

'My heart,' I said. 'Don't . . . How do you do that, anyway? That vanishing trick.'

'I keep telling you, it's all magic.'

'Actually, don't explain it, I don't want to know. That'd spoil the trick.' I moved to the drawers and stopped. 'Um . . . could you, like . . . ?'

She laughed. 'You're embarrassed! At changing in front of me. Oh my God, I can't believe you're embarrassed.'

'Nuh-uh. Not embarrassed at all. I just, uh. Just, uh, I'm used to some . . . like, being on my own when I'm . . . you know. Getting dressed.'

'Course, I haven't really seen you naked yet. Nor you me. Kind of weird, isn't it?'

I rummaged around for clean underwear and socks, a change of T-shirt. The jeans were fine – they'd do for another few days, and I especially liked this pair: I felt comfortable in them, felt secure, as if I could take on the whole goddamn world in these jeans. I said absentmindedly, 'Well, ours is a pretty weird relationship, my dear.'

'It certainly is that . . . What about the lovely Caitlin? Did she see you naked? Did she gaze adoringly on the Flood crown jewels?' Sláine giggled, putting a hand to her mouth. I laughed too, mostly out of surprise at this elegant, self-possessed girl coming out with silly naughtiness like that.

'Caitlin? Yeah, I wish.'

'Do you really wish?'

I stood and looked at her, clothes bunched in one fist. 'Actually, no. It doesn't bother me now. Nothing bothers me now. Except for . . . heh.' I smiled ruefully. 'Except for that one thing we talked about? That guy, you know yer man who controls a demon and wants to kill everyone and eat their souls and all that stuff? That's bothering me a teensy bit, I must admit.'

Sláine said, 'Mm-hm. About that. It's all going to be okay.'

'And why is it going to be okay, oh she who knows all?'

'Because, Aidan my lad, I told you before – I won't let anything bad happen to you.' She looked off. 'I *won't*. I swear it.'

***

She left me with some instructions. I was to meet her on Sunday night, at Shook Woods, in our lodge, at nine o'clock; she needed time to think. Until then I should keep my head down. Sláine and me would both mull it all over, formulate some plan of attack when we got together again, then strike hard against the enemy that night, when he – hopefully – wouldn't be expecting it. She had a strong hunch that we couldn't leave it too long after deciding our course, because *he* might somehow pick up on it, be forewarned. On the other hand, we couldn't do anything too soon because, frankly, we didn't yet know what the hell to do. We needed the time to work it out but time was short, time was ticking down. It was a hellish conundrum, and meeting at nine tomorrow was a flawed compromise but the best solution we had.

Part of me was unsure about all this. What if our villain struck in the meantime, struck at her, or worse – I'm ashamed to say this – at me? What if another of those zombie-walker things tried to turn me into a human ice lolly again? I assumed they couldn't enter my home and wouldn't show themselves in the daytime, but still I was on edge about it. Scared. Sláine could handle herself. I was a wimp with skinny arms and the physical courage of a nervous rabbit.

But I trusted her, unreservedly, instinctively, completely. Whatever she reckoned was best, I'd go along with that. Even though I got the impression that she was kind of winging it herself, that she wasn't the all-knowing super-being I wanted her to be, and was troubled by her own doubts and confusion. Didn't matter: I trusted her. Perhaps my trust, like her love, could empower Sláine to know what to do when the time came. I prayed that this was so.

It was now Saturday morning, so that gave me less than two days to prepare, I guess. To wait. To worry, or try not to worry. To put my affairs in order, should the worst come to the worst. Should I not make it past tomorrow night.

Sláine vanished in a metaphorical puff of smoke and I forgot about putting my affairs in order and got back to worrying. I knew so little about what was happening that I wasn't even able to think, 'This could all go horribly wrong.' Because I didn't know what 'this' was. Didn't know the name of our enemy, where he lived, anything about him really, and neither did Sláine. We didn't know the nature of this – shudder – demon he'd raised, what it could do, what *he* could do now he controlled it. Didn't know what we hoped to achieve, or how we aimed to achieve it. The pair of us were in the dark. But I could sense *him* out there, sense them – this nameless, faceless menace to the entire planet.

Just before leaving my bedroom Sláine had hugged me tightly, wrapping me in that cold embrace, saying, 'Listen. My powers are growing stronger – you've seen that. And, Aidan, it's you. You're enabling them, and me. Maybe it's my love for you, maybe it's coincidental. But whenever I think of you, or let my heart fill with good intentions towards you . . . I feel as if I can do anything. Defeat anyone. I feel I could change whole worlds if you asked me to.'

I don't know if this was true, or she had just said it to give me courage. Whichever, it worked. And it made me feel pretty goddamn good about myself.

Later that day I met Podsy. I wanted to leave instructions of my own with my best friend: what to do in the event of – well. That aforementioned worst coming to the worst. I said nothing over the phone, just asked if he was about for a bit of grub.

I walked through town in late afternoon, the sun thinking about setting, my nerves jangling, head swirling with emotions, a swarm of angry wasps. I checked my phone and saw I was in plenty of time, and looked up and half of John Rattigan's family was standing in front of me, blocking the pavement.

Crap.

I knew most by sight. They all looked the same anyway: cretinous expressions, Cro-Magnon faces, a brutal kind of simmer in how they held those hefty bodies. This was, I guessed, two of Rattigan's brothers, his father, an uncle and his mam – hard to know for sure, one generation didn't look much older than the next. I swallowed hard and kept walking. Don't show fear. You've every right to be here. Just ignore them. I recited these mantras and tried to convince myself they weren't here for me, that this was a coincidence.

Of course, it wasn't. Rattigan senior thumped me on the chest when I came within striking distance. He rasped, 'Hold on there. Where d'you think you're going?'

'To meet my friend,' I muttered. 'Let me pass, please.'

They didn't move. Mama Rattigan hollered to one of the brothers, 'Here, Martin, is this the fella? Is this him?'

Martin nodded and glared at me, looking fit to tear my head off and drink blood from the spurting neck-hole. I noticed a van idling across the street, yet another Rattigan brooding behind the wheel. I ignored that and channelled a smidgeon of bravery from somewhere, saying, 'Is this him what? What's the problem here?'

She didn't appear to be listening. Why would I expect a fair hearing from this band of inbred hooligans? Mrs Rattigan bellowed, 'That's the boy, is it? The one who done it.'

Another nod from Martin. The dad moved towards me, the brothers in step just behind. To my amazement, I didn't budge, didn't retreat. I *wanted* to – I've never wanted so badly to skedaddle as fast as my legs could spin – but I couldn't. Something was stopping me.

And now this something was putting words in my mouth. I barely recognised my own voice as I said, quietly but firmly, 'Back off. I didn't do anything and I'm not going anywhere with you.'

Rattigan *père* seemed dumbfounded. Rattigan *mère* screeched, 'Go *on*, Martin, what're you waiting for!?'

A different guy reached for my jacket, grunting, 'C'mere, ya little bastard. You'll answer for what you done to John.'

To my continued astonishment, I still didn't flee. I slapped his hands away and spat, 'Get your ignorant paws off me, you ape. And *back off*. I told you, I didn't touch your precious John.'

By this stage even Queen Rat was gaping in disbelief. The something inside moved my right foot forward a step, then my left, then right again. Was it adrenaline? Fear? The realisation that humanity was in mortal peril and I didn't have time for these bullshit people and their bullshit antics? I don't know. I just did what I did.

I got right up in the face of Pops Rattigan, saying, 'I wanted to, yeah. I wanted to *kill* him for what he did to me. Maybe I should have – he'd've been no loss. But I told you, I had nothing to do with your son being attacked.'

And then, and then . . . oh my God. I pushed him back, four feet, his soles sliding along the frosty pavement. My voice rising, whether through courage or panic, I yelled at the lot of them, 'Now back *off*, motherfuckers! The Guards have been told about you. If you come within fifty yards of me again they'll sling your asses in jail until Easter. It's called a restraining order, dickheads.' I was making it up on the fly, extemporising, pulling this stuff out of God knows where. I said tightly, 'Now *move*. Out of. My way.'

That something lifted the corners of my mouth and I smiled, and it lifted my hand and I patted Rattigan's dad on the cheek. 'Please.'

And . . . they did. They shuffled off, confused, unhappy, scratching their heads literally and figuratively. A gang of cavemen wondering why this evolution thing seemed to be passing them by. I continued towards the cafe, actually shaking – seventy per cent adrenaline and thirty per cent relief. Or maybe the other way around.

Fiver and Dimes, again. The muddled decor looked even more ridiculous in daylight, but the booths were still comfortable and the food was decent. For the first time since I could remember, I was ravenous. I couldn't wait for Podsy so, rude as it was, went ahead and ordered a coleslaw burger and wedges with blue cheese sauce. Not too healthy – more or less a coronary on a plate – but it tasted *great*, particularly after that little dance with the Rattigan mob. Anyway, might not be around much longer to enjoy nice food, I reminded myself. None of us might.

I was two-thirds through my meal when he got there, flopping onto the seat opposite. His shirt was askew, coat half-hanging off one shoulder. Podsy looked as dishevelled and nerdish as ever, which made me so happy I wanted to lean across and give him a big kiss, smack on the lips.

Instead I gestured to the table and, impersonating this Arab camel driver I saw in some movie, said, 'Sit, my friend, sit. You have travelled far and must be in need of sustenance.'

He misunderstood the reference. 'Been reading those fantasy novels again, yeah? They're good, all right.'

Reading fantasy? More like living inside one, Podsy.

'You okay?' I asked.

'Yeah, not too bad. Why'd you want to meet up again? I'd be seeing you at school anyway.'

The middle-aged waitress bustled in with a menu for Podsy. She gave a dirty look at his dishevelled state, a bitter, pursed-mouth expression on her bitter, pursed-mouth face. Podsy amused himself, and me, by taking ages to decide. When the waitress moved off he made a face at her retreating back.

I said, 'Never mind her. Listen, I've something important to tell you. *Really* important. Your life could depend on it.'

'Okaaaay . . . Okay. Sounds interesting. Terrifying, but interesting. Go on.'

'First, I wanna apologise. To you.'

'Right? This sounds even better.'

He settled back in his seat, hands linked over his skinny belly.

'I haven't been the friend I should have been, Podsy,' I said. 'You were always there for me, really decent. I don't mean just about the bullying and all that – other times too. You've always

265

been, just, a really good pal. Put up with my shit and made an effort with me. I know I'm a cranky git sometimes – it can't be easy listening to my moaning.'

He said playfully, 'Only sometimes?'

I smiled. 'Only sometimes. Anyway. Then there *was* the bullying, and you were like – man, you were a rock. I mean that. I don't know what I'd've done without you. Seriously.'

Podsy flapped a hand. 'Nah. I did nothing. Although in fairness, there wasn't much I *could* do.'

'That's not true. You were there, you were my friend, and that was enough. Didn't need to do any more. You showed real balls, Podsy. Could have gone along with the herd and kept your head down, or even joined in. But you didn't. You stayed true to yourself, and to our friendship. I'll always appreciate that. Always remember it.'

'Meh. I guess so.'

'No guessing needed, boy. I know you got hassled because of me. I know it – don't deny it.'

'Aidan, look at me. I'm a geek. Of below-average size, with a wonky mouth and glasses since I was four. I don't need your help in getting picked on, know what I mean?'

'Well then we're two geeks. And I'm bloody happy to be one. I'm proud to be the same as you.'

The lady returned with his food and Podsy dived into it like a starving man at a king's banquet. After a few minutes he wiped his mouth with a napkin and gasped, '*Oh* yeah. Needed that.'

'Lunch is on me.'

'Wow. Generosity *and* emotional honesty. What's got into you today?'

'Let's just say . . . I recently had a moment of revelation.'

'Well, thanks. And there's no need to apologise for anything. If you insist on doing it, I will politely accept. That's only good manners. But it's not needed. You weren't a bad friend. You were just – normal, you know? Typical teenager. Moody, unpredictable, sometimes annoying, a lot of the time really cool to be around. Don't apologise, man, it makes me feel I owe you something.'

'You don't owe me squat. I owe *you*.'

Podsy drained his Coke and said, 'All right, all right. You owe me, fine . . . You know, I really *would* have liked to've been able to get some payback on the bastards. The bullies – for giving you all that grief. And me – they gave me grief too. It was never gonna happen. I mean I'm small and feeble and can't fight to save my life. But still. A little revenge would have been nice.'

I winced, the memory of Sláine's confession rising in the back of my mind like a shadow taking physical form. 'Ugh . . . yeah,' I mumbled. 'Careful what you wish for.'

'Guess someone else did it for us, huh?'

I hummed non-committally.

'Anyway,' he went on, 'seems you're in the clear for it all now.'

'Yeah?' I said brightly. 'This's Uncle Tim talking, I assume?'

'Yep. Told my old folks off the record that they don't have any actual evidence against you – apparently, Parkinson was hoping to squeeze out a confession the other day. That didn't work, so . . . They'll likely close the investigation if there are no more attacks, which there don't seem to be. Probably keep an eye on you, though.' He grinned mischievously. 'Officially, it'll be recorded as "unexplained and unsolved".'

'That's something, I guess.'

'It *was* kind of weird, though, wasn't it? All your – our – enemies taken down like that. I know it was just coincidence or whatever, obviously you didn't assault anyone. Still, though. Feckin' *weird*.'

Did he know? Or suspect? Neither was possible – was it?

Podsy went on, 'Anyway, don't mind that. What about all this stuff you're coming out with today? Something's going on. You're not exactly the *Dr Phil*, display-all-your-emotions-to-the-world type. So – what is it?'

I rolled my shoulders. 'I can't really tell you. Yet. If ever.'

'Why did I know you were going to say that?' He squinted at me. 'You're not dying of cancer, are you?'

'No.'

'Dying of some other disease.'

'No.'

'Dying of –'

'I'm not *dying*, Podsy, full stop.' I gently banged a fist off my forehead and swallowed heavily. 'At least . . . not yet.' I pushed an envelope across the table. 'Here. Keep that somewhere safe. Like, totally fail-safe. Has your dad got a lockbox or anything? No, not there, he might see it. But somewhere.'

'I know the very place. Don't worry, nobody'll find it. Whatever it is. Um . . . Sorry, what is this?'

'It's a letter. From me to you. You're not to open it – I mean *never* – unless I don't contact you by Monday morning. Say, eleven in the morning. If you hear from me . . . '

'By phone call or text? Or in person?'

'Any. Either. Any kind of communication. If you hear from

268

me, it'll be me telling you to burn that letter. If you don't, then something bad might have happened and . . . '

'Then I read it. Got you.' Podsy put the envelope in a pocket of his bag, zipping it shut. 'Do I get any hints about what's in this? Or why, in the name of Muhammad, something bad *might* happen to you? Aidan, seriously, what's going on?'

'I can't . . . It's better you don't know yet. With any luck you'll never find out. That'd mean everything had worked out okay and there'd be no need for you to know. Oh, how I hope that's the case. We can have this stupid secret between us as a little joke. Hell, I'll tell you the whole story. By that stage it won't matter.'

He nodded. 'And in the event that things *don't* work out okay . . . ?'

'Something terrible is on the way, Podsy. It's here already, and it's going to get worse. Unless we – *I*, unless I can stop it.'

'Well, can you? Stop it?'

'I don't know.'

'Is there any way I can "be of assistance", as they say?'

'No. I don't think so. Don't worry, I have . . . I'm not totally on my own in this.'

Podsy sat back and exhaled heavily. 'Whew. Uh . . . yeah. I don't really know what to say right now. Which isn't like me at all.'

'That letter will explain everything. I don't know how much help it'll be to you guys in trying to stop this . . . danger. Maybe none. Maybe lots. At least you'll know what you're up against.'

I threw money onto the table and stood. Podsy shucked on his coat and stood too. 'So that's it? All you can tell me.'

269

'That's it. Sorry.'

'Okay, then.' He shrugged as we moved to the door, a stoical lift of his narrow shoulders, and I knew he'd do right – I knew I could rely on Podsy, trust him like I'd always done. A true friend, a real friend, to the last. How fortunate I was to have known such friendship in my short life.

For the first time ever I grabbed Podsy and squeezed him in the biggest bear hug my arms could muster. He gasped in surprise. I muttered into his ear, 'I really bloody hope I see you again so you can embarrass me by reminding me of this. Take care of yourself, Podsy.'

Then I was out the door and gone.

Hey Podsy –

*If you're reading this, I'm already dead. Well,
probably. Almost certainly. Sorry I'm so vague. The fact
is, I'm not sure exactly what's going to happen. All I
know is where I'm going: Shook Woods.*

*On Sunday night I go to the forest. To meet a dead
girl. I know, it sounds ridiculous. It looks ridiculous to
me, typing it out. The words don't seem to make sense,
but it's all true, I swear. I can see you crinkling your
nose and laughing in disbelief at this point. You think
I'm taking the mickey, that this is all a joke. It's not.
How I wish it was.*

*I'm not mad and not on drugs. You have to believe
me – this is real.*

*Podsy, you were right: Shook Woods is haunted.
Remember you said that? Said there was something
spooky and creepy about the place, like you wouldn't
know what could happen in there. Well, you were right.
The whole town is kind of strange anyway, but there's
something unearthly about the forest. Weird things
go on among those dark trees in the dead of night.
Sometimes when I'm there I feel like I'm in a dream.
No, more of a waking dream. Because you know you're
not asleep but you feel like you're still dreaming.*

*Hey it's just occurred to me, that word 'spooky': I
wonder, is it a corruption of the Irish word for ghost,
púca? They sound the same, don't they?*

Sorry, I'm rambling. Anyway, here's the facts: you

271

*know Sláine McAuley, the girl who killed herself last
November? She didn't kill herself. And she's not dead.*

*I mean she is dead, but she came back to life. Don't
ask me to explain it – I can't. I just know what Sláine
told me. She was killed by a demon, some evil presence,
which is being controlled by a guy who learned how to
do this from another guy who died during the Famine.
I know, it's getting even more absurd. Bear with me,
please.*

*The second man, as in the first man – Famine
dude – his name was William John McAuley. He was
Sláine's ancestor: her great-great-whatever grandfather.
He tried to raise a demon to do his bidding; he failed.
The lack of food had made him too weak. But, but,
but . . . Someone else succeeded. A man, we don't know
his name, found writings that'd been left by McAuley,
explaining how to conjure up this thing, this demon.
How to control it. It's made of the elements or some
shit. I don't really understand it. Some Celtic demigod,
is my best guess: part of the physical world itself, the
weather and temperature, but a separate entity too.*

*That's what's been killing those people, the cold
deaths, the hypothermia. It's not this cold snap, it's him.
Them. This asshole, the human half of the partnership,
gets power from other people's deaths. He sort of eats
their souls or something, and it makes him immortal.
He thinks it does, anyway. The guy is obviously
deranged.*

Sláine doesn't know his name, but he lives locally.

A mortal man, you get it? Someone you might have seen around town. Actually it's just occurred to me that it's probably dangerous for you to know this stuff. But someone has to, and I trust you. I know you'll do the right thing, and you'll know what the right thing is. You're smart, you'll figure something out. But sorry anyway.

This letter isn't making a lot of sense. Okay, the demon: Sláine and me are going to Shook on Sunday night to try and figure out a way to kill it, and the man controlling it. We're gonna bang heads together, then strike out into the night. Sounds kind of cool when I put it like that, but I have to admit, I'm bloody terrified. I really hope to Jesus that Sláine comes up with a plan.

The demon, or this man I guess is the brains of the operation, brought Sláine back to life. For what reason, we don't know. It didn't just kill her, like with the others. She was brought back, changed, actually improved in lots of ways. She's quite a girl. Powerful. Beautiful.

Podsy, I'm in love with her.

Again, I imagine you laughing, but not from disbelief. This time it's the opposite. You're thinking, Oh yeah, typical Aidan Flood – finally meets the girl of his dreams and it turns out she's something from a nightmare. But it's not like that. Sláine is amazing, in every way. She's so cool. (Ha ha, little private joke there.) Really funny, warm-hearted, very affectionate . . . not without her flaws, I must add, like

273

anyone. And so beautiful. I mean breathtaking, this brilliant-white, almost overwhelming, like breaking dawn on an Arctic ice shelf. I sometimes feel I could go snowblind just looking at her.

Sláine's in love with me too, by the way – she's told me. So it's not some disastrous one-way infatuation, like with the other one.

We've been sort of seeing each other since just after her body was found. That's where I've been going all those times. Sláine contacted me, she wrote a message in ice on my window. Man, I'll never forget that moment, when it all started, this crazy dream that's not a dream. Then I went to the forest and met her and we started hanging out together. It sounds so weird when I say it that simply, but that's how it was. We found some connection across the divide between life and death. We found each other. Now we might be about to lose each other again.

I don't know what's going to happen. In the long term, I mean, assuming everything goes well and we can defeat this thing. Do we have a future, Sláine and me? Sometimes I think, how could we? Like, can you imagine introducing her to the parents: 'Guys, this is Sláine, she's actually dead so there's no need to set a place at the table, and you might be waiting a while for any grandchildren.'

Then other times I think, yes, definitely, we have a future. I wonder if I only think that because I can't imagine life without her, though.

274

But don't mind that. This is what you need to know: our villain plans to go on with his killing. Forever, as far as I can tell. He wants to live forever. If me and Sláine don't bring him down, you guys will have to. I mean you, your parents, the town, the whole human race. He's coming for all of you, and won't stop.

I don't know what you can do about it. Maybe pray, maybe nuke the forest. That's where his power is centred, I think. I also have a suspicion that the cold snap is related to this demon thing. So if you can heat up the weather, maybe you can destroy it.

And how are we supposed to do that, Aidan? That's what you're asking. I don't know – again. Giant hairdryers, point them at the forest and turn the setting up to max – I don't know.

I wish you well, Podsy. Everyone. I hope if Sláine and me don't make it, you all will. Say goodbye to my parents and the smallies for me, will you? I'm not going to do that myself. I'm hoping there'll be no need.

Anyway, that's about it. I can't think of anything more to write. Good luck, man. Hope to see you soon.

Your friend always,

Aidan

WRAP THE NIGHT
AROUND ME

I fell asleep sometime Saturday night. And since I'd basically been awake since Friday morning, and the preceding months of long days and late nights were finally catching up on me until I was running on empty . . . I slept right through to late the next day. It was past six on Sunday when I surfaced, fuzzy-headed, more than groggy, feeling ill, hungover.

I'd slept for over twenty hours – and dreamed.

A slippery, woozy phantasmagoria of pleasant reverie and fearful nightmare. Violently plummeting down a wormhole of images and sounds, the sense of a sense of something. Vertigo, spinning circles, hypnotic, nausea, ecstasy.

I dreamed for hours and in dreamtime it felt like aeons. Dreamed I saw animals made of strips of bark and wood, running through the forest: deer, horses, wolves. Living sculptures, rearing their heads in anguish or howling at their mother the moon. They could see me despite having no eyes. They growled at me to keep away, but I didn't feel scared. It seemed more of a warning than a threat.

I dreamed I met Tommy Fox and he was dead, though not like the others: Tommy pointed to the back of his head, where a gaping hole let the light through. He smiled ruefully and said, 'See where love can get you, Flood? *Booooom*. Night-night . . . ' In the dream I felt bad for him. I knew it hadn't happened in reality but the empathy was real. I dreamed myself touching his arm and offering words of consolation. He smiled, his mouth a dead-black universe collapsing to nothingness, and said, 'I knew you were all right, Flood. Look after yourself.'

I dreamed *I* was dead. No, not dead – I'd ceased to exist at all. I said to myself, 'You're thinking and dreaming, therefore you are. Like the man says. So how could you not exist if you're aware of the fact?' Then I replied to myself, 'Ah – but what if these are someone else's thoughts I think I'm thinking? Answer *that*, smart guy.' Before I could reply again, I realised I wasn't smart at all, I was Clara Kinnane who was always kind of dumb at school and now wasn't only dumb but insane too. This thought made me giddy, like a hyperactive child.

I dreamed of *him*. A man, naked for some reason but it was Arctic outside, colder than deep space, absolute cold, that temperature which it's theoretically impossible to reach. Yet he had reached it, he was there now. And so was I.

I dreamed of *her*. Sláine and me had become the Paul Éluard poem I'd quoted weeks before: she was standing on my eyelids, literally, her hair was in mine and she was being absorbed into my shadow like a stone against the sky. Her eyes were always open and she wouldn't let me sleep and then she was dreaming herself and those dreams made the suns evaporate and made me cry and laugh and speak when I had nothing to say. That was a nice dream.

I dreamed that Sláine was outside my window, spectral, floating, like a vampire child in this old horror movie I stumbled across as a kid. She glowed and grew to the size of a galaxy but remained just a girl, hovering at my window. She smiled mischievously and I pressed my fingertips to the icy glass and she tilted her head and bit down on her lip. She began humming a tune, 'Dum-dum-dum-DUMMM,' three notes up and one down, simple, catchy, a real earworm. And I frowned because I knew that melody from somewhere and said to her, 'Where'd you hear that?' and Sláine said lazily, 'Oh, I don't know . . . it's just been playing in my head for a few days . . . '

And then I woke and opened my eyes and whispered to the darkness, 'Fuck me. James Bond.'

I knew who was behind it now.

Sioda Kinvara. The mystery man. Our very own Double-O Seven. Mr Fancy Cars and Leather-bound Library. How stupid I'd been.

Now that I'd worked out his identity, this madman who was playing with demonic fire and might yet incinerate us all, everything made sense. Every clue slotted neatly into place. And the musical key that unpicked all the locks: Sláine humming the same tune Kinvara had as a phone ringtone *and* played on his piano.

I mentally ran through the evidence. Kinvara had rocked into town only a few months back, from some uncertain place of origin. He was independently wealthy: big house, classic car collection, didn't appear to need a job, even gave my dad a hefty bonus for some straightforward work. Which meant he had time and means to pursue any wacked-out interests he wanted.

More pieces fell into place, memories crashing into my mind, facts, proofs. Kinvara was charming, intelligent and confident. A self-confessed bibliophile. He had a generously stocked library at home and was often in the public one, checking out strange old tomes. Believed there was 'actual power' in words and books. Could read Latin: what was it he'd said? 'Good for understanding ancient texts' – something like that.

He seemed to keep finding me in different places: outside the library, at the antiques shop . . . inveigling my father into coming to work for him before then. Following me. Stalking me.

And the final proof: Kinvara invited me to his house, apparently to check out his collection of books and maybe borrow something. What? I'd have been lucky to make it out with my privates intact and my brains where they're supposed to be. But no, he wasn't some sexual deviant: it was worse than that.

Kinvara had even laid out a clue for me, presumably figuring I'd be too thick to get it. Look up the origins of the word 'bravo', he'd said. It translated as 'wicked outsider'. Boom, boom, joke's on me.

My first instinct, of course – the sensible thing to do – was tell Sláine. But there lay the rub: I couldn't contact her. Sláine did the telekinetic, mind-to-mind communications thing, not me. I made a half-hearted attempt at 'reaching' her mentally, knowing beforehand it'd fail. Then I got suited and booted, snuck out of the house and trudged to Shook Woods and the lodge. Yes, it was risky, but this new information was too important: this could be our break, our shot at bringing him down.

Him. No need for that impersonal pronoun any more. We'd moved on to actual names now.

I reached the lodge – all clear, but no Sláine. She'd said nine, so I guessed she intended to keep to that. Still, I moaned, 'Where *are* you? Why can't you just be here, waiting around, ready and willing to take command?'

What now? I debated my situation as I hauled ass back towards town, stumbling through the darkness, my boots making the shallowest of impressions on hard-packed snow. Should I go to Kinvara's house myself, or wait for backup from Sláine? The two competing arguments pushed and pulled: urgency versus caution, risk-taking versus good sense.

Eventually I reached the town limits and stopped. I could go left towards my house or right in the direction of Belladonna Way. Time check: half-seven. Time enough to check out Kinvara's gaff and make it back to the lodge by nine. I shut my eyes and willed my feet to make the decision for me, take the pressure off poor doubting Aidan. They went right. Bastards.

I summoned up every last ounce of courage as the yards passed underfoot and Kinvara's house loomed ever nearer. Just walk by, I told myself. Start by scoping the place out. And if it seems empty . . .

I was still uncertain if I genuinely had the balls to break in. We'd find out soon enough.

Lighting a cigarette with shaking hands. Checking the time again. Nodding to a middle-aged couple I passed on the street. They might have been the parents of one of those kids Sláine attacked as they eyed me warily enough and scurried off quickly, but I didn't have time to explain that it wasn't my fault. I had to keep going.

What am I doing? You're doing what needs to be done, so shut your yaphole and quit whining.

Do your own James Bond act, I thought. 'Aidan Flood, international super-spy! He may not have the car, money or movie-star good looks, but he's ice-cold under pressure.' All this junk tumbling through my mind to keep it preoccupied and keep my courage up. I tried to remember stuff from movies or TV, about cops and spies and SWAT teams, all those tricks of the trade. Stick to the shadows. Check your exits. Always have an escape plan. Be prepared. Stay frosty. No one here gets out alive . . .

Ugh. Where had *that* come from? That wasn't even a line of dialogue – it was the title of some music autobiography . . .

COLDSTAR.

I hadn't noticed the nameplate on Kinvara's front wall the last time I was here. Maybe he'd only put it up since. Anyway, there it was, granite, a classical-style font: COLDSTAR. Stupid name for a house, but it made sense for this demented asshole. And it was another mark in the book of evidence against him.

I'd made it this far. Might as well keep going, Aidan. No guts, no glory. He who dares. Only the brave. Blah blah blah.

No lights on at the front of the house – which didn't mean it was empty. I decided to peek around the back, try and discover if Kinvara was at home. I took a look around, saw the street was deserted, and was about to dash over the lawn towards the side of the house when I had an idea. I found a large stone and flung it across the grass – not so far that it'd crack off the house but enough, I hoped, to set off any lights that worked on movement.

Nothing. Okay. Definitely no weaselling out now.

Thoughts of Sláine came to mind. Help me, I asked her. Protect me, camouflage me, wrap the night around me.

I had another look around and grit my teeth and scuttled over the grass to the corner of ColdStar, just around the side, into a shadow blacker than midnight. I stopped, breathing as quietly as I could. Then I inched along that side, moving like a gangly crab, staying in the darkness. I reached the rear corner. A large, unkempt garden. Still no sign of anyone. I hunkered down and sort of waddled along the ground, as quietly as I could manage. No lights showing back here, either, which still didn't mean anything. I could just about make out a large crow, glowering at me from ten feet away. For some reason I wasn't afraid or anxious – almost getting used to the dark bastards by this stage – and mouthed silently to it, as though the bird could possibly understand, '*Quiet* as a feckin' dead slug, got me?'

I reached a window and thank God I was crouched down because just then, I heard movement inside the house. *Shiiiiit* . . . Steps, soft but crisp on the wood floor. A man's voice singing a show tune. I recognised it from some distant memory of my mother making us watch the film this came from: 'Tonight, tonight . . . isn't just any night . . . ' A pleasant voice, mid-range, baritone or maybe tenor. It didn't sound precisely how I remembered Kinvara's voice, but then again that was speech and daytime, this was music and night-time.

Silence. I held my breath. Steps in my direction. Oh Jesus . . .

I squeezed my eyes shut and my body as low as it would go. Don't make a sound . . .

Kinvara was at the window. I could hear him even though he was silent. I could *feel* his presence, as if a shadow had weight and was leaning on me. Still afraid to breathe. The sash window popped, rolling up an inch or two, and I thought my heart was going to give out. Now I really could hear him, as he bent and put his face to the opening. He breathed in zesty winter air – don't remind me, pal, I'm nearly asphyxiating here – almost smelling the atmosphere. My leg was tingling with cramp, concertinaed up as it was. I asked myself, panicked, what would Sláine do right now? My fingers curled into fists . . .

Then he was gone. Evidently satisfied that he'd imagined whatever he thought he heard or felt, he drew his head back in and shut the window. Slowly, I eased out carbon dioxide and took in oxygen. This was a bust: Kinvara was home, there was nothing I could do. A sense of relief mingled with shame at my cowardice, but what could I do? You can't fight your essential nature.

After waiting sixty seconds for safety's sake, I crept back towards the street, padding through the shadows. And there was Caitlin Downes, of all people, when I reached Belladonna Way. She mustn't have seen me coming round the side of ColdStar, or if she had she didn't care, because Caitlin came straight over and blocked my way, saying urgently, 'We need to talk. Please, two minutes.'

I hustled her away from the house, down the street twenty yards, stopping under the camouflaging darkness thrown by a gigantic tree, so thick it blotted out much of the street light even though its branches were bare. Couldn't risk Kinvara striding out his front door, blasting out that Broadway song, and catching me staring in his direction like a paralysed, guilty goldfish.

'Uh, okay,' I said to Caitlin. 'So.'

I realised my hands were on her shoulders and removed them. A spark flared in the back of my mind: maybe I could send her over there. Ring Kinvara's doorbell, draw him from the house on some pretext, distract him long enough for me to slip around back again and jimmy that window . . .

I couldn't believe I was considering this kamikaze move. Needs must when the devil drives, I suppose, and we almost literally had the devil driving here. But it didn't matter – the opportunity passed and before I could ask, Caitlin had launched into what sounded like a rehearsed spiel, barking it out mechanically while staring at the ground.

'I was following you,' she said. 'I admit it, okay? I'm sorry . . . Was waiting outside your house earlier and you went for a walk in the woods, although why you'd go there any time, not to mind a frosty night, I don't know. But I followed anyway because I really need to talk to you. I waited out front, freezing, I wasn't going in there with or without you, but then you came out and I followed you back to town. So here we are.'

Still no mention of my incursion into Kinvara's property. I guessed Caitlin hadn't registered it because she was so single-mindedly focused on getting out whatever she needed to say. Now, I figured, we were coming to the meat of the matter.

Caitlin went on. 'Aidan, I'm so sorry. For everything that happened, for . . . ' She nodded to herself, determined. 'Yes.

For everything *I* did to you. I did it – can't blame anyone else. I was a total bitch and I know it. It's been eating me up inside for months, and you know what? I deserved it. Every bit of guilt, every sleepless night, I deserved it all. I was horrible to you, and I'm sorry. For cheating on you with that idiot, ignoring you afterwards . . . For not having the decency to give you your speak. Let you get angry and tell me you hated me, and take it. I owed you that. And . . . I'm sorry for not sticking up for you. When everyone was bullying you, I hated to see it and didn't join in, but that wasn't good enough. I should have defended you. Should have said, *I'm* the one you ought to be picking on. Me! I'm the one who did something wrong. Aidan did nothing. He was a perfect gentleman. Still is.'

She looked up at me. I didn't know what to say, if she wanted me to say anything. Caitlin whispered, 'I'm so, so, *sooooo* sorry. I have no excuse or explanation. I was . . . stupid, probably embarrassed at my actions. I felt like a fool and blamed you, in some irrational way. I don't know. I was wrong, that's the sum of it. I hurt you and I'm sorry. And if you don't accept my apology, I think I might just jump off a cliff.'

She was crying. And there, in the frozen heart of our undying winter, my own heart thawed. I had forgiven Caitlin, probably a long while ago – if I didn't know it before, I knew it now. And I was glad Sláine hadn't got around to wreaking her vengeance on this girl who almost killed me.

In a soft voice I said, 'It's all right.'

She said tentatively, 'Really?'

'Really. Forget it. I accept your apology.'

'Really really?'

'Totally and absolutely. All done, in the past, it's dead. Let it go, you'll be happier for it.'

She smiled through the tears, sniffing her snotty nose. 'Okay. Thank you . . . I know there's no chance of getting back together. I mean I'd like that but I think there's someone else . . . ?'

'There is.'

'Good. I'm happy for you, honestly. You deserve someone great.'

She stood on her tiptoes and kissed me on the mouth, a friendly sort of embrace, a farewell.

I said, 'Your lips are warm.'

Caitlin smiled, bemused. 'You sound surprised.'

'Nah, it's . . . uh, the cold night and all.' What time was it? I probably needed to get gone to Shook Woods. 'Listen, I gotta roll. Now I'm the one saying sorry. But I do, it's . . . kind of important.'

She stepped back. 'Of course. Sorry, I'm keeping you.'

'Nah, you're okay. I'll go now, though.'

'All right. Bye, Aidan. Take care of yourself.'

'You too.'

We moved in opposite directions, away from Kinvara's house, the wellspring of my nightmares. Thirty seconds up the road, I spun around and called back.

'Hey, Caitlin?'

She turned. 'Mm-hm?'

'Hope to see you soon.'

THE INFINITE POTENTIAL
OF ZERO DEGREES

I went straight back to the forest where I met Sláine as agreed, though not as agreed at nine, or at the hunting lodge. Instead she was waiting at the main entrance to Shook Woods, my phone's display showing 8.30 p.m. – I'd given myself that much time to hike in to the lodge. I was startled when I saw her there, glowing like a special effect in a movie. Unearthly, transcendental. So beautiful I thought I'd die.

She said, 'Come on, let's head,' and we started walking briskly in along the path, Sláine energised and strong, seeming taller than me, as she often did. I half-expected her to lift me and whoosh us through the forest, but she didn't. She seemed anxious somehow, hesitant. I guessed that she was lost in thought and worry about our showdown with destiny. The moment that might destroy the world. Maybe she had a plan and was going over the details. That could wait: I had urgent news to tell.

'Here, listen,' I said. 'I've worked it out. Our mystery man.'
She looked at me, said nothing, kept moving.

'It's this guy, Sioda Kinvara's his name. Some rich prick moved here a few months ago. Lives in a big old creepy house on Belladonna Way.'

'What makes you think he's our villain?'

I listed off all the evidence I'd accumulated. Sláine listened impassively. She didn't seem to be buying it, for some reason.

'Who else could it be?' I asked, impassioned. 'Besides, *you're* the one put me on to him.'

'How so?'

'I dreamed about you. And you were humming this tune, the same one Kinvara's got as his ringtone *and* I heard him play on piano. The prosecution rests, Your Honour.'

'Not the most persuasive argument, counsellor. It came to you in a vision?'

'Yeah. Dreams have meaning, didn't you know that? Like, Freud or someone worked it out. And *I* dreamed about *you*.'

She smiled at me, enigmatic, the first since we'd met: 'Did you, though . . . ?'

What did that mean? She'd really appeared outside my window, and I'd crawled over, half-asleep, insensible, thinking I was imagining it?

I shook my head and said, 'Here, never mind dreams or Sigmund bloody Freud. Kinvara's our man, I know it in my bones.'

'Yeah,' Sláine said. 'I think . . . yeah. I think you're probably right.'

'Well, great. Thanks for that show of confidence. So look, what's the strategy? I was thinking we could draw him out somewhere, a place where he's not in control. Somewhere of our choosing. Then you handle the demon some way or another, and I clock Kinvara over the head with a lump of wood.'

I laughed nervously. Sláine didn't respond. The night was darker now, a slim sliver of crescent moon lighting our way. I didn't mind. I knew Shook Woods like the back of my hand by this stage – I could have walked it blindfolded. And she was with me. Sláine wouldn't let me fall, she'd never allow anything to hurt me, I knew that. I trusted her judgment and the purity of her heart.

Still, I wanted *some* idea of what we might do.

'Eh – Sláine? Are you going to answer?'

She snapped, 'What?', frowned into space, looked away, and finally smiled at me. 'Sorry. A bit preoccupied. It's not you.' She shook her head, as if trying to loosen out whatever tensions and pressures might be in there.

'So what do you think? Draw the bastard out?'

'Um . . . you know what? Let's just go to the lodge and sit down and see where we're at. I have half a plan but I need to work out the finer points. Is that all right?'

'I . . . guess so. Yeah, okay. You have a plan? Excellent.'

'*Sort* of a plan . . . Listen, Aidan, don't worry. When it all happens, we'll know what to do. You'll know. Won't even have to think – it'll come naturally, your reaction. Just . . . have patience. Almost there.'

I said, 'Sure.' I wasn't sure, at all, but didn't feel I had much of a choice. 'At least give me some kind of heads-up, yeah? Like, wink at me or something. They always do that in movies.'

'Sure,' she said dryly. 'I'll wink at you.'

Still Sláine didn't move us at super-speed; still we walked, like regular people, silent. A bird flapped from its perch and flew across the sky. What was there to say anyway, I told myself. Whatever will be, will be, and all that. I tried to convince myself I really believed it, that I was stoical and philosophical. I think I even half-succeeded.

To pass the time and fill the silence I thought about my parents and siblings. As I mentioned to Podsy in that letter, I hadn't said goodbye. There wasn't time, as it happened, with my treks back and forth to Shook Woods and detour via COLDSTAR, but I wouldn't have in any case. My folks would have tried to stop me if they'd any idea of what I was heading into. The two little ones would have cried. So would I, probably. I pictured them, sleeping now, Sheila in her tiny room, Ronan in his tinier room, little more than a converted cupboard. I could see them, looking so small and defenceless, little mouths open, breathing softly, safe there, innocent of all the bad things in this hurtful world. I mentally blew a kiss back at my home and wished the four of them God speed. Then I wished it for myself and continued to strike out into the blackness.

It had just passed nine when we saw the lodge in the distance. The crumbling old stone, moss and ivy, the familiarity of it – how reassuring it seemed. I could feel myself tense as we came closer, though – some autonomic response I couldn't control and didn't want to fight. In fact, I welcomed it. If tonight turned to shit and my mind went cuckoo-bananas, maybe my body, my primal nervous system, would step in and continue the battle. Maybe.

We stopped at the door. I said, 'Ladies first?'

Sláine smiled wearily and gestured towards it. 'Nah, you go

ahead. It's the age of equality, after all.'

'Okay. Whatever.'

I reached for the handle, opened the door inwards. A soft light exited the lodge: candlelight, warm, organic. That was the first warning sign but clearly it didn't register strongly enough because I continued on inside. Like a dumb naive lamb being led to the abattoir.

The second warning was a sound: someone there, humming a familiar four-note refrain. 'Dum-dum-dum-DUMMM . . . ' A chill descended on me. Panic like an explosion, a thousand Roman candles cartwheeling and fizzling across my brain. But too late for panic, too late for anything, because Sláine had entered the lodge too, swiftly locking the door, and now was moving behind me, coming nearer, the cold preceding her like a warning of bad intent.

And I was looking at the face of Sioda Kinvara.

He stood by the far wall, dead centre, staring at me. I was frozen in shock, couldn't talk, my mind in turmoil, speech centres scrubbed clean of any language up to the task. We held the stare between us.

After an age Kinvara said quietly, 'It's not what you think.'

I could sense Sláine right behind me. Her voice in my ear, almost wistful, whispering, 'He's right, Aidan. It's *not* what you think.'

A twist of pain, as if I had literally been stabbed in the back, not just metaphorically. She wrenched my arm up and wrenched me around so I faced the armchair. And the middle-aged man sitting in it, holding a glass of something dark gold – and pointing a handgun at Kinvara.

Sláine said wryly, 'Told you I was working on a plan. Unfortunately for you, it's not the one you wanted me to have.'

The guy in the armchair said, 'Don't worry, Aidan Flood. I will put an end to all your troubles.'

He placed the gun on the arm of his chair and smiled with a creepy familiarity that made me feel uneasy, somewhere in the back-brain, the animal instinct part. He was familiar to me, too: I'd seen his face before . . . or something like it. I'd seen it, immobile with terror, on the man standing across the room.

'He's your brother,' I said to Sioda – though my words just floated into the chilled air, not specifically in his direction.

The gunslinger declaimed theatrically, 'Joseph Kinvara, at your service.' There was even an ironic little bow for a flourish. 'Three years younger than my beloved sibling. Call me Joe if you like, whatever suits. Sioda there got the fancy name from our parents. I'd to make do with plain old Joseph.'

He shrugged. I gazed at him, speechless. I didn't give a rat's ass about what to call him. What did I care for strangers' names, there, right at the end, at the death of everything I knew?

I gasped. 'You . . . you sold me out. Sláine. *Why?*'

She didn't answer. I would have slumped to the floor if she wasn't now holding me under my arms. One hand rapidly moving over my body, patting me down, as if I were carrying a weapon.

'Oh, Christ,' I breathed. 'I walked straight into it. Can't believe how *stupid* I was. Stupid enough to believe you . . . '

She lifted me to the bed and I flailed onto it like a drunk. Sláine went and stood next to Joseph, who rapped at his brother, '*You*. Go join him.' Sioda shuffled over and sat beside me. He

292

looked like hammered shit: dazed, exhausted, horrified.

I said to him, 'And stupid enough to have you fingered as the bad guy.'

He didn't respond, but began muttering under his breath, 'Oh God. *Please*, Joseph, stop this madness . . . '

'Shut up, Sioda. I'm getting to know my new friend here.'

I sat up straight and brought my eyes around to meet the other two. Joseph was smiling genially, a trace of a smirk. Sláine was smiling too, sardonic, almost patronising. I suppose it was justified, her obvious feelings of superiority: she *was* superior. The girl had played me like a violin, the poor lovelorn sap I was. Just like Caitlin last year. So things never really change at all, I reflected bitterly, they just take a different form. That image, the pair of them, seemed to waver somewhat in the wobbling light of several candles, cast from different points around the lodge; neither of the oil lamps were lit, I noticed, though both were filled with fuel.

I snarled at Joseph, 'And *you*. You're like a guy who came third in your own lookalike contest. Like a bad imitation of yourself.' I didn't know where that came from – I just wanted to hurt him. It didn't work.

Joseph raised his glass to me and took a hearty drink. 'Mm. Glenfiddich scotch. Really good stuff.'

I blurted out to Sláine: 'You *asshole*. Why did you *do* this?'

She shrugged and gave a gentle laugh. Joseph said, 'She brought you to me to prove her fidelity. Your life was payment for my full trust. Proof that she hadn't . . . had her head turned by someone else. Or her heart. Also, you knew too much. About me, what I intended to do.' He frowned at her, annoyed.

'My beautiful Sláine wasn't supposed to make contact with anyone. I didn't think she would; that wasn't in the plan. For some reason, though, she became – friends, I suppose you'd call it, with you. Told you the whole story. Or, you worked it out together. Whichever. It makes no difference, really, and there's nothing a young lad like you can do to stop me. But it shouldn't have happened. I did not want that. So she had to make restitution.'

'And I'm the bloody restitution.'

'Exactly.' He took another drink and seemed to relax again. 'Ah, what matter? You'll soon be dead anyway. Sláine has made her mistake, and learned from it. Isn't that right, my dear?'

She smiled at him with affection, the same look she'd given me so many times, and something strange happened: I got angry. A fire burning in my belly. I couldn't believe it. The same shit I got from Caitlin, from Rattigan and Harrington and the rest of them. Sláine and this other idiot might have seen it as something grandiose and special, but that was wrong: they were just bullies, exactly like the others. Mean-spirited, vicious, petty and callous. To hell with her, and back to hell with him and his demon.

'Blow me,' I snarled. 'Do whatever you want.'

Joseph chuckled. 'I fully intend to do what I want, my boy. Great plans for the future. Sadly, you won't be around to see them come to fruition. But look on the bright side: you were part of something magnificent. Something *vast*, almost beyond human comprehension. You were in at the start. Console yourself with that.'

'Don't think I'll bother, thanks. Who's going to do it? You or her?'

294

'Kill you? Hardly matters, really, does it?' He sniggered. 'Or do you have a preference? Perhaps you'd like your one true love Sláine to end it all. You know, it's funny. Human nature doesn't change that much. Men have always been slaves to their hearts.'

I stood and roared in fury and embarrassment, '*Get fucked*, you old creep!'

'Hm. Sláine? If you would.'

Without moving a muscle she propelled me backwards with an invisible force, slamming me against the wall. Joseph yelped in appreciation: 'Wonderful! She really is remarkable, isn't she? A fitting queen for the new world I am about to create.'

My breath came in torn, painful gasps. I didn't care. I pushed my hair off my face and slowly pulled my tobacco pouch from my pocket. I threw it at Sláine, one quick flick, without looking in her direction. She caught it, her hand moving at incredible speed.

I said sullenly, 'Feel like rolling me a smoke, your majesty? One for the road.'

I'd barely finished the sentence before she had tossed a rolled cigarette and the pouch back to me. She said flatly, 'It won't hurt. Your death. And we won't turn you into a zombie. We won't even eat your soul. I'm going to take pity on you and simply kill you. If there's a heaven, there'll be something left to go there.'

I sat in the lotus position on that mattress and lit up. My hands were shaking, but my voice was strong. 'Super. I appreciate that. Always said you were a top-class girlfriend.'

'Don't fight it, Aidan. It's easier that way. Accept your position.'

'My position? What is that, exactly?'

Sláine spat out, 'You're fodder. You're food for the gods. You're nothing. An insect to be crushed into the ground if it suits us.'

'Well, shit. If only you'd told me earlier, I'd've reconsidered this whole relationship.'

'Don't take it personally. You're no more insignificant than any other mortal. All of you are nothing more than our puppets, playthings, slaves or sustenance.'

Joseph laughed. 'That's my girl.'

Sláine smiled again. 'It's not you, Aidan my darling – it's me.'

She clapped her hands in delight. I wanted to spit in her face and tear his head off with my bare hands. I knew I wouldn't be able to do either, but I might as well have the full story, while I was alive to hear it.

'What are you, Kinvara?' I asked. 'Some kind of demon? A man who can't die? What?'

He waved a hand dismissively. 'Pff. Does it matter what *exactly* I am . . . ? You can consider me the personification of coldness. A consciousness sprung from the infinite potential of zero degrees. Heh. The iceman has cometh.'

'Very poetic and all, but that doesn't answer my question.'

'All right, then. Here it is: I conjured a demon from the depths of hell and now it inhabits me, I inhabit it, we coexist together. We are immortal, indestructible and all-powerful. We cannot be stopped and we will not stop.'

I tried to keep up a brave face hearing those words, but my

Adam's apple catching in my throat must have sounded as loudly as the bell being struck for the end of days.

Joseph went on. 'We – me, to all intents and purposes. This thing does not have a mind in the sense that you understand it. It possesses great powers but requires a human consciousness to harness them. Which is where I come in.'

He lifted his glass. Quick as a flicker of lightning, Sláine flitted over and refilled it from a large, nearly full bottle. I felt sick, seeing her subservience to this disgusting reptile. The heavenly-white ice queen of my dreams, reduced to a traitorous lickspittle. And worst of all, by her own choice.

'I kill mortal humans,' Joseph said, 'and consume their life essence. The warmth of their blood, the electricity of their brains, the force that moves them, that makes people *alive* . . . and their souls eternal. The more I consume, the stronger and more perfect I get. I intend to live forever, young man, by using this demonic power. Alas, there's a price to be paid for everything – including immortality.'

'And you're making others pay it for you.'

'No. Not completely. I have paid a price, too . . . '

He didn't elaborate. In the silence I noticed that Sioda was sobbing and moaning, his head in his hands. I wanted to slap him, tell him to man up, get a grip, give me some goddamn help.

I said to his brother, 'Yeah? Well, this's how I see it. I see a power-crazed madman who's sucking the goodness out of real, living people to feed his sick desires. I see a freak who wants to create an army of zombies that he can use as slaves.'

'Ah-ah. Incorrect. Certainly, I'll keep the odd one around – slaves, like you said. But other than that, I will simply kill, and keep killing: everyone in your town, the surrounding areas, the world.'

'You don't deny the power-crazed madman part, then?'

'Of course I deny it. Your accusation is so absurd, it's hardly worth bothering with. I am perfectly sane, Aidan Flood. Do not doubt that . . . I'm not even *bad*. Or immoral, whatever word you want to use. I know, you see all this through the old Judaeo-Christian perspective. "Thou shalt not kill" and so on. Wake up, boy. We've moved far beyond those simplistic notions. Good and evil. Pah! Is the avalanche "evil" because it crushes hundreds of people to death? I am on a higher realm now. There is no good and evil where I dwell. There is only the two of us, and the rest of you. Predators and their prey.'

I tossed my cigarette onto the floor and watched it smouldering there in the damp dirt. 'Tell me what happened, Kinvara. How'd you do all this?'

He settled back in his armchair, getting comfortable for the telling. He was enjoying this, the prick, but what could I do? Nothing. It'd kill me to admit it but Sláine had been right: I was weak, powerless, an insect waiting to be crushed.

'From an early age I've been obsessed with demonology, necromancy, the occult – much like Sláine's ancestor, though I hadn't heard of him before we came here. I read every book even remotely connected to the paranormal, every grimoire of dark magic. Islamic mystics, *The Picatrix*, *The Sworn Book of Honorius*, *The Book of Enoch*, Trithemius, Roger Bacon, John Dee, *Malleus Maleficarum*, the Bible and Tanakh, Paracelsus and Doctor Faust, *The Munich Manual of Demonic Magic* . . .

Anything, everything. Even obvious charlatans like Aleister Crowley or Anton LaVey.'

Joseph paused, regarding me with a strange intensity. He continued, 'And there's something about your town. Something strange and magical and dangerous. Something *beautiful*. I was drawn to it. And I *knew* . . . I'd been searching my whole life, and somehow I knew I would find it in this place.'

'Searching for what?'

'Wisdom. Power. *Everlasting life* . . . I'd passed through your home town a few times and it practically called out to me: "Here lies your destiny, Joseph. Here you will become great." So I decided to move permanently. Sioda agreed to facilitate my wishes.'

The other brother spoke, for the first time in what seemed like hours, his voice barely audible. 'Joseph is . . . he's always been odd. Even as a child, he was peculiar. Awkward, unsociable – just *different* from everyone else. I've looked after him our whole lives. I felt I owed that much to our late mother.'

Joseph raised a glass and said sarcastically, 'Dear Mammy. Whose money funded all this – my life of enlightened enquiry.'

'He was always a loner, since we were boys. I took him in, took care of him . . . He's lived with me for decades but I never told a soul about him. Joseph stayed in the shadows, a recluse. As far as anyone else knows, I have no brother . . . '

Joseph said roughly, 'Didn't I tell you to shut *up*, Sioda!? Before I cut your tongue out and feed it to you.' Back to me, in a gentler voice: 'It's the forest, I think. These black woods around us. The town itself is strange, there's no doubting that. You've felt it yourself, surely? But the uncanny black heart of it lies in Shook Woods. It beats, that heart – it's alive. This forest is *alive*, boy, in ways you could scarcely imagine . . . They often are. Why do you think cautionary fairy tales are usually set in the woods? That the highest concentration of serial killers in the United States is in the heavily forested north-west? It's the place where our darkest selves are realised and revealed. Where the deepest melodrama of the human spirit is played out . . . '

He was right, I reflected with dismayed horror. The woods were more than a collection of trees and wildlife: they were some kind of eerie dreamscape, a hellish netherworld into which I'd been drawn. Mysterious, ambivalent, unreal, yet strangely comforting too. The forest, I remember someone writing once, was everything those fairy tales made you feel.

Joseph snapped out of his soliloquy, smiling self-consciously. 'Anyway. We moved to your town, and then Providence took a hand. Do you understand, Aidan? This was *meant* to happen.'

I didn't like the sound of that – though, then again, what could possibly be worse than everything else I'd heard?

'The house we bought – it used to belong to one William John McAuley. Recognise the name?'

I jabbed a finger in Sláine's direction without doing her the courtesy of looking over there. 'Her grandfather. Great-great-great-something.'

'How about that?' Joseph said gleefully. 'Destiny guided us towards that building. Out of several large, private houses to pick from, all perfectly suitable, we chose that exact one. Sioda liked the library and how the garden was running wild, but that's neither here nor there. I clearly had a sixth sense.'

He stood and went on, fired up now. 'One day, while brother

dearest was out and about on his little errands, I did some exploring. And found a secret passage in that library, behind a fake panel in the wall. Do you know what was in there, Aidan Flood?'

I could guess. I began rolling another cigarette. My throat was parched but that didn't matter any more.

'McAuley's writings,' Joseph said, triumphant. 'All of them? I'm not sure. But enough. Letters, diaries, notes, records, knowledge he'd accrued, experiments and ceremonies attempted . . . things he was *going* to attempt. There were reams of this stuff, volumes of it.'

I thought about the pages that the unknown someone had deposited in my bag at the library: were they among the texts Kinvara discovered? Had my mysterious ally stolen them from him, and passed them on to me? Or were they duplicates? I decided it was shrewder not to bring this up.

He was still lecturing: 'McAuley outlined how to conjure up the demon, the precise words to say, every last crossed t and dotted i. Other parts to it too, certain metals to be worn on your person, foods to be consumed in the lead up, the position of the body, further details. No old rubbish about toad's blood or the hair of a golden child, none of that shit. This wasn't pantomime – this was *real*.'

I said flatly, 'I have no doubt.'

'McAuley had tried to do it, back in 1851. He was too weak. I don't just mean because of starvation, he was obviously too weak in *here* . . . ' He pointed to his head, then his chest. ' . . . And here. McAuley was an amateur, and he failed. He didn't have the stuff for it. But *I* did.'

His eyes darkened, something hideous and terrible in them, and I trembled with a nameless dread.

'A demon of the cold.' Joseph paused. 'There is immortality in coldness, child. Viruses and bacteria, they can survive for millions of years, more or less forever, if the temperature is low enough. Everything stops. Time stops, to all intents and purposes. And that, of course, means death stops too. Observe.'

Joseph seemed to – this wasn't possible, but I could see with my own eyes – begin *enlarging*, his body expanding upwards and out into this small room. His shape became distorted, the torso getting broader, like a caricature. And he was glowing, but not like a light – more that dark glow I once thought I'd seen surrounding Sláine. I actually cowered back, the unlit cigarette falling from my fingers, as did Sioda. Both of us stared, open-mouthed in stupefaction, as Joseph's eyes rolled and his flesh swelled like a balloon and that *thing* inside him showed itself finally.

A face of indescribable malevolence. Eyes half-closed in gloating, mindless ecstasy. Pointed ears, bald skull, naked neck and shoulders, the body surprisingly small – I'd have expected something almost cartoonishly gigantic – but radiating a sense of immense power. It hovered there, about Joseph's head, an image buzzing and fuzzing in and out like a hologram being periodically flicked on or off, surges of energy, disappearing and reappearing. A vision of hell expressed in the random shifts of electrons.

I scrunched the blanket under me in a white-knuckle grip and thought I was going to pee my pants. Then Joseph – he, they, who knew any more – spoke, two voices intertwined, something intimate about the sound, almost sensuous, that made me feel nauseous: 'Last October . . . Shook Woods and . . . called this being . . . gave *life* . . . then joined as one . . . closer than man and wife . . . soldered together . . . our very selves . . . for good and all.'

His head dropped and the thing vanished and suddenly Joseph was normal again. Well, normal physically. He was clearly as wack-a-doodle batshit crazy as the bastard spawn of Rasputin and Caligula. He shook slightly – presumably this transformation, this revelation, took something out of him. Sláine glided over and helped him back to the armchair. It disgusted me again to see her playing the servile handmaiden to this contemptible shit-bird. Sioda, meanwhile, was curled up in a foetal position, snivelling like a hurt kitten. I guessed he was in shock and wondered why I wasn't just as bad. I found my rollie and finally got round to lighting it.

Joseph took a swig of scotch and said, 'I conjured up that . . . thing you saw. Out here in the forest, in a secluded spot, not far from this room. Straight after that hallowed ceremony I went into hibernation for a week or so – sort of suspended, a demonic version of cryogenic freezing, I suppose. Ha! That notion amuses me. Hibernating, growing stronger, becoming different. Becoming *more*. Waiting, waiting, for circumstances to come into line, *exactly* right . . . '

'And then you made your triumphant return.'

'Precisely. Eventually I knew my time had come, my body knew. *It* knew. And I was resurrected. I took a few days to get used to being alive again, get my breath back, as such. Then I made my first kill.'

'Sláine.'

He nodded. She didn't react in any way. I snapped my fingers at her, snarking, 'Hey, yo. Princess. That doesn't bother you? Your boyfriend here actually *murdered* you? How romantic. I mean I really see beautiful things ahead for both of you.'

Joseph stared gloomily at a candle flame as it danced, his face a mask. 'We are bound, this demon and me. At first I wasn't . . . fully in control. But I learned. My strength grew. Now I control it. I can separate myself from the thing whenever I please. At least, I think . . . Sometimes, though. Sometimes it feels as though I'm sort of . . . losing myself, all over again . . . '

He abruptly slapped the arm of the chair. I jumped with the noise. Joseph continued, evidently back to his cocky self. 'I had to lure her out here, you know. Lovely Sláine. In the beginning I was unable to leave the woods – they sort of . . . held me. Pinioned, like the proverbial butterfly in a glass case. It took all my powers of hypnosis and persuasion to bring her to me. But that was only in the beginning. My strength grows all the time, exponentially. These days, I can kill wherever I like. The whole world is my hunting ground. I feast on the warm-blooded buffet table that is the human population.'

I blew smoke in his face, a dismal attempt to annoy him. He didn't even blink. I said, 'The way you say that, with such pleasure. Admit it, Joseph – Joe, whatever your goddamn name is – this is about more than eternal life. You're a sadistic bastard. You enjoy killing.'

'I won't deny there's pleasure to be found in it. To take another's life – and soul, in this case – yes, it's a sublime pleasure. One of the perks of the job, you might call it.' He gazed on

Sláine, and there was almost a genuine fondness in it. 'As is this beautiful woman, of course. A queen should be beautiful, don't you think? That's how all the best fairy tales have it.'

'This is no fairy tale, it's a goddamn horror story. So it was you who laid Sláine's body out under that tree. Why there?'

He shrugged. 'No reason. You have to dispose of the rubbish somewhere. That's all it was by that stage: rotting matter. The essence of Sláine was gone. It had been freed. The *real* Sláine you can see before you. Not the weak human she was before I improved her. Now she is radiant, powerful. She is triumphant.'

'I remember that man finding her corpse, the forestry guy. Clearing old growth . . .'

Joseph laughed heartily. '"Clearing old growth!" Ha! I'm the one who's clearing old growth. By the time I'm finished this world will have been remade completely. It's a new birth, my lad. A bright new dawn for a tired old world. You should think yourself lucky to be a part of it. Not that you'll *stay* a part of it for long, but still – can't have everything.'

I hopped off the bed, a renewed anger prompting me to act before I'd had a chance to weigh up the consequences. I pointed at Joseph and said, 'This is *crazy*, man. What you're doing, it's evil. And unnatural. Death is a part of life.' I turned to Sláine and started saying, 'You said that yourse—'

In an instant she was on me, her fingers at my throat. The *cold* of it, Jesus, I could feel it going through me. Unable to breathe, my body going into hypothermic meltdown.

She muttered, 'Don't move again. Trust me – if you know what's good for you, don't do anything stupid.'

Radiant, powerful and triumphant indeed. I looked into

her eyes. Nothing there but contempt. Worse, a profound disinterest. I meant zero to her – it wasn't even worth working up the energy to despise me. I never felt so small and pathetic, so unloved. So alone.

Tears came to my eyes as I realised, finally: I'm dead. And this was just a ludicrous fantasy built on nothing at all.

Sláine dropped me again. I fell to the bed and mechanically rolled another fag. What else are you gonna do, right? The condemned man always gets his last few smokes. I sniffled, saying numbly, 'Why her? Why Sláine?'

Joseph said, 'Well, someone had to be the first. And I picked Sláine in tribute to the man who made it possible: William John McAuley. In his honour, and besides which, she is a beautiful young woman in every way – fair of face, full of grace. I'd watched her on weekends home from college since we arrived in your town. I knew who she was, and that she would make a fine consort for me. My helpmeet across eternity . . . I'd also found an old ring McAuley'd had engraved for his wife Eleanor in the library cubbyhole. Put that on Sláine's finger as a token of my esteem, her great-grandmother's ring. And a little clue, maybe, for Sláine to ponder over. I know it can get dull, this immortal life, when you've nobody to share it with.'

'Why didn't you come to her straight away, then? Once her new life began. She could've started helpmeeting the shit out of you from day one. Actually, why'd you wait so long between killing Sláine and, and . . . this *rampage* of murder over the last few weeks.'

'Murder? Tch.' He seemed disappointed at my naive-weakling bourgeois morality. 'It's hardly *that*. We've been over

306

this already, Aidan. It's not murder when you squash that fly with a newspaper, is it? The two don't compare, they're not in the same universe, man and fly. That's how it is for me now: there's myself and Sláine, and then all of humanity. We are separate animals. Different universes.'

Without warning Joseph grabbed his glass and flung it at Sioda's head. The shot missed, the glass smashing into pieces off the wall behind him. Sioda recoiled further into his foetal curl. Sláine replaced the glass, a fresh drink already poured.

'Christ, that *whining*,' Joseph said. 'Shut up, damn you. Or I will give you an end even nastier than I'd originally intended.' To me he added, 'You asked me a question – why did I wait so long? The answer is simple: I was waiting for her.'

He glanced at Sláine. She remained as impassive as an Ancient Egyptian burial mask, though I noticed her body wasn't completely still, like before: she was drumming her index finger off the fabric of that fabulous antique coat. How gorgeous she looked, I thought, how divine the surface. How demonic the undergrowth.

Joseph went on, 'I had time, after all. I've all the time in the world. I will never die, so I was in no mad rush. And before I made my move I wanted to see how Sláine would . . . develop. Once she became accustomed to her new existence. I was curious: would it change her the way it changed me? Make her colder, harder? Bring her closer to the state of flawlessness that is absolute zero: unmoving, unchanging, magnificently indifferent. *Perfect.*' He smiled with smug satisfaction. 'It did. I knew it would anyway. I don't make mistakes. But that was proved when I saw what she was capable of. The way she dismantled those boys and girls, tore them apart, toyed with them, invaded their dreams, drove them mad, launched a virtual one-woman *terror* campaign . . . !' He clapped admiringly. 'Sláine may have thought it was done for you, revenge on your behalf. I know the truth, and now she does too. She attacked those kids because she *could* – and because she liked doing it.'

Out of somewhere I found the gallows humour to drawl to Sláine, 'Told you you shouldn't have done all that.' She smiled on me with an insipid pity that was worse than the violent disinterest of five minutes before.

Joseph said, 'I knew then, for sure, this was the girl for me. No compunctions, no hesitations, no miserable little moral code. Sláine, like me, had the right stuff. So about a fortnight ago – less, ten or eleven days – I began killing again. I was hungry by then. I'd waited long enough. I sated my thirst, grew stronger, my powers expanding, becoming ever more refined . . . After a week or so, once I was in the groove, so to speak, I made contact with Sláine. Told her *some* of what was going on, not all. It's more romantic to keep a few secrets from each other, don't you agree?'

Jesus Christ. Could this guy get any more deluded? And yet . . . she genuinely seemed to have fallen for him. His dark charm, the lure of eternal life. My stomach knotted and roiled like a stormy sea.

'Then I appeared to her, here, this evening. Told her everything she needed to know, and she told me everything. About your absurd intention to somehow stop me, how you were on the way to this lodge, supposedly to hammer out a battle plan . . . So, the mountain came to Muhammad, and here we are. The rest, as they say, is history. As you will soon be.'

A thought struck me and I figured I may as well ask about it: 'Are you responsible for this weather? The cold winter we've been having.'

'Seems so, yes,' he said. 'A side effect, not intended. But not unfavourable to my plans. The cold snap helped to cover up what I was doing. Freeze people to death during a mild spell and . . . well. It tends to raise suspicions. Even among the slow-witted local constabulary you're blessed with here.'

'Hell has literally frozen over,' I said dully. 'This is it, here. This is hell now.'

That amused Joseph. He chuckled and took another drink. Such a strange place to die, I thought absently, this little hut. I'd never in a million years have imagined these to be the circumstances of my demise.

'This is hell,' I went on, almost mechanically, 'and *you* are the devil, Kinvara. You're a sick bastard who should have been put down at birth. Even your own brother can't stand the sight of you.'

I gestured towards Sioda, who hadn't moved a muscle for ages. In an instant Joseph had erupted from the seat and was looming over me, towering, growing huge, the evil being inside him emerging once more, the same flicker and blur, a radioactive buzz around Joseph's head. I flinched back. I actually whimpered. I could smell the scotch off Kinvara, those sickly sweet fumes: a cloud of whisky-perfume, wreathing this hideous twosome. Then I heard them, raw thunder rising to a ragged roar, unbearable, infernal, the demon screeching in counterpoint. It sounded like the rumbling of the massed armies of hell.

'Be ... *careful* ... boy.'

Just as abruptly, the pair had merged again and the man was sitting in his chair. I was shaking, gallons of adrenaline shooting around my system but it was pointless, neither fight nor flight was possible here and I was *boned*.

Joseph said quietly, 'Your death is assured, but I can still make it painful. Or perhaps I should take your soul as well? Condemn you to the eternal wandering of a hellish afterlife. The only thing stopping me is Sláine's soft spot for you.' He turned to her. 'What do you say, my love? Shall we consume him wholly? Maybe make him one of our slaves?'

Sláine considered me with a cool, disdainful eye. 'Tch. He's not even worth turning into a zombie. Poor pathetic Aidan is only good for throwing away, like any piece of junk.'

Even now, when anger and disbelief had turned to miserable resignation, it still hurt to hear her talk like that. Were the last few months a total lie? Had none of it meant a goddamn thing in reality, outside my delusional mind?

She seemed to soften a bit, handing me Kinvara's whisky bottle and saying, 'Don't be frightened. I told you: when the time comes, you'll be all right. You won't even think about it. Have a drink. It's good for the nerves.'

I grabbed the bottle – it felt heavy, like the weight of some awful knowledge – and slugged from the neck, a measure of sickly, fiery scotch going where it was meant to, more of it dribbling onto my jacket.

Emboldened by the booze, I yelled at her through a scorched throat, flung words in her face as if they were physical things which had the power to hurt, to change, to *move*: 'The bullies.

The attacks. Even that. I can't believe I believed you, that you did it for me. God, at least that gave *some* meaning to all this bloody violence, or justification or something . . . This awful thing, but done for a good reason . . . ' I shook my head angrily. 'Doesn't matter. Clearly you were just a bloodthirsty maniac all along.'

She said evenly, 'Thirsty, yes. But not for blood. Blood is old hat, Aidan. It's silly stories about vampires. We feed off the *cold*. We create it, and in turn it gives us life. A perfect symbiosis. A dance of death that will never end.'

'Don't you regret anything? Or has your conscience frozen over, too?' I jerked a thumb in Joseph's direction. '*He* hasn't got one, that's obvious. Too long inside his own madness has turned him into Jeffrey Dahmer. But you, Sláine. Jesus, you were a human being just a few months ago. You felt love, affection, empathy. You kissed your mother goodbye and hugged your granny. You did things, physical things, emotional, just *things*. You went on the lash with your pals and ye danced together and hugged each other and had the crack and felt good. You played music and helped out with handicapped kids and shifted Tommy Fox. You and him, together, your mouth on his mouth, your hands on his body. Don't you remember that? What it was like to be a goddamn *person*?!'

I realised I was shouting. I resumed, quieter. 'You were a girl, Sláine. A human being, with warm skin and lively eyes and a heart that beat dozens of times a minute. Not long ago, that was you. You must remember what it was like. You *have* to.'

She stared at me for a long moment. Finally she said, 'Do you recall what's written above the door to this lodge? "It does

311

not trouble the wolf how many the sheep may be." I'm *not* a girl any more, that's the point. I'm a wolf now, Aidan. And the fate of the sheep doesn't trouble me.'

My shoulders slumped, then my whole body. I collapsed onto myself like a marionette with its strings cut. I'd failed, again. It was no use. I was beaten. They wouldn't listen to reason, had no moral compass. Sláine and Joseph Kinvara were the worst thing imaginable: psychopathic, immortal, all-powerful, unstoppable . . . and there were two of them, so they'd never get lonely and never get bored. And this nightmare would never end for the human race.

So I chose the coward's way out. I decided not to stick around. I'm no hero, I admit that. Better to go now, a clean break with life. Better not to fight, as she'd said. Better to hold on to my soul and hope to God there really was one. Hope that God and heaven existed.

But there *had* to be a heaven, right? Somewhere better than this.

I stood, sighed and said, 'Okay, do it. Right now.'

Neither of them moved. '*Kill me*. I'm asking you, please. Just kill me. I've had enough.'

Sioda finally glanced up from his womb-like crouch. He seemed surprised; perhaps some survival instinct lingered on, making him hope that somehow, some way, we'd both make it out of there alive.

I smiled at him, saying ruefully, 'Sorry, man. Nothing we can do now.'

Joseph went to rise from the chair but I held up a hand to stop him and looked at Sláine. 'I'd prefer if you did it.' I gave a lopsided smile and felt tears pricking my eyes. 'For . . . for old times' sake, yeah?'

She nodded and came over, standing just in front of me. Sláine ending my existence: the ultimate betrayal in a life that sometimes seemed full of them, and there was a weird kind of aptness in that. Why shouldn't the story of my shitty existence have a disappointing, unhappy ending?

'It'll be quick, Aidan,' she said, smiling, something almost tender in it. 'No pain. I won't take your soul. I won't destroy your face. Your parents will have something decent to bury.'

Amazingly, I really did appreciate this – that my mam and dad could have an open coffin at the funeral. Wow, I thought, smiling inwardly: you're actually maturing, Aidan. You're getting outside your own stupid head and thinking about other people for once. Pity this newfound maturity was coming too late, but there you go. Like I said, life's full of irony.

I appreciated it, but wasn't going to let on to Sláine. 'Good for you,' I drawled with some dying spark of defiance, one last 'screw you' to my tormentors. 'Award yourself a medal. Can we get on with it now?'

She smiled indulgently. 'Of course. One last smoke before you go? Last meal on death row?'

Before I could answer Sláine had whisked my tobacco out of my pocket, rolled a cigarette and gently slipped it between my lips. I shrugged: sure, whatever.

Sioda swung his legs over the bed and implored his brother, hands together like a religious penitent: 'For God's sake, Joseph. For the memory of our mother, stop this insanity. Don't let this boy die. You hate me, I get that, but think of Mammy, for God's sake . . . '

Joseph sniggered. 'For God's sake? There is no god any more, you snivelling little turd. *I* am God now. Carry on, Sláine. Ignore that worm sitting next to you there.'

I rose from the bed, clutching the bottle of scotch. Sláine stood before me, partly blocking Joseph's line of sight.

'That's it,' she said, as softly as a mother hushing her child to sleep. 'Accept the way things are.'

The whisky bottle in my hand. My lighter in her hand. Sioda's head back in his hands. My life, and death, in Sláine's hands.

And then, and then, right at the finish, my real 'screw you' to the pair of them – not the flip comment of childish rebellion but something heartfelt, fundamental. Something quiet and tender, and all the more powerful for that.

I smiled sadly at her and said, 'I love you, Sláine.'

There was my triumph. There I was victorious. In letting her know I hadn't changed, despite everything. My heart hadn't hardened or frozen over. I still loved her, and always would. I still *felt love*. Life hadn't beaten me, they hadn't beaten me. I was bloodied but unbowed. And I was at peace.

I smiled again, different this time – a genuinely happy smile, given the circumstances.

Sláine stared at me. She lit the rollie and I inhaled greedily, its tip glowing lava-red, engorged, enflamed. She whispered, 'The time has come. And you know what to do.'

Then she winked.

And I did. Just like that, I knew. Sláine didn't say anything more. She didn't need to. She didn't have to get inside my head with words because we were already inside each other's souls. She was lonely and I was lonely and we had ruptured the fabric of space and time. We were hearts talking across continents. Across the boundary between life and death.

I called out, 'Yo, Joey?'

His head lifted, perplexed at my tone of voice.

I returned the wink to Sláine. 'Health warning for you, pal: my smoking can kill you.'

Then the bottle was slipped from my hand by Sláine's hand and the cigarette was in my hand and she was moving, faster than a shooting star, faster than I would have thought it possible to move, spinning from me and towards Joseph Kinvara and *smashing* that heavy glass bottle across the fucker's head, an explosion of glittering shards, a volcanic splash of whisky all over his face and clothes as he howled in shock and pain, blood running from his face and mingling with the scotch. With all that alcohol.

I flicked the cigarette at him and it arced in slow motion through the air like the shining-white ape's bone in that old sci-fi movie, and before it even reached Joseph the spark ignited the fumes rising off him like a toxic spill, and he was engulfed in flame. Then Sláine was moving again, *fwit-fwit-fwit-fwit*, running angles, stretching physics to breaking point, grabbing both lamps and swinging them in turn at Joseph's head – smash-crash-*flash*, oil catching fire, further nourishing the blaze.

Hair melting off his skull, skin lifting and bubbling like fat in a pan, clothes sticking to his body. It was horrific to watch but I had to keep looking. Joseph screamed like a baying pack of underworld hounds and tried to rise but Sláine pushed him down, forcing him back onto the armchair, that tatty piece of shit, that four-legged fire hazard. The furniture went up in flames too, the fabric curling and burning to nothingness, the stuffing inside feeding hungrily on the fireball. Joseph's gun clattered to the ground.

More screams, but this wasn't just the man, it was the thing inside him too. A blood-curdling screech – not only pain, fear also. The demon was scared, and no surprise: Sláine, my Sláine, was at full fury now, fury and *love*, a force of nature, beyond nature. She thrust her hands into the inferno, ignoring the flames and wrenching Joseph out of the chair, flinging him against the wall, ancient brick bursting apart as he hit and came crashing down, dust settling on him like a pall, still burning, still screaming, a human firestorm.

I understood now why and how she could do those things to my bullies, do them for me even when she knew it was wrong. I loved her more than ever.

And Sláine loved me. She hadn't betrayed us.

She lifted Joseph from the floor and hammered his head into the wall, again and again, a whizzing blur of white violence and red fire. He swooned in agony and Sláine kept hammering. I couldn't move my legs or tear my eyes away. And I didn't want to.

A different type of fire was beginning to well up in my stomach, a pure thrill of excitement and bloodlust and vindication . . .

I hollered, almost feverish with vengeance, 'Kick his ass, Sláine! Pound his ass into the ground! *Kill him!*'

She leaped for the ceiling and Joseph's head went through the rafters, old wood shattering like crystal, flames flaking from his dying body. Sláine pulled him down and grabbed his head, her fingers like a vice grip. Her hands began to turn. Sláine gasped, 'Get out of him get out get out *get out* . . . '

316

Joseph somehow regained his equilibrium and tried to fight back, arms flailing like pinwheels of sparks from a bonfire. He was a trapped animal, crazed, acting on instinct. No longer the smooth master of a new universe. Kinvara was just another bully, a chicken-shit coward when he met someone stronger.

'Kill him!' I shouted. 'Smash the bastard's skull to dust!'

With a desperate effort she pressed harder, her throat opening with a sound like the earthy blood-roar of a woman in childbirth. Joseph gave a last unearthly scream and the thing, that accursed demon, exited his flesh and flitted away from its host, its smallish form darting out of the lodge into the sheltering blackness of Shook Woods. What d'you know? Even demons are chicken-shit when someone stands up to them.

Sláine loosened her grip and Joseph mindlessly barrelled out the door past me, a fireball, a tumble of roasting meat, no longer a man, running a few yards before collapsing into the snow, facedown. He was done for.

Silence, broken by the sound of my heavy breathing. Sioda was so far in shock by now I don't think he was even capable of that much. He stared at Sláine and babbled, 'Muh-muh-muh . . . '

I ran to my girl. There, by the wall, as plaster dust and wood splinters fell onto our heads like bizarre confetti, I threw my arms around her and held Sláine close enough to crush her. Never had absolute cold felt so warm to me. Our hearts together, a conflagration in the centre of a raging snowstorm.

She whispered, 'I have to go after it. Can't let it get away.' Then she stood, took three sharp breaths, rolled her neck, rolled her shoulder muscles. Sláine looked nerveless, resolute, incredibly capable. Incredibly powerful. I didn't think it was

317

possible, but I was more in awe of this girl than ever.

She took my hands, squeezed them, released. 'I don't have time to explain. Get back to town and stay in your house.' She aimed a thumb in Sioda's direction. 'Bring him with you. And don't leave until I contact you.'

'No way. I'm staying. Not letting you out of my sight again.'

'Just stay well back.'

'That I can definitely do.'

Sláine stared at the floor. She said quietly, 'Maybe I can free those poor souls they've already taken. Like in the stories, you know? When you kill the head vampire, you release his victims. You save them.' She looked at me, uncertain, pleading. 'It's not a vampire, but . . . It has to be worth a shot. Doesn't it?'

I nodded and gritted my teeth. 'It's worth a shot. Let's go get the bastard. Mr Kinvara, wait here. We'll be back.'

He didn't respond, or move, or do anything, except stare at the spot where an angel of death had driven his brother into hell.

Outside. The crescent moon a knife cutting through the firmament. I started to ask, 'What direc—?' when Sláine shushed me, closed her eyes, held a finger to the breeze. Her dark-grey eyes opened and she pointed into the darkness.

'There.'

Then we were running through Shook Woods, giant pines on all sides as silent and inscrutable as an alien monolith on the moon, a flying squadron of crows in relief against the sky, screaming, driving us onwards. Sláine raced ahead, I could see her flashing white through gaps in the trees, before the forest's shadow swallowed the view once more. The darkness of this place, it kind of washed over you, seeming to be more than the mere absence of light but a thing, a presence, maybe the spirit of the forest itself, standing guard, keeping watch, leaning in . . .

Then I was entering a large clearing and *there* was the demon, zipping and glowing through the night like a will-o'-the-wisp towards something odd – I couldn't quite see what because it was so goddamn dark in . . .

Sláine was covering the ground at terrific speed, making a trajectory for the demon, a missile set to explode. It glanced back, looking scared now, its malignant face full of terror and hatred and fury.

'Come on, Sláine,' I gasped, running as hard as I could, my lungs burning, legs turning to acidified jelly. 'Bring it *down* . . .'

But even as I said it I could see that the creature had reached the odd something and could see what that something was and my heart sank. We were screwed.

A door. A portal. An exit. A sort of shimmering in space, a dull, nauseating vibration. Oval in shape, maybe eight feet high, five across. This door, I somehow knew, opened onto another dimension or realm or universe, some other *place* where that demon could find escape. Could plot its return. We'd never be free, never feel safe, knowing it was over there, wherever that place was.

I kept going, pushing every last ounce of energy into it. Sláine was still gunning for the demon like a heat-seeking missile but it was halfway through the portal, one side of its body disappearing into the nothingness beyond, the image sort of being scrubbed out. It grimaced at us, a sight to make the blood run cold, yowling like a rabid cat, throwing its curse to heaven. Then it turned to go, and I knew once it was through the door would close behind it, and we'd be as damned as that hell-bound thing.

Sláine screamed, a wordless cry of grief and anger, and launched herself across the sky, practically flying, stretching for that portal to keep it open, if she could just reach it before the demon disappeared forever and *keep the bloody thing open* . . .

She didn't make it. But she didn't need to.

Because, bringing up the rear my heart had been battering my chest, heat rising there inside my parka with exertion and fear and exhilaration, and I realised that something really was battering my chest. An object, a physical thing, bouncing back and forth as I ran. I kept running and reached my inside pocket and pulled out the old locket that lady gave me, Meredith. It had remained in there all this time. I guess I'd told myself I'd find photos of Sláine and me to put in it, then got distracted and forgot about it.

It was warm. Not tepid, from being close to my body, but definitively *warm*, like a cup of tea made five minutes before. And it was . . . this might have been the moonlight playing tricks again, but the little disc seemed to be glowing, a muted throb. Warm and bright, I held it tight in my hands and ran towards Sláine as the demon vanished and she screamed and lunged, too late . . .

And I *hurled* that locket – I swear to God, it told me to do this, it practically spoke to me. I threw it towards the portal just as the creature moved through fully, my arm almost wrenching out of its socket. I threw with every ounce of strength I would ever possess. Somehow it worked. That door to another dimension remained open, just about. It was buzzing crazily now, like a swarm of molecules in hot water, straining to pull themselves apart into chaos.

Sláine's voice died away. She realised what had happened. She looked at me, smiling in a sort of pleased amazement.

I shrugged laconically. 'What? I have to contribute *something* to this effort, surely?'

She nodded once and tumbled through. The portal collapsed on itself and vanished completely. Sláine had vanished. The locket lay on the ground. I mechanically returned it to my jacket then gulped in dismay and brought chilled fingers to my sweat-soaked head and was about to scream myself, when suddenly light exploded from that spot, beginning as a minuscule point before enlarging rapidly, *whoooosh*, like a nuclear bomb. A flare of energy hurled me back, landing me flat on my ass, the light blinding me temporarily, shockwaves reverberating in my ears. I was sightless and deaf and completely ignorant.

And then her voice – celestial choirs never sounded so wonderful – distant and muffled at first but getting louder and sharper and nearer, and my vision cleared and I could see Sláine walking towards me, calling my name.

'Did you . . . ?' I gasped. 'Is . . . is it . . . ?' I was unable to say the words.

Sláine nodded, slumped to the ground and hugged me. I could almost feel it physically, her exhaustion, as though it were a black hole collapsed in empty space.

She said weakly, 'It's dead. That *thing* is . . . I followed it down into the jaws of hell and I . . . I . . . ' Her head flopped back, she moaned in pain, her eyes fluttering. 'Oh shit. I think that took quite a bit out of me.'

I squeezed her tightly. After a minute Sláine added, 'It's over, Aidan. For good. I destroyed it. I destroyed it.'

Something immense had happened beyond the door – I had the strangest sense she had *aged* in that split second, changed in some elemental way – but Sláine wasn't being forthcoming with details, so I decided not to press it. There'd be plenty of time for all that later; we had the rest of our lives to talk together, or I guess, the rest of mine at least. I broke our embrace and smiled, about to thank her. And shit, she was *crying*.

I said drolly, 'How can someone so badass get upset enough to cry?'

Sláine laughed. 'Don't know. Tiredness? Feel kind of . . . emptied out.'

'Take it easy. You must have . . . Just . . . just rest here for a minute.'

She nodded in agreement, like a child being willingly put down for her nap. I cradled Sláine's head in the curve of my arm. After another few minutes I said gently, 'It's all right. Everything is all right now. Thanks to you.'

For the first time since I'd met this strange, marvellous girl, I felt like the senior one in the relationship, the more mature of the two. I felt like an adult. And that felt good.

Gradually, she got some of her strength back, enough to fill me in on recent events: how Joseph Kinvara had appeared at the lodge, in person, that evening – around the time I'd been dreaming about her, I reckoned – and laid out his intentions for their joint world domination. Sláine hadn't time to make any sort of plan herself, or contact me; besides, she assumed he'd be able to 'read her thoughts', being in such close proximity. This was also why she didn't tell me anything en route to the lodge – he might have 'heard'. For all she knew, Joseph could have been watching from the trees the whole way in.

'It was a stupid move,' she sighed. 'Thinking we'd a day or two to work something out.'

'Yeah, but be fair, what would you expect? We're just two kids.'

She'd been forced to wing it, flying on blind hope, pretending to go along with Joseph's schemes – which included murdering me.

'He was going to kill you himself, tonight probably,' Sláine said. 'He'd already sent the walker to the cemetery, that poor O'Leary woman. I volunteered to do it instead. Prove my love for him, whatever. Which in turn was a set-up. I had to pretend to be – *interested* in him.' She shuddered. 'Ech. The *sleaze*. Made my skin crawl. But I reciprocated his romantic suggestions.'

I said, 'So you were tricking him? To get his guard down?'

She nodded. 'Get his guard down, get him relaxed, even a little drunk. And get close. I had to separate them, Kinvara and the demon inside. That was the only way I could think to nail them. Too powerful for me to face together.'

'You looked pretty powerful yourself, driving his dumb head into the ceiling.'

'Nah, they would have beaten me. Probably. I mean Kinvara'd have powers of his own, like I do. And coupled with the demon's . . . ? Anyway. Doesn't matter now.'

'No it goddamn does not,' I said with satisfaction.

She continued, 'I figured, their strength lies in the cold, right? I mean that's what the thing *was*, essentially: coldness, come to life. And what better weapon to use against that than fire?'

'Good thinking, Holmes. So this was your grand plan – set Kinvara alight and . . . '

'Plan is too ambitious a word for it. But yes. Set him on fire and hope to God it'd loosen the bonds between them. Enough for me to pummel the shit out of the mortal man and basically beat that demon's ass out of him.' She shrugged, said, 'It worked,' then smiled awkwardly. 'I promised you I wouldn't kill anyone.'

'I think in this case you get a pass, morally speaking. Counts as self-defence.' My own ass was freezing, I realised. 'You mind if I – stand up? I'm in danger of getting glued to the ground.'

We both rose.

Sláine said hesitantly, 'I think their souls – those souls Kinvara claimed? I think they're free now. At peace.'

'Me too. You did good, girl.'

'As did you. Throwing that disc – what was it?'

I pulled it out. She examined it, turning the locket in the moonlight. Eventually she said, 'Would you believe, I think I know this. Think I've seen it in an old photograph.'

'Yeah? No way.'

Sláine nodded. 'Looks like . . . I can't be sure, but it looks like this locket my ancestor used to own. Eleanor.'

'McAuley's wife.'

'The very same. An old family heirloom, you know, passed down the generations. Lost years ago, but I've seen it in pictures

324

of my great-grandmother. Eleanor's granddaughter, I guess? Not sure exactly.'

'Maybe that's why it had – power,' I said, 'for good, I mean. Maybe William John gave it to his wife as a symbol of love, and it represented, like, something good. Whatever decency was in him. This locket had held on to some of that, his love for Eleanor, his good side.' I thought of the ring Sláine wore, the one that creep had put there. 'That ring of yours meant something to Kinvara . . . I guess the locket means something to me.'

'Where'd you get it?'

'From this very interesting old dear called Meredith. Runs an antiques shop. You think she . . . ?'

Sláine gave a little smile. 'Maybe.'

I put the locket away and said, half-teasing, 'You know, you were banking an awful lot on me understanding your purpose back there. I mightn't have clocked at all what you wanted me to do, with the scotch and the fag. Bit slow on the uptake, you know?'

She shook her head adamantly. 'I knew you'd get it. I know *you*, Aidan. How you think, what you'll do.' She kissed me hard on the mouth. My fingers shot outwards in shivering bursts of delight. 'I know you better than I know myself. And trust me, when you've got this much free time, you get to know yourself pretty well.'

We laughed and I said, 'Why not just set him alight yourself? Out of curiosity. Why take the tiny risk that I'd be too dumb to follow your lead?'

She thought about this. 'I needed you there when I took

him down. I can't – I can't explain it . . . I told you before, you make me stronger, more powerful, like I can do anything. But I need you there to do it *with*. Does that make sense? It had to be a team effort. You and me, taking on the world.'

It made sense.

'Aidan, I'm sorry,' she added. 'About keeping you in the dark like that, but especially for saying those things tonight. I didn't mean any of it.'

'I know that.'

'Not one word.'

'Not even one?' I smiled and kissed her forehead. 'Listen, I have to know. Why would you give up all this power? Everything Kinvara promised you. Immortality, I mean . . . It's a lot to lose.'

Sláine frowned, annoyed. 'I told you. Because I *love* you, you moron. What, is that so hard to believe?'

I smiled again, taken aback at how simple things often were, underneath everything. When you stripped away the horseshit and melodrama. When you stopped overanalysing and started feeling and living.

'No,' I said. 'Not hard at all.'

I stretched my back and gazed at the twinkling panorama of the night sky while Sláine told me that Sioda – Mr Smooth Operator, who in reality was a bundle of nerves – had arrived shortly before I did, apparently invited by Joseph. Little did he know what his demented brother was cooking up. Little did he know about any of it. I'd have to apologise again for suspecting him.

She must have read my mind because Sláine said, 'Go back

and check on that man. Make sure he's all right.'

'What're we going to tell him? To explain all this. Explain – you.'

'I don't know. Just make sure he hasn't *done* anything. To himself.'

Sláine embraced me again and I could feel that something had changed, a hesitation in her beaming out like radiation. I thought I knew what she had to say and why she didn't want to voice it. I definitely knew I didn't want to hear it, but I forced myself to speak anyway: 'Go on. Tell me.'

'I have to go away for a while. I'm sorry.'

'Okay.'

'I'm not sure why. I just . . . it's something I need to do. Be by myself.'

'Okay.'

'Is it?'

I smiled sadly. 'Not really. How long? Do you know?'

'I don't.' She looked at me with regret. 'It's not like before. This is more . . . I can't describe it. It's like I have to find myself again, or something. Let some process of transformation take place, give it space to breathe. Be alone, and sort of . . . There's no point trying to explain it. I don't understand it myself. But it won't be forever. I will come back.'

'Ha. *Okay*.'

'Aidan, I'm so sorry for everything,' she said again. 'All these bad things that've happened to you, it's because of me.'

She was crying once more. I wiped an icy tear from her cheek and said, 'And every good thing, Sláine. Every good thing is you.'

We smiled at each other for a long time under the thin moonlight, the whole forest hushed as though paying its respects to the moment.

Finally Sláine said, 'Will you wait for me?'

I laughed. 'What? What kinda dumb question is that? You *know* I will.'

She laughed too. 'I will come back to you. I *will*.'

'I know that. And I'll be here waiting. As long as it takes.'

'I love you, Aidan Flood. Endless, boundless.'

She kissed me again, ferociously. I was drowning in it, dizzy with it all.

'I love you too,' I said. 'Ever, forever, the size of a universe.'

Then she whispered, 'Hearts talking across life and death,' kissed me one last time and with a rush of cold air was gone.

Goodbye, my love. Goodbye, my dream, my ghost, my guardian angel.

No, not goodbye. Farewell. Until we meet again. We will.

I hiked back to the lodge, further than I thought – I guess we'd run pretty quickly. I didn't quite know what to expect when I got there, but it hadn't much changed. Joseph Kinvara's charred remains still face down in the snow, the sight of them turning my stomach. Sioda still inside the room, although he'd moved back to the bed. The armchair was gutted but no longer aflame. Thankfully, the fire hadn't spread any further.

Sioda was lamping into a bottle of wine he'd found – another super-expensive brand Sláine had purloined somewhere – and looked drunk, red-eyed, torn up. But his speech wasn't slurred when he saw me and said, 'You.'

I eased inside and found my tobacco.

'The boy from the library,' he went on. 'Mr Flood.'

Sitting on a stool, I made myself a cigarette, keeping a close watch on the man opposite.

'Bravo,' Sioda said, taking another generous swallow. 'Bravo.'

Was he being sarcastic? I'd been involved in killing his brother, and what was that he'd said about loyalty to family . . . ? I tensed.

'It had to be done,' he said faintly. 'He had to die, and I didn't have the balls to do it. Didn't have the *heart*. He was family. But Joseph was evil. I see that now.' Another drink. I lit my smoke. 'I never realised the full extent of what he was doing. Thought he was just playing around with all that black magic rubbish. I love old books myself, but only as a reader. Never thought he took them *seriously*. Never thought that stuff was . . . Jesus.'

He had a look of utter disbelief, presumably not for the first time. The mind sometimes refuses to accept what the senses show it.

'Am I to blame?' Sioda said. 'I've always supported him, indulged him . . . Joseph wanted to move to this town, we moved. He asked me to check out such-and-such a library book, I did it. He spent his life skulking in the shadows – he avoided everyone – Christ, he'd even leave the house when the cleaner was due to call around – and I ignored his strange behaviour, no questions asked. Worse, I made it possible. Made all *this* . . . '

He looked at his hands as if there were actual blood on them. The moment of intense anguish passed, for now. Sioda smiled warmly and said, 'It's almost funny – how you thought it was me.'

'Yeah. That. Listen, I gotta apologise. I was way off.'

He flapped a hand, dismissing my regrets. 'Not at all, I can see why you thought it. The clues sort of added up there, didn't they? I'm . . . an eccentric man, in some ways.'

'Hey, why'd you call the house ColdStar? That totally struck me as a reference to – you know. This.'

Sioda smiled bashfully. 'Name of a racehorse I had a share in. Doesn't mean anything. I just liked the sound.'

'You really didn't know the house once belonged to William McAuley?'

'Never heard of the man until tonight. Coincidence, I suppose?'

'Okay. And why'd you employ my dad?'

'Another coincidence.'

'Or "bravo", telling me to check it out. It means "wicked stranger". Thought that was a clue too.'

'All coincidence,' he said. 'Life is full of them. Didn't Jung or someone say everything is connected, every mind and event, through the great collective unconscious . . . ' His voice faded, embarrassed. 'Or maybe . . . like Joseph thought. Maybe it was destined.'

I said, 'Why did you invite me to your house that day? I thought it was a trap . . . '

Sioda scowled at me. 'I told you, I'm no pederast.'

I said hurriedly, 'I know. I didn't mean it like that. But looking back, when I thought it was you . . . I reckoned you were planning to . . . tie me up, kill me, feed to me to this bloody demon.'

He sighed. 'I offered the use of my library because I knew

your family was . . . '

I finished his sentence: 'Poor?'

He seemed more ill at ease than me. 'Yes. I knew your parents didn't have a lot of money. For books and so on. I figured you'd get something out of it.'

'I would have. That was good of you.'

Sioda stood, swaying slightly. 'No – 'twas my little brother all along. You had the wrong man, Mr Flood . . . He'd been stalking you for a while. He told me so, this evening. Said he met you on the road outside town, little while back?'

I nodded. I remembered. So that was Joseph. No wonder my Spidey-sense was tingling.

'Saw you pass our house, got in his car – *my* car – and followed you. Hid the car, then walked towards you. Wanted to get up nice and close. And you know why? It *amused* him. He admitted this, like it was all a big joke . . . ' Sioda abruptly changed direction. 'Is she your sweetheart, that lass who was here earlier? You're a lucky young man. She's one hell of a girl.' He took a swig from the bottle and laid it on the ground. 'All the best to you, Aidan Flood. Give my regards to your dad.'

A chill ran through me as I saw he now held the gun. Did he have it all along . . . ? His thumb stroked the hammer which, I registered nervously, was cocked. Bad news. What did he think he wanted to do with that?

'Mr Kinvara,' I said softly. 'Do you . . . you wanna give me that?'

He ignored me and stepped outside, half staggering, gun swinging, a vaguely ape-like motion. The moonlight seemed brighter. Sioda moved towards it like an actor stepping into the spotlight. I gingerly stood and followed at a distance, anxiously awaiting his next act. The entire night waited, breath held.

That silence was broken by a hideous screech: the collection of burned flesh and black ash that used to be Joseph Kinvara, who I'd assumed was dead, suddenly lurched to its feet and came reeling towards me. He must have been in unbelievable pain, hardly conscious any more, driven by muscle memory and undistilled hatred of me. His blackened skin crackled as he lumbered across the snow, arms outstretched like a mummy, rasping, 'Kill you . . . *kill you* . . . ruined all . . . Aidan Flood . . . '

I stared, aghast at this fresh madness. Would I have snapped out of it in time to crack him on the head with the bottle, or dial 999 and shimmy up the nearest tree to wait for the cavalry?

It didn't matter. The gun cracked, twice, three times, five, six, as Sioda unloaded that revolver into his brother. Two to the head, pretty much blowing it apart. More to the body. Joseph dropped like a sack of shit. This time he really was kaput.

Sioda let the weapon fall, still smoking, sizzling into the snow. He said flatly, 'I love you, Joseph.' Then he walked off, nary a word or gesture to me, swallowed by the gaping black maw of the forest. I somehow knew he wouldn't be seen alive again. Only death could offer him peace now.

Alone once more but not lonely. I located my phone and texted Podsy: ALL OK I THINK. YOU CAN DESTROY LETTER – EVRYTING GONN BE FINE. A

I tapped my parka, searching for smokes, and hit the famous locket once more. I'll do it now, I vowed – put in two pictures, me and Sláine. Maybe ask her mother for a nice photo on some vague pretence. Find something half-decent of me.

My phone beeped: message from Podsy. OKAY . . . GREAT. PS EH EH EH . . . DONT KILL ME. I ALREADY READ IT. SORRY, CURIOSITY GOT BETTER OF ME.

Ha. Cheeky little fecker. I texted back: YER ALL RIGHT. SO? THINK I'M CRAZY NOW PROBLY.

NO. MORE IN HEAVEN AND EARTH, HORATIO ETC ETC . . . STRANGE STUFF THO. MUCH TO DISCUSS.

AGREED. NIGHT, PODS.

U TOO. NIGHT TO HERSELF ALSO :)

I felt a squeeze of pain in my heart. I ached to be with Sláine. I knew I couldn't for now, and that made me sick inside.

But suck it up, soldier. Tough it out. Endure. Wait for her, as you promised.

I replaced the phone and zipped up my parka. I didn't have a cap but that didn't matter because I had warmth enough and this would do and I walked back to our Ancient Greek amphitheatre and found a soft spot and it was dry enough too and then I lay down and drew my arms closer to myself and pulled that locket out of my jacket and held it near to my heart with awkward frozen fingers and settled down to wait for Sláine's return.

My eyes cast around in the darkness and landed on a white shape, tiny against the black-green moss. A snowdrop, struggling to escape the ground, gasping for life. Reaching for it. Making it.

The thaw was coming. It'd take a while but now that Joseph Kinvara and his demon were gone, I knew the cold weather would disappear too.

You did it, Sláine. You saved the world. You saved me.

Tears filled my eyes, tears of sadness and longing, tears in her absence, yet I smiled, happier than I'd ever been. I will see her again, I told myself. I will. I'll lie under the dark pines for as long as it takes, and wait for her to come back to me.

And I thought, yes, I'll wait for you here, Sláine. As long as it takes . . .

in the cold and the blackness I'll lie here . . .

in our place in the pines I'll wait for you and . . .

shiver the whole night through.

Darragh McManus

Darragh McManus is an author, journalist, playwright and screenwriter. *Shiver the Whole Night Through* is his first Young Adult book. He has previously published two crime novels: a vigilante thriller called *Even Flow* (2012) and noir-style mystery *The Polka Dot Girl* (2013). His first book was the humorous non-fiction *GAA Confidential* (2007), and he released a comic novel, *Cold! Steel! Justice!!!*, as an e-book under the name Alexander O'Hara (2011).

For more than a decade Darragh has written reviews, features and opinion columns for several papers, including the *Irish Independent*, the *Sunday Times* and the *Guardian*. Several short stories have appeared in literary journals, in Ireland, the UK and the US. He's also written a play, which has had cast readings in Manhattan and Belfast and will be recorded for radio broadcast this year.

Darragh lives in the west of Ireland and is currently working on some new YA stories. Follow Darragh at darraghmcmanus. com or on Twitter: @McManusDarragh